HIDEAWAY

HIDEAWAY

Stolen Away Series Book One

WILLOW PRESCOTT

For my three little monsters.
Thanks for driving me so crazy that escapism led to a whole fucking book.

Dear Reader,

This is a dark romance that explores themes and situations some may find unsettling or disturbing. This book contains triggers such as kidnapping, violence, rape, and elements of BDSM including: spanking, whipping, caning, and bondage. Please proceed at your own risk. For those of you who like a little darkness, enjoy my loves.

Yours Always,

Willow

COPYRIGHT

Hideaway Copyright © 2023 by Willow Prescott

All rights reserved.

Cover Design by Books and Moods

No part of this book may be reproduced or transmitted in any form or by any means, electronic or mechanical, including photocopying and recording, or by any information storage and retrieval system without the express written permission of the author except for the use of brief quotations in a book review.

This is a work of fiction. Names, characters, businesses, events, and incidents bearing any resemblance to actual persons living or dead or actual events is purely coincidental.

CHAPTER ONE

THE cool city lights turned to hazy orbs beneath the shroud of rain. Chicago's towering skyline appeared almost spectral amid the winter deluge. It was just warm enough for the droplets to resist turning to snow, but still plenty cold to leave a lingering sting of chill in its wake. Caden Ashford wiped a dampened strand of hair from his face as he tried to focus on his task.

Damn rain.

A week prior, a prospective client came to Cade with an endeavor that seemed surprisingly simple. The man needed a single, invaluable item retrieved from a relatively unprotected location. The client was, by his own accord, the rightful owner, not that Cade gave a shit about the rights of ownership. He was a procurer; the elite came to him, under the guise of anonymity, when they desired an item so exotic and singular in nature that insurmountable challenges, such as federal preservation or proprietary rights, impeded direct attainment. Cade was there to bypass the legalities and make their dreams come true. For an exorbitant fee, of course.

His endeavor consisted of three components: a library, a book, and a girl.

The location seemed relatively unchallenging for a man who had gleaned treasures from museums and collections housed in the grandest of fortresses. Endowed with a rather extensive, private assortment of reading materials, Cade had never frequented a library for public use. From his general knowledge, they were menial institutions that allowed items to be taken, abused, and returned within a specific parameter of time free of charge. In his educated opinion, any business that offered a service without the intent to capitalize was fatally flawed. The fundamentals of such an institution left Cade at an advantage; if they were inclined to let everyone in, there would be little forethought given to keeping someone like him out.

The book he was commissioned with obtaining was rare. First fucking edition rare. More than that, it was one of the older examples of printed literature, dating back to the fifteenth century. He knew enough of literary history to know that the disappearance of such a text would cause a great deal of anguish in the academic community, but that wasn't his damn problem. His client wanted a first edition Chaucer, he would bloody well get a first edition Chaucer.

The girl presented a unique challenge that deviated from his standard operations. According to his client, the book was entrusted to the keep of a single person. She was documented to be far younger than the typical university archivists, a fact which made her position as the chief librarian even more impressive. She had completed a variety of PhD's at an accelerated rate and seemed very much the bland, dry, studious sort of character that would be expected of a librarian. Cade had dealt with her type before; in his experience, mercenaries were far more preferable to academics. The latter seemed to be born with a hill to die on, whereas anyone who valued money could always be reasoned with.

The plan had been in place for a week, and it was almost time for the acquisition. Unfortunately, surveillance tended to get complicated when you couldn't see more than a few feet in front of your face. And without adequate surveillance that night, his operation would have to be delayed. Cade wasn't partial to delayed gratification in any aspect of his life. So, as far as he was concerned, the rain could kindly fuck off.

Cade took another frustrated swipe at the drenched, dark curls that had fallen into his face. Fierce eyes scoured the darkness in search of their unassuming target. A small group of students bolted from the building out into the rain, obviously eager to escape the watery onslaught and find shelter in their dormitories. Cade moved a few steps back; melding into the shadows was second nature to him. Having escaped the notice of the striving scholars, Cade advanced on the aged brick building that bore the resemblance of a cathedral. Though even if it were a sanctuary, God himself could not impede Cade in his mission.

The large, ornate windows allowed for undisturbed observance. Cade was grateful that the architects clearly had no penchant for privacy. A few older members exited the building and made quick headway for their respective destinations. After they were out of view, Cade circled around to look for any stragglers. The first floor looked clear, and the view of the second floor suggested the same. Which left the basement level and its occupants. Cade allowed himself a small shiver as he made his way through the mud and rain to a tree just out of sight. He leaned against the damp bark, set his focus on the entrance of the building, and waited.

After what seemed like an eternity of being slowly drowned, the moment Cade had been awaiting in rain-soaked anticipation finally arrived. The blurred lights ahead began to extinguish, like candles in the windows of an ancient tower being blown out one by one. The library was the most historic building on campus, and the dark neo-Gothic architecture turned eerie in the faint moonlight. A figure emerged from the large wooden doors at the entrance of the building and turned to secure them behind her.

She was quite underdressed for the aggressive weather, and her pale blue dress began to cling to her skin. On second glance, her lack of a cover was not due to under preparedness for she had a raincoat wrapped carefully around a stack of books that she held close to her chest. Clearly warmth was not on her list of priorities. Cade shook his head in disapproval as he watched her scurry away in soaked shivers. Having spent his whole life around people who valued objects over anything else, he still couldn't understand the sentiment.

She stopped suddenly and took a moment to turn penetrating eyes to the darkness where Cade hid, searching for some unknown entity that drew her unease. Cade held his breath and shrank back against the tree. Had he slipped, made some sort of sound or movement that called her attention? Cade shook his head at the notion. No, she was merely a woman of moderate vigilance who found herself walking a deserted campus alone at night and looking to the shadows for nightmares to manifest. And with good reason. Nightmares weren't the only things that lurked in the shadows.

Finding nothing out of the ordinary to satisfy her fears, the woman hurried onward. Cade checked his watch for the time. According to the surveillance work of Jace and Declan, it was the same as the last two nights, almost to the minute. Perfect. She was a creature of habit. He could appreciate that. He would, in fact, appreciate it very much when they came back in search of something very specific. Something only she could provide.

"Until next time, Miss Caine," Cade whispered in anticipation as the small figure disappeared into the rainy haze like a spirit in the night.

THE evening storm played against the window panes like the swell of a symphony. Kara quite liked the rain; it was a friendly companion to a good read, and it helped to preserve the tranquility of the library. The average student wouldn't brave the inconvenient whims of Mother Nature to obtain a hard copy text for an assignment undoubtedly due the next day. And the non-average sort were always welcome.

Kara's breath stilled in reverent rapture as she inspected their most recently donated text, lovingly caressing the time-worn spine, rubbing her thumb across the faded letters and feeling the smoothness of the binding. *Jane Eyre*—her favorite piece of literature and one in a collection of three, first edition novels by the Brontë sisters recently bequeathed to the archival department of the library. Instinctually, she drew the book close, the pale, blonde waves of her hair rippling over the discolored pages as she breathed in the intoxicating scent of aged paper and ink. It was an irreplicable smell, as though history itself was present in a form tangible to all the senses.

Carefully gathering her new additions, Kara made her way to an obscure door in the far left corner of the first floor. After unlocking the door, she turned on the lights, secured the lock behind her, and descended the steep, narrow staircase. Few people were even aware of the library's lower level, and even fewer had access to it. The realm beneath the bustle of students, keeping company with the written thoughts of men and women who had passed centuries before, was where Kara truly felt at home.

Kara and a couple senior members had offices on the lower level. There were two rooms with special equipment to study the older and more delicate texts; it was where Kara spent much of her day assisting professors and PhD students with research and examination. There was one room on that level with such limited access that only Kara, as the chief librarian, knew the entry code: the rare books archives. Kara made her way to the door, first edition Brontës still in hand, entered the five digits into the keypad, and opened the door.

She was met with a chill as she entered the repository of rarities. A temperature of sixty degrees was optimal for the preservation of

Hideaway

texts, but it was not the most comfortable thermostat setting for human tastes. Kara checked the humidity levels as she made her way to the bookshelves to find a vacant spot for their new acquisitions. After laying its sisters to rest alongside a recently donated collection of *The Canterbury Tales*, Kara couldn't resist taking a moment to inspect what lay beneath the aged cover of her favorite text. The preservation really was quite exquisite; she would immensely enjoy cataloging any unique features and comparing with other editions the library had in house.

Kara never tired of her work as the head of the archives department. The classic texts always seemed to excite and surprise her in ways that human interactions lacked the capacity. The library had been her sanctuary since she first started at the university as an undergraduate. Some had ridiculed her choice to settle into an uneventful and solitary life amid the shelves of aged texts, but in spite of her twenty eight years, Kara couldn't imagine anywhere she would be happier. And nothing quite rivaled the welcoming smell of well-worn books.

Kara's thoughts were suddenly disrupted by the sheer quiet of the room and undisturbed silence above. Assuming that *Jane Eyre* had absorbed her attention a little longer than expected, she glanced at the time.

Shit.

It was nearly an hour after closing. Kara carefully placed her text with its comrades and secured the room before heading in haste to her own office. She gathered her coat and a few books from the desk for some late night entertainment and made her way to the stairs. The rhythmic tap of her high heels meeting marble filled the great hall with an authoritative echo that seemed to challenge the empty silence as she moved swiftly to turn out the lights and make her escape into the night.

Kara was met with a damp and chilly breeze as she drew open the heavy wooden doors to the outside world. She had forgotten that the rain she'd been romanticizing from within the dry confines of the library offered a companionship of inconvenience for a long walk back in the dead of night. Without hesitation, Kara removed her coat and wrapped it securely around her books, bracing for the freezing onslaught. She'd take wet clothes over wet books any day.

It was on these days that Kara truly regretted her inability to accessorize with sensible shoes. Navigating the muddy wasteland that separated the campus from the faculty parking lot would be an adventure in pencil thin heels. Her feet had already begun to get wet as she splashed her way down the ruddy brick of the main walkway. Kara's steps faltered as an eerie sense of being watched washed over her like a chill that had nothing to do with the weather. She searched the shadows warily as she readied her keys in her fist as a weapon against any ill-wishing foe. When nothing dangerous presented itself, Kara soothed her suspicions and hurried on. She'd ask Mike to double check the library on his midnight security rounds as a precaution. She could see the luminous glow of the parking lot and her solitary car in the distance. Kara held her sharpest key at the ready until she was safely inside the confines of her car.

Should any nightly shadows choose to emerge, Kara Caine wasn't going down without a fight.

CHAPTER TWO

KARA jolted from her habitual daydreaming while sorting requests, thrust into reality with the unusual appearance of a large figure walking into the library. A pair of figures actually. It was the one in front who had captured her attention. He was clearly older than the average age of a typical student, but he didn't quite possess the quiet refinement of a university professor. He was tall, dressed in a brown, tweed suit that fit snugly enough to hint at his muscular build. Round, tortoise glasses framed his striking blue eyes that stood out starkly against his beautiful, deeply-tanned skin. His dark, curly hair was styled short and his perfectly manicured facial hair left her in doubt if she'd ever beheld a specimen who was more the epitome of debonair than the man walking toward her.

Fuck, he's coming this way.

Hurriedly, Kara fussed with her unruly blonde waves and needlessly smoothed down the front of her dress. Thank whatever powers that swirled above, she was wearing her favorite floral print wrap dress that accentuated the slight curve of her hips and revealed the perfect hint of tit. She looked more than acceptable, and from the appreciative glint in the approaching man's eyes, he noticed.

"Good evening," Kara greeted when the enticing stranger approached her desk with his companion. "May I help you with something?"

"Why yes, you may," Jace responded with a smile that bordered on dazzling. It was a practiced gesture, but it was always effective on women. "I'm Dr. Jamison, and this is my research assistant, David." Jace gestured to the younger man beside him that Kara had clearly forgotten existed. "I spoke with Anne Spade yesterday about viewing a few texts from your rare collections for an essay I'm writing. She said they would be available today."

"I'm sorry, Ms. Spade isn't available tonight," Kara replied, not sounding the least bit apologetic as she was suddenly, guiltily grateful that her colleague had called in sick and left her to attend the library alone that night. "But the rare archives is actually my department. Let me check and see if she filed a special request for you."

The notice of Ms. Spade's absence wasn't news to Jace. It was his own less than friendly suggestion that coming into work that day might not be beneficial for dear Anne's health that had encouraged the dowdy librarian to spend a quiet evening at home. It was amazing the power that could be wielded over that sort of skittish creature with so little effort. The weak and insignificant always crumbled under Jace's steely gaze like rubble beneath a boot. He took a moment to size up Dr. Caine as she rustled through some papers at the front desk. Jace doubted the small, bookish girl would require much effort to manipulate into his schemes. In fact, the whole night would probably be disappointingly easy. Compared to his usual jobs, taking a book from a librarian would be child's play.

"I apologize, I can't seem to find any record of your visit today," Kara announced in confusion after having checked the logs twice. It wasn't like Anne to forget a special access request; she was always exceedingly detail oriented.

"Oh that is disappointing," he answered, appearing unfazed. "I don't suppose you would be able to arrange a viewing tonight? We did travel quite a long distance for this opportunity."

Kara took a moment to consider his request. She was typically rigidly adherent to their appointment policy, but she didn't want to be an impediment to someone's quest for knowledge. "Of course, I can make an exception. May I see some identification for both of you and have your academic permissions form?"

A brief expression of exasperation passed across Jace's face. "Unfortunately, my assistant failed to pack the academic permissions form. It is sitting on a desk back at the university. He still has some things to learn," he said, shooting a dark look at the quiet boy beside him with ebony hair and nearly black eyes that were soft and kind. "Could you kindly forgive his oversight? We were really looking forward to collecting this data for our research. You have such a renowned collection of early editions in your library, Dr. Caine. I would hate to miss the chance to examine them," Jace pleaded in an overt attempt to appear charming and persuasive.

Kara froze in unease, trying to recall if she'd at any point given Dr. Jamison her name. She had not. "I'm sorry, to which university did you say you belong?" Kara inquired, suddenly growing inexplicably uneasy. She desperately hoped that the sinister twisting of Dr. Jamison's features was merely her imagination.

"Ohio State," Jace answered through gritted teeth, keenly aware of her change in demeanor. Maybe his task wouldn't be as easy as he thought. Which was fine with him. He enjoyed a little physical coercion, especially with pretty little doe-eyed things like Dr. Caine.

"Well, we are actually about to close for the night. I could always contact Ohio State University tomorrow and get a copy of the academic permissions form? I'm sure they'll have one on file," Kara offered in compromise, hoping to escape a scene she had an inkling could turn ugly at any moment.

"Sorry, but tomorrow isn't going to work for us," Jace answered coldly, making no move to back down.

Sensing that the situation was slipping beyond the point where she controlled the outcome, Kara made herself appear as tall as possible with all of her five feet and three inches; thankfully, her high heels added nearly another four. She put on her best mask of cold librarian authority—the one that scared the shit out of rowdy students who used her library to socialize rather than study. "The library is closing. Please escort yourselves out. Now."

"I was hoping to avoid any unpleasantness, Dr. Caine."

"Who's being unpleasant? I did say please. Get your ass out the door *now*, and I'll even add a thank you."

Judging from the dark look she received in return, maybe sarcasm hadn't been the best approach. In response to her indelicately stated request, Jace planted both of his hands on her desk imperiously. Towering above her with broad shoulders and arms hidden not so discreetly beneath the tight confines of his suit, the man was a formidable entity. Kara shrank back slightly in spite of herself. She certainly wouldn't be making an escape on account of physical merits. She could only hope Dr. Jamison didn't have the brains to match the brawn.

With a quick scan of the library, Kara made the unfortunate discovery that she and the two men were the only occupants. Mike wouldn't be making his rounds for at least another hour, so she was on her own unless she could discreetly get to her phone to call for assistance. As nonchalantly as possible, Kara reached into her pocket in search of her phone. At the same time, Jace drew back the edge of his suit jacket to reveal a handgun tucked into his waistband.

"I think it might be better if you kept your hands where I can see them, Dr. Caine. We wouldn't want any accidents to happen," he threatened harshly.

Kara froze, startling at the sight of a weapon in the library and wondering what the hell she'd gotten herself into. As it was a simple enough request to preserve the peace, Kara abandoned her search for her phone and placed her hands dutifully on the desk.

"Good girl," Jace said in patronizing tone that made Kara feel about three inches tall. "Now, I believe you were about to show us the archives?"

Kara looked at the two of them, trying to surmise what they would demand when they reached the level below. And if she would be willing to provide it. She needed time to think and formulate some sort of plan, and she couldn't do it with her back against the wall and two men staring her down intently. The lower level was her domain, and, if she took her time navigating, she could perhaps think of an escape plan by the time her adversaries realized she wasn't exactly cooperating.

"Fine. This way, please," Kara acquiesced curtly.

"Nice to see you're actually capable of compliance, with a little friendly persuasion," Jace goaded as he tapped the side she knew concealed his gun. "Just follow my instructions, and we'll be gone without a fuss, and you'll be safely on your way home."

Somehow his words didn't offer her much reassurance. Kara walked slowly, checking windows for signs of people passing by, looking for any suitable places to hide, gauging the amount of time it would take for her to reach the front door if she ran. She would have to ditch her shoes first. Running, or hiding, or much of anything really was intrinsically harder when performed in miniature stilts. But there would be plenty of time to consider the hazards induced by her fashion choices later. Provided there was a later. Having stalled as long as she inconspicuously could, Kara finally arrived at the door in the back of the library with a semi-feasible plan. All she needed was a bit of luck.

"The archives are kept on a lower level to prevent light exposure. We'll have to go down the stairs to reach them."

"Lead the way, Dr. Caine," Jace encouraged amicably.

"I'll have to retrieve the keys from my pocket," Kara warned as she reached for the side that held her keys as well as her phone.

Before she could reach either, Kara felt the hardened, boulder-esque presence of someone pressed far too firmly against her back. One hand slipped around her waist and grasped her wrist restrictively, while the other slid suggestively down the curve of her hip before dipping into her pocket. His touch lingered a moment too long before he removed the contents hidden away in her dress.

"Allow me to assist you," Jace offered smoothly as he tucked her phone into his coat and held up the keys in front of her.

Kara allowed herself a moment's glare before taking the proffered keys from his hand.

Well, there goes plan A.

She felt even more helpless without her phone by her side as she prepared to descend into the darkness below. From down there, only one way of exit was possible; she just had to make sure she got there first. Kara turned on the lights, going against her nature to leave the door unlocked behind them, and started down the very familiar path. "Watch your step; it is pretty steep," she cautioned out of habit. When they all reached the bottom floor, Kara gathered her courage and attempted to appear casual. "Do you mind if I grab a book from my office? I need to take it home with me tonight. The archives room is the last one at the end of the hall with the keypad," she offered in a perfect facade of cooperation.

"What is the code?" Jace asked with the eagerness of a sprinter nearing the finish line.

"It's 3-8-2-5-8, then press enter."

F-U-C-K-U

Kara dipped into her office and removed her shoes as the other two rushed for the last door, ready to have their prize and be done with it. When she heard the beeping of the keypad, Kara hastily started for the stairs, the urgency of speed outweighing the need for quietness. She was halfway toward the door to freedom when harsh hands grabbed her waist and jerked her over a shoulder.

"Put me down, you fucking asshole!" she shouted as she made frantic, futile attempts to escape his hold.

"Trying to make a run for it, Dr. Caine? And here I thought we were getting along. I guess you're not quite as smart as I thought," Jace seethed, the grip on her waist tightening. "Declan, go get a chair from one of the offices," he ordered his supposed assistant.

Kara tried to think of what motive these two would have for using aliases and forcing their way into the secure areas of the library. They obviously were in search of one of the rare books, but the contents of the archives weren't common knowledge. The texts catalogued in the archives were known to Kara herself, a few members of the university board, and select higher members of the academic community. Maybe it was just a shot in the dark to see if they could get away with something valuable?

"You were supposed to be an easy mark, Dr. Caine. In fact, I should already be on my way to enjoy a nice glass of whiskey. Instead, I'm having to waste valuable time dealing with your bullshit. And until I get what I want, things are going to get rather uncomfortable for you."

Considering her awkward position on his shoulder, Kara doubted the situation could get much less comfortable. "So I'm going to assume your name isn't Dr. Jamison?" Kara asked, trying to gather any information she could use.

After Declan emerged with a chair, Jace threw Kara down roughly on her ass. "That is correct," he confirmed with a smirk as he kneeled down in front of where Kara was sitting. With one swift movement, Jace reached for the hem of her dress and ripped upward and across, removing the bottom half. His hands lingered on her legs a bit too long afterward, and Kara shivered in response.

"What the hell do you think you're doing?" Kara asked in infuriation as she stared at the ruins of her favorite fucking dress.

"Easy on the shouting, or you'll get a gag as well," Jace warned as he moved to tie her wrists to the chair with the pieces he'd torn from her dress. "We can't have you trying to escape, now can we? And since it's your fault a simple job has been drawn out this much, I think you can stand to sacrifice a little clothing." Jace took a step back to admire his handiwork before Declan took him aside to converse in hushed tones. She wouldn't be moving anytime soon unless he allowed it.

Kara tested the makeshift binds on her wrists; they didn't give an inch. Dr. Jamison, or whatever his name was, certainly had practice securing hostages, Kara noted with unease. Perhaps this was a planned, professional operation and not just a happenstance robbery. Kara studied the two men before her; they were immersed in what appeared to be an argument, oblivious to her scrutiny. The assistant, Declan, looked young enough to be her student, and his face held an innocence that had yet to be marred by an intimate acquaintance with the world. He was obviously new to conning his way into academic establishments. His associate, however, bore the countenance of a man who had very few vices left to explore.

"So what exactly are you trying to acquire here?" Kara called over in an attempt to gain any information she could. She also hoped to stop whatever scheming was unfolding out of the reach of her hearing—not being privy to their secretive plotting was making her nervous.

"A collection that was recently donated to the university," Jace answered freely. Any information he had was irrelevant to her, so he saw no need to conceal it.

"Oh?" Kara continued conversationally, trying to mask her surprise. While the knowledge of what exactly was catalogued in their archives wasn't widespread, the timelines of donations were only known to a very select few.

"We're meant to retrieve an early edition of *The Canterbury Tales*. Mind fetching it from the book prison back there and saving us any more wasted time? It's probably just laying around collecting dust with a bunch of other old books too ancient to read or use or keep within a few hundred feet of the sun," he said, glancing around the lower floor distastefully. He usually worked in the realm of luxury, acquiring items from museums and private collections housed in mansions. He was getting tired of the dark, musty room and the librarian bitch.

"The William Caxton *first* edition of *The Canterbury Tales*?" Kara confirmed, unable to quell a gasp of shock. That collection was one of Avery Reed's most recent donations to the university, and it was the most magnanimous contribution the library had ever received. "It's fifteenth century for Christ's sake. That text is of paramount historical, academic, and literary significance, not to mention it's worth a fortune."

"Exactly. And?"

"*And*, I would rather fill my pockets with stones and take a stroll at the bottom of a river than deliver a first edition *Canterbury Tales* to anyone lacking the proper intentions or the skill set to handle such a delicate text."

"Trust me, sweetheart, that could be arranged," he threatened darkly as he strode the distance between them and bent to grasp her wrists, meeting her unwavering gaze with cold, violent eyes. Under his icy glare, she faltered only slightly. "However, the state in which I chuck your remains into a murky underwater grave is entirely up to you. I was tasked with getting a book out of the vault back there; the methods I use to extract your cooperation can be as creative as my twisted imagination allows," Jace added as an extra layer of intimidation, eyeing his prey greedily.

At that moment, Kara felt the first prickles of fear across her skin. She was trapped and helpless with no viable options at her disposal. And she was very likely about to be tortured for the sake of saving a piece of literature that had survived for centuries before her, and, if she had anything to say about it, would exist for many after her. She looked at Jace with all the hatred she could muster and saw a dark gleam fill his eyes in return.

Jace could tell he was getting to her; the fear coursing through her veins intoxicated his senses like a fucking drug.

Kara had an unfortunate habit of reverting to antagonism when she felt threatened, and it often escalated rather than helped the situation. Before she could repress the words, instinct overpowered common sense. "I guess you're one of those guys who can only get hard when they're beating up helpless girls," she provoked as spitefully as she could. Kara heard a growl of anger a split second before she felt, rather than saw, a hard hand meet her cheek with a resounding *smack*.

Jace is sensitive about his manhood. Noted.

"Jace," Declan warned. Jace ignored the young man's caution; Kara had the full extent of his attention.

"You're a mouthy little bitch, aren't you?" Jace asked spitefully as he considered the best retaliation for the her disrespect.

Kara's cheek stung, but the pain felt better than being powerless. She couldn't believe that she'd been attracted to that prick when he first walked in the library. Of course, he'd be a fucking psychopath. Kara watched as Jace's eyes lit with the fire of cruel machinations; he just hadn't picked which torment he would carry out. Though her words had sparked whatever hell Jace was about to put her through, Kara didn't regret them. Revenge would take precedence over retrieving the text she would sacrifice everything to preserve. And perhaps, if he went far enough, his cruelty would turn Declan to her aide. Kara took a deep breath and braced herself for Jace's assault.

"Declan, go upstairs and make sure everything is secure," Jace commanded without taking his predatory eyes off Kara.

Shit. That had not been part of Kara's plan. She needed Declan there; he was her only possible ally. The thought of what harm might befall her after being left alone in a room with Jace was terrifying. Suddenly, the fire of resolve and determination that had fueled her resistance vanished like a flame beneath the wind. Kara looked to Declan to implore mercy.

"Jace, I'm not sure that's such a good idea," Declan argued, the same fear of Jace's intentions clearly present in his countenance. He'd signed up for robbery, not assault. Or worse.

"Trust me kid, you don't have the stomach for what comes next," Jace assured the younger man. He didn't want to ruin the kid's taste for the job his first night out. Sometimes their line of work wouldn't always provide pretty solutions, but that was a lesson for another time when Declan had more experience to understand the need for force. Perhaps the kid would even grow to enjoy the violence as its own source of fun like he had.

Against his better judgment, Declan gave one last sympathetic look to the women tied to the chair and headed for the stairs. He took no pleasure in leaving anyone helpless to the whims of Jace's perverse amusement, but he didn't have the pull of rank to intervene. Declan ignored the urge to steal a last glance at the scene below as he exited and shut the door soundly behind him.

Kara tried to steady her breathing as trepidation threatened to consume every fiber of her being. Whatever harsh fate awaited her at Jace's hands, he wanted no witnesses. His violence was for her alone. Kara attempted to steel her will for the sake of preserving something greater than herself. Judging from the eager cruelty of Jace's expression, the path to academic martyrdom would not be pretty.

"You know, doctor, I'm glad you put up a fight," Jace stated amicably as he stalked toward her. Without warning, his hand shot out and made brutal contact with Kara's other cheek. Both sides of her face burned with the force of Jace's abuse, but she didn't back down or lower her gaze. "It's so much more fun when you struggle."

He slapped her again. Hard. Kara fought the first swell of tears, angered by her body's natural response to the pain, as the nauseating, coppery tang of blood filled her mouth. Cruel fingers dug into her jaw as Jace bent to draw her closer, so close that the musky scent of his cologne suffocated her senses. Kara could hear the thundering of his heartbeat, pumping with adrenaline and what she sickeningly suspected was arousal. His lips brushed against her ear almost gently, but his breath was hard and fast against her neck.

"And the victory will be so much sweeter when you finally break," Jace whispered, his voice full of dark anticipation as his fingers tightened painfully around her face.

Taking advantage of the repulsive closeness of Jace's body against her own, Kara made the most of her unbound limbs and thrust her knee up as hard as she could in the hopes of incapacitating him with a sharp hit to the balls. With a misfortune of aim, Kara's knee caught him in the hip. Grunting in pain and irritation, Jace lunged for her throat, inescapable fingers mercilessly crushing her windpipe. Judging from his unrelenting fury, Jace knew exactly what she had been aiming for. All too quickly, the room began to darken as consciousness slipped from Kara's reach.

Just as she had resigned herself to Jace's destruction, the door above opened again. A man who was not Declan emerged with a countenance full of concern. Against all odds, Kara had been granted a liberator. Jace turned to scowl at the intruder, but when he met the stranger's gaze, his stance shifted completely. Deference replaced the dominant arrogance that had ruled Jace just moments before. Kara studied the stranger as he descended the stairs with an authority that was undeniable. He didn't belong to the faculty, and he was at least a decade older than the usual student population. If he wasn't associated with the university, then what chance of fate had brought him to her aide at that moment?

"What is going on here?" the man demanded in a tone that fell between frustration and fury.

His voice held a refined lull that belonged more to the upper class of London than to the streets of Chicago. The stranger was able to meet Jace at eye level, an impressive feat as the latter was certainly over six feet tall. He didn't possess Jace's broad muscularity, but the perfect tailoring of his suit suggested his form was lean and toned. His pale face was constructed of hardened angles outlined by the slightest shadow of stubble and framed by inky waves that had an unruly tendency to fall to one side. There was a resting harshness to his expression, a furrowed brow that hinted at perpetual discontent. He had hardened eyes of captivating depth that held melded hues of green and gold, like summer leaves tinged with the whisper of autumn. Kara mentally catalogued each detail of his appearance as she would an ancient text full of undiscovered secrets. The visage of her savior would remain engrained in her thoughts for as long as she had breath to sustain them.

Kara's romanticizing of the new arrival came to an earth-shattering halt as Declan followed down the stairs at the same time as Jace's next words.

"I had it under control, Ashford. There was no need for you to involve yourself."

"Clearly," Cade replied acidly with a pointed look at Kara's battered face and makeshift restraints.

Kara froze as the realization that the two men were acquainted crept into consciousness. *Ashford.* The name of her savior turned assailant. She fixated on the name with all the black hatred she could gather as the alluring features she'd been fantasizing about turned dark and menacing beneath her gaze—tinged by the haze of contempt.

Cade felt the heat of her fury as he turned reproachfully toward Jace. "Declan contacted me with some concerns regarding your technique, and I felt obligated to come down here and supervise your handling of the situation. You know I don't like exposing my identity while a job is in progress unless absolutely necessary, but it appears young Declan's misgivings were warranted. May I ask what the hell were you thinking?"

"The bitch wasn't cooperating, so I resorted to less orthodox means of persuasion. I assumed my methods wouldn't be subject to scrutiny provided the book was obtained," Jace rationalized, shooting Declan a deadly glare.

"I see. So you are in possession of the book?"

"Not yet," Jace responded through gritted teeth.

"So this small, insignificant girl has been threatened, disheveled, assaulted, and held hostage, but you still don't have anything to show for it? It seems my top acquisitioner might be losing his touch," Cade critiqued, irritated that such a simple operation had yet to yield results, but also annoyed that Jace hadn't had the forethought to avoid a hostile, hostage situation in the basement of a public establishment.

Jace's face contorted with anger at the insinuation of his incompetence, but he bit back the first choice words that came to mind. "The girl has been stubborn. She just needs a bit of rough persuasion, and I'm more than willing to oblige. Trust me, she'll break easy enough."

"She's a librarian, not MI6 for Christ's sake," Cade said in exasperation. He too was inclined toward a rougher approach, but, unlike Jace, he knew when the situation warranted it. He looked at the girl who appeared so fragile in her bound state and assumed delicacy would be the best form of action for obtaining the text they required.

"Think you can do any better, boss? Be my guest," Jace said curtly, gesturing to Kara like she was a nicely wrapped gift.

Though that was certainly how he liked his presents wrapped, Cade wasn't sure that the librarian was the kind of gift he would enjoy. He ran a hand through his unruly waves in frustration; it was one of his tells when he was stressed. The movement caught the girl's attention, and she turned dark, disdainful eyes to his. The last remnants of Cade's cool composure vanished beneath the gaze of her wide eyes that held an all consuming fire of defiance. He smothered the unnerving urge to protect her, overcompensating with a glare that was a little crueler than intended; she recoiled from the intensity.

"Miss Caine," Cade addressed her with a smug superiority that was typically sincere, though at the moment felt constructed for the sake of preserving authority.

"It's Dr. Caine," Kara corrected matter of factly.

"Pardon?" he questioned with a smirk of amusement. The girl was tied to a chair and still preferred pride over the more logical choice of pliancy. It seemed preservation was not on her list of priorities.

"Unless, by some negligence, you've entered into this situation less informed than you appear, my appropriate title should be common knowledge." She hadn't gone through years of hard study and work to be demoted to *miss* in her last tragic hours. Being addressed by the patronizing title merely added insult to injury. "I would afford you the same professional courtesy were you to have the decency of introductions."

Kara's sharp stubbornness momentarily threw Cade off guard, but he recovered quickly. "My apologies, Dr. Caine, you are absolutely right. Caden Ashford, no title necessary, though technically Lord Ashford would be appropriate if you're a stickler for formalities. I would offer my hand, but you seem to be tied up at the moment." The last part might have been a bit much, but Cade couldn't resist.

Kara scoffed; there was no way in hell she would ever be referring to that man as *Lord* Ashford. On a positive note, if he was telling the truth, the authorities would likely have a much easier time locating some posh member of British society than an average criminal. The thought of the tables turning and getting to see that smug bastard restrained instead of herself filled Kara with the fuel to outlast whatever madness the night might entail.

"Yes, speaking of being tied up, do you think we could do away with the whole bondage bit? Can't say it's really my thing. Sorry to disappoint, Jace," Kara said in a flippant tone that contrasted her rather spiteful look at the man responsible for the restraints digging into her wrists.

Cade tried to repress a smile at the cheeky retort. Perhaps if she knew who she was dealing with, she wouldn't be making those comments so lightly. He understood that she was looking for leverage, some level of trust from him, so she could feel less helpless in the situation. Since he knew who truly held the power, Cade was willing to play along.

"Well, I am sorry Jace's efforts failed to satisfy. Perhaps you require someone with more experience," Cade offered, his response eliciting an eye roll from Jace.

"His technique was more than efficient, thanks. The setting, though, is a bit lacking in ambiance. Maybe we can continue our negotiations somewhere more comfortable?" Kara suggested, eager to get out of the windowless box she shared with three hostile strangers.

"Oh, so this is a negotiation now?" Cade asked, intrigued.

"What word would you use?" Kara questioned almost sweetly.

"No, I think negotiation sounds promising. That would imply you are willing to help us get what we need in exchange for something in return. Name your price." Cade assumed she was stalling. Declan had mentioned that the illustrious Dr. Caine refused to cooperate for idealistic reasons; she was willing to put her life at stake to ensure that the collection remained pristine. Fucking academic romantics. As if anything composed of stale paper and ink could be worth dying for.

"I'm afraid I haven't the time to conjure demands while we wait down here. Mike will be doing midnight security checks soon, and I assume you won't want to get anyone else involved in your criminal activities." It was a small bluff; since there was such limited access to the lower level, and Kara always personally secured the area, Mike only did sweeps of the two upper levels. If they stayed below, Kara and the men holding her hostage would pass undetected. She had to hope they wouldn't take that chance.

Cade looked shaken at this new information. "What is the time, Jace?"

"It's a quarter till," Jace answered, looking equally stressed.

"Can you confirm that there is security entering the area in mere minutes?" Cade asked, clearly peeved that both members of his team had failed to plan for such an occurrence.

"There is a guard that comes to check the grounds at midnight," Jace said, seeming apologetic about the oversight. "We didn't think it would take this long to retrieve the book."

Cade released a huff of irritation as he tried to formulate his next move. Thanks to Jace and Declan's neglect of time management and failure to mention extra security, there would be no opportunity to reason with the librarian as delicately as he had intended. They needed to get in and out of the archival vault as quickly as possible. The banter with the girl had been amusing, but it was time to stop playing and start pressing the librarian for answers.

"Key code. Now," Cade commanded, all trace of good humor gone.

"What happened to negotiation?" Kara asked in a panicked tone. She was quickly losing any leverage she thought she'd gained.

"You give us the code. We set you free and leave you to live your life. There is your negotiation," Cade replied, his expression hard and unyielding.

"No," Kara said as forcefully as she could, meeting him with a relentless defiance of her own.

"You really have no sense of self-preservation, do you?" Cade responded angrily. He had behaved more than civilly, but the girl was testing his patience. "If you don't cooperate with us, there will be consequences neither one of us will enjoy, you decidedly less so." Kara flinched at the threat housed in Cade's words, but she made no move to acquiesce.

Cade ran his fingers through his hair again. He didn't appreciate being forced to resort to violence, especially with a girl who looked so fragile and helpless. Though, if she could still stand her ground when met with the most imperious glare Cade could summon, perhaps she was stronger than she looked. Cade took a moment to survey Dr. Caine fully from her disheveled, pale as cream curls to her bare feet that rested on point to shy away from the cold floor. He tried not to linger on her open, overexposed thighs or the heavy heaving of her chest as her heart thumped heavily with coursing adrenaline. Cade was a master of reading people and using their drives to his advantage, so all he needed to discover was what made Dr. Caine tick. From the little he had ascertained of her character in their brief acquaintance, Cade could make an educated guess.

"Jace, grab a book from one of the shelves. Something that looks old," Cade ordered with a pointed look at Kara.

Kara couldn't decipher the meaning of the look or the purpose of Jace's task. Perhaps they meant to cut their losses by taking the most valuable books housed within reach? While the rare archives were used to store priceless texts, the library kept out a few shelves of academically significant editions on the lower level. Kara felt a shiver of revulsion as Jace ran his fingers along the spines of the books on the first row, searching for his victim of choice. He picked a rather worn, gold-bound book and handed it to his boss. Cade announced the title aloud.

"Candide. Fourth edition. Very nice. I suppose it's valuable?"

"Academically? Very. Monetarily, it is of moderate value," Kara answered vaguely. She would hate to lose the Voltaire text, but it would be a lesser devastation compared to losing the Chaucer.

"Perfect," Cade said with a malicious grin as he opened the book, ripped it in half, and tossed it on the floor. Kara's eyes widened in horror as she stared at the literary remains lying on the ground. "Care to give up the code now?" Cade pressed.

"No," Kara whispered quietly, aghast at the lengths he was willing to go to get what he wanted. Though he'd committed no act of violence against her personally, Kara felt as though she had been hit in the chest.

"As you wish. Jace, get another one," Cade ordered coldly. "Declan, go upstairs and see if you can stall our security guard."

Declan moved quickly to obey, displaying none of the hesitancy he had when asked to leave her alone with Jace earlier. Whether it was because he trusted Cade's instincts, or feared Cade's anger, Kara wasn't sure.

Jace searched a moment before he retrieved another text from the shelves and placed it in Cade's outreached hand. Cade's face filled with spiteful amusement when he discovered the author. "Is it worth revealing the code to save poor Jane Austen from becoming a heap of rubbish?" he asked with a sneer.

It was clear from Caden Ashford's face that he thought victory was in hand with his ransom of *Sense and Sensibility*. Unsurprisingly, he overestimated his leverage in the situation. Kara had no intention of yielding Chaucer for Austen. Unbeknownst to the criminal who was clearly operating on the basis of stereotypes in the literary field, Kara preferred Brontë to Austen in every respect. Additionally, *Sense and Sensibility* was hardly the masterpiece of Austen's career. Finally, though she hated to see any book harmed, that particular copy was a later edition that was in poor condition and needed to be rebound. Kara assumed the world would still turn with one less print of Austen in it.

Sorry, Jane.

"No, thank you," Kara answered with a hint of superiority. This savage game of his would fail, and he was running out of time.

Cade fixed on her with a dark glare as he easily tore the unfortunate novel in two and discarded it. He too felt the slipping of time from his favor and decided on a more rash form of action. "Jace, did you happen to relieve Miss Caine of her mobile?"

"I did," Jace answered, unsure of the motive behind Ashford's questioning. He removed the phone from his inner pocket and handed it to Cade. With Kara's unwilling help, he disabled the facial recognition and proceeded to search for something.

"I see you don't have much contact outside of work," Cade directed at Kara as he searched through her call and messaging history. She didn't like the insinuation that her social life lacked vibrancy, but she said nothing. "Do you have any family or friends that you keep in contact with on a regular basis?" he asked casually.

Kara blanched. These questions hinted at a hidden inquiry: *would anyone miss you if you disappeared tonight*? Kara wanted to lie, but she knew the evidence on her own phone would condemn her. She opted for neutral evasion. "Not particularly; my work keeps me busy. I'm at the library all the time."

"I am going to need a more concise answer, Miss Caine. Do you have any close friends or family?" he reiterated sternly.

Kara gritted her teeth as she forced a reply. "It's doctor. And no, I have no close family or friends." And Kara had never regretted her tendency toward solitude more than in that moment. Kara had spent most of her life trying to avoid intimacy in any aspect because it wasn't worth the risk of loss. After her parents, she couldn't handle that kind of devastation again.

Cade appraised the girl who seemed lost in regretful ruminations. He knew he had a couple choices; both held high risks and neither ensured he would attain the item he needed. With the clock ticking, Cade deliberated quickly and made his decision. "Jace, untie Miss Caine, please."

With shocked relief, Kara thought he might have decided to let her go, but when she saw the sneer on Jace's face as he advanced, she suspected she was in for a worse fate than getting home a little late. Jace removed a knife that he had concealed somewhere on his person, and Kara scoffed slightly at the fulfilled stereotype of a suit-clad villain walking around with an arsenal hidden secretly beneath his formal attire. The amusement of the cliche lost its touch quickly as Jace drew closer and brandished the weapon menacingly. He bent to release the restraints, nicking her skin on the last cut. The look on his face told her it was intentional.

Dick.

"I'll give you one last chance to cooperate, Miss Caine. I'd advise you to take it. A simple code is hardly worth this much trouble. No one would blame you for giving us access under duress. And, for what it is worth, I can guarantee the collection will be delivered into capable hands," Cade said, attempting to persuade her to reason before things got very complicated.

Kara rolled her eyes, refraining from yet again correcting his abuse of her name. At this point, he was clearly making an intentional effort to annoy her. Considering he required her assistance, it was not the most educated tactical move, and it made her refusal all the easier. "You are never going to lay a single, unworthy finger on a first edition *Canterbury Tales* if I have anything to say about it, so you might as well get on with it. With the efforts you've taken to stall whatever comes next, the suspense will have killed me before Jace gets a chance to do what he enjoys best. What's the matter, Ashford, don't have the balls to give the order?"

"Oh, I believe I'm satisfactorily endowed in that regard, but I appreciate your interest, Miss Caine." Cade flashed a smile that was a bit too charming to be sinister, but Kara saw a darkness in his eyes that reminded her he was a man to be feared, not toyed with. "Fetch your shoes, love. We're going for a walk."

Kara took a shaky breath before she gathered the courage to remove herself from the chair and walk gingerly across the cold tile to where her shoes lay abandoned in her office. She stepped into the nude heels as she pondered how no one gets dressed in the morning with the inkling that it would be the outfit they die in. Kara looked down at the ripped remains of her favorite floral dress and supposed it wouldn't make much difference in the end if they had.

She emerged from her office feeling slightly more dignified; at least she wouldn't have to walk barefoot to her doom. Jace took a moment to leer appreciatively at her exposed legs; she tried to cover what she could without much success. Cade noticed her discomfort and removed his own coat without hesitation and held it out to her.

"Here," Cade said as he placed the coat on Kara's shoulders.

The gallant gesture confused her, given the situation, but she took the jacket gratefully. The far too large coat covered her down to the knees as she hugged it tightly around her body, thankful to feel slightly less naked in Jace's discomforting presence. In spite of herself, Kara took a moment to inhale the scent of Cade that lingered on the collar of the coat. He smelled masculine without the heaviness of musk, refreshingly spiced like mint mingled with cedar, and a whisper of unexpected, vanilla sweetness. Kara stifled a hint of arousal, reminding herself that it was merely her body's weak, instinctual response to male interaction that she so often neglected; her body had no notion that the intoxicating scent belonged to a man of very questionable character.

"Thanks," Kara responded finally after an internal conflict regarding her feelings toward the giver.

"My pleasure," Cade answered, the picture of good English manners. The sudden impulse to offer his coat to assuage her embarrassment caught him by surprise as well, and he needed a moment to regain his impassive exterior. As usual, he covered the slip into softness by being overly harsh. "Up the stairs. Now," he commanded, giving her an impatient push forward.

Kara obeyed, frightened by the change in his demeanor, and led the way up the stairs toward an uncertain future. Cade allowed her to secure the lower level after they all emerged; appearances needed to be kept for when the security guard arrived. After Kara locked the door, Cade held out his hand expectantly for the keys. She surrendered them without a struggle, and Cade felt a measure of his control returning. Though he had dealt with insubordination before, there was something about the girl's incessant defiance that left his sense of authority feeling shattered. Hell, he hadn't even been able to slightly sway her decision to withhold the text. If Jace hadn't been an utter failure in that department as well, Cade would've taken the

Hideaway

blow to his capabilities rather personally. All things considered, Miss Caine clearly needed a lesson in compliance. And Cade was in an instructive mood.

"Wait, my things," Kara announced as they moved past the front desk.

"I don't think you'll be needing them," Cade replied. It wasn't a suggestion.

"If we leave them, Mike will know something is wrong," Kara argued. She could have neglected that bit of information and left her personal belongings as a sign for help, but she honestly didn't think assistance would reach her in time. At least she could go out in her own coat and relinquish the one she wore to the bastard it belonged to. Also, she got a moderate amount of satisfaction from disregarding the directions of the insufferable man, whatever they may be. If he told her not to jump off a bridge, she had a sneaking suspicion she would do so anyway, merely out of spite and consequences be damned.

"Fair point, Miss Caine. You may gather your things quickly," Cade conceded. He was giving her permission, so technically she hadn't achieved any leverage.

Kara retrieved her purse, wishing she was in the habit of using it to store mace or a weapon of some sort rather than a few spare books. The hardback compilation of Poe stories and poems that she carried with her now might be able to do some damage. Kara had to assume that Edgar Allan Poe would more than approve of his works being used to bash someone in the head, but her aim was unfortunately not her most adept skill. Kara quickly abandoned the rather hopeless idea of assault and gathered her coat and scarf, eagerly slipping into her own clothes and shedding the borrowed jacket that smelled enticing and unfamiliar.

"Thanks again for the use of your coat," she said sincerely as she handed it back to him.

"You're welcome," Cade answered, sliding the still warm coat back over his dress shirt. He was surprised to hear sincerity in his own voice as well.

Fully armored for the chill of a wintery night, Cade led the way to the double doors that barred their exit. He opened them and gestured for Kara. "Ladies first."

She turned back for a final glance at her beloved sanctuary before leaving the building, perhaps for the last time. Kara jumped as the sound of the heavy doors closing behind her echoed with finality, disrupting the tranquil silence that filled the night air.

"Which key?" Cade called back to her as he retrieved her ring of keys from his pocket.

"The gold one," Kara answered, not bothering to look back.

The three of them took a moment to peer into the haze of fog that loomed ominously in the distance.

"So, where to Ashford?" Jace asked his boss expectantly, more than ready to get Kara Caine somewhere private where no one would hear her screams.

Cade was met with two questioning pairs of eyes, one full of eager impatience, the other full of resigned dread. With a sigh of futile exasperation, he delivered the decision they both impatiently awaited.

"The Manor."

CHAPTER THREE

KARA awoke with heavy eyes, stiff limbs, and a tenderness in face that made her wince. She frowned when her fingers fell upon an unfamiliar nightgown that caressed her body with the softest of silks. A nightgown trimmed in delicate lace that barely covered the middle of her breasts or the tops of her thighs. *She* didn't own anything like that. Suspicious fingers trailed along the bedding that suddenly felt too soft, and her sense of unease grew. She wasn't in *her bed*.

Jolting up with a start, Kara surveyed her surroundings as her heart pounded frantically, steadily succumbing to an overwhelming sense of panic. Last night hadn't been some horrid melodrama concocted by her overly creative subconscious as she slept. It was real. Caden Ashford was real.

And the bastard had fucking *kidnapped* her.

Kara tried not to think of whose hands had removed her clothes and dressed her naked body in skimpy bits of silk and lace as she searched her body for signs of damage or assault. Apart from the cut on her wrist and the tenderness in her cheek, courtesy of Jace's assholery, everything seemed to be in good order. She rose from the bed slowly, her senses feeling somewhat hazy and dulled and her mouth unbearably dry. Desperate for escape, she tried to shake the heaviness from her limbs and the fogginess from her mind as she worked to forge a way out of her potentially life-threatening predicament.

Try as she might, Kara could remember nothing beyond walking out of the library with two terrifying men, assuming she was being led to her death. The current alternative seemed preferable, though barely. The only logical explanation for her loss of time between that moment and waking up in the morning was that the bastards had drugged her. She supposed being drugged was a traditional component of the whole kidnapping experience, but the idea of having her consciousness stolen from her infuriated her just the same.

Warily, Kara finally took a moment to observe her surroundings—or rather, her prison. It wasn't exactly the sort of room you'd expect to be used for housing captives. The bedroom was huge, bursting with bright daylight streaming in from tall windows draped with velvet, dusky-pink curtains. The walls were cream with Regency style decorative panels and crown moldings inlaid with gold. A large gold and crystal chandelier dangled obscenely from the gilded ceiling, granting the room an unmistakable air of decadence and grandeur. It was a room fit for a princess, not a prisoner.

Kara slipped out of the massive bed with its gold tufted headboard, throwing off the heavy cream duvet and discarding a mountain of satin and velvet pillows in various shades of pink. She opened a door at the far end of the room, revealing a large, private bathroom with two freestanding vanities overset with gold filigree mirrors, a claw foot bathtub with a miniature chandelier dangling above, and a walk-in shower big enough to fit three or four people. With a sudden, urgent need to use the toilet, Kara gratefully relieved herself before continuing her explorations. Opening the door beside the bathroom, she gasped in awe when she beheld the walk-in closet as big as her own bedroom back home. Floor to ceiling, the room was stocked with every imaginable item of clothing, accessories, and shoes, and another damn chandelier dangled from the middle of the room over a plush, pink settee.

Kara curiously sifted through drawers along the wall, finding a collection of scarves, sunglasses, hair accessories, and jewelry. She couldn't resist spending a moment to admire the pretty pieces of jewelry; they were clearly real and very expensive. She played with some of the rings, trying them on for fun, though they were a bit large for her small fingers. Kara paused abruptly when her gaze landed on a beautiful pendant necklace with an E initial crafted entirely of diamonds. She jolted back as though struck, the initial of a someone else's name painfully dragging her back down to reality. She was in someone else's room, touching someone else's things. The woman's perfume still lingered in the room like a Chanel scented ghost. What terrible end had befallen the woman who came before her? And would she be the next to disappear?

Swallowing her distaste for wearing a stranger's clothes, Kara searched the rows of beautiful, designer dresses for something practical and casual. She settled upon a simple navy dress that came down to the knees and seemed about her size. When she slipped it on, Kara discovered that the dress was *exactly* her size, as though it had been tailored for her. Was Cade some sort of serial kidnapper, and she just happened to be his preferred flavor of victim? The thought was terrifying and spurred her to get out of that room as quickly as possible. Kara found some flats that would allow her to run if given the opportunity; they were a half size too big, but they worked.

Contemplating escape, Kara tried the windows first; it would be the easiest route without being seen. Though they were unlocked, the view from the frosty, floor-length windows revealed vast grounds that offered seclusion for quite possibly miles. Kara was being held on a higher level which made escape from the window impossible unless she wanted to plummet to her death. Kara searched her surroundings for another way out or some object that would be useful in fleeing or, heaven forbid, fighting. There was nothing, and the most formidable weapon she could find in the whole room was a damn hairbrush.

Summoning her courage, Kara headed for the only viable option for escaping her room: the door. She turned the antique brass knob hesitantly, noticing with dismay that it was an old-fashioned sort of lock that could be accessed from both inside and *outside* with the use of a skeleton key. To her great astonishment, her door was unlocked, opening onto a long hall with a balcony view of the floor below. Kara stepped out cautiously, seriously confused as to why a prisoner was given free reign of the house. Perhaps it was all just a misunderstanding? Then again, waking up in a stranger's house with marks of brutality and missing memories of the night before wasn't exactly the sort of situation that lent itself to misinterpretation. Without a doubt, she had been kidnapped. Now she just had to figure out what exactly her captor wanted from her.

Lost in an unfamiliar maze, Kara searched for the most logical route toward freedom—preferably the front fucking door. She couldn't help but study the eclectic grandeur of her surroundings as she made her way toward the elaborate double staircase. In contrast with her usual acquaintance with the wealthy estates of donors and patrons of the university, there was nothing minimal or bland or monochromatic about the mansion she was currently being held in. Quite the opposite—there were colors, patterns, and different eras and styles of artwork thrust together in a sort of chaotic cohesiveness. Anything modern or contemporary was absent as though the owner bemoaned the very existence of anything pertaining to the present day. Vivid shades of green and blue colored the walls accented with wainscoting and trimmed with gold-inlaid crown moldings. The selections of art in the forms of paintings, sketches, framed tapestries, and a few scattered sculptures wove together intricately, reverently—like a love letter to pieces of the past. A little less delicate was the ostentatious, gold and crystal chandelier dominating at least half of the airspace above the black and white marble checkered floors of the formal foyer.

Kara's steps halted when she heard the unmistakable sound of people conversing down the hall. There was the all too familiar accent of her captor, but it was mingled with others that she didn't recognize. Kara's pulse quickened with tremblings of excitement. Perhaps Caden Ashford's guests had a less agreeable view of kidnapping than he so clearly held. Maybe, they could help her escape. It was with that hope clutched firmly to her chest that Kara rushed toward the voices that might be her salvation.

She came upon a formal dining hall, the doors wide open revealing yet another colossal chandelier composed of thousands of long, angular crystal prisms forming multiple rows of concentric circles in descending sizes. Commanding most of the space of the room was a vast, black marble table with thin veins of white streaked throughout and plush, emerald green, velvet chairs that provided space for at least twenty diners. The table was laid with a bountiful, mouth watering spread of breakfast items—pastries, fruits, eggs, sausages, bacon, coffee, and tea. Kara's stomach rumbled with the realization that she'd skipped lunch at the library yesterday, been deprived of dinner courtesy of her captors, and breakfast was due a few hours ago. With great effort, she pulled her attention away from the food and sought out the intended source of her interest. Other people. Escape.

To her great reluctance, Kara's eyes immediately settled upon Cade at the head of the table; he held her gaze with an indescribable expression—perhaps irritation and amusement mingled with something darker—before his features morphed into the very picture of gentlemanly politeness.

"Miss Caine. I'm glad you could join us," Cade greeted amicably, his hand outstretched as he welcomed her to an open spot at the table.

Breaking his stare, Kara glanced about the table. There were six men in total. Not a woman in sight, no one who could be the *E* whose dress she currently wore. Her absence sent a chill down Kara's spine. Was she wearing the gown of a woman who had already met her fate at Cade's hands? She suddenly had the urge to rip the exquisite clothing from her body and throw it as far away from her as she possibly could. Whatever Cade's sinister intentions may be, Kara would try her damnedest to make it out of that house alive.

Kara recognized three of the men from the previous night: the aggressive brute who backhanded her and tore her favorite dress, the kid who couldn't be any older than one of her students, and, of course, Cade. One of the other men looked mildly familiar, but she couldn't place where she had seen him. He was older, maybe late fifties, with gray hair, cold dark eyes, an unnerving smile that seemed too contrived, and a perfectly tailored, navy suit that emulated wealth and power as much as an article of clothing could. The older man eyed Kara with polite distaste, as though she had interrupted something far more deserving of his time. And perhaps she had.

One of the others—about her age with a slim build, unruly curly hair, and soft grey eyes framed by dark rimmed glasses—looked notedly uncomfortable, his gaze shifting between Cade and Kara, but he said nothing. The sight of the last man caused Kara to shrink back subconsciously, as though her body had assessed an undisclosed threat and warned her to seek out safety. The man was huge, dwarfing every other person at the table, the confines of his black jacket doing nothing to conceal the sheer amount of muscle that covered what seemed to be every inch of his body. The beauty of his tan skin and warm brown eyes did nothing to soften his threatening appearance; he looked as though he could quite literally snap her in two. Thankfully, of all the men at the table, he seemed the least interested in her, paying her a brief glance before turning his attention back to his coffee. Coffee that smelled deliciously enticing, causing Kara to frown with envy.

After sizing up the occupants of the room, Kara turned her attention back to Cade, who was patiently awaiting her response, his eyes still locked on her. "I wasn't aware I had a choice in the matter, Mr. Ashford, as you've taken me hostage and kept me here against my will." Kara looked around to gauge the reaction to her words, which should have been truly startling amongst normal company. The man in glasses squirmed uncomfortably in his seat, refusing to meet her eyes. Everyone else at the table seemed generally unbothered by her accusation. That bastard, Jace, even had the nerve to chuckle lightly from his spot near the head of the table. Cade watched gleefully as panic began to settle into Kara's features, a cruel smile upon his lips.

"Everyone at this table knows of your situation, Miss Caine. You'll find no help or escape here," Cade addressed her unkindly, his tone seeming to chastise the extent of Kara's naivety. "Sit," he commanded shortly, gesturing toward the empty seat beside him.

Kara bit her lip as she considered her next course of action. Clearly, the offer of a seat at the table had been an order rather than a suggestion, but there was no way in hell she was sitting beside the man who kidnapped her. Deciding upon partial obedience, Kara walked past the open chair beside Cade, past all the other useless assholes who would make no move to help her, down the row of empty chairs, until she came to the foot of the table. Loudly scraping the legs of the chair against the floor—the room echoing with the cacophony of her irritation—Kara sat down directly in front of Cade, a mere twenty feet down the table. Cade scowled at her furiously, his eyes alit with an anger that might have scared her if she wasn't so fucking over all of his shit. She was sitting, as he'd *commanded*, and that was the most compliance he was getting out of her at the moment.

"Eat," Cade barked at her, the single word sounding more like a threat than a courteous invitation.

Practically starving, Kara was quick to obey, her annoyance at being commanded like a dog soothed by the thought of food filling her empty stomach. And everything smelled so delicious, Kara could almost forget the presence of Cade and the five other accessories to kidnapping sitting around staring at her. That was, until Cade opened his stupid fucking mouth and ruined the delectable taste of a warm, buttery scone on her tongue.

"I suppose introductions are in order," Cade announced, his mask of gentility firmly in place once again.

Kara blanched as the piece of bacon she was holding fell to her plate, her hands trembling in trepidation. Everything that she knew from films and fiction told her that learning the identities of her captors was never a good sign. The more incriminating information you knew, the less likely you were to be set free. Had Cade already decided that this was where her life would end? Amongst cold strangers in a house that was too garish and grand to ever be welcoming? She had been prepared to die at the library last night, her life a not too begrudging sacrifice for the sake of preserving literary history. However, when directly faced with demise in the bright light of day, Kara couldn't suppress the quickening pulse of panic within her chest. Cade paused, a flicker of what might have been remorse crossing his face for a brief second before his mask was carefully in place once again.

"This is a matter of business, Miss Caine, nothing more," Cade offered as a consolation. "Once our transaction is concluded and I take possession of the book, you are free to go. You have my word."

Kara arched her eyebrow dubiously at his words, wondering what, exactly, the word of a criminal was worth. *Once he had the book*, she would be free. Unfortunately for both their sakes, that would never happen. In spite of her fear, in spite of being in a room full of terrifying men who would do absolutely nothing to aid an innocent captive, Kara's resolve held firm. She would protect the Chaucer text at all costs. Even if the cost was her life.

Deciding to at least get a final meal in before invoking her own destruction, Kara allowed Cade his assumptions about her agreement on the matter and began stuffing another scone into her mouth. And fuck, it was delicious. Not such a terrible way to die, all things considered.

"You'll remember Jace and Declan from last night," Cade said with a gesture in their direction. Jace winked in greeting and Declan offered a small, apologetic wave. Kara granted the latter a tight smile of acknowledgment and the former no acknowledgement at all other than an innate shiver of revulsion. "This is Braxton, our tech guy." Cade pointed to the younger man. "Ortega, the head of security." Cade waved to the monolith of a man. "And perhaps you already know of Manfred Randall?" Cade gestured to the last man with the cold eyes and too wide smile. "Randall is our legal counsel. Business and private matters."

Now that he mentioned it, Kara did know of Manfred Randall. He looked familiar because she passed his obnoxiously large face pasted on a billboard on her drive to the university every day. Certainly a man of the law wouldn't approve of a woman being kidnapped and held hostage?

"Before you get any grand ideas, he and I are very close, so you'll understand that attorney-client privilege is more important in this situation than any pleas you might make in favor of your escape," Cade stated bluntly as soon as he noticed the spark of hope in Kara's eyes; he enjoyed watching that spark fizzle and die.

"As much as I sympathize with your unusual predicament, Dr. Caine, Ashford is right," Randall addressed Kara in between sips of coffee as though commenting on something as trivial as the weather. "Legally speaking, my hands are tied."

"*Unusual predicament?*" Kara spoke for the first time since sitting down, her face contorted with fury and disbelief. "Is that what you call being kidnapped and imprisoned by a bunch of lowlife thugs?"

"Well, it isn't exactly a usual occurrence, now is it Dr. Caine?" Randall responded in a patronizing tone. "Unless you're accustomed to kidnappings in your daily life, which would be a surprising, not to mention troubling, admission if you were," he finished with a laugh as he continued with his breakfast unperturbed.

Fucking hell, he's as bad as Caden Ashford.

"What I find *troubling* is Chicago's most glorified representative of the law aiding and abetting criminals," Kara admonished through gritted teeth, but trying to draw remorse from a lawyer was a bit like trying to draw blood from a stone. Impossible.

"What are lawyers for, my dear, if not to assist the common man in understanding our nation's laws and regulations—and how to circumvent them," Randall explained with a smug gleam in his eye.

Left speechless by the level of depravity and weakness exhibited by the repulsive representatives of the male species surrounding the table, Kara rolled her eyes dramatically and revisited her plate of breakfast.

"So, now that the formalities are out of the way, we can move on to business. When would be a convenient time for you to accompany us to the university today?"

"Why? Are you running low on good reading material?" Kara inquired obtusely.

"We would like to conclude the Chaucer transferral as quickly as possible, Miss Caine," Cade commented evenly, ignoring Kara's quip entirely.

"For the last fucking time, it's *Dr. Caine*, and that's a rather elegant way to demand the theft of monumental text from a hostage librarian."

"I would like to think I'm an elegant man, Miss Caine," Cade offered with a smile that would have been absolutely pussy-obliterating if Kara didn't consider him to be such a reprehensible human being.

"If charm is your only weapon, you've come to this negotiation horribly underarmed, Mr. Ashford."

"Trust me, Miss Caine, you don't want to be acquainted with my other methods of persuasion. You'll find they are primitive, but effective." Cade fixed her with an intimidating stare, his fists flexing against the table, but Kara didn't flinch or cower, in spite of the danger laced with his words. "Certainly an educated girl such as yourself would appreciate the chance to reach a resolution with reason rather than violence."

Kara fidgeted in her seat, the tension of the moment relieving her of the last of her appetite, the food on her mostly full plate suddenly unappealing. Though she put on a brave front, she really had no idea how to handle the demands of a dangerous—and regrettably attractive—rogue and his band of merry miscreants. It wasn't a fair fight, and Caden Ashford seemed keenly aware of that fact. The best Kara could do was even the playing field, however insignificantly.

"I have questions," Kara announced finally, trying her very best to keep her voice firm and steady. She hoped she might gain some useful information, or, at the very least, stall the inevitable.

"I suppose that's not unreasonable," Cade responded thoughtfully, stroking the slight stubble of his jaw. "You may ask three."

"Where am I?" Kara asked almost immediately. Their location seemed like the most important piece of information in understanding her position, her vulnerability, and her chances of escape.

"Ashford Manor," Cade answered evasively, though truthfully. They were at his estate. He had no intention of elaborating on their exact location, but they were secluded enough that it wouldn't matter if he did.

Kara's face fell in disappointment. His answer did very little to illuminate the location of where she was being held. For all she knew, they could have left the country, and her lack of specificity had essentially cost her a question. She tried to make the most of his response, considering what information it revealed. The expansive mansion was his, not his employer's. So he was wealthy, probably well-situated in society. He spoke like a man of breeding, so why was he turning to crime to fund his endeavors? Was the life of a thief really quite so lucrative?

"So what are you?" she asked condescendingly, gesturing to the unavoidable opulence of the room. "Millionaire? Billionaire?" She'd probably wasted another question, but her curiosity got the best of her.

"I don't like labels," Cade answered shortly.

"Yes, I can understand why. Labels can get pretty unflattering for a criminal, can't they?"

"And what makes you think I am a criminal?" Cade asked smugly as he crossed his arms over his chest.

"You're joking, right?" Kara answered with a scoff. "You and your henchmen literally held me hostage, attempted to steal an incredibly valuable object, kidnapped me, drugged me, and are now holding me prisoner in some garish mansion in the middle of god knows where."

Caden smiled broadly in response, and Kara was left thoroughly regretting her impassioned tirade. Yes, he had been joking. And, rather than having its desired effect, her anger had merely amused him.

"Yes, I believe that is the dictionary definition of criminality," he concurred with a laugh.

"Fuck you," Kara spat back in exasperation. Her comment, perhaps a little louder than intended, caused a hush to spread across the room as the attention of everyone at the table turned to her. They seemed to be waiting for their boss's reaction, and Kara couldn't help feeling she had spoken too rashly.

"Someone should teach you some manners, Miss Caine," Cade responded dangerously, his eyes sparking with disapproval and something more lethal.

"Regretfully, my university never offered a course on proper female etiquette, so I settled for PhD's in Literary Theory, Archival Science, and English Literature."

"Congratulations, you spent eight years at university learning how to read a bloody book," Cade answered with a slow, condescending clap of his hands.

Kara's cheeks filled with color in a mixture of embarrassment and anger. A few snickers echoed through the dining hall, the loudest of which came from Jace's section of the room. Kara shot him a dark look before deciding it was best to ignore him completely. It had been six years in college, but Kara was not about to dignify that provocation with a response.

"And where exactly are successful criminals such as yourself educated, *Mr. Ashford?*" Kara asked, her voice dripping with sarcasm.

"Oxford. History. In my line of work, it's advantageous to know when something is valuable. Does that impress you, Miss Caine?"

Yes.

"Not really," she answered flippantly, but her eyes found his with a mixture of admiration and envy.

Cade captured Kara's stare for a moment longer than the bounds of propriety, enjoying the way she shifted nervously in her chair as though his gaze was a physical sensation that monstrously clawed its way across her skin. In one sense, she was right. He was a predator, and his claws were more than merely metaphor. When Cade decided that she had agonized sufficiently in foreboding silence, he continued with his agenda. "Well, now that we've gotten to know each other better, I think it is time to discuss the swiftest route for your return home."

"Lovely, if one of your minions would be so good as to show me the way out, I'd be more than happy to relieve myself of your generous hospitality," Kara answered far too cheerily, hoping, against her own best interests, to piss off the brooding bastard.

Cade laughed shortly; it was an ominous sound, devoid entirely of humor. "You're not going anywhere, Miss Caine," he responded darkly, the threat of imminent danger, destruction, quite possibly death wrapped within a few simple words. Cade reveled in the flash of fear in Kara's eyes, the delectable way in which she anxiously bit her bottom lip. She was scared of him.

Good. She should be. "We will be needing the book before you're granted safe passage home."

"Well then, I'm afraid we are at an impasse because there is no way in hell you're getting near that book."

"Be reasonable, Miss Caine," Cade coerced, his jaw tense with the strain of having to reason with what had to be the most *unreasonable* woman in the whole of Chicago. "Help us retrieve it, and you are free to go. Unscathed."

"Wow, that's your offer? Deliver an invaluable academic artifact into your unworthy hands, and you'll do me the favor of not harming me any more than you already have? Yeah, I think I'll pass."

"Would you prefer I offer you something more tangible? Money, perhaps?"

"Now you're just insulting me. Do you honestly think I'd be a librarian if I was monetarily motivated in any respect? I don't care about money. This house, this wealth and grandeur," Kara gestured around to the sheer excessiveness of the room, "they mean absolutely nothing to me."

Cade fumed at her from across the table, the small fragments of his self-control disintegrating with each word out of Kara fucking Caine's mouth. "Perhaps I'm not being clear enough. You *will* help us retrieve the book. It is entirely up to you how many pieces you are in when we do so."

"Already heard the death threats from the handsy asshole over there," Kara replied, throwing a harsh glare at Jace that was met very quickly with a self-satisfied grin. "Shockingly, it doesn't sound any more appealing coming from your mouth."

Cade dug his fingers into his hair harshly, feeling uncharacteristically out of control in the situation and desperate to reclaim his authority. "Clear the fucking room," Cade commanded with a curt jerk of his head, his gaze fixed intently on Kara.

The dining hall filled with the sound of chairs scraping against marble and mild dissent as the men at the table abandoned their half-finished plates of breakfast and heeded their boss's request. Breakfast aside, they were all more than happy to escape the line of fire as Cade's mood slipped from dim to dangerous.

Kara leapt to join them, quite content to be free from the lingering stares of strangers and the smoldering glare of the hateful man at the head of the table. She had every intention of stowing away in her room until death by starvation or whatever means Cade devised claimed her because she was not about to suffer the company of any man in that room ever again.

"Not you, Miss Caine," Cade reprimanded harshly. "We still have matters that require discussion."

Kara willed her body to disobey his order and escape the room with the others, but his eyes kept her feet pinned to the floor as though with the weight of a hundred stones. In complete panic, Kara watched as each man followed Cade's orders dutifully and exited the room. Jace, the obnoxious fuck, had the nerve to throw her a provocative wink before leaving the room and closing the double doors firmly behind him. She flinched at the sound; it rang with the finality of doom.

All too quickly, Kara was alone. With Cade. And it scared the absolute fuck out of her.

"Sit down," Cade ordered harshly, pointing to her abandoned chair.

After a small beat of hesitation, Kara obeyed, sliding back into the chair with huff of annoyance and a scowl of frustration. The insufferable man and his goddamn orders could go to hell. She watched Cade warily, unsure of his intentions. Beside a brute like Jace, Caden had come across as nearly chivalrous during the events of the previous evening. In the light of day, there was an obvious viciousness that lurked beneath the refined attire and smooth British accent.

"So, how long am I to remain a prisoner in this house?" Kara asked sharply, exhausting her last shred of patience for whatever

Hideaway

game he was playing. She wanted answers, and, if he wanted a mildly cooperative hostage, he would offer them.

"You have been taken care of and given many liberties, Miss Caine. You are not restricted to the house; you may go anywhere on the grounds, and they are quite vast, I assure you. You are my guest, and you have been treated as nothing less," Cade responded evenly.

"Are all of your guests kidnapped and held against their will?" Kara asked indignantly.

"You are not locked in a dungeon. You are not bound with ropes and chains," he said patronizingly as he gestured to the obvious freedom of movement she enjoyed in her seat beside him. "Though both could be arranged if it would enhance your fantasy of being my captive," he answered with a salacious grin pulling at his lips.

What the actual fuck?

Kara surveyed the dark amusement in his eyes with open mouthed horror. Her instincts told her to run, and, for once, she wasn't one to disagree. She jolted from her chair, eying the distance between herself and the door.

"Sit down, Miss Caine," Cade ordered in exasperation. "I'm not going to hurt you."

Yet.

Shaken, Kara fell back into her seat, the strength of her traitorous limbs having fully abandoned her at the sight of Cade's chastising glare.

"Now, how can we resolve this situation as amicably as possible?" Cade asked, fully intending to be reasonable. Within limits.

"I think any hope of amiability was discarded when you chose to drag me to your home against my will."

"Perhaps you're right. If it is any consolation, I don't enjoy your presence in my home any more than you do."

"Then let me go."

"You know I can't do that. You have put me in a very difficult situation, Miss Caine. You would find my easiest options rather disagreeable, and, in consideration of this, I have delayed my decision on what is to be done with you. But I warn you, the inevitable cannot be delayed forever. Your cooperation would best benefit all parties involved, yourself most of all."

"I think I have made my opinions on that subject very clear, Mr. Ashford," Kara answered firmly, rising from her chair and hastily heading for the exit, eager to avoid spending another moment alone in a room with such a man.

Cade prevented her escape easily, capturing her arm and jerking her around to face him. His expression was fierce, imperious. Kara shrank back from the unconcealed danger that lurked within his eyes, her sense of self-preservation begging her to give in to his demands, whatever they may be. As usual, her virtues of preservation and pride were at odds.

"Do not turn your back on me again, Miss Caine. You'll find I'm not as amenable on the second offense," he admonished harshly. "You were not excused, nor has our business been concluded." His eyes bored into hers as though he could coax her submission by mere force of will. "Now, you will tell me the passcode and help me retrieve the book," he commanded, his eyes cold and hard as he tightened his grip on her arm to enforce her surrender.

"*Fuck you*," Kara spat, turning away from him and whimpering when she twisted her own arm in the process.

Hideaway

Cade jerked her back toward him, thrusting her body roughly against the rigid contours of his chest. He grasped her jaw, his fingers digging painfully into the side of her cheeks as he forced her eyes up to meet his. His eyes were dark, nearly every fleck of gold extinguished by a black, all-consuming haze of fury. In spite of all of her bravery and resolute defiance, Kara trembled in his hold.

"Disrespect me again, and I will bend you over that table, take off my belt, and spank you until you remember your fucking manners," Cade threatened coldly, his tone deadly serious as his hand moved to the buckle of his belt for emphasis.

Kara stilled against him in abject horror. Fuck it, at that point, she would rather they murder her. At least being shot or stabbed would be a relatively quick and clean death versus slowly succumbing to a demise from humiliation after being bent over and spanked by Caden fucking Ashford.

"Are you going to behave?" Cade asked sharply, digging his fingers a little deeper into her cheeks.

Kara swallowed down the sickening taste of iron as the bruising pressure of Cade's grip forced her teeth to cut into the tender flesh of her inner cheek. Still stunned speechless, she merely nodded in agreement. She would have to decline Cade's demands for the book as politely as possible to prevent any of the evil bastard's cruel and unusual punishments.

Fan-fucking-tastic.

"Good," Cade replied, practically shoving her away as he removed his hand from her face. "Now, you will come with me to the university and retrieve the Chaucer text." Cade assumed Kara's nod of agreement had implied her surrender. That she was finally willing to cooperate, submit to his demands, and hand over the goddamn book. He was—apparently—wrong.

"No, I will not," Kara answered, keeping her tone respectful, but her resolve unwavering.

Her blatant denial, for what felt like the hundredth time in a span of a mere day—a day so long it seemed that perhaps weeks had passed instead—was the final rift in Cade's steady composure. His control fractured into countless shards, fury seeping in to fill the cracks as an undeniable need to destroy overwhelmed his senses. Wrapping his hands tightly, punishingly, around her upper arms, Cade forced Kara backwards toward the wall. Her body crashed painfully into the hard surface as he pressed himself against her, leaving little room to breathe and no space to escape. Trapped, Kara began to panic. Appreciating her first signs of fear and more than willing to take advantage, Cade shook her roughly as he reiterated his demands.

"Tell me the passcode, Kara," he ordered angrily, unaccustomed to having his demands so flagrantly disregarded.

"Not a chance in hell," she refused bravely, even as she shook inwardly with fear and uncertainty.

As though he were trying to contain himself before things escalated too quickly, Cade moved his hand slowly up Kara's arm, over her shoulder, along her neck, before resting his fingers tightly against her throat. The pace of Cade's breathing matched Kara's— quick and heavy, both of their bodies surging with adrenaline, hers driven by fear, his driven by rage. Cade's grip on her throat tightened slightly, simply so he could feel the thump of her pulse against his fingertips.

The ability to allow or deny the very oxygen that filled someone's lungs was an intoxicating experience; it was sheer, tangible power. Cade bent his head toward hers, their foreheads nearly touching, a gesture that might have appeared tender if it wasn't infused with barely contained violence. His proximity forced Kara to look him in the eyes. "I want you to consider your next response as though your life depended on it. Because it fucking does." He moved infinitesimally closer, and Kara could feel the weight of him against her chest. "Tell me the passcode," he said in a voice that was disturbingly impassive, while his eyes held all the threat that his tone did not.

Kara couldn't look away, she couldn't move, she could barely breathe. She was scared, and yet, she had known her answer since she walked into the room. It was the same answer she had yesterday when a beautiful, terrifying man demanded more than she could offer. No matter how many times he asked in however many ways, her answer would remain the same.

"No," she said softly, the strength of her voice breaking slightly. The fierce determination, the unflinching resolve, the stubborn willfulness—they were all gone. He had stripped them all away and left her with nothing more than a bare adherence to principle. It wasn't much, but it was enough. Kara waited quietly without the inclination to plead, entirely at the mercy of whatever Caden Ashford may intend.

Without reason, the falter in her voice shook him. In his life, he had witnessed panic and terror, he had heard screams and begging, he had seen tears, but they had never before given him pause. Her eyes were large and frightened, glossy from tears that threatened to fall, darkened with a resignation that was reminiscent of hope being shattered into a million pieces. And he flinched, drawing back slightly as though met with pain, as though he could feel her own. Cade had never had much of a capacity for empathy, so his instinctive reaction to her suffering was startling. In an attempt to suffocate his bout of weakness, Cade closed his fingers tighter around Kara's throat, squeezing as hard as he could. He watched, mesmerized, as she gasped for breath, her skin turning pink then red from lack of oxygen. Before he could finish the job, before her consciousness faded into darkness, Cade released her sharply as if the touch of her skin burned him like fire. He trembled slightly as he scrutinized his offending appendage, flexing his fingers to confirm full functionality. Everything was in working order, which meant that the problem lay elsewhere. He couldn't do it. He could not will himself to seriously hurt her, even if it was to his advantage. Somehow, the girl had gotten to him.

"*Fuck*," Cade muttered in exasperation, raking his fingers through his hair. Without another glance at Kara, Cade stormed out of the room.

The door slammed shut behind him with such force that the room seemed to tremor. Kara was left alone, her body still pressed against the wall as though the ability to function had been startled from her. Slowly, her senses reemerged with overwhelming strength. Her legs gave way beneath the crushing weight of shock mixed with relief, and she slid to the floor in a crumpled heap. In the welcome solitude of the room, her tears fell freely. She made no move to wipe them away, allowing herself a proper display of hysterics that seemed all too warranted given what had just transpired. She breathed deeply, her starved lungs working with excess enthusiasm after Cade's deprivation. Her hand traveled shakily to her throat; it felt tender and sore, as if Cade's brutal fingers still lingered, draining her of life.

And yet, he had stopped. Why had he stopped? He had threatened her with destruction if she didn't comply, and he seemed like the sort of man who fulfilled his threats in their entirety. But when she refused, he released her, even though it seemed against his very will to loosen his grip on her throat. Kara was grateful for the temporary safety, but she dreaded the next, unavoidable encounter with Caden Ashford.

Kara jolted at the sound of a door opening at the side of the dining hall. She braced herself, fearful that Cade had come to finish the job. Instead, an older woman with a small stature, full physique, faded copper hair, kind eyes, and a round, cheerful face bustled into the room. She stopped sharply at the sight of Kara in a teary mess on the floor.

"Goodness, lassy, are ye alright?" she asked in a voice full of concern as she bounded over to offer her assistance.

Kara took her hand and awkwardly stood to her feet, rather embarrassed to be seen in such a state. The woman assessed Kara appraisingly, her eyes narrowing when she noticed the marks on Kara's neck. Not one to pry, the woman made no comment as she helped Kara into a chair and offered her a napkin to dry her tears. The woman allowed Kara a moment to regain her composure before attempting conversation.

"Now, what seems to be the problem? Something that can be mended with a cup of tea? Or something stronger, perhaps?" the woman asked kindly.

"I don't think my troubles can be quite so easily mended, but a cup of tea sounds lovely," Kara answered, appreciating the kind woman's attentiveness and her rather surprising suggestion of alcohol before noon.

"Right, be back in a moment, dear," she said, scuttling back toward where the kitchen was presumably located.

In a few minutes, the kindly woman reappeared, carrying two steaming cups of tea in the most delicate china teacups Kara had ever seen in actual use. She accepted the tea gratefully, taking a long, soothing sip before endeavoring to discover who exactly the mystery woman was. Perhaps Kara had found an ally and a means of escape after all.

"You're the first woman I've seen in this house," Kara began conversationally.

"Aye, well, Mr. Ashford prefers the company of his own kind, I should think. I'm just his cook, so I stay out of their way rightly enough. The men are more than glad to see a woman at meal times, but other than that I keep to myself," the woman explained, her accent somewhat similar to Cade's with bursts of the heartiness of a Scotswoman mixed in.

"Have there been other…women. Like me, I mean," Kara asked cautiously. Maybe the woman knew about E.

"I'm not quite sure what you're asking, dear," the older woman answered cryptically, though her brow furrowed in a nervousness she couldn't mask as well as her her tone.

Kara stared at the woman, trying not to grow frustrated with what was either ignorance or a blatant condoning of Cade's actions. Clearly, Cade was into some shady shit and wasn't too far above drugging and dragging women to his house when it suited him. So was *E* a prisoner like her, or had she willingly fallen into Cade's brutal clutches?

"The room that I'm staying in clearly belonged to a woman," Kara began slowly, trying to tread carefully as she wasn't entirely sure how far the woman's blind loyalty to her employer went. "Do you know what happened to her?"

The woman looked about the room anxiously before she turned to Kara. "We don't talk about her," she whispered. "Her name hasn't been spoken in this house since it happened."

"Since *what* happened?" Kara asked in horror, an unusual iciness sneaking up her spine.

The woman's eyes worriedly searched the vicinity again. "It's not my place to say. If you want to know about *her*, you'll have to ask him. Though I would advise against ever brining her up in his presence. Mr. Ashford has changed since the incident. He's... colder."

Kara pondered her words of warning, growing more uneasy by the second. Apparently, she wouldn't be getting any more out of the older woman on the mystery girl. Kara would have to change her tactics if she hoped to get any useful information. "Mr. Ashford seems to be quite—"

Mr. Ashford seems to be quite a twat.

"Imperious," Kara finished mildly after searching for a word appropriate for the older woman's company. "Have you worked for him long?"

The woman settled comfortably into a chair and claimed the second cup of tea, enjoying a gulp as she prepared to relay the details of her acquaintance with Mr. Ashford. "Aye, since he was a wee bairn, or his mother more like. I worked at the family's estate back in Yorkshire. After he'd grown and spent a few years establishing business in America, he came back and stole me right out of his mother's house. Told me he couldn't live without my plum pudding and made me an offer I couldn't refuse. I've always had a soft spot for the lad. Him and his brother both."

Two Mr. Ashford's? How terrifying.

"Oh, I'm Mrs. Hughes, by the way. Sorry love, should have begun with that. My mind's a bit scattered some days," she added apologetically.

"Lovely to meet you, Mrs. Hughes," Kara extended her hand in greeting, "I'm Kara."

CHAPTER FOUR

AS a new day dawned, the too cheerful morning sun greeting Kara with the welcome knowledge that she had made it through another night in captivity moderately unscathed. Surprisingly, she had survived one day with Ashford Manor as her prison, but she dreaded what the second might bring. The lingering soreness of bruises splattered against the pale skin of her neck and the tenderness in her throat when she swallowed reminded Kara that her captor was a morally depraved, relentless, fucking bastard. He simply could not be reasoned with, and, consequently, she resolved to avoid Caden Ashford at all costs.

After rapidly losing her appetite at breakfast the previous morning and skipping all subsequent meals, Kara's stomach was most at odds with her decision to confine herself to her room for fear of encountering Cade. The nauseating sound of Cade's imperious voice traveling across the dining room to her quarters could only dissuade her for so long before her starving body rebelled, consequences of leaving the safety of her room be damned.

Finally, the raucous of male voices dissipated, leaving a blessed silence in its wake. Slowly, Kara cracked open her door and tiptoed out of her room. She wasn't stupid enough to linger anywhere in Cade's house apart from her allocated bedroom, but perhaps she could find solace in the kitchens with Mrs. Hughes. She'd seemed friendly enough, even if she was complicit in her employer's kidnapping of young women. At that point, Kara would accept any hint of kindness she could get.

Thankfully, she made it to the the kitchens without being accosted, the large house seeming to be empty. Mrs. Hughes greeted her warmly, dusting the flour from her hands on her apron as she turned from the dough she was kneading on the marble counter. "Morning, dear. I'm afraid you've missed breakfast," she informed Kara apologetically.

"Yes, I suppose I overslept," Kara lied. In actuality, she had no intention of ever making another appearance in the dining hall to eat with Cade and his reprehensible, criminal delinquents.

"Nae bother, there's plenty for you to eat," Mrs. Hughes reassured her, bustling around the kitchen to grab bits and bobs. She fetched a fresh loaf of bread, still warm from the oven, and sliced four, thick slices, wrapping them in a cloth. A quick pop to the refrigerator produced a selection of berries and some cold cuts of ham. "The strawberries were picked from the hothouse this morning. You can venture over there if you like. Mr. Ashford has some lovely flowers in bloom, and there are a variety of fruits and vegetables as well. It's a nice sight to see when the dreariness of winter really starts to set in." Mrs. Hughes grabbed a large block of cheddar cheese from the counter and started to slice it as well. "Why don't I get you a basket for all of this, and you can have a walk around the grounds? Some fresh air would do ye good."

"That sounds lovely, thank you," Kara answered, genuinely grateful for the suggestion of escaping the imposing walls of Cade's home. Perhaps she could even find a means of *actual* escape. "Is the estate very large?" Kara inquired, trying to get an idea of how far she would have to walk for help.

"Goodness, aye. Over twenty kilometers. Ye coudnae walk it in a day if you tried." Mrs. Hughes went to the cupboard to get a basket. "There's river that runs about a kilometer north of here that can be a rather pretty spot. It's about cold enough that it'll be frozen over. Oh, and the stables are just beyond. The horses always fancy a visitor." She began filling the basket with all the fresh foods she'd gathered, adding some apples and a thermos of tea at the top.

"I think you've packed enough for an small army," Kara laughed as she watched the older woman stuff the basket full.

"Ye need a bit more meat on your bones," Mrs. Hughes tutted back, her accent thicker and less English that morning.

Kara didn't respond to the critique because it was true. A glance in the mirror that morning had revealed a haggard ghost of a woman she had barely recognized. Clearly living in a cage did not agree with her and neither did skipping meals for the sake of avoiding the men of the house. Thanks to her wisp of a mother's genetics, Kara had always straddled the border of *too* skinny, and clearly the stress of her current situation wasn't doing her any favors in that department.

"Thank you so much, Mrs. Hughes," Kara said as the cook handed her a very full picnic basket.

"Dinnae mention it, dear. It's no trouble at all. I'm just grateful to have another woman to talk to. It's been nothing but these rowdy boys for ages."

"Does Mr. Ashford not entertain?" Kara asked, surprised at Mrs. Hughes words and trying to think of the most tasteful way to ask if Cade dated.

"Not in that way, no. Goodness, you're the first woman he's brought home in a year at least," Mrs. Hughes explained, seeming pleased by the idea of Cade bringing Kara to the manor.

Kara wondered if the woman could truly be so naive as to assume she was there of her own free will. Did she think that Cade and her were in some sort of relationship? Mrs. Hughes had found her crying in the dinning hall with the marks of Cade's anger around her throat. Is that how Cade typically treated the women he dated? Kara repressed a shiver of fear at the thought of what Cade would do to someone he didn't care for at all. How far would he go if she didn't give him what he wanted? She had a feeling that, as bad as a brute like Jace seemed on the outside, Cade had a far more deadly monster lurking beneath the surface.

"Ye can't go out like that, you'll catch your death of cold," Mrs. Hughes admonished, dragging Kara from her darker thoughts. "Here, put these on," she ordered, handing Kara an oversized coat, scarf, hat, and gloves.

Hideaway

Kara didn't have to ask who they belonged to. She could smell the intoxicating scent of Cade on every item in her hands. She was met with a conflicting desire to bring the scarf to her nose and deeply inhale the fresh, wintery scent of mint and cedar and to throw the whole pile in an open fire. "I can't wear these," Kara argued, trying to hand the clothes back to Mrs. Hughes.

"Och, Mr. Ashford won't mind. It's a dreich day. He'd rather you were warm than freezing to death outside," Mrs. Hughes brushed off, grabbing Kara a pair of tall wellies too as her heels would never hold up with wet and rocky grounds.

Kara seriously doubted Cade would mind her succumbing to the perils of the winter weather, but she listened to Mrs. Hughes and put on everything she'd offered. If Cade spotted her wearing his things, she have to worry more of dying from embarrassment than anything the cold elements had to offer.

Begrudgingly, Kara had to admit that the greenhouse was breathtaking. She'd always had a love for flowers and plants, but had never had a knack for keeping them living for long. The longest something had ever survived in her care was a cute little cactus she'd named George. George had lasted for about three months until he met his end as a result of a little overzealous watering. Clearly, plant murdering was a crime she had a one up on Cade because the greenhouse was immaculate.

Every plant was beautiful and vibrant and clearly meticulously attended. The crown jewel of the collection was a vast assortment of English garden roses spanning many different shades of color from the deepest burgundy to the palest blush. Unable to resist the lush blooms that had always been one of her favorites, Kara plucked a deep, blood-red rose from the shrub, inhaling the delicate sweetness of its petals. Careful of the thorns, Kara picked several more roses and added them to her basket, getting an irrational sense of satisfaction from plundering Cade's personal floral collection.

Having eaten her packed lunch in the warmth of the greenhouse, Kara set off in search of the stables. She hadn't been around horses in years, and she welcomed the chance to find something pleasant about her captivity. Kara quickly spotted the stables due to the sheer size of the black painted building. It was probably big enough to house twenty or more horses. She hated the thought of all those living creatures being compiled as what was probably just a status symbol of Cade's wealth. There was no way a man like Cade had the capacity for empathizing with an animal.

Kara walked into the stables with the intention of giving every single horse the love and attention they were no doubt starving for. She'd saved the apples Mrs. Hughes packed her in the hopes of finding a friend to share them with. The horses began to rustle and neigh as she approached, a little restless with a stranger in their midst. "Shh shh shh," Kara calmed them as she treaded in slowly. "It's okay. You don't need to be afraid. I'm trapped here too, just like you." Kara walked along the stalls, stopping when a particularly friendly mare stuck her head out and neighed at her in greeting.

"Hey, girl," Kara said softly, reaching out her hand to stroke the midnight black mare along the nose. "You're a pretty girl, aren't you?" The horse seemed to preen at her words. "Are you hungry? Would you like a treat, sweetheart?" Kara asked the horse as she

Hideaway

reached into the basket on her arm and pulled out a red and yellow dappled apple. The horse moved in excitement, snatching the apple from Kara's open hand and crunching down loudly. "That's it." Kara stroked her mane, loving the feel of the coarse tresses beneath her fingers. "Someone likes treats, don't they? What's your name, pretty girl?"

A loud clatter of something heavy dropping to the floor startled Kara from her one-sided conversation with the horse. Frantically glancing toward to stables entrance, Kara found herself staring into the brooding, green-gold eyes of the last person on earth that she wanted to see. "Fucking hell, don't scare me like that!" Kara shouted, having recovered her composure enough to put thought to word. Why the hell was he there? She assumed he was out working—robbing museums or thieving estates or whatever the fuck he did.

"*I* scared *you*? I would rather think I'm more surprised to find you lurking about my stables," Cade responded shortly, working to recover his equilibrium after having his chance at tranquility ripped away with the presence of an intruder in his favorite hideaway. Well, second favorite. "You're petting my horse," he informed with a dark, pointed look at where her hand continued to stroke the soft, dark mane of the sweet mare in the stall.

Kara jerked her hand away as though bitten, terrified to have touched anything Caden Ashford claimed as his without permission. The mare sought her out greedily, nudging her with her nose as if to beg for more coddling. Guiltily, Kara moved out of reach. Nothing was worth inciting Cade's anger, no matter how damn cute his horse was.

"You said I was allowed anywhere on the grounds," Kara defended, her eyes flickering with fear at the thought of having unintentionally offended or angered him. Her hand subconsciously drifted to her throat where the marks of his last bout of fury still lay upon her skin, strokes of deep blue starkly contrasting the paleness of her neck.

"I did," Cade conceded, his tone softening as he realized her tension—and the cause of it. "I'm just not used to happening upon visitors in the stables. This is where I go to be alone. I prefer the company of creatures who keep their thoughts to themselves and allow me to keep my own in turn."

In spite of herself, Kara could empathize. That was exactly why she preferred books to people. Uncomfortable with finding a common ground with her nemesis, she attempted to shatter the stirrings of kinship as quickly as possible. "Yes, I could tell from your manners that you're out of practice when it comes to human relations. Your social graces are rather rusty. Most men take a woman out to eat before holding her hostage in their excessive mansions."

"I believe we ate breakfast together yesterday, Miss Caine," Cade answered with a smile that might have been considered charming.

"Yes, but that was *after* the kidnapping, so it doesn't count," Kara answered teasingly. She was horrified with how playful her voice sounded to her own ears. Fuck, what if he thought she was flirting? Fuck, what if she *was* flirting? Stockholm syndrome was setting in so quickly that it felt normal to joke about being fucking kidnapped. She needed a distraction before she did something really stupid. Like

Hideaway

forget she was supposed to be escaping from the dark, brooding, undeniably attractive bastard before her.

"So, what's her name?" Kara asked as a subject change, feeling safe enough to continue stroking the mare who neighed happily with the returned attention.

"Sugar Cubes," Cade answered, a hesitant smile on his lips as he watched Kara whisper sweet nothings in the horse's ear.

"Sugar Cubes?" Kara questioned with a laugh. "Who named her? A five year old with a penchant for sweets?"

"In a way," Cade responded with a soft laugh of his own. "When I was a boy, I had a favorite black mare. Her true name was Midnight Fury, but she had a real obsession with the sugar cubes I would steal for her from Mrs. Hughes kitchen, hence the nickname. When I was home, I rode her nearly everyday. She passed while I was at boarding school, a couple years before I headed to Oxford. In her memory, this girl is Sugar Cubes II."

Cade moved beside Kara to stroke the horse's neck lovingly. He noticed Kara flinch at his closeness, but she didn't move away. Cade used the proximity to study Kara as she was fully preoccupied with Sugar Cubes. For all her infuriating attributes, she could appreciate an animal's company, and he had to admit that warranted at least a small measure of his respect. His gaze traveled her body, and the talons of self-hatred dug in deep when he saw the shadowy imprint of his fingers on her throat. How could she stand to be near him when he had been so brutish the last time they'd spoken?

Unbidden, Cade's fingers reached out to brush the marks marring her skin. His marks. Seeing his anger and violence written upon her body left him feeling uncontrollably sickened. He wished he could wipe the bruises from her throat as much as he wished he could wipe the moment he gave them from her memory.

"I'm sorry for these," Cade said roughly, his voice heavy with remorse and other emotions he couldn't even begin to ascribe with a label. He continued to tenderly stroke the back of his knuckles along her neck as she stood frozen beneath him.

"W-what?" Kara asked as though confused by his words, the warmth of his touch depriving her of rational thought as her heart struggled to maintain a steady rhythm and her lungs labored overstrenuously to supply her body with oxygen.

"I'm sorry for hurting you," he continued softly. "It was never my intention to cause you harm. I needed the book. I still do. But that isn't an excuse for resorting to that kind of violence." Cade's lingering fingers found her chin and gently forced her head up to look at him. "It will not happen again, you have my word." Cade's green-gold eyes deepened with the solemn sincerity of a promise that would not be broken.

And, whether it was wisdom or folly, Kara believed him.

Overcome by the stirring mix of forgiveness and trust he saw pooling in her bright eyes, Cade allowed himself to drift closer.

Closer.

Closer still.

Until his lips hovered so close to hers that he could almost taste her essence on his tongue. He could feel the radiating heat from her body penetrating his skin as though nothing, not even clothes, lay between them. Her scent pervaded his senses with the crispness of florals and the sweetness of summer berries. He could hear the rapid beating of her heart and feel the heaving of her chest against him. If he were to take an educated guess, and it would be very educated at that, he would guess that all the signs of her body pointed to arousal. Surprisingly, he could say the same of his own.

"Miss Caine, are you wearing my clothes?" Cade asked, his voice falsely stern, after recognizing the familiar items. And there was something about seeing her dressed in something of his that sent an unexpected thrill of excitement through his body. The cheeky girl was wearing *his* things, caressing *his* horse, and a quick glance at her basket revealed that she had been pilfering the best of *his* prized roses—ones he had taken the risk of smuggling to the states from his grandmother's garden back in Yorkshire. In fact, Kara fucking Caine was starting to waltz around *his* home as though she owned the bloody place. The thought made him bristle as much as it made him feel an inexplicable sense of satisfaction. It was a curious dichotomy that he hoped never to delve into any further.

"Mrs. Hughes practically forced them on me," Kara explained at his accusation, a note of tension in her tone. She couldn't tell if Cade was actually mad or not. "I'm sorry. I can take them off if you want?"

Cade chuckled. "We barely know each other, and you're already trying to take your clothes off for me?"

Kara's face turned red in mortification. "That's not what I meant—I-I just didn't want you to think I'd taken them. Without your permission, I mean." Kara shifted nervously, wishing that she'd never left her damn room, as Cade's fingers still lingered on her neck, freezing her in place.

Cade pressed himself into her, pushing her up against the stall door, unable to suppress the need to feel her beneath him. His fingers trailed up her neck and over her cheek, brushing away the stray hair in an almost tender gesture. "Kara, you know my line of work. Do you really think I'd begrudge you the theft of a scarf for a wintery day?"

"I-I don't know. Would you?" Kara asked, her lips trembling—from cold or fear or *need*, she couldn't say.

"No, love, I wouldn't," Cade answered softly, the term of endearment unintentionally slipping past his lips as he continued to stroke her cheek. "You may have anything you wish, if it is in my power to give it."

"My freedom?" Kara requested hesitantly, knowing she was treading into dangerous territory. As much as she liked this softer version of Cade, she knew gaining her freedom was worth risking his anger at the request, the jolting reminder of what exactly they were to each other—a captor and his increasingly complicit prisoner.

"No, Kara," Cade responded sharply, his expression darkening. "Not that."

"But why?" Kara pleaded. "Why keep me here? I'm of no use to you without the book, and I refuse to help you retrieve it. So why keep me captive in your fucking prison mansion if it serves no purpose for either of us?"

"I'm afraid it's complicated," he answered vaguely.

"Well, why don't you explain it for me?" Kara responded, starting to grow frustrated. "I'm pretty sure I have the comprehension skills to grasp the *complexities* of the situation."

Cade released a loud huff of exasperation, raking his hands roughly through his hair. The compulsive gesture didn't escape Kara's notice, and she studied him thoughtfully. "Fine, if you truly want to know the aspects of your current predicament that constitute an extended stay as a *guest* in my home—you are a liability, in more than one respect. Additionally, your life could be in danger from people far less civilized than I am."

Kara stifled a gasp of disbelief. "Who the *hell* would want to kill me? I'm no one. I'm a *librarian*, for fuck's sake."

"Yes, well I'm afraid the little rebellion you pulled at the university—the whole putting sodding academic integrity before your own life and safety—made you very much a person of interest for the very wrong sort of people. Does the name Avery Reed ring any bells?"

Kara's face contorted with confusion. "Yes, he's a donor and patron of the university. *The Canterbury Tales* was his most recent donation, an exceedingly generous one at that."

"As it so happens, that *generous donation* was more of a short term lease. Reed is the one who commissioned my expertise."

She scoffed at the insanity of Cade's suggestion. "I don't believe you. Why on earth would Mr. Reed do such a thing? I've met him on several occasions, and he's completely harmless. There's no chance he would associate with a criminal like you." Kara's last words were said scathingly, an attempt to injure Cade's pride, if not his feelings, of which she suspected he had none.

"You'll find good looks and charm do not equate a gentleman, Miss Caine." His words were intentionally ironic, and he was rewarded with an eye roll from Kara. "Reed needed money. You'll find even the most virtuous of men is tempted to the most desperate of things when money is involved. And let me assure you, Reed is hardly amongst the virtuous."

"Regardless, that still doesn't explain why my life is supposedly in danger."

"Reed needs the book, by any means necessary. If I prove unwilling to deliver the Chaucer text to that extent, Reed can easily find others who will." Cade's hand drifted to Kara's hair, his fingers possessively tangling themselves within the strands as he pulled lightly, just enough to get her attention. "I'd rather not let someone harm a hair on this pretty little head, so for your safety, you will remain a guest at Ashford Manor until I have decided how to resolve the situation. You will not leave the grounds. You will not contact the university or anyone on the outside. It's for your own good. Do you understand?"

"Yes," Kara answered listlessly, not entirely sure what she was agreeing to as the tingling sensation of his fingers wrapped firmly around her hair obliterated any sense of reason she might possess.

"Good." Cade loosened his hold on her hair, his touch turning gentle as he stroked the soft strands as pale and radiant as moonlight. The fairness of her hair beautifully complimented the creamy alabaster of her complexion, both strikingly offset by dark brows and lashes and eyes the rich, warm color of espresso. Cade's fingers trailed along Kara's hairline, shamelessly exploring her features as she shivered beneath his brazen touch. He brushed aside the blonde waves of hair along her temple, pausing to study her with a slight frown creased between his brows.

Kara stiffened, knowing what caught his attention—a thin, silver scar about an inch long running along her forehead and into her hairline. She styled her hair to help conceal the blemish, and most people never even noticed. Clearly, Cade was more observant than most people.

"How did you get this?" Cade asked, his voice rough as he stroked the small, raised scar gently with his fingertip. The thought of a violent lover or abusive parent marking Kara in anger had his fists clenched tightly in fury.

"A car accident," Kara answered quietly, her lips trembling. "I have others, that one is just the most noticeable. I was lucky, though. My parents, they—" Kara took a shuddering breath. "They didn't make it."

"I'm sorry," Cade responded sincerely, and it was the second time he'd said those unfamiliar words to her in a matter of minutes. What was she doing to him?

"It's okay. It was nearly a decade ago, so I'm used to the solitude by now," Kara answered mechanically. She didn't like talking about the accident. In fact, she *never* talked about the accident. The knowledge that Cade was pulling those excruciating personal details from her lips had her feeling uncharacteristically unnerved.

Cade felt the slightest twinge guilt at her confession. Admittedly, he'd been a right bastard to exploit a girl alone in the world. He had literally capitalized on the fact that no one would come looking for her. He didn't typically feel remorse—and he'd done an enormous amount of shitty things with a clear conscience to prove it—but he felt the painful stabbing of something resembling regret as he considered his treatment of Kara. The girl deserved better than being a prisoner, a pawn for the sake of monetary gain.

Well, unfortunately for her, life wasn't fair. And he had no intention of taking it upon himself to change that fact. Cade hardened himself, quelling the inconveniences of a burgeoning conscience, and brusquely asked the first question he'd thought of when she mentioned her loss. It was something he always considered when contemplating untimely death. "Do you ever feel guilty?"

"That they died?" Kara asked, a bit thrown by the question.

"That you lived," Cade clarified, his expression stoic and cold.

No one had ever asked Kara if she felt guilty for surviving. Probably because that would have been a pretty cruel thing to ask someone who had just lost both their parents. But something told her Cade didn't mind being cruel. In fact, he probably enjoyed it.

"I suppose I did at the beginning," Kara answered after a long pause. She swallowed hard, trying to overcome the emotions that swelled in her throat and threatened to choke her words. "It's hard not to when we were all in the same situation, all in the same car, but only one of us made it out alive." Kara took a deep breath, agonizing as she revisited moments in the past that she would rather bury so far down that they never saw the light of day, but also feeling an unusual sense of peace as she considered, perhaps for the first time, how her parents would feel about the life that she continued to lead without them in it. "But now I realize that they would have wanted me to live. To enjoy life. So I spend my time making sure I don't waste the opportunity I was given. That I make them proud. And most days, I feel like I do."

"You are very fortunate to be so self-assured of the purposefulness of your existence." Cade's response might have sounded cruel if his tone weren't so earnest. And he meant it. She was lucky to feel as though she survived for a reason. Cade had known loss as well, and there wasn't a single moment in which he thought he deserved to continue breathing while others around him perished. Cade didn't bemoan the fact that his existence was entirely self-centered and served no greater purpose. He merely recognized it.

The previous flames Cade had felt sparking between them had gradually been reduced to mere embers beneath a deluge of emotional turmoil—personal traumas that he had forced her to share and his own traumas that he'd chosen not to. As the passion between them gave way to an emotional communion that was verging on a depth that was out of Cade's comfort, he pulled away. He dropped his hand from Kara's hair, looking down and flexing his fingers as though he wasn't quite sure how they had made it into her blonde locks in the first place. Without another word, Cade turned around and headed for the exit, his riding gear still discarded on the floor where he left it when he'd walked in and spotted Kara with Sugar Cubes.

"Where are you going?" Kara asked, confused by his sudden retreat. He'd *touched* her. It felt as though he'd almost *kissed* her, though she might have merely imagined the closeness of his lips to hers. She'd shared some very personal details about her life, things that it physically pained her to revisit. And now he was just running away. Why the hell did that hurt so much? "Aren't you going riding?" she added, trying to sound casual and *not* as fucking desperate as she felt.

"I think the little traitor would prefer your company to mine right now," Cade answered, turning back to look at her with his standard, self-satisfied smirk firmly in place once more. "I'll see you at dinner, Miss Caine," Cade bid farewell with a small bow of his head.

Kara was left reeling, alone in Cade's stables, his horse nuzzling her shoulder to remind her that she'd held her attention before Cade came barging in. Kara stroked the horse's neck once more as she contemplated what had just transpired between her and Cade. They'd had some sort of strange, unfathomable connection. They'd bantered. He'd *apologized* for hurting her. He'd stared at her lips as though he wanted to fucking devour them. He'd caressed her neck and hair as though he wanted to do more. He'd asked her about her scars and her parents. Oh, and he'd mentioned that someone might want to *fucking kill her* and claimed she was at his house for her own protection. Could she trust him? Or was it all some new ploy to gain her cooperation? Kara had no fucking idea.

"Caden Ashford is a baffling bastard, isn't he Sugar?" Kara inquired of the dark beauty of a horse, who seemed to neigh in agreement.

And then Cade's last words finally resonated. He was expecting her at dinner. With him. And the rest of his criminal company. The exact place she'd been trying to avoid at all costs. The exact situation she'd had every intention of evading even if it meant starvation. Unfortunately, she had a very strong intuition that if she wasn't present in the dining hall for the evening meal, Cade would come up to her room and drag her down by her hair. So, dinner with Cade it was.

Fucking perfect.

CHAPTER FIVE

SHOCKINGLY, dinner had been reasonably uneventful. Cade and his all-male company had discussed business, loudly, allowing Kara to fade gratefully into the background. It was intriguing to observe Cade in his element when his glaring focus wasn't on her. He was a natural leader, everyone in the room deferring to him as if he was their reigning regent. And she supposed, in a way, he was. Declan was quiet; Ortega was too, but his silence seemed to be borne of an assertive confidence rather than the nerves of inexperience. Jace argued rather aggressively with Braxton over the best approach for infiltrating a government-owned establishment. After careful consideration, Cade agreed with Braxton, eliciting a near meltdown from Jace, who seemed to be the only one moderately interested in taking a stand against Cade. A stern, nearly deadly look from his boss had Jace firmly back in his place. Kara had laughed quietly to herself at how fucking whipped everyone was in Cade's presence. She could guarantee Cade would never get that kind of blind obedience from her. She would fight him every fucking step of the way.

Forming a routine of evasion, Kara waited until the din from downstairs had dissipated before making her way down the stairs and toward the kitchens. The remnants of that morning's breakfast smelled delicious, and she was sure Mrs. Hughes would have saved her some leftovers.

"Kara," the kind woman greeted her warmly as she drew a piping hot tray of scones out of the oven. "I was expecting ye. Those boys dinnae leave a crumb left on that table, ravenous bastards, so I made a fresh batch just for you."

"They smell divine."

"I have fresh pots of coffee and tea as well. Which would ye prefer?"

"Coffee would be lovely, thank you," Kara replied as she added jam and cream to two scones. She was so hungry that she might actually finish the whole tray before the morning was over. Mrs. Hughes handed her a steaming cup of coffee, which Kara accepted gratefully. Her time spent with the kindly cook was definitely her favorite aspect of captivity. In her daily life, Kara didn't have many people outside of work to share her time with, so finding a friend at Ashford Manor had been a welcome surprise. And she had to admit, Mrs. Hughes's gossip and whit were stellar.

"So, where are the boys off to this morning?" Kara asked conversationally as she sipped at her coffee.

"Lord if I know. They're always up to some mischief," Mrs. Hughes answered, tossing her arms up in the air as if to wash her hands clean of their shenanigans. "They'll all be back by supper time though. Mr. Ashford has already made a specific request. Spaghetti bolognese. An unusual suggestion for him, but I've given up trying to keep up with his culinary interests. He tells me what he wants, and it gets made."

It might have been an atypical request for Cade, but spaghetti bolognese was Kara's favorite meal. One of the few consistencies in her life growing up had been Spaghetti Sundays, and it was always a family affair. Even after her parents' passing, Kara honored their memory by continuing the tradition, slow-cooking spaghetti bolognese every Sunday according to her grandmother's authentic Italian recipe. The Mancini's, her mother's family, did not fuck around with their pasta sauce. But how could Cade possibly know that? Certainly it was just a coincidence?

"What day is it, Mrs. Hughes?" Kara asked hesitantly, an eerie sense of apprehension washing over her.

"It's Sunday, love. Why do you ask?"

"No reason," Kara replied quietly, trying to mask the tremble in her voice as she swallowed down her uneasiness. Sunday. *Spaghetti Sunday*. Perhaps it wasn't a harmless coincidence after all.

Disturbing Kara from her minor episode of panic, the doors of the kitchen swung open unexpectedly. Kara jolted, just barely managing to keep ahold of her coffee cup, as a villainous, devastatingly dashing, all too familiar figure strutted purposefully into the suddenly too small space she shared with Mrs. Hughes. Cade looked at Kara expectantly, a smug smile on his face.

"Miss Caine," Cade greeted in a tone that was so uncharacteristically pleasant, Kara immediately felt a strange sense of unease. "I'd rather thought I might find you *hiding* out here, no doubt engaging in the daily gossip with our good cook, Mrs. Hughes." Cade's tone was playfully chiding.

"Let her alone, ye devil," Mrs. Hughes admonished with a swat of the cloth she was using to dry her hands. "She's got no need to be wasting away her day with the likes of you lot carrying on with your business and ramblings. She's more than welcome in my kitchen, and I'll not have ye scaring her off, pushing her about like ye do everyone else in this damn house." She eyed Cade sternly as though he were still that little boy running around her kitchen with mud on his trousers and mischief in his smile. He might have grown, and he might not dabble in dirt anymore—at least of the earthen variety—but that mischief in his smile never left.

"My, you're cheeky this morning, Mrs. Hughes," Cade remarked with a laugh, his gaze warm as he looked down on the small statured Scotswoman.

"I'm always cheeky, boy. You just haven't made your way to the kitchens in a while to be reminded of it."

The subtle reprimand of her tone left Cade feeling a twinge of guilt. She was accurate, of course; he had been rather busy as of late, and the difficult situation with Kara made things even more complicated. "You're quite right, Mrs. H. Consider me well reminded. Would some of your favorite port from my next trip to Lisbon make it up to you?"

"Ye dinnae need to be getting me anything. Just show your face down here every once in a while so I can remember why I left your

Hideaway

mother, crossed an ocean, and took up residence in this bloody country," Mrs. Hughes responded gruffly, a layer of fondness hidden beneath her brusque words. "But ye ken I'd never say no to port," she added with a wink.

"Of course," Cade answered with a chuckle. "Now, I'm afraid I'll have to steal away Miss Caine."

Having been so caught up with the unusual interaction between Cade and his cook, Kara startled at being thrown back into the conversation. There was something so easy, so *endearing* in his manner as he talked with the older woman. Cade exhibited a warmth, a tenderness almost, that she'd never witnessed before. In all honesty, she hadn't thought a sociopath like Cade would have been capable of such genuine humanity. It perplexed her as much as it gave her hope for a possible escape.

"Me?" Kara questioned with squeak, wary of the darkness of his intentions. After a couple days of peace, Kara had begun to grow comfortable, forgetting the purpose of her temporary residence at Ashford Manor. Would he demand the book? Threaten her? Torture her? *Kill* her?

"Yes, you," Cade responded menacingly, earning a dark look from Mrs. Hughes before she turned her protective gaze to Kara. "Don't worry, I promise I'll be on my best behavior." Mrs. Hughes and Kara both looked at him dubiously as though they fully expected him to have crossed his fingers behind his back.

"Do I have a choice?" Kara asked hesitantly, reluctant to leave the peace and warmth of the kitchen and follow Cade into the unknown.

"No," Cade answered simply—arrogance rather than malice filling his tone. "But, I can promise you, you'll be pleased you came." Cade offered Kara his hand, expecting her to take it if she didn't want to be dragged out of the kitchen over his shoulder. Resorting to the measures of a caveman when the situation required didn't bother him in the slightest.

Kara narrowed her eyes, fully aware that Cade's statement could be taken in more than one way. Was there an innuendo woven into his words, or was Kara merely imagining things? Or, to her absolute horror, *longing* for a sexual suggestiveness from her captor? No, that definitely wasn't it. If Cade—with his lush, curly locks, and captivating eyes the color of sun-dappled leaves, and stupid fucking lips that seemed perpetually pulled into a self-satisfied smirk—attempted to proposition her, she would answer with a resounding *fuck you*. Meant as a rejection, of course, not a suggestion. And she would only marginally regret turning him down. Well, perhaps a smidge more than *marginally*, but she would survive the fucking loss.

With a sigh of resignation, Kara took Cade's hand, allowing his fingers to wrap tightly around her own. He squeezed her hand briefly, not very hard, but enough to force her to acknowledge that she was within his grasp. Kara inhaled sharply at the contact, overcome with feelings she couldn't even begin to process. Nor did she want to.

"Good girl," Cade praised with a smug grin as he pulled her toward the doors exiting the kitchen.

Those two words obliterated the small flutterings of butterflies in Kara's stomach, burnt them to a crisp with an all-consuming inferno of need. The sudden weakness of her knees would have caused her to stumble if it wasn't for Cade's firm grasp keeping her upright. She obediently followed as he led her from the kitchen, too distracted to even bid Mrs. Hughes farewell.

Cade pulled her through the dining room and, rather than heading for the stairs, led her down the right hall on the first floor. She hadn't ventured in that part of the house, and she could only contrive guesses at what lay beyond the many closed doors in the outstretched passageway. Shortly, Cade pulled her to a stop in front of a set of doors that stood out from the other plain ones that lined the hall. These two were special—tall, arched, and decorated with a tapestry of art carved into wood.

Cade reached into his pocket and pulled out an ornate, golden, skeleton key. "Here," he said as he presented her with the key, the act appearing almost ceremonious.

"What's behind those doors?" Kara asked distrustfully as she eyed the key in his open palm with suspicion. Was that where he housed the torture chamber? Would she merely be unlocking another cage that she would be forced into? Perhaps something worse than the luxurious bedroom upstairs? Maybe this was where she paid for defying his orders and safeguarding the Chaucer text.

"I promise you, nothing behind those doors will harm you," Cade reassured her, his eyes full of the utmost sincerity as they locked on to hers. "Now take the bloody key and open it."

Kara let out a breath that she hadn't even been aware she was holding as she snatched the key from Cade's outstretched fingers. Resigning herself to whatever fate lay beyond, Kara fitted the key into the keyhole and turned it counterclockwise, hearing a loud click as the lock disengaged. Not allowing herself the time for cowardice,

Kara confidently pushed open both doors, a gasp slipping from her lips as she beheld the welcome sight that greeted her.

The room was windowless. Twin, vintage, Victorian chandeliers hung from a wooden ceiling inlaid with octagonal shapes that lent the impression of honeycomb in a beehive. The only other light source, other than the dramatic chandeliers, was the dim glow of sconces along the walls, lending an ancient, atmospheric feel to the room. Gothic sculptures perched atop the corners, a mixture of angels and gargoyles as though the decorator wasn't sure whether they meant to emanate darkness or light and settled for a marriage of both. Intricately carved, gold-inlaid shelves formed eight arches around the room, some encased in glass, some open. And on those beautiful shelves—books. There were books *everywhere*. Thousands of them. Filling every shelf. Lining every wall.

He had a complete library right in the middle of his fucking house.

"It's my personal collection," Cade explained, interrupting Kara's sheer, function crippling awe. "Not nearly as expansive as the university library, of course, but I thought it might help you feel more at home while you're here."

"It's beautiful," Kara responded in reverence, the word sounding dull and hollow to her ears compared to the sheer majesty before her.

"Half of the books are far older than you. A quarter are either first editions or special publications. There's one annotated by Dickens himself if you can find it." A rare smile of genuine happiness crossed his face as he watched Kara eagerly devour the sight of the books as though it were the first sustenance she'd ever been offered.

"The library is kept locked, both for privacy and security. I have a key, Mrs. Hughes has another, and you, Miss Caine, hold the third and final key. You may use the library whenever you wish. Let it be your sanctuary or escape; you'll not be bothered while you're behind these doors."

"Thank you, Cade!" Kara exclaimed with unabashed happiness. Before she could even think to restrain her exuberance, Kara wrapped her arms around his neck, stood on her tiptoes, and placed a kiss softly on his cheek.

Cade turned rigid beneath her touch, wholly shocked by the display of affection. She had kissed him. The gesture was more gratitude than anything else—chaste rather than sensual—but he couldn't deny that her lips on his skin left him wanting more. Intrigued by the thought of how those lips would feel in other places. How she'd look on her knees with her mouth wrapped around his cock. How her skin would taste beneath his tongue. Kara's arms were still circled around his neck as she stood frozen, clearly dealing with a shock of her own. Against his better judgment, Cade reached out his hand and stroked the tip of his thumb along the curve of Kara's jaw, not missing the slight shiver of her body as she leaned into his touch as if begging for more.

She'd called him Cade, he realized after the shock of her outburst dispersed. The name in itself sent a wave of emotion flooding through his body. No one called him Cade. She certainly never had. It was always *Mr. Ashford* or *fucking bastard* if she was feeling particularly cheerful. His business associates called him Ashford. His parents called him Caden in a way that made him grind his teeth in irritation. His companions, when he had them, called him whatever he ordered them to. Only one other person had called him Cade, and he hadn't heard the name in years. Cade's eyes warmed as he drew his thumb up to Kara's lips, tracing the shape of them almost reverently.

"You're welcome," Cade finally responded, his voice husky and rough with desire. His words startled Kara from her trance, and she pulled away from him sharply, her cheeks flushed with embarrassment. Or perhaps something more carnal.

"I'm sorry," she said softly, avoiding his gaze as the mortification of what she had just done began to settle in. She'd practically accosted him, all because he'd shown her a few books. Okay, probably more like thousands of books in his own personal library. For which she now had a key. A sanctuary to escape her prison. A prison that he kept her locked in, she reminded herself in reprimand. She felt foolish. And ashamed. And…horny as fuck, but her arousal only made her feel worse.

"Kara." Cade grabbed her chin, stirring her from her self-doubt. "Do not apologize to me," he ordered, his tone stern.

Kara swallowed hard as Cade kept her chin in his grasp, his fingers digging in slightly as he seemed to contemplate something. Something that set his eyes ablaze with a heat that looked like anger but felt entirely different. It felt like a searing, insatiable hunger. Like he wanted to eat her alive—violently devour her, but make her feel good while he did it. Kara willed him to do it, silently pleading with him to close the space between them and kiss her. Touch her. Fucking destroy her, if he wanted.

A flicker of fear crossed Cade's face, and then the fire was gone, buried as his usual cold indifference took its place. He released

Kara's chin, stepping back until an appropriate amount of space lay between them and straightening his suit as a means of occupying his hands and keeping them off her. Kara felt his sudden distance as though it were a chill in the air, wrapping her arms around herself as if to ward off Cade's obvious coolness toward her.

"Enjoy the library, Miss Caine. It is at your disposal," he said, the formal titles firmly back in place. "I will see you at dinner." Without so much as a goodbye, Cade strode out of the room, his footsteps heavy and angry against the marble floor.

Kara flinched at the sound of the library doors slamming closed, sequestering her in solitude. What the fuck had just happened? Cade had nearly kissed her, she was almost sure of it. But then his features had turned harsh, and he rushed out of her newly gifted library as though he couldn't bear the sight of her. Had she done something wrong? Guilt was certainly one of the more prominent emotions surging through her body as she felt the dampness between her thighs and her chest heaved gustily in tune with her erratic pulse. What the hell was wrong with her? She was allowing herself to feel things no one in their right mind would feel for the man who had drugged her, stolen her from her home, and kept her captive in his house. Perhaps that was the problem; the sanity of her mind was slowly eroding beneath Cade's arrogant charms, infuriating smiles, and oppressively well-distributed physical genetics.

KARA anxiously fidgeted with the hem of her dress as she descended the stairs for dinner. It was an unusually bold choice for her: a silky red dress that accentuated her breasts with a very low cut in the front, a back that dipped nearly to the curve of her ass, and a skirt that flared at her hips and fell in luscious ripples down to her ankles with a subtle slit on the side that went up to her thigh. She had made her dress selection as though choosing armor and slipping into that red dress felt like sheathing herself in pure power. She'd paired the dress with subdued makeup apart from a bright, cherry-red lip that made her mouth the center of attention. Her style might have been misconstrued as seductive, but for Kara it was less about inciting sex and more about inciting confidence. The look made her feel strong, brave, and she would need both when encountering the fearsome man who waited for her in the dining hall.

The overwhelming scent of Mrs. Hughes's cooking wafting down the hall as Kara made her way to the dining room smelled delicious and familiar; it was a nostalgic reminder of Sundays spent with family, and, as much as her current situation differed from those happy, carefree memories, she still appreciated the sentimental reminder. Kara wasn't sure whether she should be relieved or disappointed when she entered the room to discover a full table. Declan, Jace, Ortega, Braxton, and Cade all turned to look at her, their expressions varied. Declan and Ortega met her with friendly smiles, while Braxton offered a brief nod of greeting. There was an unnerving hunger in Jace's lingering stare that made Kara's skin crawl, and she subconsciously put more distance between them. Cade looked at her with a heady mixture of fury and desire, his typical iciness melted away to reveal a mere human comprised of the same primal needs as everyone else.

Cade stood from his chair, and Kara had to resist the instinctive urge to turn and run for safety. "Miss Caine," Cade greeted smoothly, the words sounding far too seductive on his lips. He pulled out the empty chair beside him and gestured for Kara to sit.

Finding little cause for objection, Kara obeyed, crossing the room hesitantly until she stood beside the man she'd inadvertently kissed a few hours before. Timidly, she lowered herself into the offered chair, trying not to indulge her senses in the intoxication of the musky scent of cedar and mint that pervaded the air at his nearness. She may have inhaled a little too deeply, despite her attempted restraint.

"You look ravishing," Cade whispered by her ear as he pushed her chair in toward the table.

His words, softly breathed against her sensitive flesh, made Kara's cheeks flush and her skin prickle in arousal, but there was a dangerousness in his tone that sent a shiver down her spine. She couldn't be sure if his words were a compliment on her appearance or a commentary on his intent to assault her at the nearest opportunity. Her previous knowledge of the ruthless man implied the latter. And Kara tried, to the very best of her abilities, not to long for his ravishment with every fiber of her being.

The stifling tension of the room was broken with the grateful entrance of Mrs. Hughes carrying the first dishes of dinner, her arms full with a heaping platter of delectably buttery garlic rolls. Immediately, Kara rose to help her, unaccustomed to sitting around uselessly while being served by someone else. Her offer of assistance was sharply halted with a strong clamp of a hand on her thigh. *Cade's hand* was resting on her lower thigh, his fingers splayed across the skin laid bare by the slit of the dress.

"Stay," Cade commanded quietly, his tone firm. "Mrs. Hughes is very accustomed to handling the dinner proceedings on her own. As much as it is in your nature to help, she'd be slighted if you attempted to interfere with her job."

"Oh," Kara answered sheepishly, settling awkwardly back into her seat as Mrs. Hughes left to fetch another dish. "I'm sorry," she whispered, mortified to have almost inadvertently offended the kind cook. The incident was a reminder that Kara didn't belong, and she felt suddenly very out of place in the indulgent lifestyle that was merely a part of Cade's daily routine.

"Don't apologize," Cade said with a vexed crease between his brows. It was the second time that day he'd needed to scold her for a tendency toward self-deprecation. "You did nothing wrong."

"Sorry, it's a habit," Kara replied automatically. She realized her additional infraction when she received a stern glare from Cade in response. Left with little option other than to apologize *again*, Kara tried to smooth away his irritation with an apologetic smile. Cade didn't appear placated in the slightest.

"Don't make me put you over my knee, Kara," Cade threatened, his eyes glittering with eagerness at the idea as he squeezed her thigh to emphasize the full seriousness of his warning.

Kara gasped slightly at the reminder that Cade's hand was still on her bare leg, the pressure of his fingers sending a flood of heat straight to her core. She shifted slightly beneath him, rubbing her thighs together shamelessly in search of friction. If Cade noticed her arousal, he didn't let on, his hand still unmoving on her thigh as though he had forgotten it was there. Shyly, she stole a glance at Cade, but his attention was on Ortega as they discussed something about strengthening security on the perimeter. Biting her lip nervously, Kara gathered her courage, took an unsteady breath, and parted her legs, spreading her knees until they reached the armrests on either side of the chair.

That drew Cade's attention. He startled mid-conversation, his eyes wide with shock and something more primal as he turned toward Kara. He searched her countenance for any sign that her wide open legs were anything other than a goddamn invitation. Finding her dark eyes full of a desire and hunger that matched his own, Cade took the fucking hint and allowed his fingers to roam along the bare expanse of Kara's thigh. He didn't know what she was playing at when she came down in that bloody red dress with her tits out and her fuck-me lipstick after he'd used every ounce of his restraint to *not* overstep any boundaries in the library. Perhaps he had misjudged the game she was playing after all, if her spread thighs had anything to say about it. Maybe his prim little librarian was a little more naughty than she seemed. But if she expected him to be courteous enough not to throw her on the table and fuck her while the rest of the guys watched, she clearly didn't know who she was dealing with.

A whimper slipped from Kara's lips as Cade's fingers finally reached the apex of her thighs. She tried to focus on the bolognese, which was absolutely divine, as his knuckles brushed against her pussy, separated from his touch only by the thin lace of her panties. Cade caught her eye as his index finger trailed along the edge of her underwear; he raised a single brow, as though asking for consent to go further. Kara sucked her bottom lip between her teeth and nodded incrementally. Causally continuing his conversation with Ortega and Brax, Cade's fingers slipped beneath Kara's panties and cupped her hot, dripping pussy.

Kara moaned, a little too loudly, drawing the attention of everyone at the table. Her face burned with embarrassment as she tried to cover for the outburst even as Cade's fingers continued their assault on her pussy. "The pasta is delicious," Kara said with a nervous laugh, hoping the tastiness of the food was a passable reason to have moaned aloud at the table. A murmur of agreement from the others helped to assuage her mortification as she tried to refrain from any more audible reactions to Cade's under the table attentions.

"Fuck," she breathed as Cade slipped two fingers inside her and began thrusting them in and out at a steady pace. At that point, the others could think what they liked, there was no way she could keep her composure with Cade finger fucking her under the table like a madman. Her back arched with need as Cade spread the wetness of her arousal over her clit and began to rub in soft, circular patterns. All too quickly, she felt the tension building, the warmth in her center growing as Cade expertly strummed at her sensitive bundle of nerves. Too overcome with sensation, Kara's eyes closed as Cade plunged two fingers into her pussy and continued to rub her clit with his thumb. Regardless of the inconvenient setting, she couldn't contain her body's natural response to the perfect assault of Cade's fingers. Kara came silently, biting her lip and holding her breath to keep from screaming in ecstasy as Cade drove her over the edge of pleasure. Her thighs clamped against his hand, keeping him inside her as she spasmed around his fingers over and over until she slumped back in the chair—exhausted, sweaty, and sated.

Hideaway

Hesitantly, Kara opened her eyes to find every man at the table staring back at her.

Fucking fuck.

She had just come in front of five other men who were practically strangers. In the middle of fucking dinner. And she was too blissfully post-orgasmic to give too much of a damn about it.

"Hope everyone's got room for dessert," Mrs. Hughes announced, bursting into the room with a tiered chocolate cake.

Thank fucking god.

Eternally grateful for the distraction from her dinner exhibitionism, Kara was the first to request dessert as the conversations around the table started up again. Slowly, Cade removed his hand from Kara's cunt, her wetness visibly covering his fingers. Rather than wiping them on his napkin, like a normal fucking human being, Cade trailed his index finger through the frosting on the cake and brought it to his lips, sucking the mingling taste of chocolate and her cum as though it were his favorite combination of flavors.

"Delicious," Cade said with a mischievous smirk, his eyes not leaving Kara's.

Kara ate her dessert in silence, her thighs still quivering in the aftermath of her very public orgasm. Thankfully, everyone seemed to have moved passed the incident, apart from Cade, who occasionally flashed her a self-satisfied grin as he talked business with Jace. The insufferable man seemed to think he'd won at something, achieved some sort of victory by dominating her body and dragging an orgasm out of her while his friends watched. Well, she had no intention of bending to his will simply because he was skilled with his fingers. Incredibly fucking skilled with his fingers.

Finally, *finally* the awkward dinner came to an end as Mrs. Hughes came by to collect the cleared plates and carry them to the kitchen. Kara resisted the urge help as the Scotswoman came by to take her plate, having only her gratitude to offer for the delicious meal. Mrs. Hughes accepted her thanks warmly, her eyes glittering with an amusement that implied that she knew Kara enjoyed more than her food at the dinner table. Kara's cheeks flooded with renewed embarrassment as she waited for the room to clear so she could make her escape with some remnant of dignity.

Looking entirely disinterested as the others took their leave, Cade remained in his seat, his smoldering gaze never leaving Kara as she squirmed beneath the raw, all-consuming fire she saw in his eyes. Slowly, Cade traced his fingers over his full lips, the same fingers that had been inside her pussy a few minutes before. The subtle, sex-infused gesture had liquid need pooling between Kara's thighs all over again. She needed to escape that room before she had the poor judgment to allow him to fuck her right on the goddamn table.

Painfully prying herself from Cade's molten stare, Kara stood on shaky legs with the express intention of running for the exit. She'd relinquished quite enough of her propriety to him that evening. Before she could remove herself from the table, Kara felt the firm grasp of familiar fingers latch onto her wrist. She looked at Cade with the wide-eyed trance of a doe rendered frozen beneath headlights, a mere helpless creature caught in the orbit of something far more powerful and dangerous than she could possibly fathom. He smiled at her darkly, the grin of a predator viciously contemplating his next conquest.

"Going somewhere, Miss Caine?" Cade asked menacingly, his eyes alight with a raptorial gleam as his hand tightened around her wrist.

This version of Cade terrified her; the man who seemed accustomed to taking whatever he desired, regardless of her own willingness. She'd invited his touch during dinner, enjoyed his advances no matter how questionable they were in terms of proper etiquette. But Cade's eyes currently pinned her with a ravenousness that she didn't feel prepared to satiate. What would he do when there was no invitation?

"I'd like to go to my room, please," Kara responded, her tone pleading.

"May I come with you?" Cade asked, the weightiness of his suggestion hanging heavy in the air. His grip loosened as he rubbed his thumb softly over the bones in her wrist, feeling her shiver in response.

"Do I have a choice?" Kara asked with a quivering voice.

"Do you want one?" Cade responded sharply, a challenge in his expression.

Kara paused to ponder the audacity of his question. Did she want a choice? The most obvious answer, the most logical answer was *yes*, but she couldn't deny the inciting appeal of not being held accountable for enjoying whatever pleasure Cade might force upon her. It was a sick notion, which she dismissed immediately. Well, *almost immediately*. "Yes," Kara answered softly, not sounding entirely convinced of her own response.

"Then, *yes* you have a choice." Cade pulled Kara against his body, feeling the warmth of her skin and frantic beat of her heart as she trembled against him. She felt so small against his broad form, so *fragile*, like he had to contain his own strength to keep from shattering her into a thousand pieces. He didn't want her broken. Not yet, anyway.

"I'd like to go alone. Please," Kara answered, feeling a twinge of regret even as she said the words. In the darkest recesses of her heart, she knew that she wanted Cade, but she couldn't trust herself not to fall for him completely if she gave him such an intimate piece of herself. She needed the distance to protect her heart.

Cade glared at her, disappointment and anger marring his features. "As you wish," he acquiesced darkly, throwing away her hand as though it burned to touch her. "Run along," Cade said with a dismissive wave of his hand. His eyes glittered with the threat: *before I try to catch you.*

Heading his warning, Kara scurried toward the exit with every intention of locking her bedroom door until morning. Just to be safe. Suddenly, a nettling thought crossed her mind, causing her to turn back to the imperious man still lingering at the end of the table basking in a hazy shroud of animosity. "Cade?" she asked hesitantly. "Spaghetti Sundays—how did you know?" Because she knew he did. Cade was too calculating for coincidences to occur in his vicinity.

"I know everything about you, Kara," Cade answered simply, shrugging his shoulders as though it were the most obvious fact in the world.

Kara wasn't quite sure if she should find his confession endearing or unsettling as she ran toward her bedroom with the express intention banishing his last words from memory.

CHAPTER SIX

SHE had successfully avoided Cade the entire day after their dreadfully awkward incident at dinner. The incident in which she'd allowed him to get her off at the table and then subsequently turned him down for any further action in the sex department. He'd been pissed, and, honestly, she couldn't blame him; she was a bit mad at herself for passing up her first enticing proposition for getting laid in months. Sometimes her damned good sense and rationality was a fucking cock block.

Hence, sexual frustration was entirely to blame for her current choice of reading material as she sat alone in the library with her neglected pussy. In spite of the general stereotype regarding librarians as being purely intellectual, the book wasn't a great literary work at all. It was, to her great personal embarrassment, *smut*.

Hideaway

A firm rap on the library doors startled Kara from her complete disappearance into the imaginary constructs of a world forged entirely from words on a page. She frowned as she begrudgingly lowered the book in her hands, finding the uncomfortable experience of being coldly thrust into reality about as disruptive as being woken from a good dream. She could hazard a guess as to the identity of the ill-timed intruder. And the last thing she needed was to give Cade the ammunition for insults after catching her reading book porn.

Frantically, Kara scrambled to hide her guilty pleasure, a habit she'd developed while being an avid indulger in sexually illicit literature as a teenager. When was she worried of her parents discovering her embarrassing reading tastes, Kara would use a large, hardback bible to cover any raunchy books beneath. She supposed she was lucky to have not been struck down by some higher power for the sheer audacity. Having matured considerably since her teenage years, Kara tucked her smut beneath her chosen decoy of *Moby Dick*, composed a reasonably believable expression of innocence, and answered the intruder.

"Come in."

The doors burst open, and Cade strode purposefully into the room, his expression determined and a bit colder than usual. He looked stunning in a deep burgundy suit that she'd never seen him wear before, his usual uniform of a tie and waistcoat abandoned in favor of just a white collared shirt beneath the jacket. In a true contradiction with Cade's usual fastidious style, the top two buttons of his dress shirt were undone, allowing the shirt to billow. The man was the definition of masculine perfection in a suit and tie, but he was the *fucking epitome* of sex appeal when he was intentionally disheveled.

"Are you alright, Miss Caine? You appear to be on the verge of an aneurism."

Kara jolted from mentally undressing and devouring Cade to find him staring at her with an amused smirk. She shook her head as though that would clear the illicit images of Cade naked from her thoughts. Self-consciously, Kara wiped at her mouth, hoping she hadn't managed to actually salivate at the fantasy of Cade filling her mouth with his cock. The damn smut must be driving her mad. As she pressed her thighs together for relief, Kara found herself keenly aware that she had gone without sex for far too long. Sneaking another glance at Cade, she also realized that she might have found a solution for that particular issue.

"Cade," Kara greeted finally, hoping she was merely imaging how breathy and desperate the word sounded on her lips. "Did you need something?"

Please say yes.

"Actually, no. I'm sorry to disturb your reading of," Cade glanced at the downturned book in her lap, "*Moby Dick*." His smile widened as though he had impossibly guessed her secret. "I just wanted to let you know that I'm going out tonight."

Kara's brow furrowed as she pondered what aspect of his fucking illicit occupation would be requiring his attention two hours before midnight. "What could you possibly be working on this late?"

"I didn't say I was working," Cade responded with intentional ambiguity, a suggestive smirk playing across his lips. To be honest, he felt a mixture of guilt and satisfaction regarding the implication of his words. Guilt because he had every intention of spending the night drowning out all thoughts of Kara in the body of another woman—or two. Satisfaction because of the marked jealousy filling Kara's face at that exact moment. Whether it was sexually or in some other capacity, she cared for him. He had grown to suspect as much, and there was the proof written plainly on her troubled little face. He had to admit, seeing her worry that full bottom lip with her teeth had his cock straining in his pants.

Fuck.

He needed to get out of the bloody house.

"Oh," Kara responded finally with a slight frown, a multitudinous mixture of emotions wrapped into that one little word.

"Is there a problem, Kara?" Cade challenged with an arched brow. Daring her to claim him. Daring her to admit she cared.

"Of course not," Kara responded in a tone of false nonchalance. Because yes, *there fucking was a problem*. Cade was going out for the night, most likely to fuck around with some floozy. And she couldn't explain why the thought of Cade with someone else felt like a knife twisting in her heart, but it fucking did. "You're free to do as you like," Kara continued, her voice sounding unflatteringly bitchy to her own ears. "Unlike me."

"Don't be a brat," Cade chided, his expression darkening with annoyance that verged on anger. "You know the rules, and you know why they are in place. You have as much freedom as your safety allows."

"Oh yes, whatever would I do without your generous imprisonment. Oops, I mean *protection*," Kara responded with an eye roll before picking up *Moby Dick* and pretending to be greatly interested in an abnormally large whale.

"Kara, look at me," Cade commanded curtly, his control worn thin after just a few minutes in Kara's presence. The girl was driving him utterly mad.

With a loud sigh of exasperation, Kara lowered the book, laying it face down across her thighs, and looked at Cade expectantly. "Yes?" she answered, her voice full of syrupy sweetness and completely fake.

Resisting the urge to continue fighting her—because that could take all fucking night without either of them emerging victorious—Cade ran his fingers deftly through his dark hair and desperately attempted to tame his reaction to her relentless attitude. If she was his girl, she'd probably never be able to sit down comfortably again with how much trouble she gave him. But she wasn't his. Nor would she be. The previous night had made that particular fact abundantly clear. Whatever her feelings for him, Kara was too prim and proper to act on them and endanger her precious reputation. And she was too fucking vanilla to give him what he really needed. So, he needed to wrap things up with Kara and go find someone he could really play with.

"Come here," Cade commanded brusquely, pointing to the empty space beside him. He didn't have time for her attitude. He needed to get Kara reasonably contented and get the fuck out of there.

Surprisingly, Kara walked obediently, albeit sullenly, toward him. She stopped when she reached the exact spot he pointed to, staring up at him with a mixture of insolence and something more fragile. It was that fragment of vulnerability that gave Cade pause. He reached for her chin, gently pulling her toward him.

"What's wrong?" Cade asked softly, genuinely interested in what was actually bothering her. Was she starting to care for him in the same way he was desperately trying to avoid caring for her? So desperate, in fact, that he was willing to mindlessly throw himself at the first eager victim to escape thoughts of her. Was she hurting for the same reasons he was running?

"Nothing," Kara lied unconvincingly, pulling her chin from his grasp.

The deception, the evasion, the sheer fucking brattiness had Cade's fists curling in anger and frustration. Why couldn't she be reasonable? Why couldn't she just fucking talk to him? If she simply asked him not to go, he would bow to her request. And he hated himself for the weakness she exposed.

"Do you want me to stay?" Cade asked, his tone turning from concerned to acrid. "Is that it? Want to pay me back for services rendered during dinner last night? Seeing you on your knees might be enough incentive for me to stay." The cruelty of his words surprised him. He had never had a tendency toward meanness, at least where women were concerned. He had never needed it. Speaking with honesty, rather than modesty, the women he associated with groveled at his feet. Literally. He was proving to be ill equipped in dealing with someone like Kara who required a little more coaxing. The thought vexed him greatly.

"You're a fucking bastard, Caden," Kara admonished, the anger in her tone getting lost amid the anguished embarrassment causing her voice to tremble.

"Well, if you've got nothing better to offer, I'll be going now," Cade said coldly.

"Try not to fall off a cliff and die," Kara muttered to herself as she turned away from him with the intention of returning to her romantic novel and drowning out any lingering, poisonous thoughts of him. And what he would be doing on his night out *not* working.

"What was that, Kara?" Cade sneered as grasped her arm and pulled her back toward him. "I couldn't quite hear you. And I believe you've been warned not to turn your back on me. Shall I remind you what happens when you do?" Cade gripped her arm tighter as if in threat of something worse.

"I *apologize*," Kara answered scathingly, aware her tone might get her into trouble, but not quite caring at the moment.

"Do I need to punish you, baby?" Cade asked, his tone softening in spite of his words.

"I don't think that will be necessary. You have plans tonight, remember?" Kara answered, jerking her arm from his grasp. "Enjoy your night out, *baby*."

Cade stood still for a moment, glaring at Kara as indecision flickering across his face. Finally deciding to *fuck it*, Cade closed the space between them, fisted his fingers in Kara's hair, and forced her mouth up to meet his. He kissed her viciously—more an attack than a caress—his lips claiming her, his tongue invading her mouth and sparring against her own, his teeth demanding destruction as he sucked her bottom lip between them and bit down hard. Hard enough to taste blood mingled with the intoxicating essence of *her*.

Kara pulled away for an infinitesimal fraction of a second, the bare minimum that her dignity required, before she was moaning into Cade's mouth, eager to devour everything he had to give her. She threw herself against him, her hands clawing at his jacket, delirious with the need to get it off of him, to touch him. Obliging her, Cade whipped off the jacket in one swift movement and threw it to the floor. His lips slipped to her neck, kissing her and tasting her as his hands flew to her thighs and hiked up the hem of her dress. Kara tilted her head back, giving Cade full access to her throat as she grabbed ahold of his hair, relishing the softness of the silken strands. She whimpered as Cade's fingers trailed up to her thighs and dug harshly into the bare skin of her hips.

"Does that hurt, Kara?" Cade asked, his mouth against her ear.

"Yes," Kara answered breathlessly. "More."

Cade grinned at the need in her voice, the responsiveness of her body. Happy to acquiesce, he bared his teeth and sunk into the tender flesh of her neck, reveling in the moans he pulled from her as he bit deeply. Blindly, Kara reached for the buttons of his shirt, practically ripping them from the seams in her desperation to find bare skin. Having managed to undo the bottom half, Kara slid her hands over Cade's naked abdomen, memorizing the ripples of muscle and the sharp edges of his hip bones. Cade hissed as Kara raked her nails down his abs when he bit down particularly hard on her shoulder.

"Fuck me, Cade," Kara pleaded breathlessly, digging her hands into his hair and pulling roughly as he continued to devour the exposed skin of her neck.

"*What?*" Cade asked in shock, fairly certain he misheard her.

"Fuck me, please."

Cade stilled, his expression clouded with a mixture of anger and uncertainty. "No," he answered finally, leaving little room for misconception in his single worded rejection.

The sexually charged spell between them suddenly broken with her desperate plea, Cade pulled away harshly, nearly dropping Kara on her arse. He turned away from her, swearing to himself for letting things get so out of hand as he re-adjusted his shirt and tucked it back into his pants. He ran trembling fingers through his hair, his body still coursing with the adrenaline of what he almost did. With *her*. Under no circumstances was she available to him in that regard, and he needed to get the fuck away before thinking with his cock instead of his head really got him into fucking trouble. After picking up his jacket from the floor and sliding it back on smoothly, Cade finally turned around to face her. Kara's chest heaved erratically as she stared back at him, her features marred with shock and hurt. Her soft brown eyes were pooled with tears on the verge of spilling down her cheeks, her lips quivered until she bit down with her teeth to keep them from exposing her vulnerability, her pain. She'd never looked so devastated. And she'd never looked more intoxicatingly beautiful.

Cade gently grasped Kara's throat and pulled her toward him; she followed as though she had no will of her own. He softly touched her mouth with his thumb and pulled her bottom lip free from the sharp imprisonment of her teeth. He continued to stroke her bottom lip, loving how it had turned red and swollen from the violence of his kisses. Slowly, he pressed his thumb further into her mouth; instinctively, Kara opened for him. She allowed his finger to slip past her teeth, welcoming it with a swirling caress of her tongue.

Looking up at Cade with the tears from his rejection streaming down her flushed cheeks, Kara wrapped her lips around his thumb and sucked *hard*.

"Kara," Cade scolded, his voice rough with pent up need. "Behave," he ordered with a slight squeeze of his hand on her throat. With one last flick of her tongue, Kara obeyed and released his finger. Cade stepped away from her even as every instinct in his body begged him to get closer. "I'll be back in the morning." Cade flashed a smile that was just as charming as it was cruel "Probably." And he turned toward the library doors to leave.

"Enjoy your whore," Kara responded breezily before reaching for her book on the chair. God, she needed a fucking distraction from him.

Cade turned backed toward her in surprise. "Trust me, love, I've never had to *pay* for sex," he answered tauntingly.

"I'll add that to your list of stunning accomplishments," Kara quipped sarcastically, her eyes rolling to the heavens.

"You're keeping a list?" Cade asked brightly as though he found the idea positively adorable.

"It's incredibly short," Kara deadpanned.

"Love, I think we both know nothing about me is short."

"Goodnight, Cade," Kara said dismissively before returning to her book without a second glance in his direction. She had no intention of engaging in playful banter with a man who wouldn't deign to grant her the fuck she so desperately needed. As far as she was concerned, he could go fuck himself.

"Goodnight, Kara," he answered softly.

AN hour or two passed in melancholic silence while Kara tried to focus on literary characters fucking and not think of Cade being out for the evening fucking someone who wasn't her. It was proving to be an impossible task. The words on the page were a blur, and, when she'd accidentally re-read the same sentence for perhaps the fifth time in a row, Kara surrendered to the inevitability of *not* forgetting Cade. She bolted from her seat with a huff of exasperation and threw the *damn* book at the *damn* chair pretending that she was assaulting the *damn British bastard* instead of a helpless piece of furniture.

Kara's cathartic, albeit unbecoming, tantrum was cut short with an unusually melodic knock on the door, as though someone were playing out a tune on the hardwood. The rhythm of Kara's heart quickened at the thought of Cade returning to finish what he started. Why hadn't he left yet? Had he decided to stay? Kara's frantic heart had the sudden urge to bolt from her chest at the thought that Cade might have stayed for her.

With trembling hands, Kara unlocked the doors that she had angrily bolted after Cade walked out the first time and opened them. She flinched in surprise when she discovered who was on the other side. Jace stood before her, his wrinkled, white dress shirt unbuttoned a little too low at the top and his sleeves rolled halfway up his arms to expose the dark, inky ripples of tattoos snaking up his forearms. Absentmindedly, Kara wondered how far the ink went. This was the most she'd seen of Jace's skin, his partially unbuttoned shirt also revealing what looked like a sequence of numbers tattooed along his neck. His hand was still raised as though she'd caught him in the middle of beating down the door—which she had—and his other hand held a half-full bottle of dark liquor. Jace's eyes were darker than usual, more like the deep blue depths of the ocean rather than the pale shallow pools that usually stared back at her. Kara's skin warmed and her cheeks flushed as she watched his eyes roam her body with a lascivious gleam. He was so close she could smell the faint hint of whisky on his breath mingled with notes of spearmint. Instinctively, Kara took a step backward. Jace sober made her skin crawl with unease; Jace mixed with alcohol was a danger that had her body subconsciously begging her to run.

"I brought the party," Jace announced cheerfully, shaking the bottle of bourbon in the air.

"I'm not in the partying mood," Kara responded sullenly, breathing a sigh of relief that he didn't sound drunk. At least not yet.

"Why so serious, Dr. Caine? Mad Ashford left you to go play with his club whores?" Jace asked as he drew closer, leaning his arm across the top of the door frame. "You know, we could play too. Might be fun." Jace ran the tip of his index finger down Kara's neck, so lightly she couldn't be sure if he actually made contact with her skin or not.

"Cade is at a nightclub?" Kara guessed, too distracted by getting information about Cade to move away from Jace's touch.

In response, Jace flashed her a cruel smile that had her blood curdling in her veins. "No baby, not a nightclub. A *sex club*. And not just your run of the mill, everyone gets naked and fucks each other type of sex club. This shit is elite. Catering explicitly to kinky motherfuckers with no limits—on their bank accounts or their deep, dark desires."

Kara stood in open-mouthed silence, too shocked to come up with any clever retort. Jace's fingers trailed a little farther down; she allowed it because her body seemed to have momentarily lost control of its functions. Cade was at a sex club? A *kinky* sex club? That was so far out of her limited sexual experience that she didn't even know what to think. Absentmindedly, she wondered if that should make her feel better about Cade's refusal to have sex with her. Somehow, though, it made his rejection worse. Now she knew why he didn't want her. She couldn't even begin to understand how to be what he wanted.

"Forget about him, baby," Jace crooned as his body pressed against her, pushing her into the library. "Have a drink with me."

"Okay," Kara agreed numbly, temporarily relieved of her senses. She allowed Jace to take her hand and pull her toward the leather couch in the middle of the room. He tried to pull her onto his lap, but she had enough propriety to sit beside him instead. Jace handed her the bottle of bourbon, and she took it, lifting it to her lips and nearly choking on the burn of liquid fire spilling down her throat. "Holy fuck, how do you drink this?" she asked as she coughed on the lingering remnants of alcohol in her mouth.

Jace laughed, taking the bottle from her and drinking large gulps without so much as a flinch.

"Show off," Kara sulked, crossing her arms over her chest. She couldn't even get drunk properly.

"You can't drink it like it's water or some shit. You have to throw it back, swallow it without trying to taste it or let it linger in your mouth."

"If you don't want to taste it, why do you even drink it?" Kara asked as she accepted the bourbon and choked on another small sip. Straight liquor was revolting and needed to be doused in sugar to make it even remotely appealing.

"Because the point isn't to taste it, it's to fucking *feel* it. To forget about everything else. Hell, the world could crash and burn around you, and you wouldn't give a fuck," Jace explained after another long drink.

Kara studied Jace in surprise. His explanation was unexpected, not exactly deep, but more contemplative than she'd given him credit for. She suspected this was probably the closest anyone got to having a real conversation with Jace, and he had to be drunk to do it. Something about his words resonated with her. "What do you want to forget, Jace?" Kara asked softly, her eyes peering into his.

Jace looked away, suddenly uncomfortable with the attention that he had been begging for just a few minutes before. "You know what, guess it already worked because I can't remember shit," Jace replied after several moments, his playboy persona firmly back in place as he gave her a wink.

Kara ignored him and choked down another swallow of bourbon.

"You're doing it all wrong," he said with a laugh as he watched her struggle in a losing battle against the liquor. "Here, let me help you. Tip your head back."

"I don't know, Jace—"

"Just do what I tell you, Kara."

Kara got a little thrill of excitement from his command, but it was an empty feeling compared to how Cade made her feel—*his* demands set fire to the blood in her veins and made her want to crawl through fire just to please him. But she was trying to forget about him, so she agreed to let Jace help, tipping her head back like he asked.

"Good, baby. Now, open your mouth."

Internally cringing at being called *baby* yet again, Kara did as he asked, hesitantly opening her mouth with her head tilted up.

"Wider," Jace ordered.

Feeling positively asinine, Kara opened her mouth as wide as she could, feeling her jaw ache with the stretch.

"There you go. Stay like that. Now, open your throat, like you're about to take a cock really deep."

"Jace!" Kara screamed in indignation, moving from her position as she second guessed her decision to be alone in a room with Jace.

"I told you to stay," Jace admonished, gripping her hair and pulling her head back. "Now open your mouth unless you want me to pour this somewhere else."

Annoyed but tired of fighting, Kara opened her mouth for him. She watched him raise the bottle above her mouth without actually touching her lips. Then he poured slowly as Kara opened her throat and let the liquor slide down. That time, she didn't choke on it, and it was easier to get down.

"There, isn't that better?"

Kara nodded in agreement, her hair still held in Jace's fist.

"Do you want more, baby?" Jace asked, his voice low and sultry.

Hideaway

Again, Kara nodded. This time, the *baby* didn't bother her as much. Maybe the alcohol was working after all. Jace raised the bottle to her lips and poured, but before she could swallow, his mouth was on hers, drinking in the taste of liquor and the taste of her as they shared a burning kiss. For a moment, Kara allowed herself to forget who she was kissing. She allowed herself to forget about Cade. She allowed herself to enjoy the experience of being wanted and desired, and she opened her mouth for Jace to explore. For one moment, she allowed herself to feel sated by the feel of his tongue on hers, his hands roaming her body looking for exposed skin, his hands roaming lower still.

And then that moment shattered.

Suddenly, the kiss felt *wrong*. The feel of Jace's mouth against hers was *wrong*. The taste of him on her lips was *wrong*. The caress of his hand trailing along her inner thighs was very, very *wrong*. Because Jace wasn't Cade. And as much as she wanted to forget about Cade and what he was doing at that very moment, she couldn't let go enough to drown herself in the attentions of another man. Against reason and her better judgment, she cared about Cade. She cared about what he would feel about her kissing Jace, even when she knew he was out with someone else and giving her no such loyalty. And that nagging, unrelenting infatuation with her captor terrified her as much as it pissed her the fuck off.

"Jace, stop." Kara tried to force him away, desperate for enough space to breath without Jace's fully erect cock protruding far too closely into the vicinity of her open legs. But pushing against the firmness of Jace's chest was like pushing against a brick wall and expecting it to give way beneath the effort. It was, unsurprisingly, pointless. Trying not to panic at the precariousness of the situation she'd willingly walked into, Kara tried a different approach. "Please give me a bit of room," Kara begged sweetly as she stoked his arm—a calming gesture rather than a seductive one. "You're crushing me."

"Am I?" Jace asked innocently as he pressed his hard-on between her thighs, grinding against her body roughly. "I think you like it."

"I can assure you, I don't." Kara tried to leverage the strength of her legs against him, but the movement merely caused more friction between them as he straddled her hips. "Get the fuck off of me!" Kara shouted in frustration, her helplessness infuriating.

"Shut your goddamn mouth," Jace growled as he lowered to attack her mouth with his, kissing her with a passion that felt more like hatred than desire. He could feel the vibrations of her screams against his tongue as he muffled her protests with the seal of his mouth. His hand twisted in her hair as he held her still beneath him, taking by force everything she no longer wanted to give him. Jace scoffed at Kara's continued attempts to push him away. If she knew him better, she would know that he couldn't be denied so easily.

Trembling with the realization that Jace could truly do whatever he wanted with her and nothing and no one could stop him, Kara used the last weapon at her disposal and bit down as hard as she possibly could against Jace's invasive tongue. She continued to bite until the taste of blood filled her mouth, biting harder still until she felt Jace pull away so suddenly that she didn't register his raised hand until she felt the sting of an open palm against her cheek.

Kara gasped in reaction, though the brutal slap shouldn't have surprised her. Jace had hit her before. In fact, she'd always known exactly the kind of man he was—a brute who played upon the weakness of others. And she'd let him twist at the hurt and insecurity she had regarding Cade until she was so desperate to feel something *good* that she'd allowed him inside her head, inside her mouth, nearly inside her body before she had a welcome shock of common sense. It was a mistake that she would never make again.

"Did that feel good, Jace?" Kara taunted as she rubbed at her sore cheek. "Is smacking around someone who is helpless beneath you the trick to getting your dick hard?"

"You want to know what gets my dick hard, baby?" Jace asked, his words deceptively playful while his tone was sharp with danger. Reaching down, he grabbed ahold of Kara's dress with both hands and tore it all the way down the middle, exposing the softness of her flesh with only a thin lace bra and panties for cover. He would get to those soon too. Relishing the sight of her smooth, creamy skin, Jace skimmed his fingertips over the tops of her full breasts spilling out of her bra as her chest heaved. When she tried to stop him, he merely snatched up both of her thin wrists with one hand and forced them over her head.

"Are you scared, Kara?" Jace asked as he watched her tremble beneath his touch, his fingers trailing down over her stomach until they met the lacy edge of her panties.

"Jace, please stop," Kara pleaded, the strength in her voice nearly gone as she started to stop fighting the inevitable. People like Jace always got what they wanted. She was merely another causality in man's selfish pursuit of pleasure.

"I like it when you beg me, baby. Do it again." Jace's fingers slipped lower, stroking at her center over her panties.

Kara flinched at the intrusive contact, trying one last desperate time to wriggle out from under him. Her struggle was useless. "Please," Kara begged, her voice nearly as sob. She braced herself for the invasion she knew would come, pleading with her consciousness to escape the horrible reality of Jace's assault by way of pleasant memories or fantasies of the man she actually cared for. She pretended it was Cade lying on top of her, pressing against her entrance, preparing to fill her to the brim.

But the horrible violation never came.

Instead, the library doors flung open so hard that they ricocheted off the walls behind them with an ear-splitting *bang*. The surprise of the intrusion caused Jace to slacken his hold enough for Kara to lift herself slightly from her prostrate position on the leather couch and make eye contact with the dark, looming figure in the entrance. Her heart faltered briefly from sheer relief when she caught sight of Cade standing guard of the doorway like an ominous angel of vengeance, his face contorted with pure, unadulterated fury, his jacket discarded as though he had entered the room prepared for a fight. He took in the sight of Jace's body pressed forcefully against Kara and the obviously frantic pleading of her eyes. A call for help that he was pretty fucking grateful he had made it in time to answer.

"What *the fuck* do you think you're doing?" Cade asked, his words softly dangerous as though the overwhelming magnitude of his anger had taken away his ability to shout. The quiet deadliness of his tone was even more threatening than bellows of rage.

With a mixture of arrogance and audacity that seemed to be his signature attitude, Jace only half moved himself off Kara and stared back at Cade with an expression that could only be described as nonchalant indifference. "Ashford," Jace greeted casually. "I know you were raised in a castle, but didn't they teach you to knock where you come from?"

"In case you have forgotten, this is my goddamn house. I'm under no obligation to announce myself before entering any of *my* rooms."

"Just trying to save you from seeing something that might offend your delicate sensibilities," Jace responded with false politeness, his hands raised as though in surrender.

"Get the fuck off of her," Cade ordered sharply, his jaw tense with anger.

"Now why would I do that?" Jace asked with a smug smile as he splayed his fingers across the bare flesh of Kara's stomach, enjoying the way she shivered beneath his touch. "She practically begged for me after you left her here alone." Jace trailed his hand up to Kara's lips. "Did you know she tastes like honey, or has she not let you sample her mouth yet?"

Cade stalked toward Jace furiously. "Wipe that goddamn smirk off your face before I do it for you." He reached for Kara's hand, pulling her roughly from beneath Jace and setting her on her feet. His careful eyes appraised the state of her, searching for damage or injury. His expression darkened when he caught sight of her reddened cheek and blood on her lips. "Are you alright?" Cade asked softly.

Not trusting the strength of her voice, Kara merely nodded. Not that she was in the best state of mind to answer *that* question. Was she okay? She wasn't entirely sure. All she knew was that she was better off than she would have been if Cade had arrived a few minutes later.

"You're shivering," Cade commented in concern, his voice deep and full as he touched her trembling lips.

"Am I?" Kara responded numbly, not quite sure that she was fully present in her body, her mind seeming to have drifted somewhere else entirely.

"You are," Cade confirmed, his voice growing even deeper, almost hoarse. "And it's no fucking wonder." Without a moment's hesitation, Cade's hands fell to his shirt, hastily ripping open the buttons and sliding the white material gracefully off his well-formed shoulders. As if in embrace, Cade wrapped his arms around Kara, draping his shirt over her half-naked body and helping her arms into the far too long sleeves. The unexpected sight of Kara in *his* clothes filled Cade with a possessive sort of tenderness, as though covering her in his scent—in things that belonged to him—somehow claimed her as his as well.

Instinctively, Kara wrapped Cade's shirt tighter around her body, gratefully absorbing the lingering warmth and inhaling his intoxicatingly masculine scent. With her nakedness covered and her chilled shivers abated, Kara finally began to relax. In spite of what had nearly just happened, Cade's presence lulled her into a sense of security. Though her circumstances hadn't much changed—she still shared a room with the man who held her captive and the man who tried to assault her—Kara felt inexplicably *safe*.

Satisfied that Kara was, for the moment, in a stable frame of mind and body, Cade once again focused his fury on the prick who had tried to force himself on his girl. In all honesty, Cade would have been pissed as fuck even if it was consensual. But the fact that the arsehole had been violent, torn her clothes, and held her down made

Cade see fucking red. The bastard would be lucky if he made it out of that room alive, let alone in one fucking piece. Not wanting Kara to get caught in the crosshairs, Cade protectively tucked her behind him, pressing her to his bare back and using his own body as a shield. Reflexively, Kara wrapped her arms around his lower waist, resting her head against his shoulder.

"Now, I'll ask you one more goddamn time—what *the fuck* do you think you're doing with *my girl*?" Cade asked Jace, his voice shaking with violence. He was keeping the lurking monster of rage restrained, but barely.

"What the fuck do you mean, *your girl*?" Jace questioned, genuinely surprised by Cade's words. "You left, remember? To fuck someone other than *your girl*, if I'm not mistaken." Jace laughed, but it was cold and humorless. "You've got some fucking nerve getting pissed at me for just taking advantage of an opportunity. Sorry mate, if you leave your *toys* lying around, they're gonna get played." Jace flashed Cade a smug smile that practically begged for a punch to the face.

And that's exactly what he got. Knocked on his fucking ass.

Cade reared back for another hit while Jace was still on the ground, but Kara tugged at his arm with a silent plea not to invoke more violence.

"Jesus, Ashford, what the fuck?" Jace exclaimed in shock as he spat the blood from his mouth onto the pristine white rug in the middle of the room.

"She is *mine*, do you understand me? You do not *fucking* touch her. You don't fucking talk to her. You don't even fucking *look* at her. You're lucky I'm allowing you to continue breathing the same air as her. And if you fuck up a *single* one of those rules regarding her, you'll forfeit that privilege as well. I'll bury you on the grounds, six feet under, and you'll be alive when I do it. At least, for as long as it takes for you to suffocate as your lungs fill with earth and you spend your last few miserable minutes of life contemplating why you should never fuck with me. Do I make myself abundantly clear?"

"Fuck, yes, I get it. I don't have a fucking death wish." Jace got to his feet, noticeably less cocky than he was a few minutes before. "No pussy is worth *that* much trouble, no matter how good it is."

"Shut your goddamn mouth and get out of my sight. I'll deal with you later," Cade ordered, his last words ominous and laced with the threat of violence.

"Sure thing, boss," Jace answered obediently, suddenly very focused on self-preservation. Pissed as hell, Jace stormed toward his wing of the manor. Being hyped up, fucked up, and having nothing to stick his cock into left him feeling itching for a fight. What the fuck was wrong with Ashford? He'd never been territorial about women. Ever. Bitches meant just as little to Ashford as they did to him; it was one of the reasons they got along so well. And then that fucking prude showed up and had Ashford salivating for a taste of something he couldn't have. Ashford might enjoy working for his fuck, but Jace only enjoyed playing the game of hard to get for so long. Eventually the girl would give it up, whether she wanted to or not.

A large obstacle blocked Jace's path as he turned down the hall on the lower level toward his room. Jace looked up to see the hulking mass of Ashford's security guard glaring at him angrily. What the fuck was Ortega's problem? Did Jace accidentally lay the moves on *his girl* too?

"Bro, what the fuck are you doing? I'm not in the mood for this shit."

"You hit her," Ortega answered angrily as he aggressively threw his hands into Jace's chest, shoving him backward.

"What the hell?" Jace asked, shocked that the man was picking a fight with him over a girl. He and Ortega had never butted heads before. "I don't know what—"

"Don't fuck with me, *pendejo*. I *saw* you hit her." Ortega appreciated the look of concern that crossed Jace's face when he remembered that there were security cameras in the library. And he had all the proof he needed to put Jace in an early grave. "And if *he* ever watches that security footage, you better get on your goddamn knees and pray because Ashford will *fucking* kill you." Ortega grabbed ahold of Jace's collar and jerked him closer, his size and muscle utterly dwarfing Jace. "And I promise you, I will help him destroy you with joy in my heart."

"Fuck you, Ortega," Jace spat angrily, ripping himself from the other man's grasp.

"Watch your back, cabrón," the massive man warned before stalking away.

Jace swayed as he continued toward his room, the alcohol wreaking havoc on his nervous system. That and being threatened by a scary fucking bastard who was very believably rumored to be part of the Mexican drug cartel before Ashford got him in his pocket. Ortega had lost his shit. Ashford too. The damn bitch was making everyone in the house go fucking crazy. Someone needed to take her down a peg or two, and he knew just the bastard for the job.

❦

CADE led Kara up the stairs and down the hall in silence. Kara noticed as they passed her room and continued down toward where she knew Cade slept, but she said nothing. She also noticed the smooth contours of Cade's bare back, the way his muscles rippled as he walked in front of her, the way his pants hung low on his hips, the delectable divots at the base of his spine—she definitely didn't comment on any of that either. Cade stopped in front of his room, opened the door, and entered. Subconsciously, Kara stopped at the threshold, fearful that she was allowing herself to walk into yet another precarious situation with a man, having just escaped another. In spite of her misgivings, a gentle tug of Cade's hand had her standing in his bedroom, the door shut and unmistakably locked behind them.

"Cade, I really hope you're not about to try the same moves Jace just did. Because it's not going to happen," Kara admonished in a tone that she hoped was assertive, but she was fairly certain she just sounded desperate as hell. Because she was. Having downed a fair amount of alcohol, had her clothes ripped from her body, been possessively claimed by her equally sexy and scary criminal captor, and been subjected to Cade's half-naked body for far too long, she was undeniably down to fuck.

"Well that is good to know, as I wasn't really planning on putting out tonight," Cade responded, lightly scoffing at her presumptuousness. "Just let me put a shirt on so my substantial pectorals don't tempt your mind further into the gutter," he added cheekily. "In your defense, I understand how having both of us half naked in my bedroom might have given the wrong impression."

Drowning in humiliation at that point, Kara averted her eyes so he could have privacy to dress. "So I was given the servant's quarters I see," she commented sardonically as she took advantage of his momentary departure to his closet to take stock of Cade's private living quarters. It would be a misidentification to call the space a *bedroom* as it was nearly the size of her entire apartment, complete with a sitting room, lounge area, office space, two monstrous chandeliers, and a bed so imposing it defied description.

His clothing fully restored, Cade walked back over to where Kara stood in abashed silence. "There, at least one of us can concentrate now," he said in a voice full of emotion. He caught her chin tenderly and drew her face up to meet his. "You're bleeding," Cade said in a tone as black as death as he ran his thumb over the smudge of blood at the corner of her mouth.

"It's not mine," Kara explained hurriedly before Cade rushed out of the room and killed someone, which he was very much on the verge of doing from the murderous look in his eyes. "I bit him when he tried to force his tongue down my throat."

"That's my vicious girl," Cade praised warmly as his features softened into an expression of admiration as he continued to look over her body for signs of injury.

"Really, I'm fine," she said, trying to brush aside his concern.

Cade gave her a stern look of warning before she resigned herself to his intense inspection. He traced the faint purpled streaks that marked her jaw where Jace's grip had been too tight. He pulled away his shirt from her chest, revealing the torn remains of her dress, as he continued his search for injuries, and she shivered in response. Cade resisted the urge to try to kiss away the imprints of violence left behind on her body.

"You arrived just in time."

Kara's comment startled Cade from his private anguish. "I cannot begin to describe how sorry I am that you were treated in such a manner in my home, where I promised you safety."

"It's not your fault," she replied in a voice devoid of emotion. Kara didn't want to think about how close she had come to being raped. She felt a baseless sense of shame at having allowed herself to be put in such a vulnerable situation. She knew one thing for sure, if Cade hadn't burst through the door when he did, she would have far more regrets to agonize over.

"Well, let's get some clothes on you before I turn from rescuing to ravaging," Cade announced with the hope of distracting Kara from whatever thoughts were clouding her expression. He appreciated the lovely flush of her cheeks when she realized she was in his bedroom practically naked. "Any preferences?" he asked in regard to clothes.

"Um, just something comfortable, I guess?" Kara responded, not really in the mood to contemplate fashion options.

"Well in that case, here," he said, tossing her a matching pair of sweats that he pulled from his closet.

Kara eyed the clothes warily; there was something inherently intimate in wearing a man's clothes, and Kara wasn't sure she

Hideaway

wanted to venture into that territory, even if the act was technically meaningless. "Couldn't I just wear something from my room?" she asked, almost certain of his refusal.

"Tonight I am not leaving your side, and you aren't leaving this room. So you are left with what my wardrobe can offer, I am afraid," Cade responded, watching as aspects of his answer incited her shock. He could take an education guess at which part.

"Cade, I'm not going to sleep with you in this room," she replied, wary of misconstruing his intent again.

"Well you won't be sleeping with me. You may have the bed, of course. I'll take the floor."

Kara cringed at the thought of Cade resigning himself to a night of little sleep on the hard floor on her account. "Please, I can't let you sleep on the floor. I'm sure I will be fine in my own room," she pleaded guiltily.

"We can always share the bed if you insist," he retorted to see the color rise in her cheeks. "And do you really want to risk Jace making a late night renewal of his advances?"

"Okay, so it might not be a bad idea to have some company tonight to be safe. But we can't just stay holed up in your room for the rest of the night. What if I…get hungry?" Kara asked stupidly, desperate for literally any excuse that would allow her to escape an entire night in confined quarters with the man who had saved her by essentially declaring she was his property. It was an archaic notion, the thought of owning another person, and it should have had her thoroughly repulsed. Unfortunately, her rebellious pussy had a different response to hearing Cade say *mine*. And it was the needy desires of her irrational sex that had her anxious to leave Cade's bedroom before things got unnecessarily complicated.

"*Are* you hungry?"

"Not at the moment," Kara responded evasively.

"Well, if we manage to work up an appetite, I will happily have anything you desire delivered right to the door," Cade responded, his tone intentionally suggestive.

"But—" Kara began before being cut off.

"Kara, continue to argue with me any longer, and I'm going to assume you enjoy spending time with me in nothing but your knickers."

Kara's face filled with embarrassment for the umpteenth time, and she snatched the proffered apparel out of Cade's hands. "So are you sticking around for the show, or what?" she asked pointedly in irritation.

"Don't tempt me, love. The door on the left is the bathroom. The door on the right is my sex dungeon. Take your pick," he offered good-humoredly. Kara paled in horror. "I'm kidding. The dungeon is downstairs," he added with a sly smile.

Kara raced to the door on the left, hoping beyond reason that the manor housed no dungeon, though with a man of Cade's tastes she couldn't be sure. She opened the door somewhat hesitantly and was met with the welcoming site of a large, luxurious bathroom. A gorgeous clawfoot bathtub stood amid the white marbled floors and walls like a glittering jewel, quite literally sparkling from the downcast gleams of the crystal chandelier above. How many damn gaudy chandeliers did the man own? If suspended crystal was a fetish, Cade most certainly had it. Kara looked at the tub longingly, feeling quite sure a hot soak would wash away all of the grime of a terrible day. Well, most of it anyway.

After locking the bathroom door, Kara turned on the water and let the steam begin to fill the room. She desperately avoided the mirror as she waited for the tub to fill before slipping into the blissful warmth. With fervent need, she endeavored to wash the invisible remnants of Jace's touch from her body, rubbing a cloth against her skin with an aggression that bordered on violence. Silent tears of grief and frustration fell and melded with the warm water below. Kara wiped away the tears angrily and sank into the welcoming abyss of the watery depths.

One. Two. Three. Four. Five. Six. Seven. Eight. Nine. Ten.

She counted as she held her breath, feeling a sense of calm wash over her resulting from the oxygen deprivation induced euphoria.

Ninety-seven. Ninety-eight. Ninety-nine. One hundred.

She broke through the water with a gasping breath. The events of the day had been banished to the farthest recesses of memory, and she felt centered once again. The bath having fulfilled its purpose, Kara stepped out and wrapped herself in the plushest towel she had ever had the pleasure of experiencing. Relaxed and dry, she slipped into Cade's sweatpants and sweatshirt feeling properly cozy. Kara emerged from the bathroom in a haze of steam and found Cade casually sprawled across the bed.

"Feeling better?" he asked.

"Yes, thank you. I made use of your bath."

"And I'm sure it was never better used. This is a great look for you," he remarked, gesturing to the all too long sweatpants and baggy shirt.

"Yeah, I'd heard frumpy chic was trending," she answered with equal sarcasm.

"I think you'd look lovely in anything you wore," Cade complimented with sincerity, his voice tinged with emotion. "So which side of the bed do you prefer?" he asked, patting the space beside him.

Kara looked at him in shock, hoping that he had no expectation of her sharing his bed. "I think the floor will be fine, thanks. If I could just borrow a pillow, maybe?" she responded, the anxious wariness creeping back into her voice.

Cade mentally smacked himself in the head. Kara had just been assaulted, and he was bastard enough to be suggestive about their sleeping arrangements. "I apologize. I was trying to lighten the mood and ended up coming off as a complete prick." Cade nearly jolted out of the bed in contrition and gestured for her to make use of it without him. "I have more than earned a night of sleeping on the floor. And I'll even forsake a pillow as an act of repentance."

"It's all right, you don't have to tread so cautiously because of what happened with Jace. And I'm happy to sleep on the floor. You did save the day after all, and I don't want to displace you from your own bed."

"You get my bed; I get the floor. That's the end of it, Kara," Cade stated somewhat sternly.

Kara didn't have the mental capacity to argue with him at that moment, so she obediently crawled into bed as he began to get situated on the floor. "Pillow?" she called as she threw a grey silk cushion as hard as she could toward where he was standing. It hit him straight in the face, causing him to stumble backward slightly from the surprise impact, an astonishing feat considering her inability to aim. Kara grinned sheepishly as he glared at her.

"Attacking an unarmed man, Miss Caine? You should be ashamed," Cade chastised, his face the perfect picture of disappointment. "I have half a mind to take you to task for insolence," he added seriously, holding the pillow poised as a threat. A man so practiced with intimidation looked fearsome even when weaponizing a pillow. "I suppose, given the lateness of the hour, I will let you off easy tonight. For future notice, I would advise you not to initiate a pillow fight unless you're prepared for battle. I like to play rough, and I like to win," Cade teased, a smile cracking through his intense exterior.

Kara couldn't help but laugh at his unexpected silliness. The man was gorgeous when he smoldered, but he was stunning when he actually relaxed and let a smile replace his usual scowl. She begged her overactive heart to slow its pace before she passed out from the depth of emotions she refused to name.

"Well, the hard floor awaits," Cade said as he went to turn out the lights and head for the floor with a light blanket taken from a chair in the corner and the pillow Kara had so graciously bestowed.

Kara glanced guiltily at Cade in his makeshift bed on the floor. "Are you sure you don't want me to take the floor?"

"Go to sleep, Kara," he answered without looking up.

"You don't look very comfortable."

"Well, I am used to sleeping naked, but I can muddle through for the sake of propriety."

That comment silenced Kara easily enough. To be honest, Cade found sleeping fully clothed to be damned irritating. He preferred nudity. For both parties. After some deliberation, Cade found the boldness to request a small compromise. "Would you find it terribly uncomfortable if I removed my shirt? I'm a rather hot sleeper. The bottoms remain, I promise."

"I suppose, as my eyes will be closed, it doesn't much matter what you're wearing," Kara responded, trying not to sound flustered at the idea of Cade removing clothing. "But keep your pants on," she added hastily, afraid he would take her attempt at sounding casual as an invitation to undress entirely.

"Yes, ma'am," he answered teasingly as he reached for the neck of his shirt and pulled it smoothly over his head, tossing it on the bed. It was his wicked intent to walk over to her, naked chest in full view, and retrieve his shirt in the morning. Her expression of abashed arousal would be his entertainment for the day. With smug satisfaction, Cade attempted to settle into his bed for the night. The hard floor was truly unbearable, but the ultimate sacrifice was that such a beautiful girl was lying in his bed alone and un-fucked. Cade closed his eyes tightly and tried to concentrate on something other than the plethora of ways he could be occupying his bed's companion.

Kara stirred restlessly in the unfamiliar bed. The pillows felt too soft and the smell of Cade lingered on the sheets, arousing feelings far removed from drowsiness. She stared at the ceiling, replaying the events of the day. The violent images that came to mind didn't merit revisiting ever again, but she couldn't erase them, hard as she might try. Jace had earned a lifetime role in the cinema of Kara's memory. And, much to her chagrin, she was still forced to share a house with the asshole, eating meals with him, running into him in the hall, falling asleep a mere floor away from where his own room stood. The fact that Cade didn't have the full trust in his associate to allow her to sleep alone made Kara uneasy. She stretched out fully to feel the cold emptiness beside her. Having a bed to herself had never bothered Kara before, but suddenly she didn't want to share a bed alone with her fears.

"Cade?" she timidly probed the silence.

"Yes, Kara?" Cade answered, sounding entirely awake.

Kara took a deep breath. "Come to bed, please? Just to sleep. I'd rather not be alone at the moment, and there really is too much room in this ridiculous bed for you to be sleeping on the floor."

Cade took a moment to savor the essence of her request. She didn't ask for the one thing Cade wanted to do with a woman in bed, but somehow her plea made him feel more satisfied than sex had in quite some time. Kara's vulnerability evoked a tenderness that Cade hadn't known he possessed; he attempted to stifle those stirrings of weakness as he rose from the floor and slipped into the empty side of the bed. Kara remained turned away on her side, and Cade watched the rise and fall of Kara's chest as her breathing regulated to a more relaxed pace. The outline of her body was masked by the bulk of his damned sweat set, but she still made a beautiful addition to his bed. He longed to touch her, not sensually, but to alleviate any tensions that remained after her ordeal. Cade reached a tentative hand to her back. "May I?" he asked softly.

"Okay," Kara whispered in permission, a small tremble to her voice.

Cade placed both of his hands on her back and began to gently knead the tension away. In spite of herself, Kara moaned as his fingers pressed against her sore muscles, her body unfamiliar with such luxurious care. It seemed Cade was skilled with his fingers in every respect.

"Where'd you pick up this skill?" she asked after several minutes of relaxed bliss, surprised that such a rough man could be so delicate with his hands.

Cade moved his hands up and down her back, taking a moment before answering. "On the rare chance my mother was feeling maternal, this was how she would chase away the occasional nightmare. I suppose I still remember it as the most soothing of remedies. I thought it might help." Cade continued with his attentions in uneasy silence.

And what the fuck was that?

Cade didn't know what had possessed him to bring up his mother. The subject of his family was off limits even when he was in committed relationships, and yet, there he was sharing unsolicited, intimate details about his family like an imbecile. Something about the girl disarmed him, and he didn't like entering any situation unarmed.

"It does help. Thank you," Kara answered, her voice full. Cautiously, she turned over on her other side so she could see Cade. His eyes were honed in on her, his expression guarded and not quite discernible. He was so close that she could feel his warmth, so close that she had only to reach out to touch the bare skin of his chest. And she wanted to. Desperately.

"Don't look at me like that," Cade admonished almost angrily.

"Like what?" Kara asked anxiously, feeling her cheeks warm with embarrassment. Could he see her staring at his lips, aching to kiss him? Could he feel the heat of her skin as she burned for his touch? Did he know that, in her darkest desires, she wanted him to do exactly what Jace had been planning? Because if it had been his hands on her body, ripping off her clothes and forcing her, she would have wanted it. She wanted it so badly she had to press her legs together tightly to keep the proof of her arousal from dripping down her legs. Fuck, she was absolutely ruined for him.

"Like I'm some sort of savior or knight in shining armor," Cade elaborated, his tone scathing and abrasive. "Because I'm not. I may not approve of what Jace was about to do to you tonight, but I can assure you I'm not much better. I may sound like Prince Charming to girls like you, but I don't have a noble bone in my body. And trust me, princess, I don't save. I destroy. And I revel in the chaos."

"What if I don't want someone noble?" Kara asked softly, so softly she could barely be sure she'd spoken it aloud. "What if I don't want to be saved?"

What if I want you.

"Don't tempt me, love. I'm not in the mood to be gentle. And after the situation I just pulled you from, you're not in a state to handle what I want to do to you."

"You know what your problem is, Caden Ashford? You consistently underestimate me. I'm tougher than you think. Or hadn't you noticed in the week you've spent trying to get me to give in to your demands? How did that work out for you?"

"You know what your problem is, Kara Caine? You never know when to *shut the fuck up.*" Suddenly, Cade closed the space between them, his fingers digging into her hair as he pulled her beneath him. He hovered over her, pressing himself against her and using the weight of his body to keep her pinned. Cade's fingers roamed her body until he found her throat, wrapping his hand around her neck possessively, but not applying pressure. Not yet. "Is this what you want, love?" Cade whispered harshly against her ear. "You want me to hurt you?"

"Yes," she answered breathlessly, her pupils dilated with desire and a small dose of fear.

"You want me to take you and make you mine?" he asked dangerously, his other hand traveling between her thighs and grabbing her cunt roughly. "Once I possess someone, they're mine. *Always.*"

His words were a warning. An ominous one. But all they did was stoke the fire of passion burning in Kara's chest. For Cade, she wanted to burn, wanted the flames to consume every inch of her body. "I'm yours, Cade. I'm already yours," Kara confessed, her voice shuddering with emotion and need. The admission startled her as much as it did Cade. He stilled, as though in shock, before removing his hand from between her legs and ripping his fingers from her throat. Kara felt empty without them.

"You don't mean that. You're just a naive girl caught in a trap and looking for the best means of escape," Cade responded cruelly. "Sorry love, you won't be able to fuck your way out of this prison. I still need the book. And you're still going to retrieve it for me." Cade's words were far harsher than his actual thoughts, an overcompensation for feelings of weakness regarding Kara that he didn't want to admit or deal with.

Kara's face filled with hurt at Cade's hateful words, tears glistening in her eyes and threatening to spill. But she didn't move. Didn't say a word. She didn't trust herself to be able to acknowledge him without breaking down.

"But," Cade continued, resolved to twist the knife he'd plunged into her heart just a bit more. "If you want to fuck around to pass the time, I am happy to oblige you," he taunted, grinding his body up against her once more.

"Get off of me," Kara demanded, her voice breaking. She stared off into the distance, unable to look at the cruel, beautiful man hovering half-naked above her.

"Suit yourself," Cade answered nonchalantly, as though he really couldn't care less if he fucked her or not. As if he really couldn't care less whether she took her next breath or not. His aloofness was a facade, but a necessary one. Cade turned away from Kara and pretended to fall into undisturbed sleep beside her.

Kara remained on her back, where he'd thrown her a just few minutes before, unable to move, physically overcome with pain as though Cade's words had evoked bodily harm rather than merely emotional injury. How could he be so fucking cruel, after everything they'd shared between them? She eventually found the strength to roll over to her side, hugging her knees to her chest for comfort. She fixated on the deep, steady rhythm of Cade's breaths, finding a sort of calmness in the repetition. His words replayed in her head, cutting deeper each time she heard them. In a way, Cade's assault seemed almost more destructive than Jace's.

That night—the first time in ages—Kara cried herself to sleep.

CHAPTER SEVEN

CADE awoke in the morning feeling like absolute shite. That was, if he had gotten any sleep at all. Guilt had gnawed at his insides as he listened to Kara cry into her pillow until she finally fell into a fitful sleep. He was a fucking bastard; he could admit as much. He hadn't wanted to hurt Kara, but, in his own fucked up way, he was pretty sure he'd hurt her far worse than any damage casual sex would have inflicted.

He would have liked nothing more than to fuck her into absolute oblivion, to fuck every thought and memory of Jace out of her pretty little head. He would have obliterated her with his cock, split her the fuck open, and made her scream out his name and beg for mercy that would never be given. But *that* was the fucking problem. She wasn't like his usual fucks. She hadn't been vetted and hand picked to withstand his voracious appetites. Their relationship hadn't been planned, there'd been no agreements or discussions of limits. Hell, she didn't even know about the Hideaway. She couldn't handle him; no matter how brave or strong or invincible she thought she was, she could *not* fucking handle the things he wanted to do to her. He would wreck her. And as much as he would enjoy destroying her mind, body, and soul, he was astonished to discover that he preferred Kara in one piece more.

Cade didn't have a single fragment of selflessness or tenderness in his goddamn body, so why was he putting Kara's feelings over the needs of his cock? He needed a distraction, a way to burn out all the pent up frustration and energy that *didn't* involve him slipping his dick into the girl sleeping peacefully beside him. And he knew just the fix.

"Wake up, sleepy head," Cade called softly as he tried to rouse her, his darkness from the previous night vanished.

Kara stirred begrudgingly, desperately clinging to the last fragments of slumber before they flitted away along with the startling nightmares that had plagued her subconscious while she slept. She was exhausted, her head throbbed, her eyes felt swollen and puffy, and her heart ached with the fresh sting of rejection. Kara opened her eyes hesitantly and found the source of her heart's demise staring down at her with an inexplicable look in his deceptively lovely hazel eyes. Was it guilt? Or regret? Both seemed logical, but neither suited the character she had come to associate with Cade. Caden Ashford was ruthless and had no use for remorse.

"How did you sleep?" Cade asked, his tone conversational. Friendly. It almost masked the inner turmoil he was actively trying to avoid. Almost.

"Fine," Kara spat out, still pissed about the night before. "The bed was rather crowded," she added with a scathing look in his direction.

"Well, I did offer to take the floor, but *someone* insisted on sleeping *with me*," Cade retorted with a roguish smile on his beautiful face. The comment earned him a glare from Kara, but she refused to fall prey to his arrogant jabs. "Now get out of my bed," he commanded with a sharp clap of his hands. "We have things to do."

"What *things*?" Kara asked suspiciously. After the disaster of the night before, she was practically resolved to hide out in Cade's bedroom until he grew so tired of her that he set her free. Although, something told her that Cade offering her freedom was about as likely as Jane Austen coming back to walk the earth in zombie form. So *moderately* unrealistic.

A spark that seemed almost reminiscent of actual happiness filled Cade's eyes as his full lips stretched into a wide grin. "I'm taking you riding."

IN what was becoming an inconvenient habit, Kara once again found herself outfitted in Cade's clothes. Casual horse riding attire was one of the few things not to be found in her well-stock closet. It was a surprisingly warm and sunny winter day, so she wore one of Cade's thick, woolen sweaters with the sleeves rolled up to her wrists, a pair of black yoga pants that she had managed to find in the back of her closet, and a pair of the most sensible boots she could find. The black leather boots still sported a short heel, but the only other option had been a rather risqué pair of thigh-high, stiletto boots. Whoever her predecessor had been, she clearly wasn't the outdoorsy type.

Forgoing her usual routine, Kara had decided to forget the makeup that morning and pulled her hair into a simple ponytail. Being comfortable and relaxed while walking silently with Cade in the open air felt surprisingly nice. Lovely, even. Cade seemed altered when he stepped into nature. Calmer, as though he shed his usual cloak of dominance and assholery and just allowed himself to enjoy his surroundings. Kara couldn't help but admire the rare view of Cade without his usual three piece suit and tie. He wore brown jodhpurs, a simple white sweater, and beige riding pants. His pants were tight, clinging to his body and revealing every muscular curve of his ass and thighs. She tried not to ogle his sinfully attractive body, but—since he was walking ahead of her—why not take advantage of an opportunity to study the way his perfectly taut ass swayed with every stride?

"Would you like to take a picture, Miss Caine? It would last longer," Cade playfully chided without so much as looking behind him.

Turning bright red all the way to her ears, Kara squeaked in mortification before hurrying her steps to match Cade's. Did he have eyes embedded in the back of his freaking skull or something? Thankfully, they were close to the stables entrance, and she would have something to distract her from the shame of being caught checking out her captor. Kara immediately went to say hello to Sugar Cubes while Cade made himself busy getting the gear ready. The dark horse recognized her immediately, sniffing her hands as though she expected treats like last time.

"Sorry, girl. That tyrant dragged me down here before I could snatch you some apples from the kitchen. Next time, I promise," Kara crooned as she stroked the horse's mane.

"Who is a tyrant?" Cade asked, sneaking up behind Kara and placing his hand on the back of her neck. His touch was gentle, but barely, as though he was holding himself back. He wondered if she could feel the contained threat of destruction in his hold.

Kara jumped at the surprise attack, steadying herself by grabbing ahold of the stall door. "None of your business," Kara answered spitefully, though a little breathlessly. "I was talking to Sugar. No boys allowed." She waved him away as though he would listen to her demands.

Of course, he didn't. "Watch yourself, Miss Caine," Cade cautioned, his eyes glittering with malice. "I came armed." He twirled a black riding crop between his fingers threateningly.

Kara gulped nervously at the sight and resolved to be on her best behavior. At least until Cade put down the fucking horse whip. "So, which one is mine?" Kara asked to change the subject, gesturing to the other horses stomping in their stalls.

"Oh, I think I have the perfect one for you," Cade answered mischievously, heading toward the back of the stable. He stopped in front of the last stall, nodding toward a large, white stallion. "You two hellions should get along nicely."

Kara gawked at the sight; the stallion was huge, one of the largest she had ever seen in person. There was no way she'd be able to mount him unassisted. "What's his name?" Kara asked, making it clear that she wasn't backing down from Cade's challenge. It was a fucking low blow to pair someone as small as her with the largest horse in the stable, but she would show the bastard. There was nothing quite so thrilling as proving Cade wrong. In fact, it was becoming the very thing she lived for.

"Avalanche," Cade answered with a smirk.

Named after a deadly barrage of snow and ice. Fantastic.

"Cute," Kara replied sarcastically, attempting to mask her trepidation at being forced to ride the white, snow-death stallion. Cautiously, Kara stepped toward the horse with her hand outstretched. The stallion snorted at the approach, but slowly let down his guard enough to nudge her hand. Softly, Kara trailed her fingers through his coarse mane as the horse adjusted to her scent. "There you go," she encouraged. "You might look scary, but you're a sweet boy aren't you?" Avalanche reflexively nodded, making Kara laugh. "Yes, you're so good," she continued to sweet talk while rubbing his back.

"Huh," Cade muttered, the sound surprised and annoyed.

"Yes, Lord Ashford?" Kara asked in a snarky tone, pausing her attentions with Avalanche to study the brooding man beside her.

"He likes you," Cade explained with a note of astonishment.

"And this is surprising *because*? I'll have you know I'm very well liked outside of your general vicinity, people and animals included," Kara answered with a pout, crossing her arms over her chest.

"I'm sure you are," Cade retorted in a tone of thinly veiled sarcasm. "Avalanche doesn't like anyone."

"Not even you?" Kara asked incredulously. She assumed the man possessed the ability to glare anything into submission.

Hideaway

"No, not even me," Cade answered with a laugh.

"So you paired me with a stallion who hates everyone, *why?*" Kara asked in annoyance, though she knew she really shouldn't be surprised. Clearly the man made it his mission to torment her.

"I was testing a theory," Cade replied vaguely as he continued to study her, a dissecting expression marring his too lovely face.

"And what was your conclusion?"

"Wouldn't you like to know?"

"Possibly." She was actually unendurably curious to know what he thought he had discovered about her. But she tried not to seem too keen as she waited for his response. She was met merely with silence and a mischievous grin. "Wait, you're really not going to tell me?" Kara asked in exasperation.

"You know, I don't think I will," he retorted smugly.

"Whatever, I don't even care," Kara answered as she brushed him aside and devoted her attention to the white horse in the stall. Avalanche neighed happily as she stroked him again. Even though Cade said the stallion wasn't very social, the horse warmed to her touch immediately and wasn't nearly as threatening as his namesake. She supposed she had a knack for melting icy creatures.

Adopting the strictness of an instructor, Cade meticulously showed Kara the intricacies of horseback riding. Of course, if the presumptuous bastard had even thought to ask, he would have discovered that Kara had been riding since she was ten. She was a little out of practice since her years at university, but getting back into the saddle was rather like riding a bike—muscle memory did all the work. Strictly for her personal amusement, Kara played dumb and let Cade *teach* her how to ride. If she was being honest, a small part of her also enjoyed having a legitimate excuse to get close to him, to feel his body against her as he showed her how to mount and sit and lead. It didn't escape her notice how his hands lingered on her hips longer than necessary as he helped lift her onto Avalanche, how his fingers grasped hers a little too tightly—like he didn't want to let her go—as he showed her how to hold the reins. She was fairly certain that he was enjoying their lesson as much as she was.

They'd been riding for nearly an hour, basking in the rare winter sun and enjoying the tranquil silence of each other's company, undisturbed other than the ambient sounds of nature bustling about them. For someone who often spent the majority of their time indoors amid dusty manuscripts and aged books, Kara appreciated having the opportunity to reacquaint herself with the outdoors. And she supposed the current view was fairly enticing in all his dark, brooding glory. After fully relaxing into her company—away from his men and obligations and illicit undertakings—Kara noticed that Cade's face lost its usual harshness and rough edges. His smile was *almost* soft, his entrancing, hazel eyes *almost* warm as he looked over at her with something far removed from his usual malice or mischief in his expression. The inexplicable look in Cade's eyes caused Kara's hands to tremble on the reins as heat flooded her face —and damned arousal flooded between her thighs.

Against all reason and sense, Caden Ashford had the power to obliterate her traitorous heart with a single glance. So, naturally, she had to formulate some counter-attack against the bastard. Feeling daring, Kara nudged Avalanche, urging him to go faster. The horse obediently picked up speed. Glancing over at Cade, Kara's eyes glimmered with a spark of challenge. She'd always felt a surge of rivalry regarding Cade, an ever-lingering desire to put the pompous British bastard in his place. One of the many detriments of spending her days as a prisoner in his house was that the playing field was never quite even. But in that moment—enjoying a rare instant of freedom with the wind in her hair, a powerhouse of a beast beneath her thighs, and nothing before them but the vast expanse of nature—Kara felt as though victory was finally within her grasp.

"Kara, no," Cade said sternly, his voice a warning as his brow furrowed in disapproval at her initiation of a race between them.

Clearly, her challenge hadn't been accepted. Well, perhaps he needed a little push. Kara dug her heels into Avalanche's sides, spurring him on and feeling her adrenaline mount as the white horse transitioned into a gallop. "Good boy," Kara whispered sweetly against the horse's ear as she stroked his side. Avalanche was fast, gliding across the open plains as though he longed to fly. At that speed, he practically was. Kara closed her eyes, enjoying the rhythmic sound of hooves thundering against the earth and the wind lashing at her hair. It was somehow peaceful and exhilarating at the same time.

"Kara, stop!" Cade called harshly from behind her.

If he was behind her, that meant she was winning. As she spied the outline of the stables in the distance, Kara held on tightly to the reins and coaxed Avalanche to go just a little faster. The raucous of muttered curses and beating hooves signaled that Cade was gaining on them. But he wouldn't beat her. Not that time.

"Kara Caine! Slow down this instant before you get yourself thrown and killed," Cade thundered at her, his tone a combination of panic and fury.

Ignoring his warnings, Kara maintained her speed and raced to be the first one to the entrance. With a slight squeal of satisfaction, Kara came upon the sables, reining in Avalanche to a brisk trot as they made it through the open doors. Her chest heaving with the exertion and excitement, Kara dismounted the horse and loosened the cinch, rubbing her hand down the stallion's back and whispering words of affirmation. Kara rolled her eyes as she heard Cade storm in behind them huffing in irritation. She looked over her shoulder to give Cade a smug smirk before taking hold of Avalanche's reins and leading him toward his stall at the far end of the stable. The horse deserved a treat for being such a good boy and out-running the big, bad, man with a habit of underestimating her.

"What the bloody hell was that errant display of stupidity?" Cade yelled at Kara from the other end of the stable.

"I believe it's called winning," Kara called back, not bothering to turn around.

Ignoring Cade and his obvious sour mood, Kara tended to her horse. She removed the saddle and bridle and ran her hands over Avalanche's legs to ensure he was in good shape after the ride. Kara brushed her fingers through the horse's mane, loving the coarse texture of his hair against her skin. "Are you thirsty, boy?" Kara asked, stroking the horse's forehead and looking at him patiently as though she expected a response. Avalanche merely snorted, which Kara took as a *yes*.

Hideaway

While Kara filled a pail of water, Cade came up behind her, his own horse promptly stalled and tended. In his hand, Cade furiously clutched a plaited leather riding crop. His face darkened with anger, Cade drew back his arm and swung the crop with his full strength at Kara's unsuspecting backside. The leather made contact with her arse with a loud, satisfying *thwap*, but the sound dulled in comparison to the surprised, pain-filled shriek the lash dragged from Kara's lips. Startled, Kara lost her hold on the bucket, water splattering everywhere and drenching her boots and pants. She turned toward Cade, her expression aghast as she rubbed at her smarting backside.

"What the fuck was that?" Kara shouted angrily, still in disbelief that he'd struck her.

"What the fuck was *that*?" Cade thundered back, gesturing toward where she'd been racing him. "You could have been injured or worse."

"I was having a bit of fun! Something that's been sorely lacking since I arrived at this godforsaken manor!"

"Fun? Does your idea of fun always involve the potential for fatality?"

"I knew what I was doing, Caden," Kara retorted sharply.

"Yes, you are clearly more experienced with riding than you implied, Kara," Cade answered as he grimaced with disapproval at her duplicity on that subject. "But that doesn't make your actions any less reckless. I ordered you to stop, and you ignored me."

"I don't take orders from you," Kara scoffed. "I'm not your employee. I'm not your girlfriend. So you can shove your orders up your ass and fuck off."

Charging toward her, Cade closed the space between them so rapidly that Kara flinched. He pressed his body against her, his hand wrapping tightly around her throat—the strength of his hold threatening and enticing all at once. Cade still held the riding crop in his other hand, and Kara eyed it warily.

"You are under my protection and under my roof; therefore, you do fucking take orders from me. And when I tell you to stop behaving dangerously and carelessly, you fucking listen." With his hand still firmly wrapped around Kara's throat, Cade trailed the tip of the crop along Kara's body, dragging it down her breasts, along her hips, over her arse, across her thighs, and back up until it rested under her chin. With the flat end of the crop, Cade forced Kara's chin up, tilting her head back until she was staring up at him.

"The next time you disobey me and put your safety at risk, I will whip you fucking senseless. Do you understand me?" Cade threatened coldly, his fingers digging tightly into her neck to emphasize his seriousness.

Kara stared at him in open-mouthed horror, the shock of his threats, his hand enclosing her throat, and the lingering sting on her ass stunning her into silence. Clearly expecting a response, Cade reprimanded her silence with a sharp tap of the crop to the underside of her chin. Kara flinched, but she couldn't escape his hold on her throat as his fingers squeezed tighter.

"I said: do you fucking understand me, Kara?" Cade repeated sternly.

"Yes," she choked out. "I understand, Caden."

"Good. Now, get your arse inside, go to your room, and stay there until I feel you've properly learnt your lesson."

"You're fucking *grounding* me?"

"Behave like a willful child, and you'll be treated as such."

"Fuck you," Kara spat before turning on her heel and storming out of the stables. Kara realized her mistake as soon as she felt the sharp, punishing sting of Cade's riding crop against her ass. *Again.* "Ow! That fucking hurts!" Kara screamed at him in unmitigated fury as she rubbed the abused flesh of her backside.

"Good. It's meant to," Cade responded without an ounce of remorse. "Now go before you earn another." He jerked his head toward the stable exit, dismissing her coldly.

With an unbecoming stomp of her foot and a huff of irritation, Kara rushed out of the stable, eager to escape the presence of the insufferable, overbearing, abusive, arrogant, unjustly attractive bastard. She struggled with irreconcilable urges to murder Cade violently and fuck him in the exact same manner. She wasn't sure which urge was the strongest, the most logical, or the most probable. But she sure as fuck needed to do something to him. And preferably, it needed to hurt.

A figure loomed in the doorway as Kara approached the front steps of the manor. Jace lounged casually against the banister, a lit cigarette in his hand, his eyes unnervingly locked on hers. Kara was more than aware that her appearance was less than presentable—her hair was wind-ravaged, her skin was flushed with exertion and lingering anger, her boots were muddy, and her pants were soaked from the knees down. She was cold, wet, her ass was sore, and she was pissed as hell. The last thing she needed at that moment was to be dealing with Jace's passive aggressive shit.

"What the fuck are you looking at, Jacen?"

"Looks like someone had a hard ride," Jace drawled in a sultry voice, his eyes raking over her body and taking in the disheveled state of her hair and clothes. "Or perhaps *you* weren't the one doing the riding?" he questioned suggestively with a raised brow.

"Fuck off, Jace," Kara answered, the sexual innuendo riling her up more. Because she hadn't slept with Cade, and she would be lying if she said she hadn't been pleasantly entertaining the idea most of the afternoon, right up to the moment Cade hit her with a fucking horse whip. "There isn't a single man in this house that tempts me to anything other than murder and torture of the most gruesome variety."

"Careful, baby. Some of us would consider that foreplay," Jace answered seductively, a full smile playing upon his lips.

"You're deranged," Kara scoffed with a roll of her eyes. Of course he would enjoy the threat of bodily harm.

Sick prick.

"Quite possibly. Does that turn you on?"

Was he fucking flirting with her? After the shit he'd pulled yesterday? "Not in the least. I prefer people in full possession of their mental faculties, thanks."

"Don't knock it till you try it."

"Yeah, thanks for the unsolicited advice, but I need to get to my room." Fuck, why did she tell him that she was going to her room alone? "Boss's orders," Kara explained, hoping to cover her misstep and remind Jace that Cade knew exactly where to find her.

Jace took a long drag of his cigarette as his eyes burned into hers with a heat that somehow made her shudder. Finally he stepped aside, making room for Kara to pass. "Run along like a good little girl," he taunted as she scurried past him and through the front doors without another glance.

Darkness had fallen before Kara finally heard a knock on the door. Cade had punished her with confinement in her room for nearly eight *fucking* hours. During those hours, she'd not even been allowed the courtesy of tea and a biscuit from Mrs. Hughes. Kara was bored, hungry, and fucking pissed.

Without waiting for a response—which she wouldn't deign to give the bastard anyway—Cade barged in through the door. Not giving him a moment's notice, Kara remained in her perfectly posed position in the bed, pretending to be greatly enthralled with a novel she'd actually already read. The man would have to forcefully pry the book from her fucking fingers if he wanted her attention because she certainly had no intention of willingly looking upon his hateful face.

"Kara," Cade said slowly, his tone holding a blatant warning that she better watch her attitude.

Well, fuck him.

Kara continued reading. Or rather, staring at the jumble of words on the page. Because in spite of her best efforts, every traitorous atom in her body seemed fixated on Cade's presence whenever he entered the room.

"*Kara*," Cade chastised, his voice firmer this time. "Put the book down and look at me."

In spite of her resolve, Kara found her cowardly limbs lowering the book slightly in response to the command in Cade's tone. She peeked up at him from the top of the pages, raising a single brow as though challenging his goddamn nerve in demanding anything from her, before returning her attention back to the pages.

With an angry grunt of irritation at her pettiness, Cade quickly stormed toward Kara, snatched the book from her hands, and tossed it across the room. Kara's gasp of disbelief sounded at the same time the book clattered loudly to the hard floor.

"What the hell is your problem?" Kara raged at his audacity.

Clearly unbothered by her outrage, Cade painfully grasped Kara's jaw and forced her eyes to meet his. "When I tell you to look at me, you *fucking* look at me. Is that understood?" Cade gripped her jaw tighter as Kara remained silent. Testing him for what felt like the hundredth time that day. And at that moment, he *really* wasn't in the mood to be dealing with her shit. "Answer me," Cade ordered through gritted teeth.

"Fuck. You."

Before Kara had a moment to think or react, Cade grabbed her arm, pulled her over his lap, and delivered a loud, *hard* slap to her backside. Kara shrieked in protest as she frantically squirmed to get out of his hold. Cade expertly threw his leg over hers, caging her between his strong thighs, and wrapped his hand tightly around her wrists, stretching her arms out on the bed in front of her. With her properly subdued beneath him, Cade raised his hand and spanked her again. Harder. Kara felt tears fill her eyes at the shock and pain and

Hideaway

humiliation of being splayed over Cade's knee and punished. She trembled against him, her tears washing away any rebellion she might have had.

Kara flinched when she felt Cade's hand on her again, but that time it was gentle. Silently, he rubbed the sting from her bottom, allowing her a moment to come undone and piece herself back together. Slowly, Cade's hand drifted to her back as he tenderly coaxed the tension from her muscles like he had the night before. Kara shivered as she felt his hand slip under her shirt and his fingertips lightly trace circles across her bare skin. How could he be equal measures of harshness and gentleness? How could he punish her like a brute and then treat her with the tenderness of a lover the next moment? And why did his intoxicating melding of darkness and light draw her in like a moth to a deadly flame?

"Must you always fight me?" Cade asked softly as he continued to stroke her back.

Kara remained silent. Not out of obstinance, but because she really didn't know why she always felt the need to push back against Cade, even with the simplest things.

"I'm sorry I didn't come get you earlier," Cade continued, his apology surprising her almost as much as he surprised himself. He *had* meant to allow her a reprieve from her room after a few hours, but then Ortega had shown him something that completely obliterated any thoughts he had other than retribution. Perhaps she would approve of his afternoon activities, but he didn't really give a fuck if she didn't. "I was detained by a matter of urgency." Cade lifted Kara up until she was sitting in his lap and brushed away the stain of tears from her cheeks. "Will you forgive me?" Cade asked with sincerity, his eyes unusually kind as he gazed down at Kara.

Kara frowned, her brow creased in confusion. "So you're apologizing for grounding me, but *not* for hitting me?"

"I'm not apologizing for either," Cade replied with a scoff as his eyes took on their typical, arrogant glint. "You *deserved* to be sent to your room, and you *deserved* a spanking. I'm merely apologizing that the amount of time spent in confinement was more than you'd earned. That was a mistake on my part, and I take full responsibility."

Kara didn't really know why he felt he had the right to punish her in any respect, but she decided to take the proffered olive branch, meager as it was. "So, does this mean I'm free to go? I'm fucking starving."

"Well now, we can't have you wasting away," Cade answered as a smile softened his features. "Go get dressed for dinner," he commanded with a light swat on her arse.

"*Yes, sir*," Kara grumbled sarcastically as she rolled her eyes, trudging toward the closet to obey his fucking orders. Why did he have to be so damn bossy? Clearly, the man was accustomed to being around robots, not *actual* human beings.

Cade leisurely lay out on Kara bed as she changed, uncharacteristically deciding to let her cheeky attitude slide. For the moment, anyway. Casually, he rested with his arms above his head as he caught brief glimpses of Kara changing in the large closet. She hadn't closed the door, so he, in turn, didn't make any effort to avert his gaze from her naked body. The flashes of creamy, bare skin and the exposed curve of her ass, still pink from his hand, were enough

Hideaway

to get his cock rock hard. It took a measure of self-restraint to keep from reaching down and stroking his firm length as he watched her. It had been too long since he'd plunged his cock into a warm, wet pussy. Briefly, he allowed himself to imagine using Kara's. How she would feel swallowing his huge cock with her tight cunt. How she would scream in pleasure and agony when he split her open and filled her to the brim. How she would strangle his fucking cock while she orgasmed with him deep inside her. How his cum would cover her cunt and spill down her thighs, marking her as his. *Only his.*

"Are you ready?" Kara asked as she entered the bedroom, dressed in a deep emerald dress that accentuated her breasts and small waist and flowed loosely over her hips down to her ankles.

At the sound of her voice, Cade startled from his fantasies, the interruption leaving him desperate, ravenous, and with a dreadful case of blue balls. Swallowing back the heavy thickness of desire that lingered in his throat, Cade appraised Kara's appearance. Though he'd purchased that particular dress, he'd never seen it on. *She*, he had discovered soon after, had rather a distaste for green in comparison to her complexion, so the gown had hung forgotten in the closet and never been worn. On Kara, the hue was stunning, contrasting the darkness of her eyes beautifully and making the pale exposure of her skin seem almost luminescent against the silky, jewel-toned material. "You look lovely," Cade remarked finally, his voice raw and almost tender.

He masked the unintentional softness by grasping Kara's arm firmly, possessively. His gaze lingered on her breasts, which he was realizing were too exposed. In fact, everything was too exposed, and he wanted to take every inch of bare flesh and cover it. If anyone was going to have the privilege of seeing Kara's body, it was going to be him. And only him. "If anyone at that table looks at you a *second* longer than necessary, I'll take their fucking eyes," Cade threatened as he dragged her toward the door.

Their entrance to the dining hall brought with it the delicious scent of thyme and rosemary blended with the sweetness of honey and the savory warmth of roasted pork. If there was one thing Kara could appreciate about her captivity, it was Mrs. Hughes's cooking. The woman was a damn culinary angel. The rumble of her stomach and the watering of her mouth at the sight of food momentarily distracted Kara from the most startling detail in the room. Jace sat at the end of the table, an expression of pure animosity marring his already brutalized face. Large black and purple bruises were splattered haphazardly across his jaw, cheekbones, and around his swollen eyes. A bandage was taped across what appeared to be a cut in his left eyebrow and his nose, which seemed twisted at an abnormal angle. His lip was split gruesomely, the blood still looking bright red and fresh. Clearly, someone had beaten the absolute shit out of him.

Kara looked at Cade in shock, assuming he had been the obvious assailant, and checked him for injuries. His face was in perfect order; she would have realized earlier if he'd borne any signs of an attack. Upon closer inspection though, Kara noticed that Cade's knuckles were red and bruised, the skin cracking in a few spots. Apparently, from coming into contact with Jace's face one too many times. "What the hell happened?" Kara asked after she'd finally recovered from the surprise of Cade's brutal attack on his business partner.

Cade took in the sight of Jace's destroyed face with overwhelming satisfaction as he pulled out a chair for Kara and then seated himself beside her at the head of the table. When he'd asked Ortega for the library security footage of the night before, he hadn't expected to be so overcome with rage as he watched the events with Jace and Kara unfold. Even at that moment, the barely diminished fury boiled in his blood calling for more retribution.

"Jace harmed you," Cade explained evenly as he set about filling his plate with food. "In doing so, he broke my rules." Picking up his fork and knife, Cade pointed the tip of the blade in Jace's direction. "*That* is what happens when my rules are disobeyed."

"Jesus, Cade, you didn't need to half kill him," Kara muttered softly, still stunned by Cade's violence. And she didn't miss the insinuation in Cade's words. He hadn't wrecked Jace for her in some misplaced need to defend her honor. No, he'd beaten Jace because he'd challenged Cade's rules, and, therefore, his control. She wondered if he would inflict the same violence on her if she dared to disobey him.

"Insubordination will not be tolerated," Cade answered sharply as he cut into his meat, the knife loudly scraping against the plate. And it was true, Cade didn't allow for disobedience among his men. But that wasn't why he'd gone into a blind rage and pummeled Jace's face into oblivion. No, that was because Jace had dared to touch Kara. Not only did Jace try to take what was his, against her fucking will, he had hurt Kara. Every time Cade closed his eyes he saw that bastard raise his hand and slap his girl across the face. It made him want to beat Jace all over again.

"Men and their violent delights," Kara huffed with an eye roll as she began devouring her food. After nearly an entire day spent in her bedroom, she really was starving.

"Yes, and speaking of, Jace has something he would like to tell you. Don't you, Jace?" Cade asked, fixing the man at the end of the table with a withering glare.

"I'm sorry," Jace replied sullenly, glaring right back at Cade.

"Why are you looking at me? *I'm* not the one you hit and nearly raped," Cade chastised angrily. Everyone in the room, especially Kara jolted at his blunt words. Until that moment, only Ortega and the parties involved knew the full extent of the previous night's incident. Declan and Brax looked between Jace and Kara with surprise and horror written plainly on their features.

"Now, apologize properly, Jace," Cade commanded coldly.

Jace looked at Kara with a small attempt at contrition. "I'm sorry, Kara."

Not quite knowing how to respond the apology—because there was no way in hell she could forgive him for what he'd done—Kara merely nodded curtly before turning her attention to Cade who was gazing back at her with an expression that almost seemed protective, in a fierce, aggressive sort of way. She didn't know what to think of the conundrum of a man whose chaotic mood changes were constantly ripping her in opposite directions. First he saved her from Jace, then he treated her like a whore, then he took her out alone on an almost romantic riding excursion, and then he fucking whipped her and sent her to her room. Cade beat the shit out of Jace—making it seem like it was only a matter of control regarding his rules—but then he forced Jace to apologize *to her* as though he cared about her feelings. And at the moment, Cade was staring at her with such passion and fire in his mesmerizing hazel eyes, it felt as though he *cared* about her.

The constant tumult of their interactions was driving Kara mad. It made her feel like doing something drastic to sway the confusing relationship between them one way or the other. She could think of one sure way to test Cade's true feelings for her, but the consequences could be disastrous. Steeling her resolve, Kara decided it was the only way.

She was going to fuck Caden Ashford.

Shyly, her skills at seduction sorely underdeveloped, Kara slipped her hand from the arm of her chair and lightly placed it across Cade's thigh. The constantly composed, stoic man with perfect social graces actually jolted in his seat at her unexpected touch. Kara had to stifle a laugh at the knowledge that she could affect him so visibly as he sharply turned toward her, his eyes swarming with disapproval mixed with a hint of intrigue. Kara offered him a sly smile in response, running her thumb gently along the center of his thigh.

She'd never been the one to initiate contact. Any of their brief moments of passion had been instigated by Cade's sudden lack of control before he carefully pieced his composure together and left her aching and wanting. Now that she was the one making the move, Cade seemed thrown. It was only a minuscule, fractional crack in his cool facade, but it was there just the same. Kara trailed her fingers further up, greedily seeking the firm bulge between his thighs, but before she could reach his cock, Cade grabbed her hand and tightly intertwined his fingers with hers. He tugged their hands down and rested them safely upon his knee. Kara looked up at him, disappointment and confusion marring her features.

"Are you no longer hungry, Kara?" Cade asked, a mischievous smile pulling at his lips. He liked games, but only when he was the one orchestrating them. As much as he would enjoy Kara's hand on his cock, that wouldn't be happening unless under circumstances *he* controlled. He could admire Kara's bravery, but he didn't want her seduction, he wanted her submission. He wanted to control her body, to demand his own pleasure and forcefully tear orgasms from her body with his mouth and fingers and cock while she screamed and writhed in ecstasy. If he chose to take her, it would be *his* way.

"I'm actually feeling a little tired," Kara answered, feeling anything but tired. She felt as though she might burst from excitement and need. "Maybe we could go up to bed?"

"But we haven't had dessert," Cade responded quietly, his voice rough and deep as his eyes suggestively trailed the exposed skin of Kara's breasts. He raised a single brow as though challenging her to offer herself instead of dessert. It wouldn't get her what she wanted, but she would look adorable trying.

"O-okay," Kara replied breathlessly, recognizing the salacious glint in his eyes, but not feeling courageous enough to act on it with so many witnesses. She tried to retrieve her hand from Cade's grasp, but he kept her trapped, squeezing her fingers together in warning any time she tried to squirm away.

Mrs. Hughes brought out apple crumble with custard for dessert, and Kara tried to force herself to enjoy it as Cade still held her hand under the table and she contemplated what might possibly happen after dessert. She devoured every crumb before placing her fork on the empty plate and sneaking a glance at Cade. His eyes were fixed on her as though they had never left, warmth and desire and a touch of something dangerous filling the green-gold depths.

"More tea, Kara?" Cade asked, gesturing to the empty tea cup beside her small plate.

"No?" Kara answered uncertainly. Was he stalling, or merely attempting to torture her?

"Mrs. Hughes!" Cade called loudly toward the kitchens.

Mrs. Hughes rushed into the dining room, clearly at her master's beck and call. "Aye, Mr. Ashford?"

"More tea, please," Cade ordered, enjoying watching Kara's face fall in disappointment.

Yes, the bastard was definitely torturing her.

Kara burned her mouth sipping down the hot tea as quickly as possible while Cade took leisurely sips and conversed with Brax and Ortega. He still held her fucking hand under the table, but didn't acknowledge her beyond a slight squeeze of her fingers now and then. Kara felt herself slowly go insane with impatience. Right when she was about ready to start stripping off her clothes—witnesses be damned—in an effort to capture Cade's attention, he rose from his chair, the others following suit.

"Come," Cade addressed Kara softly, never taking his hand from hers. "I'll take you to your room."

They were both silent after bidding everyone goodnight and walking up the stairs toward their rooms. Trying to calm her nerves, Kara focused on the gentle way Cade held her hand in his as he pulled her toward her room. She took a deep breath as he opened the door, not exactly sure how to gather the words to ask for what she wanted. Because what she wanted was *clearly* deranged given the circumstances. Cade dropped her hand and waited expectantly as she hovered in the doorway without going in.

"Stay with me tonight," Kara told him quietly, unsure of whether it was panic or anticipation stealing the breath from her lungs and setting her heart pounding so loudly she could hear her pulse in her ears.

"I sleep in my own bed, Kara," Cade scolded, his tone prickling with subtle irritation. He didn't like being the subject of someone's demands. And he didn't like the quiver of vulnerability in her voice; it made him feel irrationally protective of her.

"Then can I come with you?" Kara asked, her small voice hopeful. "Please?"

"I sleep alone," Cade answered firmly, leaving little room for negotiation.

"You didn't sleep alone last night," Kara reminded softly, peeking up at him from behind long, dark lashes.

"That was different. Those were extenuating circumstances, and I didn't want you to be alone." He had other reasons for bringing her to his bed the previous night, but he didn't want her to be privy to *those* reasons any more than he wanted to acknowledge them in the first place. The girl made him weak. So much so, that he had broken his own cardinal rule of sleeping alone. There was no way in hell he would allow her to instigate a second offense.

"Well, I don't want to be alone tonight," Kara pleaded, glancing around the emptiness of her bedroom as though the sheer expanse of loneliness would swallow her up. "Please, Cade?" She timidly reached out and placed her small hand on his arm, wrapping her narrow fingers around the wide breadth of his bicep. Cade sucked in a sharp breath at her touch.

"What will you give me?" Cade asked, his tone cold as he glanced at her hand on him before turning calculating eyes toward her.

"Give you?" Kara asked, her lips trembling as she considered the possible insinuation of his words. He expected her to bargain for a place in his bed?

"Yes, Kara, what do you have to offer me?" Cade said slowly, patronizingly, as though conversing with a child. "I am a man of business, after all. Nothing comes for free." A salacious grin spread across his full lips. "Not even you."

"W-what do you want?" Kara responded anxiously, an equal mix of nervousness and arousal twisting in her belly at the thought of Cade's demands.

"Hmm," Cade hummed, pausing as though carefully thinking it over. "I'm not quite sure at the moment. Let's just say you'll owe me a favor at some point in the future." Cade's eyes glittered with sinister satisfaction at the thought of her at his mercy, forced to give in to his desires, however dark they may be.

"A free pass for a man like you sounds dangerous," Kara answered hesitantly, biting her bottom lip in indecision.

"Oh, it's most assuredly dangerous," Cade replied with no intent to quell her fears. He was a dangerous man. And she should know exactly who she was getting into bed with. "Question is, is it worth it?" Cade offered her his hand, like Hades beckoning her to the depths of the underworld.

With a final *fuck you* to any lingering thoughts of rationality storming about in her mind, Kara took a deep breath and placed her hand in Cade's. His fingers wrapped around Kara's tightly, almost painfully, as his ominous smirk grew impossibly wider. Well, if she was going to hell, she might as well enjoy the ride.

As soon as they entered Cade's room, the atmosphere altered, growing heavy and almost suffocating with tension. Cade withdrew his hand and left Kara standing in the middle of the room as he went to his closet in search of a change of clothes. Anxiously shifting on her feet, Kara stared at the imposing bed in the center of the room, thinking of what it would be like to be taken by Cade and fucked roughly against the dark, silk sheets. She startled from her daydream when something soft and cotton hit her in the face. Cade's shirt, she discovered upon closer inspection, which he had just thrown at her face. Clearly, he wasn't in a tender mood at the moment.

"Put it on," Cade ordered firmly. "I like seeing you in my clothes."

Kara glared at him, her expression of annoyance quickly morphing into appreciation when she realized that he'd already changed and was only wearing a pair of low-riding sweatpants that highlighted the delectable v-cut that trailed downward from his prominent abdominal muscles. With the naked curve of his ass peeking out from the waistband of his pants, she was pretty sure he wasn't wearing underwear. And at that moment, she didn't want to be wearing any fucking underwear either.

Rather than going to the bathroom to change, Kara gathered her courage and kicked off her heels right where she stood. Holding Cade's gaze, she reached behind her back and slowly unzipped her dress, letting it fall to her feet in a puddle of fabric. Though she stood before him in only her bra and panties, Cade's eyes never once left hers to roam over the nakedness of her body. Raising her brows in surprise at his stoic display of composure and control for a heterosexual male with a dick between his legs, Kara took it one step further. She wanted to smash his fucking control to pieces. She unlatched her bra and tossed it on the growing pile of clothes in front of her, her pink nipples immediately stiffening into hard buds in the cool air. Still, Cade didn't falter as he continued to focus on her face, the smallest hint of a smile on his lips the only sign that he knew her tits were out. With a sigh of annoyance, Kara hooked her thumbs into her panties and swiftly slid them down, stepped out of them, and threw them at Cade's bare feet. And in reaction, she got nothing. *Absolutely. Nothing.* He just stared at her with that same infuriating composure he seemed to cling to as though it was the very essence of life.

"I said, put it on, Kara," Cade commanded again, his voice sterner than the first time.

Feeling her self-esteem slowly decimate into nothingness, Kara bent to pick up the shirt. Suddenly eager to cover her nakedness, Kara quickly slipped into Cade's shirt, fastened every button up to the neck, and wrapped her arms around herself to ease her trembling. Maybe the whole *sleep with Cade* plan hadn't been the best idea after all. *He* certainly didn't seem to think so anyway. She gathered the last remnants of her pride and met Cade's gaze expectantly as though awaiting his next command.

"Would you like to use the bathroom first, or shall I?" Cade asked, his tone softening.

"I'll go," Kara answered swiftly, thankful for a chance to escape the embarrassing situation she'd created and have a moment to brush her teeth and calm her nerves in peace. She made a dash for the bathroom and shut and locked the door behind her.

Finally alone, Cade allowed some of the uncertainty he'd been feeling to creep into his face. It was tiring having to constantly erect a mask of composure when his emotions bubbled so close to the surface, desperate to burst through. With Kara in his vicinity, in his fucking bedroom, he had to be even more careful. He knew what she wanted. It was painfully obvious when she stripped herself bare for him, offering him her exquisite nakedness like a sacrifice to a bloodthirsty god. Well, she wasn't wrong there. He thirsted for her, he craved to devour every aspect of her essence. And when he was satiated, there would be nothing left of her.

Cade bent down and picked up the panties the cheeky girl had thrown at his feet. He groaned when he felt and smelled the wetness of her arousal on the material. Cade picked up the rest of Kara's clothes and deposited them in the hamper in his closet for Mrs. Hughes to launder. And he placed Kara's damp knickers in his underwear drawer for safekeeping. Since she had practically given them to him, she wouldn't be getting that particular pair back.

Sitting down on the bed, Cade contemplated what exactly he was going to do about Kara. He knew he couldn't give her what she wanted because she couldn't give him what he needed. She was too pure, too delicate, too fucking innocent to be able to handle the darkness that he needed to occasionally let loose and allow to gorge. His appetites required a willing victim, and he was fairly certain Kara would go running if she knew how he wanted to use her—and

Hideaway

he really couldn't allow her to run from him. So he would give her what he could, let her sleep in his bed, give her the warmth of his embrace if she so desired, but he wouldn't, under any circumstances, allow himself to fuck her. Because fucking her had the potential to break them both.

In a cloud of steam, Kara exited the bathroom—still dressed in his shirt, thankfully—smelling clean and minty, her gorgeous face washed free of makeup, and her eyes noticeably red and puffy, as though she'd spent the majority of her time in the bathroom crying. That was two days in a row that he had been the cause of her tears, and it made him feel like a fucking bastard. In that moment, Cade wanted to do anything to wipe the sadness from her face, but he knew giving her what she thought she wanted would only hurt her worse in the long run. As much as it twisted at his insides, he preferred being a bastard that day to save her future pain.

"Are you finished?" Cade asked as he headed toward the bathroom.

Avoiding his gaze, Kara nodded. She was seriously considering whether she should bolt while Cade was in the bathroom brushing his teeth, but figured her pride had already been irreparably destroyed so she might as well stay. She settled into the same side of the bed that she had slept on the previous night, diving under the covers and hating how much she loved being enveloped by his delicious scent. Quickly to avoid being caught, Kara switched the pillows, snuggling her face into the one Cade had used last night, the scent of cedar and mint lulling her into a sense of calm tranquility.

All too soon, the bathroom door opened and Cade stepped into the room still wearing only his sweatpants. His dark hair still dripped from being washed, sending rivulets of water cascading down the ripples of his abs. Kara bit her lip to stifle an irrepressible moan at the sight of him. He was devastatingly, breathtakingly beautiful—like an avenging angel, all darkness and light, cruelty and tenderness, destruction and salvation. A single look from him could shatter her as much as it could bring her heavenly bliss, and she would happily take ruin or rapture at his hand.

"Where would you like me? On the floor, or in the bed? As it was your bargain, you are free to choose," Cade asked as he tried to decipher the confusing concoction of emotions scattering across her face.

"The bed," Kara answered softly, uneasy with the reminder that she'd made a deal with the devil—and he had yet to collect.

"As you wish," Cade acquiesced before turning off the lights and climbing into bed. He turned away from her, giving his attention to his phone as he went about his nightly ritual of answering emails and concluding work related tasks. He wasn't usually so inattentive when he had company in his bed, but Kara wasn't his typical fuck, and he desperately needed a distraction from the fact that she was lying in his bed with her pink pussy bare and free for the taking. If he allowed himself to think about her wet cunt, he would go fucking insane before he snapped and fucked her until she passed out.

Kara stirred impatiently in bed; sleep was the farthest thing from her mind at that moment as she waited for something—anything—to happen. Cade remained fixated on his stupid fucking phone, something she still hadn't been allowed the privilege of using while at the manor, she reminded herself with chagrin. He showed no interested in her whatsoever, even though she'd practically begged him to fuck her. He'd offered to do it the day before with no reservations, so what had changed?

"Cade?" she called quietly into the darkness, pleading for some glimpse of the passionate, intoxicating man who had lately been edging her feelings dangerously toward something more than mere attraction.

Any semblance of *that* Caden Ashford seemed to have vanished amid a storm of dark, brooding silence. She could think of no cause for the abrupt change in Cade's demeanor. Fearful that she had done something to upset him, Kara anxiously studied the unmoving form lying as far from her as was possible without the risk of crashing to the floor. His back was bare, the dark sheet barely upholding the bounds of modesty as it draped slightly below the twin indentations above his backside. His shoulders appeared to be sculpted more from stone than flesh, broad with smooth curves. His back rippled with muscles Kara hadn't known anatomically existed, making the indentation of his spine more pronounced, like a linear valley amid mountains. There was a soft curve to his hip that continued below the obstruction of the sheet, tempting her gaze further down. The man was so frustratingly beautiful in every aspect that Kara's heart seemed to ache just from looking at him.

"Go to sleep, Kara," Cade commanded shortly, his tone somewhere between anger and deep annoyance.

"I am sleeping," she answered unconvincingly.

"No, you aren't. I think your eyes might have bored holes in me by now."

"Well, I'm sorry if my gaze offends you. Perhaps I should return to my own bed as you obviously find my presence so unbearably repulsive," Kara responded bitterly.

"You're in this bed by *your* demand, not mine. I'm under no obligation to enjoy the experience."

Her feelings properly wounded, Kara fell silent. He was right, of course. The stirrings of attraction and arousal that had begun to blossom within her were unwarranted, undesired, and, worst of all, unreciprocated. Kara's eyes pricked with tears brought on by embarrassment mingled with self-pity; she brushed away the signs of weakness angrily.

With a suddenness that startled her, Cade rolled over to face her, his body so close that the crisp scent of his cologne assaulted her senses like a wave crashing against her. Kara shivered inexplicably, the intensity of his gaze penetrating deep to her core with a power that couldn't be explained. Somehow, she felt as though she would follow anywhere those piercing, green-gold eyes led her.

"I apologize, that was a little more harsh than you deserve," Cade said softly, most of the previous sharpness faded from his voice.

Kara barely recalled the offense, his closeness having banished all thoughts of the past to hazy memories. He seemed troubled as his eyes searched hers, an unfamiliar crease residing between his brows, altering his expression with a severity that would have been alarming if she hadn't already resigned herself to whatever intentions he might have in store. His mouth curved with an amused smile that didn't match his darkly intense eyes, as though a conflict of emotions warred within him. Without thinking, Kara raised her hand to his forehead and stroked upward, willing the pensive furrowing of his brow away.

The unpredictability of her touch obliterated any inhibitions Cade might have possessed, and he reached for her desperately, capturing her face in his hands and forcing her lips up to meet his. Kara let the kiss consume her, feeling as though every fibre of her composition melded with Cade's the moment their bodies collided. His mouth was conquering—warm, demanding lips claiming her as his, tongue penetrating deeply as he explored the undiscovered territory of her mouth, unsheathed teeth meeting with the tender skin of her bottom lip with such force that Kara couldn't suppress a moan. The primal sound drove Cade deeper. With a passion that bordered on violence, he grabbed her hair and twisted tightly, locking her in place beneath him. His other hand moved roughly over her body, vigorously exploring every piece of her as though he were trying to commit her to memory. Kara's breath hitched in anticipation as his hand traveled lower; her lips grew more eager against his, urging him further.

The moment ended too soon. Without explanation, Cade broke off the kiss and pulled away sharply, leaving Kara breathless and aching for more. Disentangling himself from her embrace, Cade rolled onto his back and stared dismally into the darkness, refusing to acknowledge Kara's presence or what had quite nearly occurred between them.

"*Fuck*," Cade breathed as he ran his fingers through his hair, his breathing left heavy and uneven after their encounter.

Kara stared at him in complete bewilderment. What the hell had just happened? Or almost happened? Cade's kiss had caught her off guard, nearly as much as her own fervent response to his touch. She wasn't sure if she'd ever felt something quite so electrifying as his hands on her skin; she needed more, a hollow emptiness lingering in the absence of his body against hers. She watched as Cade's chest rose and fell deeply, she heard the quickened pace of his heart beating in his chest; it was a frantic rhythm that mimicked her own. He had been just as aroused as she was, so why had he stopped? Kara reached her hand across the distance between them, longing to pull Cade back from whatever dark place he had vanished to.

"Unless you want to be thoroughly fucked this instant, do not touch me again," Cade said dangerously, still refusing to look at her.

Kara drew her hand back swiftly, startled by the raw, uncontrolled violence in his voice. Cade's words rang with warning, not that any cautionary disclaimer was warranted in that regard. She knew exactly who and what she was dealing with; she had already witnessed and experienced all the terrible, threatening aspects of being in Cade's vicinity. Since that fateful day he came barging into the library, she had been taken from her home, drugged, and dragged out to the middle of nowhere entirely against her will. She spent every day living in a prison of his design because his former client had every intention of doing far worse things to her if he got the chance. With certainty, being thoroughly fucked by Caden Ashford would be the most agreeable event to occur since he had crashed so disruptively into her life.

What Kara didn't know was that Cade regretted and despised every single fucked up detail that formulated their short acquaintance. Every despicable thing he had allowed to happen that led to her lying in his bed at that very moment. The lack of control that led to the unforgivable act of kissing her and making her feel the same burning need that he had been struggling against for longer than he cared to admit. The things he would do to her if he had her consent. The things he thought about doing even if he didn't. If the girl had any sense, she would run as far away from him as possible. If he had any decency, he would set her free and allow her to vanish into a peaceful existence somewhere boring and insignificant. Somehow, he guessed neither of them had the capacity for either.

Having expended her patience for laying in frosty silence while Cade ignored her to brood over whatever dismal thoughts swirled around in his mind, Kara gathered her courage and decided to tempt fate. Self-preservation be damned, she reached across the wide expanse between them and brushed the exposed angle of his hip with her fingertips, following the v-shaped crease etched into his torso downward until she reached the waistband of his pants. Her fingers lingered there, suggestively tracing a line along his lower abdomen, bracing herself for his reaction.

With a sound that almost resembled a growl, Cade captured Kara's wrist tightly, pushed her on her back, and positioned himself on top of her with his knees locking her hips in place. Roughly grabbing her other wrist, he forced both of her arms above her head, stretching her out as far as she could go. In spite of herself, Kara struggled against him, innately spurred to panic by the inability to move, pinned beneath the weight of Cade's body. As she discovered her own defenselessness, Kara felt the first prickles of fear.

"Is this what you want, Kara?" Cade asked in a tone that was somehow both seductive and sinister, lowering his head close to hers as though he meant to kiss her.

"Yes," Kara answered softly, biting her lip to keep it from trembling with the nervousness she felt radiating throughout her entire body.

"Are you sure? I am, in no respect, a gentleman in the bedroom."

"You're not exactly a gentleman outside the bedroom either."

"My love, you wound me," he answered with feigned injury.

"You're stalling," Kara accused pointedly. "What's the matter, Ashford? Are you scared?"

"No, love," he answered, sounding resigned. "But you should be." Without giving her another moment to reconsider her decision, Cade reached for the shirt she wore and ripped it down the middle sending buttons scattering around the bed.

"Cade!" Kara exclaimed in exasperation as she watched him demolish the only clothing she wore into a heap of threads.

"Don't speak," Cade commanded firmly, the sternness of his eyes proving that he was incredibly serious about his unusual demand. He needed some display of submission from her, and surrendering her voice was the very least she could do. Ever the strong-willed, outspoken girl, Kara looked at him as though she was contemplating all the different ways she could torture and dismember him, but she respected his order. Good. She was learning that obedience was the only way she would earn what she wanted from him.

Pleased with her silence, Cade released her gaze and allowed himself to admire the view he had stubbornly ignored during her earlier strip tease. The delayed gratification and the complete control he possessed in the current situation made the delectable sight all the sweeter. His lust-filled eyes ravaged the most intimate parts of her body, devouring the sight of her nakedness with a hunger he wasn't sure could ever be appeased. Kara was undeniably lovely with perfect, milky skin that seemed radiant as though bathed in moonlight. Her breasts were surprisingly large and almost too full for her petite frame, her rosy pink nipples hard and practically begging to be sucked and bitten. Her waist was narrow, her hip bones jutting out a little too sharply and lacking in softness. Cade made a mental note to make sure Mrs. Hughes got her to eat more. Her thighs were the thickest part of her body, soft and curvy and demanding that he sink his teeth into the pale flesh and run his tongue along the smooth skin. Between her thighs was a small, meticulously groomed patch of blond curls that covered a pussy so wet and needy that he could see her arousal glistening on the top of her thighs. Clearly, his girl was fucking desperate to have his cock inside of her, and the knowledge of her desire sent all the blood in his body rushing straight to his aching dick.

"Cade, please," Kara pleaded in impatience, thrusting her hips upward with a desperate need to be touched.

As soon as she said the words, Kara swiftly felt the tight grip of Cade's hand against her mouth, stifling any of the expletives she might have attempted to use. Cade's face was stern, almost angry as he glared at her darkly and squeezed his hand harder the more that she struggled beneath him. Frantically, Kara writhed helplessly beneath the weight of his body and hand, uncomfortable with her current position even more now that she couldn't move or speak.

"Not another word, Kara," Cade commanded forcefully with a punishing press of his fingers against her cheeks. "If you disobey me again, I'll have to think of a way to punish you." His eyes lit with malice as they traveled across her exposed body, conjuring creative retributions. "I already have a few ideas, so you'd better not tempt me."

Tyrannical asshole.

Frustrated and exhausted, Kara let out a sigh of exasperation and stopped fighting. With an arrogant smile of victory, Cade ran his thumb from one hip to the other, tracing an invisible line across her trembling body just above her aching pussy. Teeming with anticipation and a small measure of nervousness, Kara lifted her hips to meet his touch, yearning to feel his fingers lower. She was fairly sure he was teasing her, stroking his fingers close enough to her pelvic region to be suggestive, but not accurately enough to provide satisfaction.

And he was, of course.

Kara groaned impatiently against the hand Cade still held over her mouth, and he laughed with gratified amusement. "Very keen, aren't you, love?" he taunted, continuing to caress the length of her hip.

Refusing to be bated into giving the hateful man a chance to inflict whatever unusual punishments he had devised, Kara ignored the question in restless silence. Cade assessed her response with surprised approval, deciding that obedience deserved to be rewarded.

"Is this what you want?" Cade asked seductively, sliding his fingers down from her mouth, over her breasts, across her abdomen, below her hips, and, finally, between the folds of her dripping, wet cunt.

Kara moaned loudly as Cade's fingers brushed against her clitoris, grateful that his hand had found a more useful occupation than keeping her mouth in check. Years of experience had taught Kara that men should be certified with a specific level of experience before being allowed to play with a woman's pussy. Prodding, unskilled fingers did more harm than good, so the first stroke of the clit was always a test of expertise. After a few blissful moments, Kara could emphatically say she knew one thing to be true regarding Caden Ashford: the man knew his way around a clit even better than she did.

Cade reveled in the moans of pleasure that he dragged from her; they were perhaps the loveliest sounds he had ever heard, especially as he had waited so long to enjoy them. She was incredibly responsive to his touch, moving her hips in rhythm with the circular motion of his fingers, her body rising slightly as he edged her closer to release. When she was seconds away from climaxing, Cade's hand stilled. He preferred to let her build slowly; delaying gave her body a chance to savor the sensation, to allow the orgasm to penetrate every sense and every nerve. An exasperated sigh of disappointment from Kara suggested that she did not agree with his strategy.

Kara trembled from the loss of the orgasm, her body singing with electric, uncontrollable need. Cade didn't delay for long; she soon felt his fingers slip inside her, sliding easily with the wetness of her arousal. Kara gasped at the sensation of being filled and stretched from within as Cade penetrated her with two fingers before adding a third. He moved his other hand to his mouth, wetting his fingers before continuing to caress her clitoris with concentrated, circular strokes. The dual stimulation left Kara feeling as though she was being set aflame from the inside with a delicious warmth that seemed to radiate through her whole body. The brink of her climax arrived quickly; she lifted her hips off the bed as she rose to meet it before plummeting with a cry of desperation as Cade once again deprived her of his fingers *and* her orgasm.

He was going to fucking kill her with need if he didn't stop his torture soon.

She whimpered when Cade once again touched her aching, oversensitized skin, biting her lip to keep from begging for the orgasm he kept denying. If she broke his rule of silence, the cruel bastard probably wouldn't let her come the entire night. In that moment, she couldn't be certain if that wasn't his plan all along. Obviously, he was a sadist who enjoyed giving her agony more than pleasure.

Maybe she could conceal her pleasure and come without him knowing?

The loud scream that escaped her lips the moment Cade's lips wrapped around her throbbing nipple and sucked it against his teeth proved that she wouldn't be very successful at masking her pleasure when he controlled her body as though he owned it. The pressure in her core was building at an alarming rate as Cade's tongue rolled over her tight nipple, his fingers continuing to pound wetly inside her pussy as his thumb assaulted her clit with expert precision. She was nearly there, and she wanted to orgasm so much that it physically hurt.

"Are you close, Kara?" Cade asked, his voice rough and raw as he continued to stimulate her in all the right places.

Kara shook her head, refusing to let him know just how close she was. Her eyes closed as she begged to go over the edge of release without him knowing, without him stopping her before she surrendered to the overwhelming pleasure. A sharp slap to her clit snapped her from her concentration as her eyes flew open to gap at Cade. The bastard had just spanked her fucking pussy.

"Don't lie to me, Kara. *Are you close?*" Cade demanded sternly.

"Yes," Kara answered, the single word coming out as a sob. If he denied her again, she might pass out from exhaustion.

"Do you want to come?"

"Yes!" Kara nearly screamed, the desperation and need consuming her like fire until they were the only things her body could feel.

"Then be a good girl and come for me," Cade ordered, his voice warm and soothing and sexy as fuck. He lowered his mouth to Kara's tit and bit down hard on her nipple as he thrust three fingers deep inside her cunt while his thumb rubbed tight circles around her clit. He felt her pussy clamp down on his hand, strangling his fingers as she obeyed his command.

Kara cried out as she came harder than she ever had in her entire life as wave after wave of pure ecstasy conquered every nerve in her body. Cade continued to thrust and bite and rub as she allowed the orgasm to consume every thought, word, breath, and heartbeat. He prolonged his assault until every ounce of pleasure had been wrung from her body, continuing until her skin was so sensitive that his touch turned painful.

"Cade," Kara begged breathlessly, her face wet with tears she didn't know she'd cried. This time, she longed for a reprieve from the stimulation.

"Yes," Cade answered deeply, loving the sight of her trembling and soaked beneath his fingers, tears of ecstasy painted beautifully across her flushed-red cheeks.

"Please," she begged, too far gone to form a complete thought. She just needed a moment to breath without his hands on her, driving her toward insanity once again.

Understanding her unspoken need, Cade removed his fingers from inside of her and brought them to her mouth, trailing the wet fingertips along her lips. "You look beautiful when you come undone," he whispered, his eyes full of adoration and desire as he admired the orgasmic flush spread across her skin, leaving her with a pink tinged glow that suited the creamy paleness of her complexion perfectly. "I believe it is my turn, love," Cade announced huskily, his voice practically incinerating with need.

"I don't suppose we could sleep first?" Kara asked sheepishly, already exhausted and overstimulated and nowhere near prepared to take his cock in her still throbbing pussy.

"Not a fucking chance," he answered darkly, desire burning in his eyes. Cade slid his pants down until they rested on his lower hips, not bothering to entirely undress before fucking her. It was a power play, a subtle way of asserting his dominance and making her feel a little disadvantaged as she lay fully naked beneath him. When he looked back at Kara, he realized that her attention was not on him, but on the massive length and width of his cock. Typically, Cade had the courtesy to provide a disclaimer on his size before intimacy, but everything about the night seemed to be deviating from protocol.

Kara eyed his cock warily; in all of her not so vast experience, she had never had anything of *that* size inside her. She was rather certain he would break her. Actually, she was *positive* he would break her.

"Don't worry, you're built to stretch," Cade offered in reassurance as he lowered himself on top of her, supporting his weight by gripping the headboard above her.

Somehow, the notion did nothing to placate her nervousness as she felt the tip of his cock at the entrance between her legs. "Wait, condom!" Kara cried in alarm.

"Are you on birth control?" Cade asked impatiently, damning himself for forgetting yet another part of his usual routine. A fucking important part.

"Y-yes."

"Have you slept with anyone recently?"

"No…"

"Neither have I," Cade said as he took her bottom lip into his mouth and sucked it hard against his teeth. "No condom. I want to feel you bare against my cock." His mouth crashed against hers, bruising her lips with the brutality of a kiss that was demanding, devouring, all-consuming. He stole her breath, refusing to allow her the chance to replenish her lungs as she suffocated beneath the weight of his passion. Without breaking contact with her lips, Cade slipped his hand down her body till he found the wet heat between her thighs. He plunged three fingers into her dripping cunt, scissoring and stretching them inside of her to prepare her for his size. His thumb drew circles over her clit, dragging her toward the edge she'd crashed over mere minutes before. Unable to wait any longer, Cade broke their kiss, allowing Kara to catch her breath in heaving gasps. "Are you ready for me?" Cade asked deeply, his voice husky and coarse.

"Y-yes," Kara answered breathlessly, closing her eyes as she braced herself for the impact.

With no attempt at gentleness, Cade thrust inside her forcefully, penetrating deep to her core on the very first stroke. She winced as he tore through her, her soft cry of pain mixing with his groan of ecstasy as her tightness constricted around him.

"*Fuck*, you feel good," he whispered against her ear, sending shivers down her spine.

Unable to control his fervid need, Cade rammed into her at a punishing pace, his thrusts at the very brink of violence. Kara might have been frightened of his intensity if it didn't satiate the fierce desires she felt growing within her every time he entered her body. Desperate to penetrate deeper, Cade grabbed her arm and twisted her over onto her stomach. Taking ahold of her hips, he pulled her up to her hands and knees and began fucking her from behind. This time, they moaned in unison as Cade reached unfamiliar territory deep within her. Cade's hand dug into her hip with bruising strength as he slammed her ass against his thighs to meet his thrusts. His other hand traveled up her back, searching for her hair as it swung against her shoulders rhythmically. Cade grabbed ahold of the pale blonde waves and pulled sharply, her soft cry sending a surge straight to his cock.

Using his knees to force her legs further apart, Cade's hand slid down from her waist, dipping into the wetness between her legs and swirling it around her clitoris. He continued to fuck her hard as his middle finger worked steady circles around her clit, pushing her toward the peak of pleasure again. Cade's thrusts grew faster and harsher as Kara's breathing became heavier. Without warning, her senses exploded with a crashing climax that left her whole body shaking from the intensity. Not far behind, Cade plunged inside her with a ferocity that obliterated any of her ability to balance. Undaunted, he merely picked her up by the hips and pulled her onto his cock, her own ability to participate irrelevant. Cade exhaled loudly as he found his release, his fingers digging deeply into her skin as he spurted his hot cum inside of her, marking her and possessing her. He held Kara's body against him—both of them breathless, trembling, and sated—and stayed inside her until finally his cock wasn't as hard as a steel rod. Gently, he pulled out, feeling her body stiffen at the emptiness, and watched with primal pleasure as his cum dripped out of her pussy and trailed down her thighs. And fuck if that wasn't the best sight he had ever seen.

Feeling his cock thicken already at the sight of his cum painting Kara's skin, Cade released a groan of annoyance before flipping Kara on her back and crashing down on the bed beside her. As much as he already ached to be inside of her tight cunt again, he knew Kara was too tired for another round. So, out of pure chivalry, Cade denied himself another glance at her glistening, pink pussy.

"*Fuck me,*" Cade said in content astonishment as he absentmindedly ran his fingers through his sex-ruffled hair. His prim little librarian was a shockingly good fuck. One of the best he'd had, and the list was *very* extensive.

"I believe that is exactly what I just did, Lord Ashford," Kara answered with a very self-satisfied smirk on her face.

"Very funny, Kara," Cade replied with an uncharacteristic eye roll. He turned toward Kara and subtly searched her body for marks or signs of injury. Although he had tried to go easy on her, Cade knew he was naturally rough during sex. Because he always fucked women with rough sexual preferences, it was never a problem. Everything was always discussed beforehand, agreed upon, and signed on for the sake of keeping his lawyer happy. But Kara was different. In fact, everything about his relationship with Kara went against his typical practices. He felt her chipping away at his control one sliver at a time, and the unfamiliar uncertainty he experienced around her was driving him toward insanity.

"Are you okay?" Cade asked with a furrowed brow, not quite sure how to proceed with Kara post-fuck. "I didn't hurt you, did I?"

Kara stretched out happily from her fingers to her toes. "I'm okay. Better than okay actually. I think a thorough fucking is just what I needed."

CHAPTER EIGHT

THE blissful scent of coffee wafting through the air roused Kara from the deepest, most peaceful slumber she'd ever had. Honestly, the past few nights spent in Cade's bed offered the best sleep she'd had in a while, in or out of captivity. And there was something about *that* word that had Kara cringing in distaste. Did she still consider herself to be a prisoner? Technically, she couldn't leave, even if she wanted to; she knew having sex with Cade wouldn't have altered her circumstances *that* drastically. But she no longer wanted to view him as a villain, nor herself as a victim. She was—hopelessly, stupidly, naively—falling for him, and it hurt her sense of pride to be reminded that she was merely a captive developing misplaced feelings of affection for her captor.

Stockholm Syndrome is a fucking bitch.

Unknowingly interrupting an inner turmoil of epic proportions, Cade walked around to Kara's side of the bed, setting a steaming cup of coffee on the bedside table. "Good morning," he greeted pleasantly, his voice soft and warm as he sat down beside Kara on the bed.

"Is it?" Kara asked nervously, not quite sure how to act around the all too attractive specimen of a man after he spent most of the night —and a majority of the last seventy-two hours *inside* of her. Would things eventually go back to the way they were? Was she a temporary bit of fun, a moment of weakness, or did the sex mean something to him? She knew it meant something to her, but she didn't know how to navigate the complexities of falling for her *fucking kidnapper.*

"From where I'm sitting, it's pretty damn brilliant," Cade answered with a smile, reaching over to brush a soft wave of hair from Kara's cheek.

Hearing his words, Kara relaxed slightly. At least he didn't regret what they did. That was a start. "So, what now?"

"*Now,* you drink your coffee like a good girl, go put on something that *isn't* mine," he enjoyed her slight blush as she looked down at his dress shirt wrapped around her naked body, "and then you join me for breakfast. It will be just the two of us as the others are preparing for an assignment we have later today."

"Wait, you're leaving?" Kara questioned, unable to conceal the disappointment in her words.

"I'm afraid I do have to work on occasion," Cade answered teasingly. He noticed her expression fall, doubt and hurt etched into her features. He gripped Kara's jaw and forced her to look up at him.

"Hey, my leaving has nothing to do with you," Cade reassured her. "These last few nights have been perfect. *You* have been perfect. And I have every intention of making it back home as quickly as possibly so that I can make you come so many fucking times you're begging me to stop. And then, I'll fuck you into oblivion."

Kara felt her breath hitch and her bare pussy dampen at the sheer, explicit deliciousness of Cade's words. "Do you promise?" Kara asked, her voice breathless and needy as she considered all the ways she could get him to skip the leaving part and fulfill all his threats right that moment.

"I promise," Cade pledged seriously. If there was one thing he didn't fuck around with, it was sex. "Does my girl need a sign of good faith?" he asked, reading the desperation in her taut body and clenched thighs. "One more orgasm to hold you until I return and use you so hard you can't walk or sit or move without thinking about me being inside that tight cunt?"

Kara didn't even have the decency to be shocked by his words. All she could feel was an exquisitely painful, breathtaking need to be pleasured, filled, and used by the beautiful man beside her. "Yes, please."

"Spread your legs, love. Let me see how soaked that pussy is for me," Cade commanded, crawling over her until he sat in between her bare thighs and sliding his hands up her hips.

With an electrifying shock of arousal and a whimper of anticipation, Kara obeyed, spreading herself for him as wide as she could. Licking his lips, Cade dove between her open legs and devoured her—kissing, licking, and biting as though it was the first and last time he would ever taste anything so delectably satisfying.

His hot tongue lapped at her entrance, savoring the earthy tanginess of her arousal, before he thrust his tongue inside her, his cock hardening almost painfully when he heard Kara's sweet whimpers of need as he impaled her with his mouth. Kara's fingers twisted in Cade's hair, holding him captive between her damp thighs as her moans grew loader and more frantic. Feeling her body begin to tighten beneath him, Cade withdrew his tongue and slapped her pussy, the sound of his palm meeting with her dripping cunt loud and unmistakably wet.

"This pussy is mine, isn't it?" Cade asked ferociously, his voice unrecognizably animalistic as he replaced his tongue with three of his fingers, shocking her with the sensation of being completely filled as he viciously pumped them in and out of her. "Isn't it, love?" he repeated, emphasizing his words with three sharp thrusts of his fingers, splaying them as wide as they could go inside of her. It might have hurt if she wasn't so completely consumed with arousal and need.

"Yes!" Kara exclaimed, completely incognizant of his words. She just wanted him to shut the fuck up and use his mouth for better purposes.

Satisfied with her response, Cade gave her what she wanted. He lowered his mouth to her clit and sucked hard, scraping the sharpness of his teeth over the hard nub. With his teeth wrapped mercilessly around her clit, Kara came as screams of ecstasy poured from her lips. Cade felt her clench tightly around his fingers as she fell apart, riding his hand shamelessly as she enjoyed a tsunami of pure bliss. Finally satiated, Kara fell back against the bed limply, her chest still heaving from the aftermath of an otherworldly orgasm.

She stared at Cade with sex-hazed eyes, her expression somewhat sheepish after having come undone so completely, so *loudly* in his presence. She had never in her life been quite so expressive during sex; perhaps it was because Cade was the first man to do it right.

Slowly, Cade withdrew his fingers from her drenched, pulsing pussy, enjoying the way she winced when he pulled out, as though she wanted to keep him inside her forever. With a mischievous glint in his eyes, Cade lifted the three fingers still dripping with her cum to his mouth and sucked on them, licking away every last drop of her arousal as Kara watched him with a conflicting sense of horror and lust. "Goodbye has never tasted so fucking good," Cade proclaimed as he bent to kiss her, allowing her to taste herself on his lips. She kissed him back with a bloody fervor that demanded goodbye never come at all.

BREAKFAST had passed too quickly; it was one of their rare moments alone while not fucking, and Kara had enjoyed every minute of it. Anxiety began to creep in at the idea of being left unaccompanied in the sprawling mansion without Cade. Mingled with the anxiety was a disturbing sense of excitement—*she would be left alone in the mansion without Cade.* The intoxication of Cade's presence often stifled the rational part of Kara's consciousness that reminded her she was still a captive in a cage. With the knowledge that Cade would be gone, that reasonable part of her being was jolting into awareness, planning for an escape. Kara tried her best to quell the annoying nettling of reason and focus on Cade's last moments with her before going on a grand adventure to scheme and pillage or whatever the fuck he did. His criminal activities were also something she tried to ignore to the best of her abilities, particularly when his cock or tongue was inside her. Morality was a pesky intruder when it came to fucking.

"Promise me you won't leave the manor," Cade ordered, his voice stern and intimidating and leaving very little room for negotiation. Actually, as far as he was concerned, there *was* no room for negotiation. "It's not safe right now," Cade continued almost pleadingly as he grasped her throat gently, *possessively*. "I hate having to leave you." Cade's grip tightened slightly as he moved his other hand to softly trace the shape of her lips, committing the prominent points of her cupid's bow to memory. "If I had it my way, I would imprison you in my bed, torture you with my mouth and cock, and never let you escape no matter how much you beg." His lips found the tender spot beneath her ear and kissed lightly, teasing her with a need for more. "And it would please me very much to hear you beg," he whispered darkly as his teeth grazed her earlobe.

"Forget work. I like your idea much better," Kara replied, breathless with lust as his lips continued down her neck.

"Sorry, love," Cade answered in a tone that was decidedly unapologetic; he got rather a thrill from denying Kara what she wanted, making her crave him and need him. And when he returned, he would deliver everything she could possibly imagine and more. "I do still have a professional reputation to maintain. And it would be inadvisable to keep this particular client waiting. He is a significantly powerful man with rather a reputation of being a tyrannical bastard."

"Hmm, sounds like someone else I know," Kara quipped before her words were stolen as Cade's mouth slammed on hers, his tongue forcing its way beyond lips and teeth and aggressively demanding her surrender. His kiss was consuming and demanding, depriving Kara of strength, will, and even thought. Everything she was seemed to dissipate until she was nothing more or less than his. Only his.

"Promise me you'll stay at the manor," Cade commanded when he'd finally allowed them the chance to breathe. His hand captured her chin and forced her to meet his gaze. His eyes were darker than usual, they demanded submission and searched for any hint of deception in her countenance or her answer.

"I promise," Kara answered solemnly. And in that exact moment, brief and fleeting as it was, she meant it.

"Good girl," Cade responded warmly, pinching her chin playfully before releasing her. "I'll try to get the assignment finished as quickly as possible. And *you* aren't allowed to finish until I'm back. Is that understood?"

"Are fucking you serious?" Kara scoffed in disbelief as she took a couple steps backward, trying to put space between them. "You aren't some orgasm overlord. If I want to fucking come, I'll fucking come. I have no intention of signing the rights of my body over to you, no matter how fucking bossy you are."

Cade closed the distance between them in a single, angry lunge. "Watch that fucking mouth," he warned, his voice deceptively calm. "You said your pussy was mine, remember?"

Kara had the vaguest recollection of saying something of the sort whilst in the throes of a mind shattering orgasm, but there was no way in hell she'd allow him to hold that against her. "Declarations during sex don't fucking count. That was the pheromones speaking, not me."

"Regardless, your cunt belongs to me. No one is allowed to touch it without my permission, and that includes you. If you disobey me, I will know, and you will be punished."

Possessing literally no ability to formulate a response to *that*, Kara merely stood in stunned silence, her chest heaving against Cade's as her heart pounded frantically with anger and lust and everything in between. What the hell was he doing to her? Before she could spout a clever retort or a witty insult or even a beautifully simplistic *fuck you*, their stare down was interrupted by the sound of someone clearing their throat as an awkward way of announcing their presence.

"Ah, just in time," Cade greeted the person standing behind Kara.

Kara turned to see Declan shifting nervously as he watched his boss pressed intimately against her body, the room charged with anger and the lingering remnants of sexual arousal. Immediately, she stepped away from Cade, smoothing down her dress as a means of calming her emotions and hoping she appeared more presentable than post-orgasmic. Declan's gaze shifted to the floor, as though he didn't want to be caught looking at Kara; the self-preservative move was understandable given Cade was likely exactly the sort of territorial Neanderthal to take offense at someone having the audacity to look at *his things*. The thought made Kara scoff aloud.

Cade fixed her with a glare before his expression turned decidedly smug. "Declan is going to be your babysitter while I'm away. He is responsible for keeping you out of trouble, so go easy on him." Cade laughed at the horrified expression on Kara's face at the idea of being treated like a mischievous child. "You," Cade ordered, pointing at Declan. "Do *not* let her out of your sight. Lock her in her room if you have to."

"Cade!" Kara exclaimed, understandably outraged. There was no way that fucker was going leave her locked away while he was gone. The manor was enough of a prison without adding more bars and padlocks.

"Be good," Cade commanded, bestowing a woefully unwelcome kiss on her forehead. "I'll be back tomorrow."

"CHECK," Kara announced in a bored tone, languidly moving her piece across the chessboard. Playing a game had been Declan's idea. Something to relieve the awkwardness of being the active jailer of someone being held against their will. And something dull enough not to incite the jealousy of his scarily aggressive employer. As she was about to win her third game in a row, chess was clearly not the kid's forte.

As Declan studied the board with an overly concentrated expression, Kara pondered why the hell she was contentedly sitting there playing games with him instead of trying to escape while she had the fucking chance. Yes, she'd promised Cade she would stay put, but that was before he'd given his little minion permission to lock her away. She was, after all, a captive. Even if her captor's fucking skills were unequivocally incomparable, shouldn't escape be her ultimate priority?

Working up her nerve and her less than adequate acting abilities, Kara turned pain filled eyes to Declan as she grasped at her temple in false agony. "Fuck, my head," she groaned dramatically.

Declan jolted to his feet in concern. "What is it? What's wrong? Are you hurt?" he asked anxiously.

Kara had to cover a smile at the poor kid clearly worried that his boss's plaything might succumb to death or injury on his watch. She knew his fear of Cade was nothing to scoff at, but she simply couldn't fathom why everyone treated Caden fucking Ashford like he was a god. Well, she'd at least try to use that fear of Cade's wrath to her advantage. Declan wouldn't want Cade to come home to his *toy* in less than pristine shape, now would he? "I've got the most dreadful migraine coming on," Kara explained, keeping her voice strained and weak as she covered her eyes. "I get them somewhat regularly, but they're exacerbated by stress. My current situation, as you can imagine, doesn't help matters." Kara cast a glance at Declan, and he had the decency to look guilty at the implication.

Perfect.

"I have a doctor's prescription that usually keeps the migraines from becoming too crippling, but it's in my purse upstairs in my room." Kara paused to moan pitifully. "Do you think you could go get it? I'm not sure I have the strength to stand right now."

Hideaway

Declan's expression was plagued with uncertainty and unease. "Umm, I don't know. Ashford said I wasn't supposed to let you out of my sight."

"*Please*, Declan," Kara pleaded, allowing her voice to tremble. "Does it look like I'm in a state to go anywhere? If I don't take the medication, I could black out, and then you'll have to explain to *Ashford* why you let me pass out in his game room."

"Okay, okay I'll go get it. Just stay here, okay? Don't try to get up; I don't want you getting hurt," Declan responded frantically as he moved toward the exit.

"I'll be right here," Kara agreed with a wincing smile. It was her second lie of the day. Or perhaps the third. She was losing count. As soon as Declan was out of sight, she rushed out of the room, knowing she had bought herself between five and ten minutes to make her escape. She hurriedly headed for the detached garages that she'd discovered while exploring the grounds. They were somewhat removed from the main part of the house, so she knew it'd take at least three minutes to get there if she sprinted.

Thankfully, Kara found the doors to the sprawling car storage unlocked. Turning on the overhead lights, she was shocked by the superfluous number of automobiles sitting unused in the garage. There were at least fifteen cars; some were clearly vintage, collectible items, others were flashy and sporty, about four were black, sensible sedans that looked more for business than pleasure. Having no interest or knowledge in the types of cars housed in Cade's excessive collection, Kara looked for the most nondescript vehicle she could find. Settling on a black Audi, she quickly snatched the keys from a rack on the wall and started the car. Shockingly, her plan was working. With maybe three minutes left until Declan sounded the alarm, Kara pushed the button for the garage door and flew down the drive.

Belatedly remembering that she would have to pass gate security, Kara slowed the car to a reasonable pace before stopping in front of the iron wrought gate—the one thing between her and escape. She knew Ortega and Braxton were with Cade on his assignment. They'd left behind minimal security who'd likely been commissioned to keep people *out*, not keep people *in*, so she hoped there was a chance she could slip by without an incident. Shockingly, *miraculously* the gates opened, and Kara sped out into the open road toward freedom. She felt a twinge of sympathy for the poor bastard who opened the gate. One thing was certain, they'd be lucky to escape Cade's wrath merely unemployed.

CHAPTER NINE

FOUR hours. She enjoyed four fucking hours of freedom before the wolves descended. Her first stop after escaping had been the university library. In hindsight, it probably wasn't the most logical choice of sanctuary, but she hadn't *exactly* been looking for a place to hide. She'd just wanted a moment to breathe without the suffocation of being under watch all the time. As utterly insane as it sounded, she'd had every intention of returning to Ashford Manor after checking in on her colleagues, her work, and ensuring the security of the rare texts. Perhaps she'd made a mistake in assuming the choice to return would be her own.

"Hello, Dr. Caine," a dark and familiar voice slithered from behind her, leaving a trail of goosebumps in its wake.

Fuck.

Kara turned sharply to find Jace leaning nonchalantly against a bookshelf with an unmistakably smug grin on his revolting face. Kara's fingers turned white as she clawed at the book in her hand with uncontainable fury. Cade had sent his fucking minions after her. And not just any of his infernal employees. Fucking. Jace. Kara took a cautionary step back from the threat of the man before her. Even if she ran, she wouldn't make it very far before he caught her. Aware that she was trapped, Jace took another step toward her.

"Don't worry, I'm not allowed to touch you. Ashford wants you in perfect condition so he can rip you apart himself."

Kara shivered at the insinuation, walking backward until her body collided with the hard frame of the bookshelf against the wall. Jace followed, filling the space between them until he hovered over her. True to his word, he made no move to touch her.

"I've never seen Ashford lose control. He's always so collected. So calculating. I wonder if there will be any pieces of you left to dispose of after he's finished punishing you for your betrayal?" Jace continued tauntingly.

The frost of fear delved into Kara's veins, her heart momentarily forgetting its purpose as Jace's words twisted through her thoughts like a knife. "How did you even find me?" Kara asked bitterly.

"You're not very hard to guess, Kara. This is the first place we looked."

"We?" she asked, her voice alight with a small spark of hope. If Jace wasn't alone, maybe she could appeal to his companion for safety.

"Me and Declan. Someone had to drive back the damn Audi you stole. The kid left with the car as soon as we got here." Jace leaned

Hideaway

in closer until his nose nearly brushed hers. "So you can wipe that fucking smile off your face. You won't be taking advantage of that idiot's weakness again. You've no car and no escape. You're coming with me." Jace brushed past her and moved toward the doors that barred Kara from freedom. "I'd appreciate it if I didn't have to use force," he called back to her.

Immobile, Kara clung to her spot by the wall. Thoughts of Cade's anger and retribution left her terrified, and she lacked the will to walk willingly to her doom. Jace turned to face her with a mischievous glint in his eye.

"Actually, that's not true at all. I would like nothing more than for you to make me drag you out of this place by your hair, kicking and screaming. Ashford asked me not to touch you, but not if it interfered with his most important command: *bring the bitch back*. So what's it gonna be, Kara? Do you want to come quietly, or do you want to make my day?"

Kara bit her lip anxiously as she contemplated Jace's ultimatum. Regardless of her decision, she knew the ultimate outcome would result in her being dragged back to face whatever hell was in store for her at Ashford Manor. The best she could hope for was depriving Jace of the satisfaction of taking her by force. She knew the sick fuck loved the fight; he had told her as much when she became very well-acquainted with the back of his hand the last time they enjoyed each other's company in the library. For him, she would swallow her anger and pride and walk out of that building with all of the composure and sickly sweet submission she could muster. "I'm ready to go now," Kara announced primly, pushing past Jace and leading the way out of the library.

A flicker of disappointment crossed Jace's face as he moved to follow Kara. He had expected fire and fury. A shrieking, clawing beast that he was ordained to subdue. Kara's usual stubbornness set his blood singing with violence. But the calm obedience with which she returned to captivity left him reeling. His whole body ached with the sudden loss of a fight, his veins coursing with unnecessary adrenaline. Kara fucking Caine had unceremoniously killed his buzz, and he was fucking pissed.

Kara kept walking without a second glance at Jace. She wasn't aware of his personal choice of vehicle, but she didn't need to ask. She simply walked toward the most conspicuously out of place car in the library parking lot and waited expectantly by the passenger side door. Jace unlocked the red Porsche with an annoyed grunt that suggested she was taking all of the fun out of his grand mission of acquisition. Good. Because she had every intention of behaving like the perfect little captive for the duration of their trip back to the manor.

They both got in the car, the area feeling rather cramped as mutual feelings of anger and annoyance filled the space between them. Repelled by the closeness of Jace's presence, Kara moved away as far as she physically could in the closed confines, resting against the window as she bid farewell to the familiar sites of campus. The heavy musk of Jace's cologne pervaded the air, drawing forth grim memories of the last time he had been far too close for comfort. She rolled down the window, beckoning the fresh air to save her from suffocation and ruminations. The start of the ignition brought with it blaring, distasteful music that committed atrocities against her eardrums. The sheer aggression of the song seemed to suit Jace's

Hideaway

overall characteristics perfectly. Noticing her irritation, Jace turned the music up. Rolling her eyes, Kara braced herself for what was sure to be the longest car ride of her life.

"You ran, but you didn't try to hide," Jace commented aloud, breaking the silence of the past thirty minutes in the car. "You actually escaped. You could have gone anywhere. You could have disappeared, gone somewhere we couldn't have found you, at least not right away. Instead, you went to the first place you knew we would look. Why?"

"Why do you care?" Kara asked defensively, keenly aware of quite how asinine her actions sounded when spoken aloud.

"I don't care. I'm just curious. Why throw away your one chance? Do you enjoy the thrill of danger that much?"

"I didn't run," Kara admitted quietly.

"Excuse me?"

"You said I ran, but I didn't."

"How else would you define stealing a car and sneaking out of his house without telling anyone where you were going?"

"I needed time to myself. I needed to check on my work. I needed a small taste of freedom, yes. But I wasn't running. I had every intention of returning tonight after settling things in my office. I hadn't thought anyone would notice. But, of course, Cade found out and sent in the damn calvary," Kara finished with a sigh of irritation.

"You promised him you'd stay. And, for some unknown reason, he trusted you."

"I know," Kara agreed, guilt settling in heavily as she remembered her pledge to Cade. Why did she feel so devastated for stealing a moment of freedom and breaking a promise to her captor? She was entitled to freedom far more than he was entitled to her trust, and yet, the thought of hurting him made her heart feel like it was being crushed in her chest. Jace looked at her appraisingly, reading her thoughts as though they were written plainly on her face.

"Shit, Ashford really did fuck you up, didn't he? You didn't run because you wanted to stay—*with* him," Jace said with a laugh devoid of humor.

Kara sat silently, ignoring his derision. What could she say? The entire situation was precisely as ludicrous as Jace had so eloquently put. She was fucked from the moment she and Cade allowed their relationship to become physical. Crossing the bounds of captive to lover had twisted their relationship into something indescribable, straddling the boundaries of both. She had allowed herself to forget the true role Cade played in her life, and her reckless naivety would come at a price.

Every minute brought them closer to Ashford Manor, closer to the man who would forever steal her freedom. Every second, she tried to make herself hate him, willing away the memories of tender moments shared between them. But try as she might, her heart could not be hardened, her treacherous emotions thrusting her open-armed toward the man holding the keys to her cage rather than beckoning her toward escape.

The gates of Cade's lair came into view far quicker than anticipated, signaling the time for dreading and delaying the master of the manor's wrath had come to an end. The first prickles of fear crept across Kara's skin as she watched the metal bars close behind them, creaking with finality. Cade would be pissed that she had broken her promise. He would be furious that she had run from him. She wasn't sure how possessive he felt about his cars, but there was a good chance he might be more than peeved about her dabbling in grand theft auto. All in all, Cade had sound reasons to be angry with her, but she had no intention of begging for forgiveness because she took advantage of her one chance at freedom as soon as he had his back turned. She refused to apologize for doing what any self-respecting captive would have done. Whatever issues Cade had with her illicit afternoon activities, he could take them and fuck off.

Kara's unflinching resolve lasted about as long as the ride up the narrow drive, vanishing as soon as the white stone towers of the manor loomed ominously ahead. Jace opened the car door for her, less out of chivalry and more to force her out of the security of the vehicle to which she was desperately clinging. Without laying a hand on her, he herded Kara toward the double stairway at the entrance of the manor. She climbed the steep steps solemnly, feeling like Hardy's Tess on her way to the gallows, innocent by virtue if not by deed. Kara stalled by the front of the imperious, carved doors before Jace pushed past her and knocked three times with the ostentatiously formal, golden knocker fashioned into a roaring lion's head. With little delay, Mrs. Hughes opened the doors, greeting Kara with a pitying smile.

Crossing the threshold, Kara looked upon the prison with which she had become familiar. Though the manor was extravagantly beautiful, she had missed the welcome simplicity of the library. Kara longed for another day spent amid the encompassing smell of books and warm glow of sunlight through open windows rather than the glare of chandeliers and the empty echo of vast halls.

"Ashford said to bring you to him as soon as we arrived," Jace informed her curtly.

"Given the events of the day, I'm assuming I don't have a choice in the matter?" Kara asked, feeling the irritation that had been growing during the duration of her ride back with Jace beginning to consume her. If Cade wanted to demand her presence, he had better be prepared to deal with the consequences. Whatever anger he might be feeling, Kara was sure she could match it in full after being dragged back to his house like an escaped convict.

"Boss's orders," Jace responded, his lips curling into a smile of cruel amusement.

"He's in his study," the older woman informed Jace, obviously apprised of their current situation and not at all at ease with it. Mrs. Hughes touched Kara on the shoulder kindly, an almost maternal gesture, as though she might impart some small measure of strength with which to weather the coming storm known as Caden Ashford.

Kara gave her a weak smile in return and trudged onward behind Jace. She hadn't explored much of the monstrous house, so she considered it as an opportunity to familiarize herself with the many facets of her prison. Preoccupied with her mental mappings of twists and turns, Kara nearly ran into Jace as he stopped abruptly in front of double doors that seemed much like the others along the hall. Jace knocked twice to announce their arrival.

"Enter," responded a decidedly ill-tempered voice from the other side.

Jace opened the door to reveal a visibly enraged Cade seated behind a large, mahogany desk, his arms splayed authoritatively across the smooth wooden surface as he continued a conversation on his phone. As Cade preferred to keep his work private, Kara had never had the opportunity to visit his study. The room suited him. Dark, emerald hued walls were transfixed with antique cabinets with glass panes exhibiting an eclectic variety of collectibles and artifacts on either side of the immense desk polished to perfection. A large, abstract painting hung directly above the desk, the sparse brushstrokes of white and grey evoking the bleakness of a winter night. Synchronizing with the decor of the rest of the manor, an ebony chandelier draped dramatically from the center of the ceiling. The pristinely organized, somber opulence of the space enveloped Cade's personality perfectly.

It seemed rather foreboding that Kara had been taken directly to Cade's inner sanctum upon their arrival. Whatever his feelings regarding her little excursion that afternoon, they were severe enough to warrant disrupting his work. How was he even at home when he had scheduled time with a client until the following morning? Had the client canceled? Or had Cade abandoned a client that he himself had described as undeniable for the sole purpose of rushing back home to deal with her transgressions himself?

Fuck, perhaps she was in more trouble than she thought. Kara fidgeted nervously, feeling awkwardly like a child awaiting chastisement, as Cade's conversation drew to a close. She clung to the hope that he would listen to reason before rushing to judgment and fury and retaliation. Unfortunately, reasonability had yet to be his strongest attribute.

"Handle it," Cade finished shortly as he ended the call, tossing the mobile on the desk in irritation.

An anxious chill washed over Kara as she realized she was next in line to receive Cade's furious attentions. She shifted restlessly beside Jace, waiting for the anger she knew would come, pondering what form her punishment would take. Continuing to ignore her presence, Cade ran raked his fingers through his hair viciously. Noticing a disarray on his desk, Cade took a moment to tuck the papers into tidy stacks, the small, orderly task allowing him to regain a semblance of composure. Finally, he stood, fingers deftly closing the front buttons on his suit as he turned to look at Kara for the first time since he had bid her a tender farewell that morning when her promise to stay remained chaste and unbroken.

Cade's eyes were darkened with the depths of icy ire, cold and fiercely unforgiving. Kara withered beneath the fury that encompassed his entire body like an aura, longing with every fiber of her being to look away. Refusing to give him the satisfaction of cowering, Kara ignored the instinctual impulses to beg or run and held his gaze with a steady bravery that hopefully masked her true terror.

"You may go, Jace," Cade instructed his associate without releasing Kara from his violent gaze.

"I'll apprise you of the details later, Ashford," Jace replied as he turned to go.

"Shut the door on your way out."

Jace gave Kara a suggestive wink before abandoning her to Cade's mercy and shutting the door firmly behind him. Kara found

Hideaway

herself alone in the room with Cade, trying unsuccessfully to avoid a tremble of apprehension. "Cade, I'm—"

"Stop," he interrupted angrily, cutting off her attempt to offer excuses or apologies. "I didn't give you permission to speak."

Cade's hands ached to throttle her or force her over the desk and deliver the thrashing she so desperately deserved for breaking her promise. He couldn't trust himself to touch her, yet. The rage coursing through his veins demanded violence, and he couldn't be sure of his ability to stop once the price justice demanded had been exacted. He didn't want to hurt Kara to the point of ruin, so he would try his utmost to keep a safe distance between them until his anger had quelled enough to discipline her reasonably.

He moved to where a chair rested in the corner of the room and dragged it rather loudly across the floor until it stood in front of his desk. "Sit down, Kara," he commanded, gesturing to the newly situated piece of furniture.

"I would prefer to stand, thank you," Kara answered firmly, having no intention of allowing him to put her in a position of feeling small and powerless as he towered above her.

"It wasn't a suggestion," Cade responded darkly.

"Well, I've never been very good at following orders."

"Clearly. If you were, we couldn't be having this conversation."

"How is it a conversation if I'm not allowed to speak?" Kara replied with determined defiance.

Cade slammed his fists on the desk in frustration. The aggression of the act shocked Kara, and she shrank back slightly. Cade was gratified to read the fear in her eyes. At least she had some notion of common sense. He intentionally used the desk as a barrier between his anger and her. Cade didn't trust himself to handle her with the haze of fury clouding his judgment. She had broken her promise. She had run right into the precarious situation he had been trying to protect her from. She had risked his reputation, his business, his employees, and her personal safety, and the possible consequences of her reckless betrayal sent all gentleness and rationality out of his being.

"Why can you not follow even the simplest of instructions? Have you not an inkling of self-preservation?" Cade asked in exasperation.

"Is this still about sitting in the chair?" Kara asked, trying to make light of the situation.

"No, it's not about the fucking chair," he growled. "But yes, I would have a much easier time maintaining control if you could make some effort to cooperate."

"Oh heaven forbid, Caden Ashford isn't in fucking control! Do I have your parents to thank for your supremely inflated sense of self-importance, or are you a self-made asshole?"

Kara could see from his face that she had gone too far. His movements seemed almost feral as he strode toward her. Kara backed away in panic, trying to escape the line of fire, but his steps matched two of her own. Within an instant, Kara felt her back pressed up against the wall, Cade's body holding her there. He grabbed her shoulders, unable to resist giving her a slight shake.

"Why are you so fucking reckless, Kara?"

"Let go of me, Cade," she demanded as fiercely as possible, trying to ignore the sting of fear she felt beneath the strength of his hands. "You're hurting me."

He loosened his hold on her, unleashing his pent up frustration on the wall beside her head. His fist met the hard surface with a loud *bam*. Kara flinched. She sensed that only a thin tether of self-control had kept him from hitting her rather than the wall. His body physically quivered with rage, but he contained himself. Barely. The violence that lurked so close to the surface was beginning to burn through. Self-preservation demanded that she tread carefully. As usual, she ignored the instinct, fear spurring her toward fight rather than flight.

"You should work on those anger management issues," she goaded with a pointed glance at the fist that still rested on the wall a few inches from her head.

"My issue is with managing my librarian, not my anger," Cade responded darkly. He was clearly still seething, and her glib attitude was not diffusing the situation.

"Perhaps you should find a new librarian," she suggested flippantly.

"Trust me, if there were any others to be had, you would be gone," he replied evenly. His words inflicted more damage then he intended; Cade could see the hurt written plainly on her face. She had, against his better judgment, become something more than just a job, but that was part of the problem. Cade ran his fingers through his hair as he tried to control his rage before he said or did anything he might regret. He had to make her understand the severity of her actions. "You promised to stay here, Kara," Cade reprimanded, finally getting to the heart of the matter.

"I don't think I should be held to oaths made under duress," Kara replied spitefully.

"Under duress?" Cade questioned with an incredulous scoff.

"Yes, under duress. As I am a prisoner in this damn house, every move I make is under fucking duress."

"I seem to recall you begging me to stay and fuck you this morning. I don't believe anyone forced you to sleep with me. Or keep coming back for more. You wanted it."

"I'm a good actress," Kara answered disdainfully.

Cade narrowed his eyes. "I see."

Without warning, Cade's lips were on hers—hot, possessive, and entirely conquering. His tongue forced its way past her defenses, invading her mouth violently. His teeth collided with flesh, impatient and hungry as they drew blood from her full bottom lip. Her mouth filled with the taste of him, heady and familiar and completely intoxicating. Kara allowed herself to briefly melt beneath his touch before pulling back and slapping him as hard as she possibly could across his presumptuous face.

"Get the fuck off me!" Kara shouted in disgust. What had possessed the impudent bastard to kiss her like that?

Immediately obeying her request, Cade took an intentional step backward, putting space between them once again. He moved his hand to the side of his face emblazoned with the red print of her fingers, stroking the sting thoughtfully, a smile slowly playing across his lips. Rather than looking pissed, Cade was positively gleeful, as though a slap to the face was exactly what he had been after. "You, my love, are no actress. When you dislike someone's advances, you protest quite freely. And quite loudly. You came to my bed willingly. You can attempt to convince yourself otherwise, but I have all the proof I need," he finished, rubbing his sore cheek for emphasis.

Kara merely glared at him, any hope of challenging him obliterated to ash. She hated him for taking advantage of her weakness and manipulating the intimacy of their relationship.

"As I was saying, when you broke your promise and went to the campus today, you risked very grave consequences. Both for yourself and for me."

"What do you mean?" Kara asked, confused.

"Avery's men were at that library, Kara. Yesterday. What would have happened if they were there today when you foolishly decided to make an impromptu visit alone and unprotected?"

"Wait, what are you talking about? I thought you *were* Avery's men?"

"Yes, but we didn't exactly follow through on delivery, now did we? Avery had no intention of permanently relinquishing that text, and he's fucked without it. He'll do what it takes to get it back, and he's more than willing to employ people with far fewer moral scruples than I."

Kara scoffed aloud at the idea of Cade representing a moral standard.

With a chastising glare, Cade continued. "His agents have been regularly visiting the university, presumably waiting for you to show up after having little luck finding you at the literary conference in Canada you're supposedly attending according to Braxton's hacking skills. If any of them saw you with Jace today, they'll know your location and that I am involved." Cade watched as the realization that she might have endangered more than just herself began to sink into Kara's consciousness.

"Well, I would have been more careful if I'd known. Shit, Cade, why didn't you tell me?"

"I didn't feel it necessary to worry you with the knowledge that you were being hunted. I had it under control, and I told you not to leave the manor. You should have trusted my judgment and not disobeyed."

"Well, I just assumed you were being a control freak; it is basically your fundamental characteristic."

"Much as blatant irrationality for the sake of appearing independent is yours."

"You literally had your lackey come and forcefully drag me back to this prison because I decided to get some air for a few hours. A little independence would be a nice change."

"Prove you're capable of obeying reason, and I'll consider it."

"And we're back to this again. I swear your outrage has far less to do with my brush with danger than it does my audacity to disregard your authority. I've seen the power you wield over those around you; hell, even Jace is wary of inciting your displeasure. It's as if your very presence extinguishes free will. Thank goodness I'm still able to express my right to rebellion."

"You speak so rashly because you have yet to experience the consequences of my displeasure, but trust me, you will." Cade's threats were interrupted by a brisk knock on the door. "Not now," Cade commanded loudly as he grabbed ahold of Kara's arm and dragged her toward his desk.

Kara tried to resist, but his grip was relentless and his countenance completely devoid of mercy. For all her defiance, Kara was beginning to dread the consequences of pushing him too far.

Hideaway

Cade's eyes shone with a determination that implied he had finally decided upon the manner of Kara's reckoning. And she knew it would not be pleasant.

Someone burst through the door, providing Kara with momentary salvation. It was Declan. Cade turned the full brunt of his fury on the poor boy, giving him a deadly glare that made Kara shudder and Declan eye his escape route warily.

"I said we were not to be disturbed," Cade thundered angrily, his hand still painfully constricted around Kara's arm. The boy was already next on his hit list after the events of the day, and his interruption was not helping matters.

Declan gulped nervously before answering. "Jace says that it's urgent. It's about the December client."

Kara rolled her eyes, terror temporarily giving sway to annoyance. Of course Jace would offer up the poor boy like a sacrifice to the mercy of Cade's wrath rather than risk interrupting Cade himself.

Cowardly bastard.

Cade took a moment to determine the best course of action. He needed thirty minutes alone with Kara. Thirty minutes and her disobedience would be reprimanded, his need for retribution would be sated, and he could complete the order for the December client with a clear conscience and a clear head. But he had already stolen time from one of his highest statured clients to fly home and deal with the Kara fiasco under the guise of a work emergency. If Jace was demanding his attention, Pascal was probably getting restless. Cade ran a frustrated hand through his dark hair.

"Fuck!" Cade yelled in exasperation, causing both Kara and Declan to flinch. Begrudgingly choosing to put work before his personal issues with Kara, Cade pulled Kara viciously toward the door.

"Follow me," Cade ordered over his shoulder to Declan.

Cade dragged Kara down the hall, around the corner, past the library, and up the stairs. She struggled to keep up with his rapid pace, tripping slightly on the stairs, but his vice-like grip on her arm kept her upright and continuing forward. Declan trailed obediently behind them. To her relief, Cade turned toward her room rather than his own. Kara's relief was short-lived as he opened the door to her room and thrust her inside, the force of his push throwing her to the floor. Kara gaped at him with unabashed outrage.

"Do not fucking move from this room until I return," Cade thundered, pointing his finger at her in emphasis.

"And when exactly will that be?" she questioned angrily, not taking kindly to being manhandled and given orders.

"When I bloody well feel like it!" Cade yelled, equally incensed.

With no further goodbye, Cade turned on his heel and left the room, slamming the door behind him with shattering force. With nauseating dread, Kara heard the scrape of a key turning on the other side of the door. Even when Cade had first taken her hostage, she had never been locked in her room. For the first time since she had arrived at the manor, Kara was truly imprisoned.

"Cade!" Kara called in panic. "Let me out! You can't lock me in here."

"On the contrary, love, I can do absolutely anything imaginable to you, and there is nothing you can do to stop me. I treated you as my guest. I gave you my trust. But you have disregarded my hospitality and broken that trust. So now, you will be treated as the prisoner you so enjoy claiming to be."

"Cade, please," Kara pleaded, the stubbornness and fury vanquished, replaced with quivers of fear.

"You've brought this upon yourself, Kara" Cade answered stonily. "Declan will be here to guard the door. And I assure you he has every intention of fulfilling his duties and redeeming himself of this morning's lapse in judgment. Do not talk to him. Declan is under strict orders to call me immediately if you attempt to disobey my orders."

Kara heard the sound of footsteps receding and then nothing. "Cade?" she called into the emptiness. "Cade!"

There was no answer. She was alone. Locked in a room with no escape and a monster for a jailer.

CHAPTER TEN

THE minutes ticked past slowly. Or perhaps they were hours. The sun had yet to shed its nightly cloak, the moon still a looming orb of gloom, signaling morning had yet to arrive. Kara had very little with which to fill the vacant hours of ennui. She had no phone, there was no television in her room, there wasn't a single book to offer a kindly reprieve from the tedium that was now her wretched existence. Cade had successfully entombed her in a crypt of boredom, a true testament to his obvious cruelty. Kara had allowed her lust and ill-fated attraction to Cade to cloud her judgment regarding his true character. It was a mistake of deadly proportions and one that she would not make again.

With little else to distract her thoughts, Kara was keenly aware that she was starving, her last meal being breakfast with Cade that morning. Apart from a cup of black coffee at the library, she hadn't

Hideaway

had any sustenance since. Contemplating the risks of disobeying Cade's orders yet again, Kara summoned the courage to ask Declan if she could be allowed to venture downstairs for dinner. She would have eagerly accepted a mere crust of bread delivered to her door, but dinner might give her an excuse to escape her confinement, even if only briefly.

"Declan," Kara called sweetly, her mouth pressed against the door where he waited on the other side.

"Shit, Kara. You aren't supposed to talk to me. I don't want either of us getting into more trouble with Ashford," Declan answered anxiously, his voice a harsh whisper.

Kara rolled her eyes. How exactly was he in trouble? She was the one locked away and guarded. For what infernal reason did everyone tread so carefully when it came to Cade? Sure he was imperious, ill-tempered, and pretentious, but not so very threatening. He was a mere man, endowed with as much or as little power as he was allowed to take. Unlike the men who followed him, Kara had no intention of allowing Cade to dominate her fear.

Gritting her teeth, Kara tried again to reason with the Caden Ashford acolyte. "I'm sorry if I got you in trouble with Cade earlier. I didn't mean for you to be blamed for my leaving," Kara apologized with partial honesty. She had planned to be back before Cade found out, eliminating the need for anyone to be blamed or punished. She'd felt bad for using the kid's gullibility to her advantage, but the guilt was mitigated by the fact that Declan was actively enabling her imprisonment.

"It's okay. I was stupid. Shouldn't have let you out of my sight," Declan responded with an embarrassed laugh.

"You were empathetic and kind. You should never have to apologize for possessing such worthy attributes. You should get the hell out of here before any goodness disappears entirely," Kara answered truthfully, repressing a shudder at the thought of the sweet kid turning into someone as merciless as Jace.

There was an uneasy pause before Declan answered. "Well, you really shouldn't be talking to me. Boss's orders and all."

"I know. It's just…I haven't had anything to eat since breakfast. Do you think you could let me go downstairs for dinner? I'll come right back to my room, I promise," Kara pleaded. The degradation of having to ask permission to keep from starving left her feeling bitterly indignant.

"I don't know, Kara. I'd have to ask for his approval."

"He seemed rather busy with work today. Certainly you don't need to interrupt him to ask if I'm allowed the common courtesy of sustenance?"

"His orders were very specific," Declan informed her, denying her request not to involve Cade with an immediate call to his superior.

Fuck.

Kara weakened in defeat, knowing how the sadistic bastard would likely respond to her request.

"Hello…Yes, sir…No, she hasn't left her room….She's asked if she can eat dinner downstairs…I called you immediately…Yes, I understand…Yes, sir, I'll put her on speaker."

"He wants to speak with you," Declan told her, his tone wary.

"Kara," a muffled voice came from the other side of the door, the angry address unmistakably Cade's.

"Yes," Kara answered, careful to keep her tone even, not allowing her frustration and hatred to seep in.

"I see you decided talking to Declan was worth disobeying my orders, yet again."

"Yes," Kara responded simply, the answer obvious.

"And you seem to think I'll allow you to leave your room? Allow you the pleasure of eating when all you have brought me today is vexation and insubordination?"

"Yes," was Kara's third monosyllabic answer.

"Disobedient brats do not deserve dinner, Kara."

"Fuck you!" Kara shouted angrily, his demeaning attitude finally breaking through her collected composure.

"I promise you'll regret that disrespectful outburst. Very soon, in fact," Cade warned ominously.

"Declan," he redirected, finished indulging Kara with his attention.

And that was the last Kara heard from either of them.

IT was a few hours shy of dusk when Cade finally arrived home. He was weary, frustrated, mentally taxed, and longed for nothing more than to collapse into bed and allow slumber to overtake him. But he still had one manner of unresolved business, and sleep would have to wait.

Cade's previous fury from that afternoon had cooled to a mere echo of anger over Kara's transgressions. The passion had subsided in favor of calculated retribution. Unlike the heated interaction in his study, Cade could now trust himself to punish Kara fairly and without malice. He was no longer out for blood. He would be satisfied with a small measure of pain as payment for her betrayal. Kara had committed a number of sins that day, and the time of judgment had come.

From the top of the stairs, Cade could make out Declan's sleeping form; he had passed out on the floor, his head resting on Kara's door frame. Cade released an exasperated sigh of disapproval, making a mental note never to put Declan on guard duty again. He'd deal with the kid later; doling out one punishment in the early morning hours was more than enough in his sleep-deprived state. For the moment, Declan would escape unscathed. The insolent girl on the other side of the door wouldn't be so lucky.

Cade lightly kicked Declan in the side, startling him awake.

"Ashford! You're back?" Declan asked in surprise as he jolted upright, his heart racing with the shock of being thrust into consciousness as well as nervousness at being caught sleeping on the job.

"Clearly," Cade responded shortly, lifting his hand to massage the weariness from his temple. "Go to bed, Declan. We'll be having a discussion in my office in the morning."

"Yes, sir," Declan replied guiltily. "Goodnight, sir."

Cade waved him off without another word, summoning his last stores of energy for what was sure to be an uncomfortable confrontation. His face settled into unforgiving stone as he unlocked

Hideaway

the door and entered Kara's room. She lay peacefully on the bed, any angers or fears she had regarding him melting away in the sweet bliss of slumber. Cade had entertained the hope that she would wait up for him, as eager to clear the animosity and dissension between them as he was, but he didn't begrudge her the desire to sleep away the stress of a long day.

He walked toward Kara quietly, treading lightly so as not to wake her. His caution was illogical as he would be doing just that in a few moments, but he enjoyed getting the chance to watch her while she was free of mouthy insults and infuriating obstinance and all the other traits that came with Kara being conscious. Cade sat beside her on the bed, unable to refrain from brushing a stray strand of pale blonde hair from her forehead. Her skin was warm, inviting, and the smallest bit flushed as Cade continued to run his fingers lightly along her cheek. She was beautiful, heartbreakingly so. Her biting temper, so blatantly incongruous with her own fragility, drove him mad while also igniting a tenderness in him that he didn't know existed. He ached to wrap his arms around her, feel her warmth against his body, and fall into tranquil sleep beside her. The enticing temptation almost banished any thought of broken promises and punishments.

Almost.

"Kara," Cade said firmly, loud enough to startle her from sleep.

She blinked at him with bleary eyes, her sleep-addled mind searching for the reason for Cade's untimely awakening. Slowly, consciousness brought with it the unwelcome reminder that she had pissed off the man single-handedly in control of her future, and he had promised retribution. Instinctually, Kara buried her shame-tinged face in the cover of the pillow in the unrealistic hope that the bit of fluff would shield her from Cade's ire. Unsurprisingly, it did not.

"Look at me, Kara," Cade commanded calmly.

Cautiously, she peaked at him from behind the pillow, anxious of being subjected to the same explosive anger he'd exhibited in his study. To her relief, the fire in his eyes had cooled, replaced by something as hard and frigid as ice. His gaze wasn't one of cruelty, but dispassionate determination. This version of Cade could be reasoned with, she just had to approach him with an appropriate balance of rationality and remorse. Or so she thought.

"Cade," Kara greeted warily, her voice still laced with drowsiness. "I thought you had business in New York for a couple days. How did you make it back so quickly?"

"I got things settled. Jace is handling it now," Cade answered, his voice tired and drawn as he ran his fingers through his hair. "Did you think you would escape so easily? I told you I would be back to handle your punishment."

"I thought being locked in my room with no dinner was my punishment," Kara said quietly, lowering her eyes.

"No, love, that was merely the overture. The true orchestration of your punishment begins now."

Kara's heart stuttered in terror at the words dripping with ominousness. "What are you going to do?" she asked fearfully, trying to inconspicuously slide away from where Cade sat on the bed.

Reproachfully, Cade captured her arm and pulled her closer toward him. She quivered slightly beneath his grasp, trepidation plainly written across her face. Cade wondered what exactly she thought he was going to do? What horrors did she suppose he was capable of? He may occasionally be a bastard, but he wasn't a monster.

"Let's go over your transgressions, shall we? Then perhaps we can ascertain a fitting judgment." Cade waited for her nod of acknowledgment before proceeding, counting each sin with the lift of a finger. "First, you broke your promise. You told me that you would keep within the safety of the manor, and you lied to my face. Second, you ran from me. When you were first brought here, you were allowed free reign permitting you didn't leave the premises. You disobeyed. Third, you jeopardized my business by risking exposure as well as depriving a client of my very valuable time when I had to rush home to deal with your misbehavior."

Kara stared at the three damning fingers Cade held before her, a tally of her crimes. She remained silent, assuming anything she said would merely be used against her. She couldn't argue with his recounting; the details were true. Hell, he'd even made her feel marginally guilty for her recklessness. But that didn't mean she was prepared to pay the price.

"Well, Kara? What do you think is a suitable punishment?" Cade asked, genuinely interested in her opinion.

"I don't know," Kara answered miserably. She had no desire to damn herself, but she was equally petrified of having Cade decide her fate.

"In that case, I'll decide for you," Cade said threateningly as he rose from the bed.

In one quick pull, Cade ripped the covers from Kara's body, sighing lustily as he beheld her near nakedness beneath. She wore a delicate silk nightgown that barely brushed the tops of her thighs, the soft blush color an exact match for the flushed rosiness in her cheeks. Transparent lace trim framed her breasts, allowing a seductively teasing glimpse of the dark pink of her nipples. The nightgown was pushed up to her hip on one side, revealing scanty knickers of the same see-through, pink lace. Cade's gaze transfixed hungrily on her pussy, the outline of her sex entirely visible. It would require an unbelievable level of self-control to keep from fucking her the minute her punishment was concluded.

"Stand up," he ordered sharply, sexual frustration making his voice harsher than he intended.

Reluctantly, Kara sat up, folding her arms over her chest to conceal the nipple revealing negligee. The thin, transparent material of her nightwear left her feeling like she was entering a battle without armor. Using one arm for support and the other for cover, Kara stood, meeting Cade's gaze as bravely as she could under the mortifying circumstances.

"Hands at your sides," Cade commanded, stripping her of another layer of security and comfort.

Embarrassment flooding her cheeks, Kara forced her arms down, her fingers clenching tightly at the bottom hem of her nightgown. She shifted anxiously from one foot to the other as Cade painfully drew out the dread of whatever retribution he had planned.

"Follow me," he directed after a long moment's pause, turning to walk across the room.

Kara followed him hesitantly, confused when he halted in front of the desk in front of the far window. She searched Cade's countenance for a hint of what he had planned. Did he want her to write something? How would that satisfy the debt he insisted she pay for her disobedience?

"What did I say would happen the next time you risked your safety by willfully disobeying me?" Cade asked sternly.

Kara thought back to his words at the stables, the blood draining from her face as she remembered the consequence to which he was referring. Surely he wouldn't?

In answer to the question she thundered at him silently, Cade reached for his belt buckle, unfastening it and pulling the belt from his hips at an excruciatingly languid speed. "Well, Kara? Surely you remember?"

"You said you'd—" Kara's voice momentarily abandoned her as she tried to get out the words that tasted of bile. "You said you'd whip me."

"That's exactly right." As his eyes seared hers with the dangerousness of his intentions, Cade folded the heavy leather belt in half and slapped it once against his palm as though he were displaying his showmanship.

The resounding *thwap* made Kara gasp aloud in sickened horror. Abandoning quiet submission the moment she heard the wicked belt meet skin, Kara started to look around frantically for a means of escape. She desperately ran for the door, and Cade made no move to stop her. He stood by the desk calmly, the doubled belt hanging sinisterly in his grasp.

"I would suggest you not run from me a second time, Kara. I don't think you'd enjoy your punishment being twice as hard."

Kara spun around to face him, her face contorted with indignant fury. How dare he think he could physically punish her for breaking a few rules? In case he hadn't noticed, beating a grown woman for disobedience hadn't been socially acceptable for at least half a century. Her heart clenched at the fact that what he threatened to do to her had ever been permissible at all.

"There isn't a chance in hell that you're going to touch me with *that*!" Kara shouted at him as she maintained a safe distance from Cade and his weapon of choice.

"You're right, I'm going to do a good deal more than touch you with it. You've earned yourself a proper thrashing. Now come here," Cade ordered, snapping his fingers.

"No," Kara denied with a firm shake of her head.

"Do not make me ask again, Kara. Here. Now," Cade almost shouted, loudly tapping his index finger on the desk for emphasis.

Kara didn't move an inch, locking her arms over her chest in a blatant stance of defiance as she stared at Cade with unshakable fortitude. Cade mirrored her posture, crossing his own arms as he attempted to glare her into submission. Both were equally matched in obstinacy. Neither of them spoke. Neither of them wavered. They were at an impasse, each of them willing to stand there all night if that was what it took to prove a point.

Cade broke first.

"Fine, you insufferable woman! If you won't own your mistakes and pay the price, I'll have to use a substitute."

"What exactly does that mean?" Kara asked, worried by his cryptic suggestion.

"It means, Kara, that since you do not accept responsibility for your actions today, I will have to find another to carry the blame in your stead."

"Who could you possibly find guilt with other than me?"

"I believe Declan was tasked with making sure you didn't leave the manor," Cade continued, his eyebrow raised with a hint of a challenge.

Kara's face drained of color, her heart twisting as she began to understand Cade's intentions. "It isn't Declan's fault that I disregarded your orders. You have no justification for taking out your anger on him. My decisions were mine alone," Kara pleaded, confused to find herself defending the boy who merely an hour before had been standing guard at her locked door, enforcing her imprisonment.

"You're right, it was you, not Declan, who recklessly ignored my orders and carelessly endangered everyone involved. However, since the guilty individual refuses to submit to the consequences, my punishment must fall on someone else," Cade shouted back, seething with frustration.

Cade thrust his fingers through his dark locks in irritation, desperately striving to find the serenity with which he had entered the room. Kara, in her infuriatingly characteristic belligerence, had taken a battle axe to his composure, and he was struggling to gather the pieces. Slowly, painstakingly, Cade centered himself once again, turning to Kara with sternness, but not anger.

"You have the next ten seconds to get your arse over here, bend over the desk, and accept the punishment you've rightfully earned. Or, I'll march downstairs, drag Declan out of bed, and have him thrashed in front of you and everyone else in the house." He wasn't bluffing. Cade had every intention of dragging the kid out into the courtyard and beating him senseless if it meant Kara would take a hard look at how her need to challenge the rules put herself and others in danger.

Kara shifted anxiously, faced with two excruciating choices. She couldn't fathom consensually allowing anyone to beat her, least of all a man she had willingly allowed into her bed. The perilousness of her current situation certainly had her reconsidering all of her recent life choices. She had fucked her captor, even developed some sort of murky feelings for him. Now, in punishment for the single sensible judgment she'd made in weeks, the Neanderthal was threatening to hit her with a belt. Every survival inclined instinct within her body screamed for her to run. And she longed desperately to obey. But Cade wasn't playing fair. In a very underhanded move, he had brought Declan into a matter that should have been settled between the two of them. Regardless of her fear and humiliation, she couldn't allow Declan to be used as a whipping boy for her mistakes.

"Time is up, Miss Caine. What is your decision?"

"I'll take the whipping," Kara answered quietly, her voice quivering with dread.

"Good," Cade said as a smug smile spread across his face. "Thank you for finally being sensible." He patted the top of the desk cheerfully, welcoming her to join him and looking more like he was inviting her to tea rather than a beating.

"It's not like you gave me much of a choice," Kara responded bitterly as she walked toward him.

"I believe a choice is exactly what I gave you."

"Let's just get this absurdity over with. I'll remember you get off on beating women the next time I feel even remotely tempted to get into your bed again."

Cade captured her wrist and gently pulled her toward him. Warm breath caressed her neck as he wrapped his fingers lightly around her throat and leaned down to press the softest kiss in the hollow behind her ear. "Careful love, you might enjoy it too," he whispered seductively.

"Not a chance in hell, you depraved bastard," she replied venomously and tried to pull away from his touch.

"Harsh words, love. Let's see if I can soften you up a little. Face me," he commanded.

Reluctantly, Kara obeyed, turning to meet his appraising gaze. The glitter of amusement had left his eyes, and he wore a steady mask of determination.

"Why are you being punished, Kara?" Cade asked, capturing her chin in his hand to keep her from shying away from the question or his attention.

"I broke my promise and I ran and I put everyone at risk," she answered, her cheeks flushed with embarrassment as he left her feeling like a scolded child.

"And what, Kara, are the consequences of your behavior?"

Her eyes begged him not to demand further degradation. She had already submitted her body for his castigation. He could at least leave her dignity intact.

"Answer the question," he demanded coldly.

"You are going to hit me with your belt," she replied as she nearly choked on the words, strangled with mortification.

"Precisely. Now, apologize and request your punishment."

"You can't be serious," Kara scoffed as she shook her chin from his grasp, her fear momentarily forgotten in the wake of his sheer audacity.

"Oh, I am deadly serious," Cade informed her, his face dark with intensity.

Kara groaned in anguish, hating the man before her with every molecule in her body. She wished she could take back every pleasant thought she'd ever had about him. She especially wished she could take away every memory of the reprehensible bastard being inside her. And, more than anything, she wished she could take back the twisted irony of enjoying his body so much that she would possibly consider fucking him even after he hit her.

"Should I go get Declan?" Cade asked, growing impatient.

British bastard.

"Fine! I apologize for disobeying your orders. Please be so good as to whip me," Kara conceded finally, hoping she had adequately concealed the sarcasm in her voice. The malicious grin on Cade's face implied that she hadn't.

"Well, if you insist, love. Bend over the desk."

Kara stood before the ominous desk. There would be no more stalling. No more delays. No more arguments. It was time for her to pay. She felt Cade's hand on the small of her back, gently encouraging rather than forcing her to lower herself onto the desk. She complied reluctantly, bending at the waist and laying her upper body across the smooth mahogany like a sacrificial offering for his whims of retaliation. The surface of the desk was unforgiving, cold, and too hard against the soft warmth of her skin. The angular corners bit painfully into the tender flesh of her abdomen, connecting with her hip bones any time she shifted or adjusted her weight.

Cade placed the belt on the desk in front of Kara, noticing her startled jolt of fear when it landed on the wood with a loud *thud*. Kara eyed the detestable implement warily, distracted to the point that she didn't notice Cade move behind her. She felt him press the length of his body against her, cringing mentally even as her traitorous body leaned slightly into his embrace.

His hands softly traced the outline of her body, stroking from her shoulders, down her sides, dipping into the indent of her waist, over her hips, and, finally, across her backside. His touch lingered there, rubbing concentric circles across her ass, demanding her relaxation with his massaging fingers. Involuntarily, Kara obeyed, raising her hips to lift her ass into his tantalizing touch. She froze when she felt his hands slip under her nightgown and slowly raise it above her hips. She shivered when Cade's fingers hooked into her panties and gently pulled them down her legs, stroking her thighs and calves along the way. Placing the softest kiss on her right ankle, Cade lifted her feet one at a time and helped her step out the panties.

Kara was naked from the waist down, fully exposed and prostrate to whatever Cade may demand. And in that moment, much to her complete bewilderment, she very much wanted him to fuck her. Feeling him pull away from her, Kara heaved in distress as Cade walked back to the desk and picked up the belt. Her stomach turned as she watched his fingers flex tightly around the smooth, brown leather, the simple act corrupted with the threat of impending violence. She stifled begs and pleas as they crept cowardly up her throat, demanding to be released. She knew, at that point, no words would save her.

The lethal sound of leather cutting through air was the only warning Kara had before the belt landed harshly on the very center of her ass.

One.

She gasped at the sensation resonating across punished flesh. Unquestionably, it had hurt. A lot. But there were layers beneath the singular feeling of pain. And it was confusing as hell. Cade's sensual caresses had left her feeling open to sensation, insatiable for touch. And somehow, even though that touch was punishing instead of gratifying, her body had welcomed it rather than finding it wholly disagreeable.

After making sure Kara was composed enough to proceed, Cade whipped her again. Harder.

Two.

She flinched at the contact of leather with skin, but remained unyielding. Aiming for the apex of her thighs, Cade hit again.

Three.

She pressed her thighs tightly together, squirming against the edge of the desk. "Please," Kara begged breathlessly, though not entirely sure for what. For Cade to stop hitting her? For him to continue the onslaught that left her feeling tortured and tingly all at once? For him to put down the damn belt and fuck her hard against the desk? Another lash hit her high on the ass, dragging a soft moan from her lips.

Four.

Cade's brow furrowed as he stilled his hand momentarily, surprised to find Kara's utterances echoed lust more than anguish. Clearly not fulfilling his duty adequately, Cade put his full weight into his next swing, the belt landing on the tender skin of her thighs.

Five.

Kara whimpered softly, this time in pain. *Six.* Every lash pulled her farther from enjoyment. *Seven.* Slowly, arousal gave way to anguish. *Eight.* Rather than his arm tiring, Cade's strength seemed to grow with every blow. *Nine.* Each strike of the belt was harder than the last, as though exacting her pain and submission fueled him. *Ten.* Kara began to shake beneath the brutal assault, tears threatening to spill.

"Please," Kara pleaded again. This time, she was entirely sure all she wanted was for the whipping to stop.

"You don't get to ask for mercy now, Kara." Cade layered another blow across an already sore welt on her ass. A blot of deep red blossomed against the purpling bruises as he broke the skin. *Eleven.*

Kara cried out softly.

"You should have considered the consequences when you broke your promise." He hit her quickly in succession. *Twelve. Thirteen. Fourteen.*

Kara felt her cheeks dampen with tears she hadn't realized she'd shed.

"You should have thought of the ramifications when you ran from me." The lashes grew harder still. *Fifteen. Sixteen.* Kara's chest heaved with silent sobs as she struggled to absorb the pain Cade delivered. How much more could she bear? How many more blows would she have to take before Cade was satisfied?

"Do you regret disobeying me now?"

Kara struggled to remain standing on trembling legs as he whipped her hard across the thighs. *Seventeen.*

"Answer the question, Kara," Cade commanded, striking her again. *Eighteen,*

"Y-yes," she sobbed in response.

He hit her again. So hard. *Nineteen.* Kara's nails dug into the top of the desk; faint scratches marred the smooth surface from her gripping it so tightly.

"Are you going to disobey me again?"

Cade drew his arm back and delivered a blow with such force that Kara's entire body shuddered. *Twenty.*

Kara mentally pleaded that Cade had satisfied his need to punish her having delivered a score of lashes. She didn't think her body could withstand much more. She knew the strength of her mentality had depleted to the point of defeat. Her slippery grasp on self-control was very close to being vanquished, and she was about to start screaming beneath the wicked blows of Cade's belt, personal dignity be damned. Though she could not speak to the actions of her future self in their entirety, Kara knew, in that dreadful moment, nothing in the whole expanse of the world could have provoked her into crossing Cade again. She would bend to his every desire, submit to his every request, provided she never had to feel the sting of the belt across her skin again.

"N-no, sir," Kara answered, choking on tears. Her unusual address had been an unconscious decision, the word startling her as it escaped her mouth. Cade hadn't asked for the title of formality, but something about the situation—his authority and her unavoidable submission— pulled the word *sir* from her lips.

Cade stilled at her response, his face awash with surprise as he shifted the belt in his grasp. Her words disarmed him as much as they stoked the burgeoning stirrings of passion and need that had begun the moment he bent and bared Kara over the desk. With those two, simple words, Kara had sealed her fate. She had provided him with the proof that he couldn't conclude her punishment. Not quite yet. She was close, so incredibly close to giving him everything. Her absolute surrender. "To truly learn your lesson, I think you need to be taken past your breaking point. One lash more than your limit to truly part with your self-detrimental disobedience once and for all."

Kara cried softly at the harrowing meaning behind his words. He wasn't done yet. He was going to keep hitting her. And she wasn't sure she could continue to take it. The next lash came so hard and so fast, Kara barely had time to register the sound of it hissing through the air before it struck mercilessly on the already broken skin of her backside. *Twenty one.*

Kara broke.

A scream tore from her throat, every last shred of composure completely obliterated beneath the overwhelming agony. Unable to resist her body's need to purge itself of the pain, she wept loudly, the pent up anguish escaping along with the tears. Kara had never allowed herself to cry with such abandon, not even after losing her parents. She had always managed to maintain control. And there she was, coming undone in the audience of a man she currently loathed more than anyone else on the godforsaken planet.

Panic stole the air from her lungs as Kara heard the rustle of the belt behind her. She couldn't possibly take another lash. She would certainly collapse or pass out or both. Could Cade truly be that cruel? The harsh bite of leather on her tender, bruised thighs answered her question. *Twenty two.*

Yes, yes he could.

When she heard the belt clatter to the floor, her tears fell abundantly, this time in relief. Was he done? Was it finally over?

"Kara," Cade breathed, his voice thick with emotion as he drew toward her. Having finished his unsavory task, Cade wanted nothing more than to tell Kara how proud he was of her unyielding strength, her submission, her complete surrender. His arms ached to hold her, to smooth away any lingering pain or embarrassment. Cade didn't regret his actions. Kara had earned the punishment, and he hadn't hurt her more than was duly necessary to exact her remorse. But the sight of Kara trembling as she remained bent over the desk, her cheeks stained with tears and the deeply colored marks of his belt written prominently across her skin, twisted at his insides in unusual ways.

Kara flinched as she felt Cade's touch at her hips, wary of being forced to endure more pain at his hands. Gently, almost reverently, his fingers found the hem of her nightgown and drew the soft material down over her legs, granting her the dignity of being covered once again. Kara sucked in a breath as even the silkiness of the thin dress felt like sandpaper on her tender and bruised skin. Cade's hands lingered on her thighs, stroking as though attempting to soothe, and Kara felt the anger rising within her to the point of bursting at his pretense of tenderness.

Hideaway

How dare he touch her like that after what he just did?

"Get your fucking hands off of me," Kara commanded coldly, her tears evaporating in the wake of her blossoming fury.

A flicker of hurt crossed Cade's face as he swiftly rescinded his touch, backing away slightly to allow Kara to rise and get her bearings without feeling suffocated.

Kara lifted her head gingerly, her right cheek feeling like it carried the bruising imprint of the desk after being crushed against the hard wood for such a long period of time. Her fingers were stiff as she pried them from the sides of the desk, identical deep red lines etched into the middle of her palms from grasping the sharpness of the edges. The overextended muscles of her body protested as she slowly lifted herself. Kara couldn't even imagine what the backs of her thighs and backside looked like, but they hurt like fucking hell. Standing straight with all the pride she could muster, Kara wiped the tears from her cheeks, smoothed the unruly mess that was her hair, and straightened the nightgown to appropriately cover what little it could of her breasts and thighs. Having fully composed herself, she directed the complete extent of her ire at Cade, meeting his cautious, questioning gaze with dark, hate-filled eyes.

She despised Cade. Completely. Irrefutably. Irrevocably. Every space in the entirety of her now hardened heart was reserved for the unfathomable loathing of the detestable man.

"Kara," Cade warned, disapproving of her misplaced anger.

"Do not say my name. You are unworthy of addressing me."

"*Unworthy?*" Cade questioned with a raised eyebrow.

"Would you prefer another adjective to describe your reprehensible character? I can think of several that are far less courteous and far more apt," Kara spat back, defiantly crossing her arms over her chest.

"Mind your attitude, Kara," Cade cautioned, feeling his anger rising to match her own.

"Or what?" Kara asked bitingly. "You'll beat me? *Again*?"

"Do I need to beat you again?"

Kara flinched at the threat, cursing herself for the habit of talking herself into an even worse situation. Biting back a spiteful retort for the sake of her already wounded backside, Kara settled into a stance that was a little less confrontational. "No," she answered quietly, the fiery outrage cooling to embers.

"Good. Because I would find no pleasure in having to punish you again. I've had a very long, tiring day, and I would like nothing more than to administer aftercare and go to bed."

"Aftercare?" Kara asked warily, fearful to be met with some other form of torture. "What the fuck is that?"

"I need to tend to your welts," Cade answered as though it were the most obvious thing in the world.

"If you actually gave a damn about my well-being, you wouldn't have given me welts in the first place!" Kara shouted back, entirely confused by his methodology of wanting to hurt her and then help ease her discomfort. Was he a sadist plagued with a messiah complex as well?

"As previously discussed, you earned them. But that doesn't mean I want you to suffer unduly," Cade explained as he moved closer to her with an outstretched arm, longing to touch her, comfort her, make her see reason. "I understand you're upset—"

Hideaway

"I'm not upset, I'm fucking livid," Kara replied hatefully, slapping his arm away from her in aversion.

Cade stilled where he stood, stunned and perplexed by her over abundant expressions of aggression and anger. Why was she acting as though she had been wronged in some way? It wasn't as though he had assaulted her in anger. He had calmly requested Kara submit to the whipping she'd earned. She had consented. "You accepted the punishment," Cade said confidently as though his assessment would prove the illogicality of her feelings and would put an end to their argument.

"Like I had a choice! If you think I willingly gave you permission to beat me, you're insane."

Cade's jaw clenched tightly in frustration. He ran a hand through his hair as he tried to formulate a response that would inspire rationality in the increasingly confounding woman. "You broke your promise," he reminded her, confused as to why he had to constantly reiterate her transgressions—her own bloody decisions—that had brought about the punishment she apparently found so offensive.

"Yes, I broke my promise," Kara affirmed through gritted teeth, annoyed to be readdressing the minor events of the day, yet again.

"You ran."

"Because I'm a fucking prisoner! That's what sensible prisoners are *supposed* to do."

"You knew there would be consequences if you were caught," Cade replied darkly, the harshness in his voice covering for the faint stabbings of guilt he felt at her accusation of being a prisoner. If he was entirely honest, that was exactly how he had treated her all day.

The knowledge did not sit well with him, but he resolved to deal with it at a moment when he was more rested and less exasperated.

"I knew you would act exactly like the domineering twat you're being right now," Kara responded bitterly, turning dismissively to walk in any direction that Cade wasn't.

Cade caught her viciously by the arm, jerking her around to face him and entrapping her tightly against his chest. "I have warned you not to turn your back on me, Kara Caine," Cade rebuked in a tone simmering with violence. "And I would thank you to watch your filthy fucking mouth."

Kara struggled against his hold, but battling against the strength of his arms was like trying to demolish an iron wall with bare fists. Finally, Kara conceded and went still against him. The moment Cade felt her submit, he relaxed his hold, stepping back so he could look at her face. Unsurprisingly, her eyes glittered with unconcealed hatred. Gently, Cade brushed his knuckles along her cheek, willing the tension in her expression and anger in her eyes to dissipate. He bent down until his forehead hovered a mere breath above her own, gazing deeply into her eyes in an attempt to disarm the defenses he watched her forge higher and more impenetrable with each passing moment.

"You earned your punishment. You paid for your disobedience. Now get over your self-righteous anger and let me tend to your injuries before they get worse," Cade entreated almost amicably, as though offering a truce.

Taking advantage of his softening attitude, Kara pulled herself from Cade's loosened grasp and threw her fists into his chest, shoving him away as hard as she could. Surprised by her aggression, Cade stumbled back slightly before regaining his balance.

"I would rather drink a hemlock cocktail than have your hands on me again after what you just did," Kara retorted spitefully.

Cade stepped toward her slowly, intentionally keeping his movements unthreatening as he reached for her again, driven by a singular need to right things between them, despite believing his actions were completely justified. Kara matched his step forward with another step backward, refusing to allow him to close the space between them.

"Get the fuck out of my room and let me suffer in peace, Caden," Kara ordered, her tone one of unflinching resolve.

Cade's jaw clenched tightly at her insolence, but his expression slowly softened into resignation. He had gotten what he came for, she had paid for her sins, and the least he could do was allow her privacy to lick her wounds. He had taken enough from her for one day. "As you wish," Cade agreed shortly. "There is arnica cream in the top drawer of the bathroom vanity. It can be applied topically to ease the pain and swelling from the bruises, though you may find it difficult to apply yourself."

"I'll manage," Kara answered curtly, eager to be free of his presence.

"Very well," Cade said in a mildly disapproving tone, making his way toward the exit. He opened the door, turning to glance at Kara one last time from the threshold. Cade knew she expected an apology, and he wished he could bestow one for the sake of smoothing things between them. But he regretted nothing of his actions, only that her choices had warranted them. Regardless of her feelings, her punishment had been an unfortunate necessity, and he would do it again if required. With nothing left to say, Cade walked out of the room, shutting the door quietly behind him.

Kara tensed anxiously, waiting for the scrape of the lock turning to announce that she was once again a prisoner. But the dreaded sound never came, just the soft tap of retreating footsteps. Alone at last, Kara sighed heavily in relief as she forgetfully fell back onto the bed in exhaustion. She yelped out loud, agony searing through every nerve in her body as her battered skin collided with the bed linen under the full weight of her body. Jolting upright, Kara headed for the bathroom in search of anything that would offer relief from the pain. Opening the drawer, Kara sifted determinedly until she found the tube labeled as arnica. Her nose crinkled at the strange, medicinal smell, but at that point she was willing to try anything. Standing in front of the full length mirror, Kara turned and gingerly lifted her nightgown to inspect the severity of the damage. She gasped sharply at the horrifying reflection.

Fuck.

Deep purple and maroon blossomed across her entire backside and thighs, speckled with pricks of red where Cade had delivered the harshest of lashes. He had marked her body with a collage of bruises, welts, and blood blisters. She knew the belt had hurt, but she had no idea Cade had delivered that level of destruction. He truly was a vindictive bastard. She would never forgive him for hurting her. She would never forgive herself for sleeping with him. Somehow, the intimacy that they had shared made the offense so much worse.

Hesitantly, Kara applied some of the cream to her fingertips and began to rub it on the welts. She inhaled sharply as the sting from the cream set in, pushing past the discomfort to thoroughly cover her injuries. Begrudgingly, she had to admit Cade was right about the challenges of self-application. The angle was difficult to manage, relying on only the mirror for direction, and she found it hard to brace for the incoming sting and apply the cream liberally at the same time. Difficulties be damned, she wouldn't allow Cade to touch her again. Not after what he put her though. She still couldn't believe that he had hit her with a belt. Worse, that she had allowed it. Perhaps the weeks in captivity were fucking with her rationality.

Having completed her task as adequately as possible, Kara walked achingly to the bed. Learning from her previous mistake, she slid awkwardly onto the bed on her stomach, careful to keep her nightgown from touching the punished flesh. Kara pulled the duvet up to only the bottom of her thighs, risking the chill of the winter night rather than the abrasion of fabric on her tender skin. Too exhausted to process her physical discomfort, Kara closed her eyes and willed sleep to come and steal away thoughts of Cade.

Twenty two. The bastard had hit her *twenty two* times. And that was exactly how many times she would stab Cade in his most valued appendage with the nearest pointy object the instant he put himself within an arm's reach of her.

CHAPTER ELEVEN

IT was hunger that at last drew Kara from her den of despondency. She was nearly resolved to starve for the day rather than subject herself to the sight of Cade's abhorrent face. But, as she would eventually have to make her descent into humiliation at some point, Kara chose to cross hunger off her list of emotions keeping rage and misery company. She planned to entertain the latter two for the foreseeable future.

It seemed an endless walk down the stairs to the large, unwelcoming foyer. At that moment, Kara desperately wished that the garish chandelier that hung above would unlatch itself and fall on her appreciative head. There was a ruckus coming from the dining room with shouts of good humored banter and Cade's hateful voice among them. Taking a deep breath and gritting her teeth in irritation at the sheer audacity of the bastard to find himself so pleasurably entertained, Kara entered the dining room. The clatter of utensils scraping against plates stopped instantly, and the din of voices fell silent. Kara stared into a sea of eyes marked by amusement and intrigue; Cade's eyes held something more, but she couldn't discern what. Attempting to ease the rocky tension between them, he rose gallantly to pull out a vacant seat for Kara. She ignored him completely, making her way to the opposite end of the table and as far away from Cade as she could manage. Cade's face fell slightly, his expression a mixture of injured feelings and concern, but he said nothing.

Jace openly studied Kara as she walked about the room, his eyes roaming over every inch of her body with an intensity that differed from his usual leering. There was a calculated appraisal in his gaze that made her even more uncomfortable than usual, Jace's eyes narrowing angrily as though her appearance had been deemed unsatisfactory in some capacity. Whatever the fuck that was about, Kara ignored him as well. The others merely stared, lacking the proper manners to avert their gaze after an unsavory amount of time spent gawking. Kara rolled her eyes as though she shouldn't have expected anything more from Cade's criminal underlings and made her way toward the table laid with breakfast. Thankfully, the murmurs in the room began to grow once again, conversations of market values and possible acquisitions dispersing the silence as Kara set about appeasing her hunger in peace.

"You still seem to be in one piece," Jace commented darkly, his scathing gaze moving from Kara to Cade, an open challenge in his eyes.

"Leave it alone, Jace," Cade dismissed shortly. "Kara's actions have been dealt with."

Refusing to get involved in their argument, though she seemed to be the topic of the disagreement, Kara made her way around the table to fill her plate with pastries, fruit, and yogurt. Deciding that she would call even more attention to herself by eating while standing, Kara eyed her chair warily, sucked in a deep breath, and sat down. She winced as the chair came into contact with the bruises of twenty two lashes courtesy of Caden Ashford's belt. A bitter laugh from Jace made Kara look up frantically in panic and embarrassment. Jace stared back at her viciously before transitioning his contempt to Cade.

"She lied to you. She ran from you. She put every single one of us at risk. And she walks away with nothing more than a fucking spanking? When did you go so goddamn soft?" Jace thundered at his boss.

Kara wished she had never left her room and simply allowed starvation to claim her. She felt the burning heat of mortification fill her face, her appetite entirely lost. There was no denying that the entire room now knew exactly what had transpired between her and Cade the night before. The public discussion of her retribution left her feeling doubly punished. Her eyes hesitantly found Cade, his face darkened with anger rather than embarrassment.

"Watch your fucking tone, Jace. The matter doesn't concern you, and I would suggest you keep your unsolicited opinions on my methods of discipline to yourself," Cade responded coldly.

"Like hell, it doesn't concern me! I was the one who had to retrieve your little pet when she ran away from home. She's a professional liability, and every minute she spends among us is an added risk. She should have been forced to retrieve the book by any means necessary, and we should have fulfilled our agreement with Avery. Then we should have been well compensated and bid good riddance to the pain in the ass librarian. But no, you're too fucking cunt struck to follow through."

"Get. The fuck. Out," Cade commanded with icy rage, jolting to his feet so abruptly that his chair fell to the floor behind him.

"Fuck this shit," Jace muttered angrily as he shoved away from the table before storming out of the room.

"Would anyone else like to share their unwarranted opinions on my authority?" Cade asked angrily as he glared about the room, four pairs of wide eyes fixed on him.

Ortega and Brax both shrugged silently, clearly not nearly as interested in Kara and Cade's personal drama as Jace was. Declan glanced at Kara guilty, clearly conflicted about how Cade had handled her disobedience, but he wasn't brave enough to challenge his boss. Silently, he shook his head in surrender. Kara glared at Cade openly, apparently the only one with enough balls to defy the overbearing bastard. Though she didn't give voice to her thoughts, she made sure Cade could read the hatred simmering brightly in her eyes.

"Good," Cade announced threateningly, his gaze fixed on Kara. "Then breakfast is fucking concluded. We have work to do." Cade strode toward the exit without sparing a second glance at anyone in the room. He knew they would follow. Or there would be fucking hell to pay.

AFTER that god awful breakfast, Kara made it her mission to avoid every despicable male presence in her vicinity as though her life depended upon it. She had attempted to ignore Cade entirely, but inhabiting the same house regretfully came with inevitable interactions. Even so, that didn't mean she couldn't treat the entire situation like a proper bitch. Anytime Kara and Cade shared breathing space, everyone was subjected to the burning hatred that radiated from every fiber of Kara's body like a fiery essence. She didn't feel the need to bother with the pretense of civility when everyone knew exactly what had transpired between her and Cade, and she would ensure they all knew explicitly how she felt about the arrangement.

That also meant forgoing any and all sexual activity with the worst bastard of them all, a fact which her pussy bemoaned far more than she did. The abstinence had given her clarity, allowed her to focus once again on finding some means of escape rather than focusing on all the pleasure she could be receiving at the mercy of Cade's cock. And mouth. And hands. Okay, maybe she did still *occasionally* fantasize about being fucked into a catatonic state by her captor, but she was at least trying to get her priorities straight.

The silent treatment was getting to Cade; she was beginning to see the cracks in his perfectly cool composure. He liked to be the one in control—actually, he demanded it. And Kara was stripping away that control bit by bit with every cold shoulder, ignored greeting, and silently enjoyed meal. And she did still eat with the others, merely for the sake of proving to everyone that Cade couldn't control her behavior or her attitude even if she was his prisoner. It was her fun little way of undermining his authority in front of his men. And it was working perfectly. She could see the others looking doubtfully between her and Cade, wondering why he was allowing her insolence to go so far. And honestly, she wondered why too. Why hadn't he just tried to beat her into submission like he had the other day? Maybe he realized that, try as he might, he couldn't break her. Or maybe, he missed the sex enough to strive to get into her good graces once more. But she had a feeling Cade's allowances had their limit. And the sinister glare he gave her at breakfast that morning suggested that his mercy would be running out sooner rather than later.

Kara spent the afternoon in blissful, Cadeless tranquility. The bastard and his band of obliging delinquents left the house right after breakfast, off to pillage and plunder or whatever the fuck they did to afford their luxurious lifestyle. Finally alone, she drifted through the manor with ease, exploring all the undiscovered rooms of the huge house without the weight of watchful eyes. In the absence of the cacophony of men's voices—one in particular—the manor seemed haunted by emptiness. As her imagination turned the winding halls and unfamiliar alcoves eerie and sinister, Kara neglected her explorations and headed for her safe haven.

As she turned the corner toward the library, Kara was startled by the rough assault of a firm hand clasped onto her arm, jerking her into the shadows and thrusting her toward a large, overpowering body. She found herself staring into the hardened eyes of the man she'd been trying to escape for days. "Cade!" she exclaimed in frustrated surprise. The bastard had stayed behind, no doubt to entrap her and force her compliance. "What are you doing here? I thought you left with the rest of the rest of the minions for New York?"

"I had a more pressing matter that required my attention," Cade answered evenly.

The implication stirred at the tension in her core that seemed ever present when he was near. Kara's eyes narrowed at the idea of *her* being a matter that needed his attention, but she didn't further engage in the conversation.

Cade released a frustrated sigh. "So what is it going to take for this needless sulking shit to end? I'm at my fucking limit with the silent treatment and death stares."

His phrase called to mind a similar one he'd used while administering a punishment she would never forget, and Kara was tempted from her vow of silence. "Well, if you're at your limit, I guess you just need one more," she replied as scathingly as possible. With the most murderous glare she could summon, Kara tried to jerk her arm free from his hold and walk away.

Cade's grasp held firm, refusing to let her get away that easily. Instead, he pulled her unwillingly toward the wall and trapped her with a firm hand on either side of her shoulders and his chest pinned against hers. His gaze held hers, and, in that moment, she could not find the strength to look away. "I will ask you one more time. What, Kara, will it take for you to make it past that minor episode of discipline and start behaving like a functioning human again?"

Kara's sense of indignation tingled at the accusation that her current behavior was anything *less* than human functionality. Heaven forbid, someone hold a grudge against the great Caden Ashford. Given his less than glowing personality, she was likely keeping company with a great many people who wished the man eternal damnation. Still seething, Kara took a moment to ponder his question. What exactly would it take for her to move on for the sake of enduring his company with a little less disdain? An apology seemed like the obvious solution. Though, considering Cade's character, that occurrence bordered on the edge of impossibility. Also, Kara doubted a meager apology would alleviate the feelings of animosity that had been festering since Cade had taken it upon himself to beat her into submission. No, she was out for blood. With a newfound delight for revenge, Kara settled on a compromise that was just as unlikely as an apology—though it held the possibility of being a great deal more cathartic. "How about you let me hit *you* with a belt?" she offered with a raised brow, a hint of challenge ringing in her voice.

Cade's face contorted with surprise that turned contemplative. Withholding an immediate answer, Cade reclaimed Kara's arm and drew her down the hall toward the closed doors of his study. He had an air of determination, but Kara didn't comprehend his intentions, the uncertainty of the situation leaving her uneasy. Practically dragging her into the room, Cade left Kara in silence by the edge of the desk and went to shut the door. Whatever was about to transpire, he required the privacy of closed doors.

Cade turned and walked toward Kara purposefully. He seemed to sense the fear in the room and absorbed it with a small level of amusement. He stopped, inches from Kara's still form, and addressed her with a look of pure intensity. "The punishment you received at my hands was not for my pleasure, as you seem to imagine. It served a purpose, and I won't apologize for it. However," he paused, placing his hands tenderly on either side of her face, willing her to read the sincerity in his eyes, "if it will help heal the bond of trust that I regretfully and unintentionally damaged, I am willing to offer you this."

Kara piqued with anger at his sheer denial of an apology, but that morphed into confusion when she considered how exactly Cade planned to absolve himself of the deed that had waged war on their relationship. As if to answer the question housed in her eyes, Cade reached for his belt with an undefinable expression and laid it down on his desk.

Kara drew a sharp intake of breath, apprehension and anxiety rolling over her in waves as she stared at the terrible implement lying there so threateningly. Though she had challenged Cade and given him a fair amount of attitude, she hadn't expected it to be enough to warrant another punishment. "Please, not again," Kara pleaded, looking up at him fearfully.

"You look so pretty when you beg, love," Cade whispered softly, brushing his thumb across her cheek. "But the belt isn't for you this time."

Cade met her wary eyes with an expression that was a combination of resignation and amusement as he reached for the buttons of his shirt, undoing them at a leisurely pace one by one. Fully unbuttoned, Cade removed the shirt and threw it unceremoniously on the floor. He stood before Kara fully naked

Hideaway

from the waist up, his dark pants riding low on his hips with the belt removed. He was a breathtaking site of sheer masculinity that demanded admiration—imperiously broad shoulders, a smooth, muscular chest, rippling abs, and the perfect outline of a V at his hips that drew her eyes unwillingly downward. Kara cursed the disarming effect that his body had over her own and felt the icy shards of animosity that had shrouded her heart against him slowly start to melt away. Searing her to the very core with a final provoking glance, Cade turned away and faced the desk, taking a firm hold with both hands and exposing his naked back and shoulders.

"Do your worst, darling," he provoked, his tone implying that he wasn't worried in the least about Kara's capacity for violence.

Kara's heart stopped, literally forgetting its function within her chest for a mere second as she processed Cade's intentions. Certainly he could not expect her to hit him? Not methodically, repeatedly, as though to purge his sins from his body; the idea was barbaric and preposterous. And yet, there lay his belt ready for the taking, his naked form willingly offered. She had asked him for this, had thought that only violence in turn could quell the anger that raged so fiercely within her. And in that moment, Kara was losing her nerve.

"Having second thoughts, Kara? Is beating someone not quite as enticing as you had imagined?" he questioned scathingly as he kept his back to her.

Damnit, he had called her out. Now she was determined to hit him, if only in a futile attempt to beat the smug pretentiousness out of his all too attractive body. Kara reached for the belt; it was heavier than she expected. After some practice testing the weight of it, Kara drew back her arm and threw the doubled end of the belt at Cade's naked back with some force. The blow landed with a mild thud across the center of his back.

"Certainly you can do better than that, love. I thought you hated me? Prove it," he goaded almost angrily.

His comments served their purpose of riling her up, and Kara threw all of her might into the next lash, hitting him squarely on the shoulders and leaving an angry red line across the entirety of his back. Having gained some confidence, Kara threw the next blow with more ease, marking his lower back right above his hips. She aimed the fourth lash at the middle of Cade's back, striking directly against the indented curve of his spine. Kara found little fulfillment in the administering of pain, but a silent need pushed her on, seeking some semblance of surrender on his part. If she could find the smallest crack in Cade's hardened, self-assured exterior, then maybe she could allow herself to trust him again. She swung again, an empty gesture, searching for some reaction from him. She hit him again. And again. And finally, as a blow hit the tender skin of his shoulders twice marked, a soft grunt of discomfort escaped Cade's lips. And that, small as it was, was enough a sign of surrender for Kara to consider her task complete.

She dropped the belt instantly as though its leather burned her skin and moved toward Cade in an offering of reconciliation. Her hands reached to touch the hot, reddened skin, marveling that those were *her* lashes on his back. As much as she hated the thought of hurting him, there was a primal satisfaction in seeing her marks on his skin. She reached desperate arms around his chest, hugging his back close to her front. Cade tensed in response. "Oh shit, I'm sorry," she said, instantly pulling away. "Does it hurt?"

"I think I'll live," Cade answered sarcastically as he turned around slowly to face her. "Much to my surprise, you've got a killer swing, love. I should reconsider the next time I hand you a weapon while you're mad at me. You might just kill me if I gave you the chance."

"I might," Kara answered confidently as she agreed with him. His light hearted manner set her at ease a bit, though she still harbored some feelings of guilt at having given in to her more vindictive nature.

Cade saw the furrowing of her brow and drew a finger to her temple to smooth the worried crease away. It was such a simple gesture, but it held a tenderness that awoke Kara's repressed feelings of desire with a sudden ferocity. Cade watched as the glint in her eyes transformed into need, and he matched her carnal hunger wholeheartedly. His firm hand captured Kara's neck and drew her mouth to his; she welcomed his devouring lips and lost herself to the kiss that righted all wrongs. Kara clawed at his bare chest needing more, no, *all* of him right in that moment. Her hands moved lower and lower until they found their prize: the button of his pants. In one skilled movement, Kara had the buttons undone, and Cade found himself with his pants at his knees.

"Let's even the playing field a bit," he said as his hands made quick work of removing and tossing her blouse aside.

Kara felt overwhelmed with gratitude as she considered how, by his willingness to lend control and submit to a measure of pain, Cade had reestablished the equality in their relationship once again. Gone was the fear that he would try to bend her to his will—in its place, Kara felt renewed trust and appreciation. And she had a very enticing idea of how to make that appreciation known. Meeting Cade's eyes with a look full of mischievousness, Kara dropped to her knees, reached for the waistband of Cade's boxers, and tugged them down. His massive cock sprang free, his impressive length nearly hitting her lips before she even settled her mouth on him. Kara gave his dick one slow, tantalizing stroke and then took him into her mouth. Cade released a primal growl of need and pleasure as he felt her hot mouth constrict around his cock as she ran her tongue along his length. Kara grinned as well as she could with her mouth full of cock and took Cade in deeper, fighting her gag reflex as he slid down her throat.

Cade placed a hand on Kara's head, half steadying himself and half guiding her onward, as he closed his eyes in rapture. Kara was skilled, more so than he would have expected from a lonely librarian who supposedly spent all her time in the solitary perusal of books. Then again, he supposed there must be literature written on the subject of oral pleasure. And if that was how Kara learned her blowing skills, they should definitely make it part of the university curriculum. Kara's pace quickened, and Cade could feel himself on the verge of release.

"Easy there, love. This isn't where I plan on coming right now," he cautioned as he lifted her up from her knees and placed her none too lightly on her back on the desk in front of him. "I've fucking missed this pussy." Cade's hands traveled up Kara's skirt and savagely ripped her lacy knickers right off of her. He grabbed both of her thighs in a firm grip as she wrapped her legs around his waist, pulling him closer. He paused with his cock pressed against her already soaked cunt. "Ready for me, love?" he asked, his voice raw with need.

Kara nodded her consent, and Cade buried himself inside her as deeply as her body would allow. She moaned at the delicious feeling of being so exceptionally full, and Cade thrust faster in response, pounding into her wet slit with a brutal pace that caused her back to scrape against the surface of the desk. The burn of the wood against her bare skin merely heightened her arousal, the pain melding with the pleasure in a tantalizing symphony of sensation. Cade's rough hands found Kara's bra and ripped it down to her stomach, causing her naked breasts to spill free and bounce against her chest in rhythm with his thrusts. His fingers latched onto her hard, aching nipples, twisting and pinching with such ferocity that Kara whimpered at the hurt in her sensitive buds even as she wanted more of Cade's torture.

"You like that, baby?" Cade asked roughly, his fingers pulling even harder on Kara's nipples.

"Yes," Kara answered breathlessly, resisting the urge to close her eyes and submit to the ecstasy.

"Tell me what you like, love. Beg me for it," Cade commanded, his chest heaving above her as he stilled and waited for her answer.

"Please..." Kara moaned.

"Please *what*? Be specific, or I'm happy to fuck this tight cunt and not let you come at all."

"Please touch my tits...make it hurt...please," Kara begged desperately as she writhed beneath him.

"Good girl," Cade replied, slamming into her so fast and so hard that the only thing keeping Kara from flying off the desk was his hand gripping her upper thigh so tightly that he'd definitely leave his fingerprints in bruises on her pale skin. His other hand traveled back up to Kara's tits, groping and pinching one before reaching over and slapping the other. She shrieked at the stimulation as her pussy clenched around his cock, strangling him tightly as she rode out her orgasm with almost pained whimpers as Cade pinched both of her nipples until her orgasm subsided and she lay breathless and exhausted against the desk.

Not giving her a moment to catch her breath, Cade grasped Kara behind the knees and threw her legs over his shoulders. "Keep them there," he ordered as he placed the head of his cock at her entrance and thrust inside her so deeply that she screamed.

"Stop, it's too much!" Kara protested as she tried to squirm away from the huge cock that felt like it was impaling her to her very organs.

Cade held her in place with his hands digging into her upper thighs. "You can take it," he told her as he continued his punishing assault on her pussy. "Can't you, love?"

Kara nodded, her eyes glistening with tears as she shattered beneath the overwhelming sensation of being so savagely, exquisitely fucked. She had never been so aroused in her entire fucking existence. She went over the edge again, Cade joining her almost instantly as he groaned with his own release, the desk shaking beneath them. He hovered above her as they tried to regain their breath in synchronized heaves.

"Well that was certainly diverting," Cade said as he crashed down on the desk and pulled Kara against his chest so he could feel her raging heartbeat against his.

"That's one word for it," Kara responded breathlessly, her chest still heaving irregularly from the exertion.

"Truly, I give it top marks. I really should endeavor to engage in make-up sex more often," he teased as he brushed her sweaty hair away from her cheek.

"Or you could just have sex without the argument," Kara countered.

"But where is the fun in that?"

Kara enjoyed the tenderness of Cade's caresses before she gathered the courage to ask the question at the forefront of her mind. "You…you said that you didn't punish me for your pleasure, but I'm pretty sure you enjoyed getting to take a belt to my ass. How am I supposed to reconcile those contrasting facts? Do you get off on hitting me or not?" Kara bit her lip nervously as she suffered the long silence before Cade composed a reply.

"The answer to your question is complicated. But, putting it simply, I would never hit you purely for my pleasure. I am willing to be a corrective force if your behavior warrants reproach, but I would never hurt you to satisfy my own personal needs. The pleasure I experience while punishing you is a byproduct of the experience of exacting total submission. It is much like the pleasure associated with sex, with the act of overcoming another body with your own and eliciting their release. It is an intoxicating adrenaline rush steeped more in power than pain. Though, if you ever wanted to explore the two together, I would be more than happy to oblige." Cade stroked Kara's cheek thoughtfully. "How did you feel when you were hitting me?"

"I didn't like it," Kara answered immediately, having no need to consider her response. Even though she thought she hated him at the time, she felt no pleasure in causing Cade pain. She had a hard time imagining how anyone could enjoy inflicting pain, even when a small voice in her head reminded her that it wasn't exactly logical for her to enjoy receiving pain from Cade's hands as much as she did. She supposed they were both fucked up in their own ways. Or perhaps the kinky bastard was rubbing off on her.

"That's because you don't crave power like I do," Cade answered darkly.

Kara had a premonition that she hadn't even begun to comprehend Cade's need for power and control.

CHAPTER TWELVE

CADE entered the dining room, momentarily glancing up from the work email he was reading on his tablet. He was startled to find the room much altered from its usual state as an orderly space of both business and sustenance. Tall candles lined the length of the table; their flames flickering against the darkness lent a warm, unequivocally romantic haze to the room. Instead of the usual fullness of dining company, the table was set for only two, Cade's usual place at the head and the place beside his. An arrangement of flowers, roses from the garden in shades of blush and burgundy, adorned the center of the table. The unmistakable scent of wine, lamb, and root vegetables wafted from the direction of the kitchen; it was a nostalgic smell, reminding him of Yorkshire and autumn and long walks in the countryside that ended with a hearty meal beside the fire to banish the damp cold. Cade was shaken from his reminiscing as the coordinator of the evening's welcome deviations entered from the kitchen.

"What's all of this?" he asked casually as Kara walked in from the kitchens, an oversized apron wrapped around her waist. They had spent the last few days in undisturbed peace, enjoying each other's company, christening about half of the manor with the most sinful fucking they could contrive, *even* in the library, and finding an easy rhythm of living alongside each other. Kara never used her own bedroom anymore, having moved into Cade's room without so much as a discussion. It had just happened organically, much as Kara was growing into a natural part of Cade's everyday life. In fact, he was beginning to forget what his existence had been like before she crashed into his life like a raging hurricane and destroyed everything in her wake. But nothing had prepared him for such a display of utter domesticity. The sight of Kara in a fucking apron sent all of the blood in his body rushing straight to his suddenly hard as hell cock.

Kara's cheeks flushed with the tinge of embarrassment. Or perhaps it was the rather large glass of wine she had downed as she waited for Cade's arrival. "I thought it might be nice if we had dinner, just the two of us," Kara responded shyly.

"Like a date?" he inquired teasingly. "Why, Miss Caine, are you trying to seduce me?"

"Do you require seduction, Lord Ashford?" Kara replied, the slightest smile breaking through her attempt to maintain a countenance of complete seriousness. She tried to conceal the slip with a hand to her lips, managing very much to look like a guilty child stifling giggles after sneaking a sweet.

In spite of himself, Cade found her ineptitude for coyness endearing. "Not at all. Against my better judgment, I find myself completely beguiled already," Cade answered with sincerity. The declaration, though true, troubled him. He could see his words jarred Kara as well, but she recovered her composure quickly.

"Well," she responded after the slightest awkward pause. "Just wait until you try dinner. I've been told my true powers of seduction lie in the kitchen."

Immediately, Cade conjured images of how he could make use of Kara in the kitchen, and it certainly was not for cooking. There was a sizable marble island in the middle of the kitchen that would suit his fantasies quite well. Thoughts of fucking her over the table were interrupted as Cade processed the entirety of Kara's statement. She had *seduced* someone in that manner before. Was it a past lover? A current one? Hell, she could have a fucking assortment of men for all he knew. And he didn't like *that* thought one bit. His pleasant thoughts of fuckery shattered by the treacherous blade of jealousy, Cade sulked as he dwelled on imagined adversaries for Kara's attentions. He did not care to share his possessions, least of all her.

The shadow of disappointment that passed over Cade's face was not lost on Kara, though she couldn't have guessed what caused it. She tried to revive the air of happy banter that Cade's curious mood change had dulled. "Would you like a glass?" she asked hospitably, gesturing with the bottle of wine in her hand that she had quite forgotten. "It's an excellent year, or so Mrs. Hughes tells me. I relied on her considerable expertise for tonight's menu."

"Yes, where is our venerable cook this evening?" Cade inquired, just noticing that she hadn't made her usual appearance to announce dinner.

"I gave her the night off. She works far too hard, and I thought she deserved an evening to herself."

"You gave my employee the night off?" Cade asked incredulously with a raise of an eyebrow. "And under whose authority are *you* giving orders? Perhaps we need to have a discussion concerning your position here, Kara. Ashford Manor has only one master, and you are looking at him."

The sternness in Cade's eyes left Kara feeling chastised and embarrassed. "I'm sorry," she stammered. "I didn't mean any disrespect. I've just missed cooking and didn't see any harm in letting Mrs. Hughes have a break. I apologize if I overstepped."

The wounded anxiousness in Kara's face tugged at Cade's heart, which seemed to be growing consistently softer since their acquaintance. Perhaps he had been too hard on her regarding Mrs. Hughes. The guilt of being the one to turn her happiness into distress was unsettling, and he longed to make amends. "Forgive my shortness; it's been a long day," Cade responded finally as he moved behind Kara, wrapped his arm around her waist, and placed a soft kiss on the side of her neck. "Here, allow me," he said as reached for the bottle of Sangiovese.

"Nope," Kara replied, pulling away from him. "I'm serving you tonight. Sit, please." She pulled out Cade's chair from the table and gestured for him to take a seat.

Hideaway

"As you wish," Cade answered with a laugh, sitting as requested. The irony of his following her orders after the confrontation between them just moments before was not lost on him.

Kara reached for Cade's wine glass and poured as professionally as she could before placing the glass delicately on the table beside him. "Your wine, sir," she announced in a tone of false formality.

"That's more like it," Cade answered in amused approval. She had no idea how much he liked it. "So, what's on the menu for tonight?"

"You'll see," she answered with a mischievous smile as she placed the bottle of wine on the table and whisked off to the kitchen.

Cade listened to the clatter of dishes and cutlery coming from the other room with curiosity. The whole playing house charade appeared to ignite a sort of giddy excitement in Kara. And it suited her quite well. There was something appealing about watching her bustle about the house in her apron and high heels, cooking for him and serving him, the perfect picture of a housewife. The scene was fun for a night, but a night only. He had a cook for cooking, maids for cleaning, and the only role in his house suited for Kara was in his bed. So, Cade had every intention of getting Kara out of that bloody apron—and the rest of her attire—as soon as possible.

The echoing tap of high heels across the marble floor announced Kara's arrival, her hands full with a dish that smelled heavenly. She placed her masterpiece on the table and watched for Cade's reaction.

"Shepherd's pie?" he asked in pleasant surprise.

"Uh-huh," Kara answered, feeling very pleased with herself.

"That's my favorite," Cade conceded. Clearly, she had done her research.

"I know," she replied smugly as she dished out a serving for Cade and herself. "I asked Mrs. Hughes what you liked best, and she gave me the recipe. She said you asked for shepherd's pie so often as a child that she was surprised you didn't turn into one yourself."

Cade wondered what else the old battle axe had told her. He had no idea that Kara had become such good friends with his cook. The idea unsettled him, though he didn't know why. Mrs. Hughes was practically family. Hell, she probably knew him better than his own mother after all those years, not that it was saying much considering the type of mother the great Lady Ashford was. And perhaps that was the problem. Cade was a private person; Kara knowing little details like his childhood longing for a peasant's dish left him feeling exposed. He would have to speak to Mrs. Hughes before she revealed any other intimate information regarding his personal life.

"Allow me," Cade offered chivalrously, rising from his seat to pull out Kara's chair from the table.

"Thank you," she answered graciously. "Please, eat before it gets cold."

Happy to acquiesce, Cade tucked in eagerly. It was delicious, indistinguishable from Mrs. Hughes's best work in the kitchen. Kara Caine was a woman of many talents.

"Well, how is it?" Kara asked, anxious for his opinion.

"Mmmm," Cade answered in a guttural sound of approval. "It tastes like home. Well, the good parts of home anyway."

"Are there bad parts? Of home, I mean," Kara asked, her face a mixture of kindness and sympathy.

Cade groaned inwardly; he abhorred talking about the past, even less so when it meant disrupting a delectable dinner. Although he supposed he brought it upon himself. He shouldn't have said a damned thing about home, it just slipped out. "Just your standard story of family dysfunctionality. Lady Ashford didn't care for motherhood, Lord Ashford didn't care for monogamy, soon neither of them cared for their marriage. I was often considered a minor inconvenience in their pursuit of things they truly enjoyed. After a time, I adjusted my expectations for parental affection and managed tolerably well. I had nannies and Mrs. Hughes, and eventually there was boarding school and university. I left home as soon as the opportunity in America presented itself, and fondness rarely draws me back."

"Mrs. Hughes said you have a brother. Does he live here, or is he still in England?"

Caught off guard, Cade lost his composure completely, the cutlery he held in his hand dropping to the plate with a loud clatter. "Fucking Mrs. Hughes," Cade said angrily under his breath, not low enough to escape Kara's notice. He took a moment to collect himself before answering. "No Kara, my brother does not live here or in England. He died, angry and broken and intoxicated, and he is lucky he didn't take anyone out with him in his destruction." Cade ran his fingers through his hair in irritation. "Are you quite finished with the investigation into my personal affairs?"

Kara was devastated, the color draining from her face in mortification. In merely trying to get to know Cade, she had unintentionally gouged open more than one wound of his past. "I'm sorry, Cade," she whispered sorrowfully. Their dinner had consisted of far more apologies and far less romance than Kara had imagined. Cade wouldn't look at her as she reached across the table to place her hand on his before he pulled away sharply. "I understand loss, Cade. You know I do." Her voice was broken, her eyes pleading.

Realization dawned on him, and it was Cade's turn to feel guilty. Her parents. Of course. He had been so focused on the inconvenience of having to relive and retell his past hurts that he had been completely insensitive to her experiences with pain and loss. Twinging with remorse, Cade grasped her hand and held it tightly. "Of course you do, Kara. Forgive me, again. I am not myself tonight. I prefer to keep the past in the past; bringing ghosts into the present only allows them to haunt you further." Looking deeply into her eyes, Cade saw his words had soothed the sorrow, but there remained a guarded caution in its place. "In recompense, I'll permit you to ask me one personal question of your choosing. This is a rare offer, so I'd suggest you ponder your query carefully."

"Can it be anything?" Kara asked, her eyes alight with excitement at the possibilities.

"Anything at all. Though I warn you, some answers may be harder for you to hear than for me to give. My life has been full of diverse experiences and interactions, a fair number of which would not appeal to your delicate tastes."

Kara sat in stunned silence for a moment, shocked by Cade's offer to divulge personal information. The man valued privacy almost as much as he valued control. So what did she want to know most about the enigmatic man she had somehow become entangled with? His darkest secret? His darkest deed? Did he make a habit of kidnapping women, or was she the first? Did he keep a staggering tally of the women he had fucked? Was she one of ten? One hundred? More? The thought of others raised a question that she'd stuffed far down beneath the surface of her consciousness the moment she'd started to develop feelings for Cade.

What happened to E?

"Have you ever killed someone?" Kara asked brashly before she could even try to form the question with more finesse or detail.

"Yes," Cade answered simply, his voice devoid of any emotion one might associate with the confession of murder. "Does that frighten you?"

"I could scarcely call myself human if it did not," Kara responded shakily. She stared down at her hand, still firmly held in Cade's. Did he kill *E*? Was she wearing the clothes of a murdered woman?

"Do you wish to leave?" Cade asked courteously.

"I'm not sure," Kara answered truthfully. She *should* want to leave. She should want to run as far away as possible and never look back. But something kept her grounded, something that common sense and intellect and rationality could not overcome.

Cade could see Kara grappling with reason and emotion, the two battling for dominance, and he sympathized. He supposed natural moral instincts dictated that Kara remove herself from whatever their relationship may be. That was the last thing he wanted her to do, but the decision must be hers alone. "Would it help if I added that her death was not my intention?" Cade elaborated, hoping, perhaps selfishly, that he could keep Kara a while longer.

"It was an accident?" Kara asked in clarification, allowing herself to breathe for the first time in what felt like ages.

"On my part, yes, a tragic one, though I still blame myself for the outcome."

"You can't possibly blame yourself for an accident, Cade. I tried after what happened to my parents, but in the end you have to accept that there is nothing anyone could have done to change it."

"Unlike the car accident that took your parents, I wasn't blameless in her death, Kara. It wouldn't have happened if it weren't for my actions, and I will always carry the guilt with me. I have learnt to accept it, much as I hope you can accept me in spite of it."

Kara thought a moment before answering. "For now, I can accept the man that I know, however mysterious and fragmented the pieces of your composition may be."

"For that, I am very grateful," he answered, his eyes tender and thoughtful as he gave her hand a light squeeze. "Now, Miss Caine, we've spent a fair amount of time delving into my dark past this evening. It seems hardly fair for you to escape unscathed."

"Trust me, I am quite the open book," Kara said with a laugh.

"We shall see. Tell me, what is the most devious deed an upstanding academic such as yourself has ever committed?"

"You eat, and I'll think. Deal?" Kara said as she took a bite of dinner herself.

"Deal. The shepherd's pie really is quite delicious," he said as he started eating as well. "Mrs. Hughes might have some competition if you intend to stay."

"Very funny," Kara answered with a laugh, confusing Cade as to whether she was laughing about the cooking or the staying.

"Time is ticking, Kara," Cade reminded as he finished what was on his plate.

"Give me a minute!" Kara responded shortly, never liking to be rushed when she had an assignment.

Cade went for a second portion of dinner, watching in amusement as Kara scrunched up her eyebrows in concentration. She was considering all her misdeeds from birth, no doubt. He was sure it was a compilation of late book returns, missed stop signs, jaywalking, and maybe even a drink or two underage. The idea of Kara being capable of anything truly deviant was unfathomable.

"Time is up, Miss Caine."

"It's doctor, for fuck's sake! If you're going to be weirdly formal so frequently, you might as well use the appropriate title," Kara declared with a huff.

"But where is the fun in that, Miss Caine, when I know it irritates you so much?" Cade answered with a bastardly smirk. "Let's hear it. Worst thing you've ever done. Astonish me."

"Okay, no judgment?"

"After my own admissions, I hardly have any standing to judge."

"Okay," she started, taking a moment to brace herself for the confession. "I had sex in the library, during open hours, in the Children's Literature section." Kara looked away in embarrassment.

Cade laughed so loudly and so hard that his eyes watered. Insulted by his amusement, Kara punched him as hard as she could in the arm, though the assault had no effect on his laughter, which continued. With a huff of irritation, Kara gathered the dishes, silverware, and remnants of their dinner into a single stack, appreciating the loud sound each item made as they clashed together, an obvious signal to Cade that she was pissed. Grabbing the two wine glasses in a single hand and the tower of dishes in another, Kara stormed out of the room and into the kitchen.

Cade listened to the ruckus ensuing from the kitchen without a single twinge of guilt. At times, Kara was so delicately sensitive he feared she'd fall apart in his hands. Other times, Kara was so fiercely strong and defiant that a man less brave than himself would hesitate to cross her. At that moment, she was a conflicting concoction of the two. There was something endearing about her storming about like some imperious force as though those four inch heels made her the biggest, most imposing person in the room. They did not, but he wouldn't be the one to deprive her of the delusion.

Kara entered the dining room once again, drying her wet hands on the apron around her waist before settling into her chair. Having a moment to herself in the kitchen seemed to have slightly improved her mood, which now hovered a touch above sulking. She leveled a gaze at Cade, daring him to approach their previous conversation at his own risk. If he had a modicum of decency, Cade would have heeded the silent warning. He did not.

"So," Cade began, pausing for dramatic effect, "that's the worst thing you've ever done? You humped next to 'Humpty Dumpty?'"

"Hilarious," Kara responded with an eye roll.

"You got dick on 'Hickory Dickory Dock?'" Cade continued, self-impressed with his wit.

"Are you finished?"

"You," Cade stopped to think for a moment, "diddled by 'Hey Diddle Diddle?'"

"Stop it!" Kara berated in irritation. Clearly he wasn't taking her seriously.

"Have you seen the titles of nursery rhymes? They're overtly suggestive. Truly, that is the most disreputable thing you've done in your entire life—you've banged in the kiddie corner at the library? Wait, did the children watch? That *would* be fucked up."

"Of course not! We did it in the Children's Lit section because it's always empty at the university. And, in case you weren't aware, having sex in a public place is illegal. I think taking the risk of being seen and arrested to enjoy a quick fuck is a level of impropriety not to be taken lightly," Kara argued with as much dignity as she could.

"Yes, you do lead a very provocative life, Miss Caine. I worry my honor as a gentleman might be impugned by our mere association," Cade responded with an admirable attempt at keeping a straight face.

"You're such a bastard, Caden," Kara berated with a scowl.

"Yes, you've mentioned that. *Repeatedly.*"

"Alright, enough about me," Kara announced as a change of subject. "Did you save enough room for dessert?"

"I believe I could rouse an appetite for something sweet."

Kara rose to retrieve the cake she had made from the kitchen, but Cade stood quickly and grabbed her hand before she could make her way from the table. He pulled her close, her body tightly wedged between the table and himself with no room for escape.

"Cade, what are you doing? The dessert is in the kitchen."

"Correction," he answered, locking his hands around Kara's waist and sliding her onto the smooth wooden surface behind her. "Dessert is on the table."

"Cade!" she half-shrieked, half-giggled.

Cade embraced her, his hands moving along her back as he searched for the laces of the apron, his fingers moving deftly as they untied, removed, and threw the apron on the floor. Next, his hands found the laces that wrapped her dress slightly above her waist. With one quick pull, the bow was undone. Cade opened her dress, easily revealing the bare skin and bits of pink lace underneath. He sighed in appreciation. Kara saw the hunger in his eyes; his raw desire ignited something deep within her, a carnal intensity that she had never quite experienced with anyone else. Perhaps because no one else had ever thrown her on a table and declared her dessert.

No longer satisfied with the mere sight of her, Cade brought his lips to her neck, drinking in the taste of her with the ferocity of a man whose thirst could never be quenched. Her skin was burning with warmth though she shivered beneath his touch. She smelled of violets and strawberries. She tasted of salt and earth. Cade's mouth trailed kisses across the exposure of Kara's breasts. He moved lower, planting a line of kisses down her abdomen. He nipped at the curve of her hip before capturing the edge of her panties with his teeth, tugging to pull them down to her thighs.

Kara inhaled sharply as Cade exposed her sensitive pussy. With a skillful move of his hand, he slipped off her knickers entirely and tossed them over his shoulder. Cade trailed a single finger down the length of Kara's leg from hip to heel. He grasped both of her ankles and pulled her to the edge of the table, spreading her legs, bending her knees, and placing her feet flat on either side of the table. Kara was left bare and spread wide open before him; it was without a doubt the most exposed she had ever felt in her life, lying naked on a table like an object to be examined. It was both excruciatingly uncomfortable and exhilarating at the same time.

Cade admired the exceptional view for a minute before drawing his chair close to the table and positioning himself between Kara's open legs. He looked up at her and offered a mischievous smile before diving into the soft folds of her cunt. Kara gasped as she felt his mouth on her, his skilled tongue caressing her clitoris with a perfection of speed and position. She moved her hips in rhythm with the circular motion of his tongue. Her hands slid into his hair, pulling him closer. She moaned—a sound of desire and desperation and unadulterated need. Cade grasped her thighs tightly, his fingers digging into the tender skin as he locked her in position beneath his mouth. Kara was close; her back arched, her legs tensed, her toes curled. Cade felt the tightness of her body and moved to push her right over the edge of ecstasy. Simultaneously, he sucked hard on her clitoris and plunged two fingers inside of her wet slit.

Kara came loudly, eagerly meeting Cade as he thrust his fingers inside her and lapped at her pussy until he had rung every ounce of pleasure from her body. Kara collapsed on the table, orgasm flushed, sweaty, elated, and exhausted. Cade smiled in appreciation, licking his lips as he savored the taste of her on his tongue. Kara closed her eyes and enjoyed the briefest reprieve before she felt Cade's cock ram inside her. Kara moaned at the sensation of being filled completely, her pussy still tight and spasming from the orgasm. Cade moved quickly, fiercely. He grabbed her legs and pulled her down till she hovered halfway off the table. Kara reached above her head and clung to the edges of the table to steady herself. Cade slammed into her hard, grasping her hips and pulling her as close as possible. The table squeaked loudly in protest as they fucked their way to euphoria. When they came, it was in unison, their moans of pleasure melding together as they surrendered to the discovery of an ecstasy that seemed only to be found within each other's bodies.

After finishing, Cade laid Kara down gently and pressed himself against her, hovering over the table and supporting himself with an elbow on either side of her head. He bent to place a kiss just below her chin, stroking his thumb along the curve of her jaw. He was growing increasingly appreciative of Kara and her many talents, sexual and otherwise. As surprising as it was for a man of his experience, he had never fucked where he ate his dinner. The experience had much to recommend itself, and that table had just become his favorite piece of furniture in the whole damn manor.

"Tired?" Cade whispered against Kara's ear, rousing her from whatever thoughts had been occupying her attention.

"Mmhmm," she answered with a nod, sounding blissfully happy.

"I see you enjoyed dessert as well," he said with a laugh.

"I enjoyed the sex, though, technically, you were the only one who *ate* dessert."

"My apologies, Miss Caine, you are quite right. Allow me to remedy the situation," Cade responded as he rose from the table, picked up Kara at the waist, and put her over his shoulder.

"Cade! What are you doing?" Kara yelped in surprise as she was jostled in the direction of the kitchen.

"Getting you dessert," Cade answered as he kicked open the kitchen door and walked through. He set Kara on the counter a little roughly beside a lovely cake decorated with candied lemons and edible flowers from his hothouse. "Ah, see, dessert," he said, gesturing grandly at the cake as though he had just magically produced the cake from thin air.

Kara laughed at the welcome silliness. "It's beautiful. Made it yourself, did you?"

Hideaway

"Absolutely. Only the best for you," Cade answered seriously before very determinedly beginning to rummage through the cupboards in the kitchen.

"And what is the purpose of this grand expedition?" Kara asked in amusement as she watched Cade systematically search through the vast collection of cabinets in the manor's kitchen.

"To my great personal embarrassment, I rarely venture into the kitchen," he answered, continuing to look around. "Mrs. Hughes has always provided everything, so there was never any need."

"Of course not," Kara responded with an eye roll. He really was a pampered prince. Or lord, or whatever. Realizing that her dress was still completely open, she tried to cover up as Cade rustled around the kitchen; she crossed her legs to make up for the fact that Cade had left her panties lying somewhere on the dining room floor.

"Eureka!" Cade announced triumphantly, holding up two coffee cups.

"Does Caden Ashford actually know how to make coffee?" Kara questioned doubtfully.

"He can manage," Cade answered with a touch of chagrin. "And none of this," Cade chided, noticing that Kara had fixed her attire. He walked over to her and quickly undid the bow, opening her dress. Sliding a hand between her thighs, he spread her legs open. When Kara resisted, he spread her open wider. "Stay like this," he commanded with a stern look.

Kara greeted his bossy attitude with a glare of disdain, but she obediently kept her thighs positioned where he placed them on the counter. Modesty was something she was growing less accustomed to the more time she spent in his company. She glanced over at Cade as he fiddled with the coffee machine and its accompanying accessories, smiling in amusement as she considered the unexpected disadvantages that came with a life of privilege. At some point, she'd have to ask him for an account of all the basic life skills he had made it well into adulthood without acquiring. As the delicious smell of coffee filled the air, it was apparent he had somehow won his battle with the brewing machinery.

"Your coffee, m'lady," Cade said as he carried over two steaming cups of brown liquid that did indeed resemble the aforementioned beverage.

"Is it safe to drink?" she asked, eyeing the coffee cup suspiciously.

"It's coffee beans and hot water. I doubt there's much I could do to render it dangerous for consumption."

"Never doubt your abilities," Kara answered with a sarcastic laugh.

"Just drink," Cade said, rolling his eyes as she hesitantly took a sip.

"Mmm, tastes good actually," Kara confirmed in surprise.

"See, I know what I'm doing," he answered, giving her a light nudge on the shoulder. "Now, forks."

"They're in the second drawer to the left," Kara instructed, feeling magnanimous enough to save him from another scavenger hunt in the kitchen.

Cade came back with a single fork in his hand. "We can share," he declared mischievously.

"I should have known you would try to put something in my mouth."

Hideaway

"An excellent idea for later," Cade answered with a salacious smile. "But for now, cake." Cade indelicately thrust his fork into the side of the cake and scooped up a piece that was a fair amount bigger than bite-sized. "Open up," he instructed.

With a measure of embarrassment, Kara opened wide, feeling rather like an infant being spoon-fed. Cade fed her the forkful of cake, getting a smudge of buttercream on her cheek as he put it in her mouth. Kara tried not to giggle as she struggled to chew the huge piece of cake with as much ladylike decorum as possible. As doubtless was his intention, she did not succeed. Cade wiped the frosting from her cheek with his finger, bringing it to his mouth for a taste.

"Mmm, delectable," Cade judged in approval. "I think I'll have to try some more," he said as he drew close and kissed the sugar sweetness from her lips.

"My turn," Kara announced, snatching the fork from Cade's hand as he went in for another kiss. "Open up," she mimicked, digging into the cake to achieve the largest bite possible.

Cade obeyed dutifully, downing the cake in what appeared to be a single gulp. Dissatisfied with the ease in which he had consumed his portion, Kara swiped her finger along the side of the cake and deposited a large dollop of frosting directly onto Cade's nose. She stifled a giggle as Cade stood there in stunned silence for a moment. Collecting himself, Cade launched a counterattack and buried his face between her breasts, smearing the frosting across her chest.

"Oh no, I seem to have made a mess," Cade said with a devious grin. "Here, let me clean you up." Cade unfastened the front clasp on Kara's bra—she was lucky to have made it that far into the night with it on—and set about kissing, nipping, and licking her tits until any remnant of frosting had been wiped clean.

"I believe you've tasted quite enough of me tonight," Kara scolded as she fought to push him away from her breasts.

"What can I say, you're like a craving I can never satisfy."

"Well, the only craving I care about satisfying right now is my sweet tooth," she said as she dug the fork into the cake, this time taking a bite for herself.

"Allow me," he said, stealing the fork from her hand and shoveling another bite into her mouth. He quickly fed himself before thrusting more cake into Kara's mouth.

"Slow down," she choked out with her mouth full.

"With your body this exposed, you aren't going to make it much further tonight without being fucked. So unless you want me to take you here on this counter, eat up."

"Yes, sir," she answered obediently after a quick gulp of the remaining food in her mouth.

The words sent a jolt of excitement to more than just his cock, and Cade stood transfixed by the beguiling, baffling women who had serendipitously stumbled into his life. Or rather, she had been dragged into his life against her will, kicking and screaming along the way. And yet, there she sat, of her own volition, wrapped within his arms, her eyes full of warmth and hunger, her rosy lips begging to be kissed. He did kiss her, long and hard. She tasted like lemons and violets and sweetness. Their kiss deepened as Cade pulled Kara close and twisted his fingers in her hair. Cade wanted more. He wanted to consume her, body and soul. The feeling was both exhilarating and terrifying. When he finally pulled away, they were both breathless with desire and need. Cade tenderly ran his thumb along her bottom lip, swollen from the passion of their embrace, and turned his darkened gaze to meet hers.

"I'm rather fond of you, Miss Caine," Cade said softly after a moment of heavy silence, his voice deep and rough. It was a simple confession, but Cade's eyes burned with a depth of affection which seemed a great deal more than fondness.

"I'm rather fond of you too, Lord Ashford," Kara retorted in the most dreadfully pompous British accent she could summon.

"God, is that really what I sound like to you?" Cade asked as he laughed out loud. He appreciated her attempt to lighten the mood of the room, which had been steering dangerously toward seriousness. Fuck, what was happening to him?

"Oh no, you sound much worse," Kara answered teasingly.

"Alright, enough of your cheek. Time to get you to bed," Cade announced as he lifted her off the counter.

"Ready to go to sleep already?" Kara asked with a suspicious raise of a brow.

"My love, you will be lucky if I allow you to sleep at all tonight."

CHAPTER THIRTEEN

KARA practically hobbled down toward the dining hall, still feeling the lingering imprint of Cade's massive dick deep within her womb. Every muscle in her body ached in protest of Cade's delicious abuse. Throughout the night, he'd made her come so many times she lost count of the number of orgasms he forced from her needy pussy. Her neck was covered in hickeys, her breasts sported the red marks of his teeth, and her hips bore the bruises of his fingers from where he held onto her and fucked her like a madman. She was relatively certain she'd been kidnapped by a villain in possession of the highest sex drive in the whole damn world.

The bed was empty when she woke up, so she assumed Cade would be preoccupied with work and wouldn't spend the day bending her to the will of his overactive cock. Good. As much as she missed his company when he was busy with clients, her poor pussy could use a reprieve. The table was full when Kara walked into the dining room, the men already in heated discussion. She tried not to pay too much attention to the details of their business talks; she had enough difficulty rationalizing that she enjoyed fucking her captor without being reminded that he also did illegal shit for exorbitant amounts of money. One thing at a time.

Drawing a collection of reproving glares, Cade broke off his conversation, rose from his seat, and pulled out the chair to his right, gesturing for Kara to sit beside him. She blushed as she felt the attention of several pairs of eyes on her as she walked toward Cade and sat down, hoping that she'd concealed the hickeys enough to prevent everyone in the room from knowing that she was fucking their boss. Although, from the lingering, molten intensity of Cade's stare at that moment, she was almost completely sure it was obvious what the two of them did behind closed doors. Or on the fucking table. The same table from which they were all currently eating breakfast. The inappropriate memories of the night before sent a shock of arousal and need straight to her overused pussy as heat flooded her pale skin.

"Good morning," Cade whispered seductively against her ear, his lips so close it was almost a kiss.

"Morning," Kara answered softly, looking around guiltily as the others at the table stared with expressions lacking in amusement. It wasn't her fault that their boss had a perpetual hard-on and she was the only female in the house other than Mrs. Hughes. If they were annoyed, they could take it up with *him*.

Cade's hand inconspicuously caressed her lower back as he pushed in her chair before taking his seat with a slight smirk on his lips. The man was utterly incorrigible. Kara subtly kicked his leg under the table as a warning to behave in front of the others. In retaliation, Cade reached across her seat and pinched her thigh so hard that Kara had to stifle a yelp. Concealing his mischievousness with a blank expression, Cade turned back to Jace to continue the business Kara's entrance had interrupted, keeping his hand on Kara's thigh as a threat for any further insolence. Kara rolled her eyes in annoyance and set about filling her plate with breakfast.

The chaotic cacophony of men's raised voices halted with the trill of a phone ringing. Kara looked to Cade in surprise. He didn't allow the use of phones at the table; it was one of his many ridiculous, controlling rules, and the men abided by it religiously, always making sure to keep their electronic devices tucked away during meal times. The most unusual aspect of hearing a ringtone at the dining table was that it was coming from Cade's pocket. His movements stiff and full of tension, Cade pulled out his phone and looked at the caller.

"*Fuck*," he breathed before swiping the screen to answer it. "Ashford," Cade answered brusquely. He waited impatiently as the person on the other line rushed out an explanation. "Damnit, I knew this would turn into a fucking shit show. Have you heard from Jensen?" He waited as the caller barked out something. "*Fuck*. Don't do anything else right now," Cade ordered, shoving his chair hard across the floor as he stood abruptly. "No, leave it. I'm heading over." Cade motioned for Brax to follow him as he stormed toward the exit, phone still in hand.

Hideaway

Ortega checked his phone and left soon after, though Kara couldn't be sure if his departure was related to Cade's miniature explosion. She found herself hoping that it wasn't, before chiding herself for being empathetic towards Cade's work stresses. He was probably just having issues stealing a priceless piece of history or depriving some unsuspecting elite of their family heirlooms. God, she seriously needed to be rethinking her relationship with such a depraved man. Unfortunately, her pussy was morally bankrupt at the moment.

"What was that about?" Declan asked as he looked toward the dining room doors with his dark eyes wide in surprise. He wasn't used to seeing Ashford lose control like that. In fact, before Kara arrived, he'd never seen his boss lose his cool.

"You don't want to know, kid," Jace answered cryptically. "You might want to eat up. We'll probably be shipping out soon if that call was who I think it was."

Kara resisted the urge to press Jace further about what he knew about Cade's sudden departure. Cade kept her in the dark regarding that aspect of his life, and that was exactly how she wanted to keep it. Brushing aside her inconvenient interest in Cade's dark business matters, Kara tried to focus on her breakfast. Desperate for a hit of caffeine to lift the morning mood, she reached for the coffee carafe, jolting when she felt the brush of fingertips against hers. Realizing that Jace had reached for the coffee in the exact same moment she did, Kara pulled her hand away sharply, hating the feel of his skin against hers and the memories his touch conjured.

"Sorry," she responded hastily out of habit, not entirely sure why she should be apologizing for reaching for something at the same time as him. Social etiquette was a peculiar construct.

"It's all right," Jace answered with an air of gentility that didn't quite suit him as he lifted the carafe and reached for Kara's cup. "Allow me," he offered, filling her mug before she had a chance to decline.

"Thanks," Kara answered suspiciously, again feeling obligated to be cordial and polite with the man who tried to assault her.

"Let me guess, you take it black?" Jace asked, his eyes glittering with a dark sort of amusement.

She did take it black. But there was something about Jace having the audacity to correctly assume her taste in something as simple as coffee that had Kara gritting her teeth in irritation. So she did the least logical thing she could think of: she lied. "Cream and sugar actually. Heavy on the sugar," Kara responded sweetly as though she hadn't just requested a revolting concoction for the sake of disappointing the smug asshole.

"Sweet and light, huh? I'm surprised, Dr. Caine. I would have thought you preferred something more…dark," Jace implied suggestively as the brightness in his eyes turned sinister.

"Nope, nothing dark here," Kara answered uncomfortably, hoping she was imagining the innuendo in his words as she gulped down the far too sweet coffee.

Jace was silent a minute, studying her thoughtfully in a way that made Kara's skin crawl. She looked for a distraction, latching onto the only other person in the room. "Hey, Declan, could you look up the forecast for today? I was hoping to go riding if there isn't any more rain and it's not too muddy from yesterday." Spending time outside with the horses was always a nice diversion from her life as a pampered prisoner.

"Sure," Declan answered helpfully with a smile that was a little too eager as he pulled out his phone.

Kara had a sneaking suspicion that the boy had a bit of a crush on her. She recognized the bright look in his puppy dog eyes; she'd gotten rather used to ignoring it with students over the years. Declan was sweet and inexperienced, and Kara wondered for the hundredth time what on earth had led him to associate with criminals like Jace and Cade. They'd crush his innocence before it even had a chance to bloom.

"Lucky for you, it'll be mostly sunny the whole day," Declan declared brightly before setting down his phone and grabbing another scone off the tray in front of him. "I could walk down there with you if you'd like some company?"

"Thanks, Declan, that's really sweet of you," Kara replied kindly, trying to think of the easiest way to turn him down for his own good. If Cade caught her traipsing about the countryside alone with one of his men, it might not go over very well for either of them. "But you should probably stay close to the house, just in case Cade needs you."

"Oh yeah, that's true," Declan answered, sounding a little bit disappointed.

"Yes, I'm sure Ashford would be *lost* without Declan here," Jace intruded into the conversation scathingly.

"I don't recall asking for your opinion, Jacen," Kara spat back.

"Dude, I didn't know your full name is Jacen," Declan commented in amusement, the sarcasm in her response completely going over his head.

"It's not," Jace answered in annoyance. "Dr. Caine just likes to pretend that she's smarter than everyone else. Isn't that right?"

"I do *not* think I'm smarter than everyone else," Kara retorted angrily.

"Oh, I think you do. I think you're a spoiled little princess who thinks they're too good for the rest of us."

"Fuck you, Jace," Kara said with a bitterness that was a front for her hurt feelings. She was *not* spoiled, and she did *not* think she was better than everyone. Jace was just being a dick like usual.

"Is that what you want, baby? You want me to fuck you? Or is Ashford already doing that for you?"

Declan looked at Jace in shock while Kara looked at him with nauseated embarrassment. "I'll take that as a yes," Jace answered smugly, judging the warmth flooding Kara's cheeks as confirmation of his accusation. "I was wondering why he put you in *her* room, but the answer is obvious now. He wants to use you like he used her."

Kara blanched at Jace's words, the breakfast in her stomach suddenly revolting. "W-what do you mean? Who is *she*?" Was Jace talking about *E*? Did he know her? Did he know what happened to her?

"Hmm, I see Ashford didn't tell you. That's interesting," Jace answered vaguely, nodding his head as though understanding something that no one else in the room did. "You are full of surprises, Dr. Caine. I didn't think you'd be into that sort of thing."

Hideaway

"How did Cade...use her?" Kara asked softly, terrified of his answer.

"Well, it's no fun if I tell you, Kara. You'll have to figure it out," Jace replied with a malicious smile.

Kara looked at Declan, but he was clearly just as confused as she was. As much as it terrified her, she was going to have to ask Cade about E. She didn't like Jace making threats that she didn't have enough information to understand. The general unease in the room was disrupted when Ortega barged in through the doors with an expression that Kara had started calling his *business face* fixed sternly upon his features.

"Boys, let's go. Ashford is already in the car," Ortega shouted across the room, clearly not in the mood for patience that morning.

Declan jumped to his feet instantly while Jace downed the rest of his coffee and then followed suit. The three men hurried out of the room, keen to obey their precious dictator's command, leaving Kara alone to enjoy the rest of her breakfast in unexpected peace. The silence of the dining room broke with a slight buzz that sounded distinctively like a phone vibrating with an incoming notification. Kara's heart stuttered for a moment, overwhelmed with what was certainly false hope because there was no way in hell that one of her captors had left a phone within her reach. Already braced for disappointment, Kara searched her surroundings for the source of the buzzing, freezing when her eyes fell on Declan's spot at the table. Lying forgotten on the table beside an unfinished glass of orange juice, there was a phone.

Declan had left his phone. And perhaps given her a chance at freedom in return.

Kara ran to the black device, not sure how much time she had before the men came back. She knew that she might have only minutes and needed to think quickly. After turning the phone on, there was a password prompt when face recognition obviously failed. Without unlocking the phone, she could still make an emergency call to the police, but that option didn't offer much chance of success. The manor was gated and monitored by security. Cade would have more than enough warning before the police set foot on the property, he had enough men and resources to keep her hidden or move her to another location, and when he finally dismissed the police's concerns, Cade would be fucking pissed at her. And since she didn't have any other numbers memorized, the call option was basically useless. She would have to try to crack Declan's code, knowing full well that the statistical chances of her success were slim at best. Just for the hell of it, Kara started with the easiest combination she could think of.

1-2-3-4-5-6.

Holy shit.

Against all fucking odds, the phone unlocked. What the hell was Cade doing with a kid who protected his phone with a password based on *numerical order*? With a sense of urgency, Kara considered the best use of the lifeline in her hand. She wasn't sure if she was in a position to escape Cade completely; he was too powerful, and the manor was too secure for her to be able to slip away again. Evading Cade's clutches would take far more strategy and advantage than a mere phone could provide. In fact, the more she thought of it, the less convinced she was that the phone would be able to offer any

Hideaway

form of escape. The best she could do was to ensure the safety of others threatened by Cade and his illicit affairs with Avery Reed.

She first sent a quick email to her sister to tell her that she was alright and warned her to be careful about anything shady or out of the ordinary in her life. She couldn't be too careful about mercenary bastards using her sister as a weakness against her to retrieve the Chaucer text. Next, Kara drafted an email to Anne, her closest associate at the university library.

Dear Anne,

I am sorry to have not corresponded sooner. The literary conference in Canada has been very full-on. I recently became aware of a threat to our archived texts. As a precaution, I would like to implement extra nightly security and have identification checked before admittance to the library during opening hours. Also, please rescind Mr. Avery Reed's access until further notice. Thank you for your diligence, and I hope to see you soon.

Kind regards,
Dr. Caine

As soon as Kara sent the illicit email, there was a rustle from the kitchens. Startled, she threw the contraband phone on the table and moved back toward her seat. She settled down just in time as Mrs. Hughes bustled into the room to clear the breakfast plates.

"Where has everyone run off to?" Mrs. Hughes asked, more in conversation than surprise.

"Work emergency, apparently," Kara responded, resisting the urge to roll her eyes at what Cade considered *work*.

"Och, it's too bad they've left ye all alone. Would you like to join me in the kitchen? I can teach you how to make those scones you sneak up to your room after breakfast," Mrs. Hughes offered with a kind smile.

Kara's face reddened slightly at having been caught sneaking extras of her favorite treat at the manor. "How did you know that? I thought I was being careful," Kara answered with a laugh.

"Not much gets past me, even if I am getting to be an old lady."

And Kara was pretty sure that was true. "Well come on, old lady," Kara joked as she rose from the table. "Teach me how to make those magic scones of yours."

THE guilt of having gone behind Cade's back left Kara on edge all day. Technically, she knew that she'd done nothing wrong. She had merely done what was reasonable, but she couldn't get rid of that nagging voice in her head that said Cade trusted her, and she had betrayed him. Conflicted and frustrated, Kara found herself in the library trying to drown out the nettling guilt with Hardy, like an addict turning to their poison of choice. It felt good to wallow in misery amongst literary characters who were best acquainted with its bitter taste.

Suddenly, the library doors slammed open so violently that Kara literally jumped from the sofa she was lying on. Cade stormed toward her, flinging the doors shut behind him with such force that the room seemed to tremble. She wasn't sure if she'd ever seen Cade so discomposed; his hair was disheveled as though he'd run his fingers through it one too many times, his typically perfect attire was slightly askew as though he'd actually run to library to find her, his face was darkened with fury, and his eyes bored into her like twin flames bent on her destruction. Clearly, Cade was fucking pissed.

Shit. Shit. SHIT.

He knew. Somehow, the fucking omniscient bastard knew what she'd done that morning. And he looked about ready to murder her for it. Cade halted his steps a short distance away from Kara. He wasn't quite close enough to touch her, his hands flexing viciously like he was seriously considering throttling her and just barely kept his antsy fingers from wrapping tightly around her delicate neck.

"Kara," Cade greeted her coldly, his voice soft and deadly. "Can you explain why I received a call from Avery Reed today saying he knew I was keeping you at Ashford Manor and demanding that I turn you over to him immediately?"

How the fuck did Avery know?

"No?" Kara answered hesitantly, the word coming out as a question as she shifted anxiously on the couch. She probably had a good idea of how Avery found out, but she wasn't about to give Cade a reason to punish her. If he was asking her, maybe he didn't know exactly what happened. She could work with that.

"No?" Cade repeated, his tone dangerous. "Care to take any guesses? I'll give you a hint—apparently the university library changed their protocol for admittance, under guidance from their chief librarian regarding a threat to library property." Cade threw her a glare that sent her insides liquifying with fear. "The chief librarian would be you, would it not, *Dr. Caine*?"

"Y-yes," Kara answered, a nervous tremor in her voice. It wasn't like she could deny blatantly obvious facts.

"So tell me, Kara, did you contact someone outside of the manor?" Cade's resolved expression made it clear that she was doomed regardless of her answer.

"Obviously not. You have me under fucking lock and key. I don't even have my phone," Kara lied convincingly. There was no way he could prove that she had done it.

"I'm going to ask you one more time," Cade threatened as he stalked toward her, stopping directly in front of Kara and grabbing her hair tightly in one hand as he made her look at him. "If you lie to me again, I guarantee you will not like the result." In warning, he pulled sharply on her hair, causing her to wince. "*Did you* talk to someone outside of the manor?"

"*No*," Kara answered spitefully. She was sick of his threats and his demands and the way both made her traitorous pussy slick with misguided desire and need.

"Wrong fucking answer, Kara." Using his hold on her hair, Cade flipped her onto her stomach, her knees landing roughly on the hard floor. Before she could think or protest or catch her breath, Cade picked up the novel beside her, threw her dress up over her hips, and slammed the hardcover book against her nearly bare arse.

Kara writhed beneath him, shrieking in shock and discomfort. Surprisingly, being hit with a book really fucking hurt.

Hideaway

"Now let's try this again. Did you contact someone?" Cade asked sternly, his hand poised to deliver another swat with his weapon of choice should he not approve of Kara's answer.

"Y-yes," Kara admitted, flinching in preparation for his reaction.

"Very good. That wasn't so hard, was it?" Cade answered agreeably, staying his hand as long as she cooperated. "How did you do it?"

"What do you mean?" Kara asked in confusion, the humbling situation of being bared and bent over the couch causing her concentration to scatter.

"How exactly did you manage to contact someone? As you said, I confiscated your phone as a precaution. So how did you message the university?"

Kara bit her lip as she contemplated the best way to approach Cade's question. She didn't want Declan to get in trouble. She'd already brought Cade's wrath against the kid once before, and she didn't want to make a habit of using Declan as a scapegoat for her actions. So she conjured the most reasonable explanation she could think of without selling out Declan for leaving his phone within reach. "Your work computer. I snuck into your office and sent an email." She whimpered when she felt the hard smack of the book against her ass.

"My office is locked and my computer is password protected. You never would have managed to access one, let alone both. Would you like to try again, or should I spank you until you remember?" Cade asked, emphasizing his words with another firm slap on Kara's arse.

"A phone!" Kara cried out, desperate to escape another punishment. "It was a phone."

"Good girl," Cade praised, soothingly rubbing his palm over her stinging backside. "Whose phone?"

Hoping to protect Declan, Kara remained silent.

Smack! "Whose phone, Kara?" Cade demanded impatiently. He needed to know if one of his employees had betrayed him and willingly aided Kara. "Answer me." *Smack!*

"It was Declan's phone," Kara admitted miserably. The bastard was going to beat the answer out of her sooner or later, so there wasn't much use in fighting him. "It wasn't his fault. He left the dining room in a hurry and forgot his phone on the table." Kara felt herself growing angry that she even had to justify her actions to the man holding her prisoner. "You can't exactly blame me for taking it when I had a chance," she muttered bitterly with her face still pressed against the couch.

"I can't blame you?" Cade reiterated angrily, his voice growing fierce. *Smack!* "Can I blame you for putting your safety at risk, *again*?" *Smack!* "Can I blame your blatant stupidity for essentially gifting your location to Reed on a silver platter because every message you send is traceable?" *Smack!* "Can I blame you for going behind my back and lying about it?" *Smack! Smack!* "It seems as though there is a great deal I should be blaming you for. You *and* Declan, but I'll deal with him later."

"No, please don't," Kara begged, her voice breathless and choked with tears. "Please don't punish Declan. It wasn't his fault. He was distracted and worried after you stormed out at breakfast." Kara trembled with remorse and dread. "He's just a kid."

"Yes, a *kid* you seem to take great pleasure in exploiting. This is his last strike. I need to do something about his constant lapses in judgment before he endangers himself or my business."

Kara gasped at the thought of Cade doing something drastic to handle Declan. She couldn't bear to be the cause of his suffering. "Please, Cade, it was my fault. I'll...I'll take the punishment. I deserve it."

"You certainly do, but that doesn't mean Declan is off the hook."

"Just don't hurt him. Please," Kara pleaded as convincingly as she could while still bent over.

"Fine, for now, I won't do anything to him. I'll send him to Prague with Jace and let him handle the little bastard. I'll let you decide if that's mercy or not."

Since Jace was involved, Kara assumed it was probably the furthest thing from mercy. Cade was terrifying, but he was reasonable. Jace was an entirely different type of monster. Kara braced herself when she felt Cade sit down on the couch beside her; he grasped her wrist and gently pulled her over his knee. She had agreed to accept her punishment, and she would try to suffer it with as much decorum as possible.

"When you are careless and irresponsible, you put yourself and everyone around you at risk," Cade lectured as he pulled Kara's knickers down to her ankles, admiring the faint bloom of pink already spread across her naked arse. "I refuse to allow that kind of immature behavior. Maybe this will help remind you to think before you act," he finished ominously.

The sickeningly familiar sound of Cade's belt sliding free from his pants squelched Kara's ten seconds of submission. She fought him as though her life depended on it, wildly flailing her legs to break free from his hold and digging her nails into the arms holding her down until she was almost certain she drew blood. Cade fought her just as hard, though his overwhelming strength put a quick end to her struggles. He viciously dug his fingers into the bare skin of her hips and dragged her back over his knee, trapping her beneath him with one of his legs as he pinned her down. His hand snaked out and snatched her wrist, twisting her arm painfully behind her back to keep her still. His other hand tangled in her hair and pulled sharply, causing prickles of pain across her scalp. Kara whimpered against the roughness of Cade's hands; she was truly, terrifyingly helpless beneath him.

"Do not. Fucking. Move," Cade growled angrily, twisting the fingers in her hair tighter for emphasis, causing her to cry out.

"Wait, please," she begged frantically, breathless from their struggle and ensuing panic.

"This isn't a negotiation, Kara. You knew your actions would have consequences. You knew you would be punished. Remorse won't save you now, love," Cade answered mercilessly, releasing her arm and reaching for his belt again.

"Stop, please!" Kara pleaded desperately as she felt the brush of leather against her skin. "I know that I made a mistake. I shouldn't have taken Declan's phone. I'm sorry."

"Saying *sorry* isn't enough," Cade reprimanded sternly before drawing back his arm to deliver the first blow of the belt.

"Please," Kara sobbed pitifully, distantly aware that tears had begun to fall, but too intent on escaping Cade's wrath to feel ashamed of them. "Please, Cade, I'm begging you. Please don't use the belt."

Startled by the anguish in her voice, Cade stayed his hand. Gently reaching for her shoulders, he lifted Kara up until she was sitting on his knee, grasping her face with both hands to search her expression intently for signs of manipulation or truth. His thumb moved to brush a stray tear from her cheek before slipping down to stroke her full bottom lip. "What's this, Kara? You're brave enough to go behind my back, defy my orders, and lie about it, but you're not brave enough to accept the punishment you deserve?"

"I-I know I deserve punishment," Kara admitted quietly, stumbling slightly over the words as she tried and failed to avoid his gaze. "But not with the belt, please."

"I see," Cade answered thoughtfully, nodding his head as though mulling it over. A ruthless smile crept across his features as he happened upon an intriguing enhancement to Kara's suffering. "In my experience, begging is most impactful when done on your knees, wouldn't you agree?" he challenged with a raised brow and a pointed glance at the floor in front of him.

Feeling tears of frustration invade her eyes at the humbling insinuation, Kara swallowed her pride, slipped from Cade's lap, and slid down to her knees between his open legs. She stared down at the floor, twining her fingers together anxiously as she awaited Cade's next command. She felt his fingers grasp her jaw and lift her head upward to look at him. His gaze was imperious and almost cruel. Involuntarily, she shivered beneath him.

"Well, Kara?" Cade asked expectantly, his tone harsh. "Beg for mercy." He stared at her with eyes of ice and stone, cold and impenetrable. "If you dare."

"Please don't whip me, Cade," Kara implored, her voice trembling as she gazed at him with large, pleading eyes.

"You look so pretty in tears, love," Cade admitted with indiscernible emotion roughening his tone, his features softening barely as he captured a tear from Kara's heavy lashes and rubbed the wetness across his lips, savoring the taste of salt and fear. "So pretty on your knees to please me."

Cade stroked her cheek, and Kara couldn't help but lean into the caress, lulled by the tenderness in his voice and touch. Couldn't he forget about the punishment and allow her to quell his anger with pleasure rather than pain? Sensing her thoughts, Cade deprived her of his touch and reached for his belt, laying it threateningly across his lap in front of her. Kara eyed the implement nervously.

"Now, why should you be allowed to escape your punishment?"

"I'm not asking to escape punishment. I'm just asking you not to use your belt on me."

"And why is that?" Cade asked, genuinely interested in why such an unassuming item could inspire such fear in his unshakeable librarian. Sure, he wielded the accessory in more instructive ways than its intended purpose. Sure, it temporarily hurt like the fucking blazes. But certainly it wasn't more than she could handle? She risked death for a goddamn book, for fuck's sake. She could handle having her arse warmed a little after the shit she pulled that morning.

"The last time you…" Kara paused to swallow the mortification of having to dredge up the memory of her first punishment, "whipped me, it was too much. Too much pain. Too much emotion. You wrecked me, Cade. And that's exactly what you meant to do. One lash more than my limit, remember? You used your belt to break me, and not just physically either—no, that would have been too easy." Kara heaved a heavy sigh before continuing. "I have a feeling you went easy on me the first time compared to what you want to do to me now." She took a moment to glance at him accusingly. "I'm not sure I can trust you not to fucking kill me this time."

"Kara, I have no desire to harm you. You should understand that by now," Cade answered reproachfully, hurt by her lack of trust.

"Oh, so beating me is just for giggles, then?"

Cade grabbed her jaw firmly, growing increasingly irritated with her attitude. "I don't punish you to aimlessly entertain myself, I punish you to correct destructive behavior before you cause yourself harm," Cade answered sharply, inadvertently digging his fingers deeper into her skin.

"I'm sorry, you must have missed the part where I am a full-grown adult capable of making my own fucking decisions," Kara thundered back, her anger at the ridiculousness of the situation growing rapidly. "I don't need your correction or your rules or your fucking punishments. I don't need someone to parent me, so go look elsewhere for someone with daddy issues to exploit."

"Careful, Kara. You're meant to be talking your way *out* of a whipping, not giving me a reason to hit you harder," Cade warned, his voice deadly calm while his eyes burned with fire.

"I'm sorry," Kara apologized hastily, shrinking back from violent tension in his body. She knew she wouldn't be able to argue her way out of being punished by Cade if he thought she deserved it. Hell, maybe she did deserve it, but there was no way in fuck she was taking that shit laying down. If she couldn't appeal to his sense of reason—like he fucking had any—she would appeal to his transactional side. Barter for mercy. Make him a deal he couldn't refuse.

"I'll do anything," Kara offered, three simple words that had the power to destroy in the wrong hands. And Cade's hands certainly weren't the right ones to endow with such limitless power, but she was desperate. Cade's eyes sparked with wicked curiosity, and Kara knew she might have a chance of victory, at least momentarily. Until she was subjected to whatever *anything* Cade devised.

"I'm intrigued," Cade responded, trying to keep his features neutral, but failing to hide his excitement as Kara upped the stakes in their game. "Elaborate?"

"I'm willing to submit to anything, any form of punishment you deem appropriate for my reckless behavior. Anything but your belt."

Cade took a moment to ponder her proposal. It was tempting, he had to admit, even if the belt in his hand begged to be reacquainted with her backside. "Are other forms of physical punishment acceptable?"

"No," Kara amended, trying to sound firm and unshakable, even though she was afraid of demanding too much. "Nothing that hurts."

"So no *physical* pain?" Cade asked in clarification.

The way he asked made Kara feel like she needed to be worried about him hurting her in ways that weren't physical. "Anything but physical pain," Kara answered in agreement.

"Well, I think I can work within those parameters," Cade announced in a tone of vengeful glee. "But, as this apparently *is* a negotiation, I have an addendum. To soothe my need for prompt justice, you allow me one lash of the belt. Then the remainder of your punishment can be deferred to another time."

"That sounds reasonable enough," Kara accepted warily, body already tense for the pain she'd just agreed to endure. Though she was relieved to have escaped the brunt of his punishment for the moment, she seethed at the idea of Cade sneaking in the belt just for a show of power and control. She'd won, but he somehow made her feel like she hadn't.

Fucking asshole.

Cade offered his hand, gently helping Kara to her feet; the gesture would have appeared gallant if it weren't for his next words. "Turn around and grasp the side of the couch," he commanded sharply.

Biting her lip anxiously at the knowledge of what was coming, Kara faced the arm of the couch, digging her fingers into the leather to brace herself against Cade's vindictive intentions for her ass.

Cade stepped back to admire the view. There was very little beauty in the world that superseded the delectable sight of Kara bared and bent over before him. And his cock was in firm agreement. Since Kara's bargaining had swindled him out of every lash but one, Cade had every intention of making that single lash count. He drew back his arm and put all of his considerable weight into delivering the one blow. The belt hit Kara's skin with a thundering *thwap*, leaving an angry red welt in its wake.

Kara cried out, stunned by the sheer force of the belt slapping across her ass. It felt as though all of Cade's anger and frustration and disappointment had been poured into a single blow, and her body protested the viciousness of the assault. Incredibly grateful that she was only forced to endure one lash, Kara stood up and attempted to gather her remnants of dignity as best she could.

Unfortunately for her, Cade preferred her dignity in shambles.

Cade pulled her tightly against him, pressing his body firmly into the contours of her own. They were close enough that Kara could feel the hard bulge of his cock jutting into the softness of her belly. She gasped slightly at the intrusion, her body instinctively reacting to his need, though she wondered if he was hard from the feel of her body or from the punishment he inflicted on her.

Cade captured her chin, forcing Kara to look at him—a mischievous glint in his eyes. "Now say: *thank you, daddy, for my spanking,*" Cade ordered with a sadistic smile, clearly not allowing her previous comment regarding daddy issues to go unpunished.

"I hate you," Kara whispered under her breath with an angry huff.

"What was that?" Cade asked scoldingly, raising a single eyebrow as though daring her to challenge him and risk another punishment.

"Thank you, *daddy*, for my spanking," she said through gritted teeth, choking on the words as though they were barbed wire in her throat and nearly perishing with mortification.

"You're very welcome, baby girl," Cade replied, pinching her cheek indulgently, the act so infantilizing that Kara physically cringed. "Now, go clean your face and get ready for dinner."

Gritting her teeth, Kara turned to leave without another word, yelping as Cade sent her off with a firm slap on her already stinging backside.

Fucking. Prick.

CHAPTER FOURTEEN

FEELING sore, horny, and thoroughly vexed in a way only Cade—in his magnificent assholery—was capable of achieving, Kara slid into her room and slammed the door a little louder than necessary. The resounding bang of the door hitting the adjoining wall gave her some measure of satisfaction as she replayed her recent humiliations at the hands of her captor. A captor who she also had the ill-advised misfortune of fucking on a somewhat regular basis. She was aware of her idiocy on that account and had every intention of rectifying the situation as soon as another opportunity presented itself. Another opportunity being a sizable cock attached to a man in possession of at least adequate moral scruples and a modicum of human decency. And perhaps less of a tendency to take out his frustrations on her ass.

Rubbing at her mistreated backside, Kara headed for the bed with every intention of sleeping straight through dinner and avoiding Cade's smug face until at least the next day. She paused when she discovered that the bed wasn't entirely empty. A large, black box elegantly adorned with a black satin bow lay at the foot of the bed, the package looking dreadfully out of place as its darkness contrasted the rest of the bright and cheerful room. Kara eyed the mysterious parcel warily. Her recent behavior was hardly befitting a present, so she couldn't begin to fathom what lay within the box or who had left it. With a sigh of determination, Kara strode toward the present and tore off the attached card, solving the mystery of the gifter without actually mitigating any of her confusion regarding the gift.

Wear this tonight. Pair with black stilettos. Dinner is at eight.
Don't be late.
-C

Still dubious of Cade's intentions, Kara untied the silk bow and lifted the top of the box. Inside, a gorgeous Dolce & Gabbana dress lay nestled in layers of black tissue paper. She gasped audibly as she carefully pulled the dress from its wrappings and held it against her body lovingly. The dress was exquisite, certainly unlike anything she'd ever owned or worn before. It didn't escape her notice that, while everything else she wore had belonged to someone else, this was the first item of clothing that Cade had purchased specifically for *her*.

Her anger momentarily forgotten, Kara excitedly undressed and slipped into the new dress. As she expected, it fit her perfectly. The dress offered decidedly little coverage with sleeves of sheer black lace that dipped slightly below her shoulders, a satin corseted bodice featuring a lacy see-through panel in the middle, and a mere hint of eyelash lace at the hem that just barely graced her mid thighs. It was without a doubt the most expensive and exposing piece of clothing she had ever worn. Slipping out of the dress, Kara eyed the clock on the bedside table. She had a few hours until dinner, plenty of time to shower and put in some extra effort into her makeup and hair than usual.

Feeling refreshed, smooth, moisturized, and perfumed, Kara slid the new dress back on. Inspired by the seductive black lace and the lingerie-esque bodice, Kara lined and shadowed her eyes in smoky shades and painted her lips a deep Bordeaux. A quick glance in the mirror revealed the faint shadow of bruises peeking out from the black lace on her shoulders. Kara traced the marks mindlessly, entranced by the brand of Cade on her skin. For reasons she couldn't logically explain, Kara pulled her sleeves down her arms a little bit lower, finding an unusual satisfaction in seeing the dark fingerprints against her pale skin. A sign that she was his.

As she entered the dining hall's double doors, Kara's cheerful stride came to a sudden, horrified halt.

Cade was not alone.

Seated at his left was a man that Kara had never seen at the manor before. He was tall, taller than even Cade, with deep, oceanic blue eyes and hair the palest shade of blonde. He looked European, possibly Scandinavian. Both men stopped mid-conversation and turned their attention to her as she entered the room. Kara shifted uncomfortably beneath their appreciative stares and anxiously fidgeted with the hem of her skirt, unsuccessfully attempting to coax a few more centimeters of coverage over her practically bare thighs. She never would have worn the damned dress if she'd known Cade had company that night. What the fuck was he thinking? She felt displayed, like an item for auction for the benefit of the mysterious guest across the table. Hell, perhaps she was. Kara shot Cade a panicked look.

"Kara, please come in," Cade greeted casually, ignoring her obvious anguish. "This is my friend, Finnian," he continued, with a gesture toward the man beside him.

In uneasy silence, Kara remained where she stood. It was a surprising disclosure that Cade was emotionally close enough to another individual to consider them a friend. It was an even more confounding occurrence that Cade would have invited said friend to an intimate dinner in which he had personally dressed her in attire befitting a high-end escort. For someone as private as Cade, the whole situation seemed out of character. Planning her escape, Kara eyed the exit warily.

"Are you going to wait by the doors all night?" Cade asked, growing slightly impatient. "Come here."

"I'm sorry, I didn't know you had company. I can come down after you've finished with your friend," Kara responded, turning toward the hall in an attempt to excuse herself.

"Kara. Here," Cade ordered firmly, punctuating the command with a snap of his fingers.

Kara turned back sharply to balk at Cade's astonishing arrogance. "I beg your pardon?" she asked in disbelief. Had he really just snapped at her like a dog to be beckoned to his side? If he wanted a pet, she'd get him a fucking golden retriever.

"I am not going to ask you again, Kara. Come here. *Now*."

Against her will, Kara's body heeded Cade's command, one footstep at a time, until she found herself standing before him.

"That's better. Next time, you should do as you're told immediately. I don't appreciate repeating myself. It looks bad for company," Cade said in a patronizing tone.

Kara scoffed aloud, but said nothing in response. The man, Finnian, gave Cade a look that seemed to hold both a question and a challenge. From the determined set of his features, Kara assumed that Cade had accepted the unspoken challenge. When he turned his attention to Kara, Cade's face was that of a stranger's. His eyes were cold and calculating, his mouth stern, his expression merciless. Instinctively, Kara wanted to draw back, but she felt frozen in place beneath his gaze.

"This afternoon, you and I came to an agreement," Cade began.

Kara felt the blood in her veins turn cold with trepidation.

"Tonight is *anything* else."

Kara could do little more than perish slowly with dread and hope that she hadn't been better off taking the whipping than whatever sadism Cade had planned for the night.

"Kneel," Cade commanded.

"I'm sorry, what?" Kara asked in confusion as though she didn't understand the context of the word.

"Get on your knees," he elaborated patiently. He knew this would be difficult for her; her stubbornness made him relish the moment even more.

She hesitated, pleading eyes searching his for any hint of mercy. She found none. With a sigh of resignation, Kara awkwardly bent to the floor, one knee at a time, struggling to achieve the act gracefully with the height of her stilettos and the shortness of her hem. Her body quivering with embarrassment as Cade and Finnian witnessed her humiliation, Kara sat on her heels with her bare knees on the cold marble floor and waited.

"Very nice," Cade said, nodding in approval. "Now, as your behavior recently has been recklessly immature, tonight will be an exercise in obedience. You are not to speak unless spoken to, and you will address Finnian and myself as *sir*. Do you understand?"

"Okay," Kara agreed hesitantly.

"Disobeying already, Kara?" Cade reprimanded with a disapproving tsk. "Try again."

"Yes, sir," Kara answered grudgingly through gritted teeth, mentally contriving various, agonizing deaths for them both.

"Good. Mrs. Hughes left dinner prepared in the kitchen; you may go and fetch it," Cade ordered with a dismissive wave of his hand.

As much as she wanted to tell him to *go fuck himself*, Kara swallowed the words and attempted to escape her position on the floor with as much decorum as possible. She breathed a sigh of relief as the kitchen door closed behind her. The interaction with Cade moments before had left her shaken and anxious of what else he might have in store. She had never considered him a cruel man, but tonight he seemed intent on shattering her pride into pieces.

Finding a welcome, open bottle of white wine on the counter, Kara pulled a glass from the cabinet, filled it generously, and drained every drop before slamming the empty glass on the counter. It was possible Cade would detect the unavoidable flush of the wine in her cheeks, but it was a risk she was happy to take. There was no way she was walking back into that room entirely at the mercy of a British sociopath without drinking something to settle her nerves.

Finally remembering her required task, Kara looked for the dinner Mrs. Hughes had prepared. The delicious scent of prosciutto and truffle led Kara to the oven where everything was being kept warm. There was prosciutto wrapped chicken, truffle risotto, and roasted asparagus beautifully laid out on two plates. As her presence would make three, Kara bitterly assumed her punishment for the night would include starvation. It was incredibly trusting of Cade to have commissioned her with the task of procuring his dinner, for if Mrs. Hughes happened to keep any poison on hand in the kitchen, there was a great possibility Kara would have used it.

Carefully balancing a large plate on each hand, Kara reentered the dining room with dread. Cade and Finnian looked at her expectantly, and she tried not to falter as she brought the plates before them. After she set the food on the table, Cade summoned her with an imperious *snap* and pointed down to the floor beside him. Kara rolled her eyes as she followed his command and stood at his side.

A single raise of his eyebrow suggested that she should not be standing.

Gritting her teeth to keep from saying anything that would earn her further punishment, Kara kicked off the ridiculous stilettos and slipped into position on bare knees and feet. This time, she was marginally more comfortable. Cade looked amused at her dismissal of the formality of shoes in the dining room, but he didn't address her further.

The men conversed about art while Kara counted the number of streaks in the marble floor to keep from focusing on the uncomfortable twinges of pain in her knees. Cade was clearly well-versed in many, unconventional forms of torture. It was almost enough to make her more receptive to his rules and requests in the future.

Almost.

Her aimless mental tallying was interrupted when she heard her name being called. Kara looked up from the floor to see Cade waving a forkful of food in front of her face. She shook her head in refusal, any appetite she had momentarily obliterated. There was no way she was going to let Cade hand feed her in front of a stranger while she knelt at his feet. The act was too infantilizing and embarrassing even without an audience.

"Kara, eat," Cade commanded, bringing the food to her mouth.

"No thank you, sir," Kara responded bitingly, turning her head away.

"It was not a request. Eat."

Choking back repulsion and shame, Kara opened her mouth and allowed Cade to feed her. She chewed, the food tasteless in her mouth, and swallowed dutifully. Cade continued to feed her intermittently with himself, taking great pleasure in watching her

Hideaway

swallow her pride with every bite. He noticed that she was very receptive to *that* corrective approach. Beating her seemed only to stoke the fires of her anger and rebellion, but humiliation left her silent and compliant. In the future, he would keep in mind that her pride was more easily chastised than her body.

"More wine please, Kara," Finnian requested in a slightly accented voice, lifting an empty glass and gesturing toward the bottle on the table.

Kara looked at Cade, as if for permission, and he nodded his approval. She rose and walked on bare feet to where Finnian sat. Keenly aware that the man was scrutinizing her every move, she lifted the wine bottle gently and filled his glass as carefully as she could. As she finished, a single drop of red wine escaped the bottle and landed on the table.

"I'm sorry," Kara apologized quickly, realizing too late that she had forgotten Cade's rules for speaking.

"It's alright. Allow me," Finnian responded chivalrously as he used the napkin from his lap to dab at the spot before it stained.

Kara stood in stunned silence, unsure if should apologize again for breaking the rules or hope that no one noticed. Judging from the knowing look on Finnian's face, he was well aware of her misstep. Kara knew she was at his mercy and prayed he was more forgiving than Cade.

"Thank you for the wine, Kara," Finnian said, dismissing her without reproach.

"You're welcome, sir," she replied softly, truly grateful to have escaped unscathed.

As Kara walked back to return to her place on the floor, Cade seized her arm firmly and turned her around to face him. She shifted uneasily as he studied her face with stern, condemning eyes. He lifted his other hand to her warm, reddened cheek, and Kara had the sinking sense that she had traded one perilous situation for another.

"You are flushed tonight," Cade commented in a tone of thinly veiled accusation.

Fuck.

"Am I?" Kara answered nervously.

"Quite. Have you been drinking?"

Fuck, fuck, fuck.

"Of course not, sir. It's just uncommonly warm tonight," Kara responded in an attempt to sway him from his suspicions, however accurate they may be.

"And yet, your hands are freezing," Cade answered damningly, clearly not persuaded by her evasion.

"I suppose the unexpected strains of this evening have left me feeling overwhelmed and overheated," Kara replied as she tried to pull away from his touch, holding firm in her denial of the truth. She assumed she was safe, in spite of the lie, wagering that Cade would not push her further in front of his friend.

"I see," Cade answered dangerously.

Had he not promised that afternoon to refrain from physical punishment, Cade wouldn't have had any reservations about bending Kara over the table that instant and spanking the deception out of her while Finnian watched. As it was, Cade would have to think of a more creative approach to remind Kara that he was not a man to be trifled with. Cade stepped behind Kara, moving his hand from her

Hideaway

arm to firmly grasp the back of her neck. His other hand traveled gently up her back, almost like a caress, until he reached the top of her dress. He captured the zipper and pulled it down slowly, leaving her dress completely unfastened and her back bare. Kara gasped, frozen and powerless beneath his hands.

"Remove your dress," Cade whispered softly in her ear.

"No," Kara answered in shock, holding her dress tightly to her breasts so it wouldn't slip off her shoulders.

"If you're so overheated that your cheeks are blazing, you should welcome the relief of removing some of your clothing," Cade explained tauntingly.

Kara blanched at his words, knowing that her own deception left her with little chance of escaping his command. She should never have underestimated Cade. "Please, sir," Kara pleaded desperately, the embarrassment of what he suggested unfathomable.

"Did you have a drink, Kara?" Cade asked plainly, his lips still pressed against her ear.

"Yes, sir," she admitted weakly in defeat.

"At last, we have the truth. You will not lie to me again, do you understand?"

"Yes, sir," she agreed sheepishly.

"Good girl. Now, take off your dress."

Kara turned around sharply to look at him, aghast that Cade still made the same request.

"The confession does not absolve the sin without penance, love," Cade instructed with the pretentious air of a man without fault. "Come now, hesitation merely prolongs the discomfort of the situation."

It was easy for him to say, having made it through the night without degradation, reproach, or the removal of his clothes. Kara regarded him hatefully as she contemplated her options, which were not plentiful. Disregarding her dignity and pride for what felt like the hundredth time in the span of an hour, she turned away from Cade and let go of the dress she had been clutching tightly to her chest. The dress fell to the floor, leaving Kara in only a revealing black bra and black lace panties. She cursed herself for wearing the seductive pair for Cade's pleasure, assuming she would have an opportunity to reveal them in a far more intimate setting than in front of company in the dining hall.

"You may return to position," Cade dismissed with barely a glance in her direction. Undressing her wasn't about gratification or exploitation, it was about power.

Using her arms to cover what she could of her exposed body, Kara stepped out of the dress and made her way around the table to her designated place at Cade's right side. She sank to her knees, grateful for the first time that night that her place on the floor might put her below their notice or attention. She tried to tell herself that she was no more exposed than she might be on a beach in front of throngs of strangers, but Kara couldn't seem to mitigate the humiliation she felt as she knelt practically naked at the disposal of two fully clothed men. Hot tears of shame slipped down her cheeks before she brushed them away in irritation.

Kara sat in abject misery as Cade and Finnian continued their discourse, oblivious to her discomfort. Eventually, misery turned to anger. After a time, anger fizzled into emotional indifference. No longer being overwhelmed by emotions made way for the physical realization that she was very cold, very hungry, and very tired. Kara wrapped her arms around her chest for warmth and nestled her head in the curve of her shoulder, allowing her eyes to close briefly as she waited to be released from the purgatory of the evening.

A scrape of chairs against the floor startled Kara from her momentary respite. Both men had risen from the table, apparently making their way to Cade's study to continue their discussion. Finnian headed for the doors, but Cade remained in the dining room to address unfinished business. "I'll be there in a moment, Finn," Cade called to his friend.

Finnian's gaze lingered on Kara, his expression unreadable though hinting at mischief, before turning from the room.

Kara waited in place expectantly, more than ready to be free of the evening's excruciating torture. Cade stood above her, but Kara kept her eyes on the marble floor, avoiding his gaze with a sulkiness that masqueraded, perhaps unbelievably, as subservience. Cade caught her chin between his thumb and forefinger and gently forced her to look at him. His eyes were warm and alit with something that very much resembled adoration; Kara felt her irritation soften slightly in spite of herself.

"Don't move from this spot," he commanded with a wicked smile before turning to follow Finnian out of the room.

Any momentary feelings of congeniality toward Cade evaporated as Kara found herself kneeling on the cold, hard floor. Alone. The minutes ticked by slowly. Literally. The large, faceless clock mounted to one of the walls obliterated the tranquil silence of the empty room, its shifting gears sounding with a rhythmic auditory assault that tallied every second of torment suffered. Cade knew exactly what he was doing when he allowed her to escape the belt that afternoon. He no doubt relished the challenge of contriving punishments not nearly as forthright and quickly concluded as a whipping. Instead, Kara had been subjected to prolonged torture, one borne of her own obedience to Cade's commands. Something about her willing participation in his punishment made the humiliation and discomfort sting a bit more. Next time, she would forego the negotiations and simply submit to the fucking beating. Which, now that she considered it, might have been his exact intentions behind the whole theatrical production. Forcing her to her knees. Treating her like some sort of pet or slave. It was so over the top so ridiculous so entirely *Cade*. He'd forced her into ready compliance without having to lay a finger on her. He could fuck her body like a pro, but he could fuck her mind like a goddamn rockstar.

Well, fuck him.

And that was exactly what she wouldn't be doing ever again, not while she was in possession of her life and her sanity. That bastard had seen the last he was ever going to see of her pussy, so she hoped he enjoyed the view while he had it. And while she appreciated the adequately skilled appendage between his legs, the world was full of cocks *not* attached to psycho egomaniacs. She'd get over the loss.

Three thousand, six hundred excruciating ticks later, Kara found herself still sitting bare-kneed on the cold floor. A fucking hour had passed, and Cade still hadn't come to dismiss her. Did he plan on leaving her there kneeling all night? Her heart stuttered in panic at the thought. Minute by minute, Kara's resolve faltered. After another thirty passed, she was willing to submit to anything Cade could possibly imagine if it would get her off the fucking floor. Forget abstinence, she'd take his cock any way he gave it if he did it on a bed and let her sleep afterward. Slowly, the incessant din of the clock grew quieter, fading alongside consciousness as slumber struggled to overwhelm her senses. Her eyelids grew heavy. Her head lolled. And, at last, she slipped into sleep.

"K ARA," a soft voice called through the void, disrupting the peaceful darkness.

"Hmm?" she answered half-awake, begrudging the interruption.

"Kara," the voice called again, this time louder—clearer.

Suddenly, Kara recognized the voice invading her dreams. Anxiously, her eyes flashed open to find Cade staring down at her, his expression surprisingly gentle as he stroked his knuckles against her cheek. Kara straightened her posture quickly, casting her eyes downward in submission. She hadn't meant to fall asleep before Cade returned, and she was afraid of what further discipline she may have brought upon herself. Cade's fingers traveled slowly down Kara's cheek, curving under chin and gently pressing her head upward. His eyes found hers, and there was nothing threatening or malicious in his gaze. Cade's golden-green eyes were warm and indulgent, having lost the sadistic glimmer he sported earlier in the evening. Kara couldn't help but melt beneath him, relieved to be dealing with the familiar side of Cade that she actually enjoyed rather than the cold bastard she'd been subjected to all night.

Cade couldn't help but smile as he watched Kara soften before him. Instinctively, Kara nuzzled into Cade's arm as he continued to stroke her beneath her chin, unencumbered by the thought that she was behaving like a good little pet. After allowing her a moment of tenderness, Cade grasped Kara's jaw firmly and demanded her attention. "Have you learned your lesson, love?" he asked sternly.

"Yes, sir," Kara responded obediently without a moment of hesitation.

"Are you going to lie and behave recklessly again?" Cade questioned as his grip on her jaw tightened slightly.

"No, sir," Kara answered somberly, and she'd never spoken two words with more sincerity.

"Good girl," Cade crooned, chucking her under the chin. "Now, come here." Cade offered his hand to help Kara escape the uncomfortable position she'd been holding for over two hours. Kara accepted his assistance gratefully, rising shakily and stumbling as she struggled to stand on numb feet. Without a second thought, Cade swept Kara off of her aching feet and into his arms, holding her tightly against his chest.

"Thank you," she whispered into his chest as she nuzzled against him, allowing herself a momentary weakness for which she could berate herself to her heart's content in the morning. Typically, Kara would have protested such a masculine gesture that left her feeling weak and helpless, but at the moment she was willing to accept any gallantry that would enable her to make it up the stairs and into her welcome bed without using her abused appendages or her last stores of energy. Bidding adieu to her last remnants of dignity, Kara snuggled into the warmth of Cade's body, burying her cheek into his chest and welcoming the rhythmic beat of his heart against her.

"Are you tired, sweetheart?" Cade asked softly as he pressed his lips to Kara's hair and inhaled the sweet scent of her.

Kara merely nodded against his chest, too physically and mentally worn to form the words of a response.

"Well then, let's get you in bed."

Kara hoped she was imagining the hidden meaning in his words, an insinuation that promised more than sleep.

Cade placed Kara gently on the bed. Having already deprived her of half her clothing downstairs, Cade stripped Kara of her knickers and unhooked and removed her bra, his pace languid and savoring. Reverently devouring the sight of her nakedness as though it wasn't a view she afforded him on a daily basis, Cade brushed his fingertips over the curves of her breasts, claiming them as his own. "So beautiful," he murmured to himself as though the merits of her body still astounded him. Because they did. Kara was, undeniably, the most tantalizing creature he'd ever entangled with, and he had every aim to keep her. Leaving her on the bed, Cade vanished into the adjoining bathroom.

"Don't lay down yet," he ordered with a raised voice from the other room.

Obediently, Kara sat on the edge of the bed and tried not to close her eyes. It was a difficult feat. Quickly, Cade returned from the bathroom with a cloth in hand. A makeup wipe, Kara noted with surprise.

"Close your eyes," Cade commanded gently, smoothing the cloth over Kara's features and starting to wipe her face clean.

Cade's hands were skilled as though he'd taken care of a girl in this capacity before. He probably had, Kara noted with a flicker of irritation.

"You did so well tonight, love," Cade commended as he stroked the cloth across her eyelids and removed the dark, heavy makeup.

"I-I did?" Kara stuttered in surprise, his words of praise catching her off guard. She'd only suffered through a night of his torture—a punishment that she'd earned—and not very graciously at that.

"You did. Such a good girl," Cade answered, softly pressing a kiss against each eyelid.

Kara didn't respond, but his words warmed her straight to her core. Embarrassingly, she felt the heat of arousal pooling between her clenched thighs as Cade stroked her face and called her a *good girl*. God, the man made her weak in every sense of the word.

"Lie down on your back," Cade instructed as he went to dispose of the cloth and retrieve something else from the bathroom.

Kara obeyed hesitantly, excitement rapidly overcoming her fatigue as adrenaline coursed through her veins at the thought of what Cade might do next. Fear and anticipation battled for dominance as Kara lay on her back and stared at the ceiling, waiting for Cade's return. After some minor clatter and sounds of rummaging, Cade walked into Kara's bedroom entirely naked and holding a small bottle of oil. Kara shot Cade a dark look. There was no fucking way she was doing *that* tonight.

"It's not what you think," Cade said with a laugh as he correctly interpreted the source of Kara's glare. "It's massage oil."

"Oh," Kara answered blandly, her face awash with relief. "You want a massage?" She wasn't exactly in the mood to be rubbing him down when all she wanted to do was sleep, but she'd happily accept it as an alternative to having anything shoved in her ass.

"No, the massage is for you," Cade explained, sitting down on the bed, reaching for one of Kara's sore feet and laying it across his thighs.

"Why are you taking care of me?" Kara asked with a suspicious raise of her brow. "I thought I was being punished? Shouldn't I be left to suffer the consequences of my disobedience or something?"

"You've already been disciplined, Kara. I'm not going to continue punishing you; I'm not a complete bastard. I told you before that aftercare is an important part of the process," Cade explained as he poured a small amount of oil into his palm and warmed it between his hands.

"So really you get some sort of sick satisfaction out of breaking me just so that you can put me back together?"

"I suppose that's one way to look at it," Cade answered with a grin, unperturbed by her attempt to make him question or feel guilty about his methods. He knew he was perverse, and he was completely unencumbered by the knowledge. "Do you want the massage or not?"

Kara took a quick moment to weigh her pride versus the ache in her feet. Her choice was simple. "Yes, please," she pleaded, closing her eyes in bliss with the first delicious stroke of Cade's skilled thumbs across her heel.

Cade worked out the tension in her muscles dexterously, applying the perfect amount of pressure to have Kara moaning in ecstasy.

After tending to her feet, Cade moved to her legs, deeply digging his palms into her calves, balancing on the edge of pleasure and pain. Kara writhed beneath him, the excruciating euphoria of his touch almost too much to bear. She couldn't withhold a whimper of desire as Cade's hands stroked and kneaded up her thighs and over her hips.

"Does that feel good, love?" Cade asked smugly, continuing to rub his fingers along her hips as he bent to place a kiss on her inner thigh.

"Uh-huh," Kara agreed breathlessly, her eyes closed in rapture as she gave in to the sensations overwhelming her body.

"Spread your pussy for me," Cade commanded softly, pressing another kiss higher up on her thigh.

"What?" Kara asked, confused and half-lucid thanks to his tantalizing attentions. A chastising slap landed directly on the sensitive spot between Kara's thighs, eliciting a sharp shriek of surprise as she moved a hand to cover the tender, stinging flesh.

"I said: open your legs wide, spread apart your pussy lips, and let me see that needy, wet cunt like a good little slut," Cade ordered, each word even and controlled as though he weren't saying the dirtiest, most demoralizing words Kara had ever heard spoken aloud.

And the worst part? She absolutely loved it.

Instant, liquid hot need overcoming any remnants of shame or self-consciousness, Kara did as she was told. She raised her knees, bringing her heels up toward her ass and opening her legs as wide as she could. Slowly, she slid her hands down her stomach, her fingers trembling as they rested against the throbbing mound between her thighs. She slipped her thumbs between the folds of velvety flesh and parted them, revealing the most private parts of herself for Cade's hungry perusal. The act was so deliciously deplorable that Kara already felt her arousal dripping from her entrance and sliding down between her ass cheeks.

"Goddamn, if that isn't the loveliest sight I've ever seen," Cade declared as he devoured the view of Kara spread out before him, his eyes dark and ravenous. "Makes me want to have a little taste."

Kara squealed as she felt his hot mouth latch onto her, his tongue sliding up from her entrance to her clit, swirling over the aching bundle of nerves and sending shocks of electricity through her entire body. Kara arched into his mouth, begging for more. Cade was more than willing to concede, his tongue conquering as he thrust inside her, relishing the clench of her muscles around him as she spasmed with need and arousal. Feeling her body tense as her climax approached rapidly, Cade moved his mouth to her clit, sucking the nub into his mouth as he replaced his tongue with his fingers. He thrust two fingers deep inside her, relishing her uncensored moans as they pierced the silence of the room.

"Are you close, baby?" Cade asked as his fingers slammed inside her deeper, harder.

Kara could only nod breathlessly in response, her teeth digging into her bottom lip in an effort to contain the unbecoming shriek of ecstasy that was threatening to spill from her lips, torn from her body unwillingly with the excruciating bliss of Cade's fingers and mouth on her body.

"Come for me, Kara," Cade growled in command, his words vibrating against her clit before he took the nub into his mouth and sucked hard, his teeth scraping against the delicate bundle of nerves as Kara writhed beneath him in agony and pleasure.

Kara screamed as the orgasm exploded through her, wave upon wave of pure pleasure rippling through her body as she spasmed around Cade's fingers still thrusting inside of her. She shuddered against his tongue as he continued to lap at her pussy and wring every drop of ecstasy from her sensitive clit.

When her orgasm subsided, Cade slid on top of her, straddling her thighs as he swiped a thumb over his mouth to wipe his face clean of her lingering arousal. Then he put his finger to his lips and sucked her juices off as though they were the remnants of a delicious meal. "Such a good girl, coming so prettily on my fingers," Cade whispered in approval as he stroked her swollen bottom lip. "Would you like to come on my cock now?"

Kara nodded eagerly, desperate to be filled with his cock and his cum as he used her for his own release. Wasting little time, Cade lined himself with her entrance and slammed his cock inside her, burying himself to the hilt in a single, merciless thrust. Kara cried out as he stretched her tight, still spasming pussy, forcing her to accept his entire length. Having Cade inside her was equal parts torture and rapture, and she was desperate for more.

"You're so tight, love. Can you take it?" he asked, thrusting into her slowly. "Can you take all of me?"

"Yes," Kara answered fervently, meeting his thrusts and willing him to take her harder. "Fuck me. Make me come, please."

"Since you beg so nicely," Cade answered roughly, a dangerous glint in his eye.

Abandoning all pretense of gentleness, Cade hammered into her with a force that was near violent. Digging his fingers into her hips deep enough to bruise, he dragged her down onto his cock, thrusting into her over and over at a punishing pace. Needing to penetrate even deeper, desperate to be further inside her than any man had ever been, Cade grabbed her ankle and draped her leg over his shoulder. He continued his rhythmic assault of thrusts before throwing Kara's other leg over his shoulder and impaling her so deeply she screamed.

"That's it sweetheart, scream for me. I want to hear as my cock tears you apart." Cade slammed inside her over and over, feeling her body begin to tense again with need. "Who owns this pussy?" he demanded, his voice rough with arousal.

Kara didn't respond, too overcome with the sensation of him moving inside of her and another orgasm cresting. Cade commanded her attention with a light slap of his palm against her cheek. Her gaze darted immediately to his, her eyes wide in shock but not pain.

"Who does this pussy belong to, Kara?" Cade reiterated, punctuating each word with a sharp thrust of his hips.

"You!" Kara almost screamed, her voice breathless and hoarse as her orgasm hovered just out reach.

"Give it to me, baby," Cade growled, all rhythm lost in his all-consuming need to tear her climax from her body and lay claim to it like a conquest.

Left with nothing but primal instinct, he rammed into Kara frantically, demanding her pleasure as much as he did her surrender. That time, she came silently, her very breath stolen by the overpowering sensation of complete, full-body ecstasy. Cade climaxed alongside her, shuddering as he pumped inside her, filling her with his cum before pulling out and shooting the rest of his release across her stomach in thick ribbons of white. Marking her. Claiming her.

"You're mine," Cade said harshly, his voice thick with passion as he spent the last of his orgasm and heaved breathlessly above her. "Say it." He nipped at Kara's ankle, her legs still hiked over his shoulders.

"I'm yours," Kara agreed, her voice equally breathless as she basked in the afterglow of her second orgasm.

And, to her utter bewilderment, she meant it.

CHAPTER FIFTEEN

A crushing weight on her thighs and an urgent need to pee woke Kara from her near coma. Cade's leg was wrapped around her waist, his arm thrown over chest and holding her close to his body. And Kara could not move an inch beneath his weight, the predicament suffocating and endearing at the same time. Who knew Caden Ashford was a cuddler? Although, he probably just considered it using his body to keep her imprisoned while he slept—for the sake of preserving his reputation as a heartless bastard.

Kara struggled to displace Cade's wayward appendages, her body protesting as she used abused muscles. She felt as though she'd been torn apart from the inside out. Her back, legs, and neck were stiff from enduring her lengthy punishment on the floor. Her pussy felt tender and raw, her womb ached as though it had been split open.

Cade seemed hell bent on fucking her into an early grave or dying while trying. Not that Kara minded; she could think of worse ways to die.

Finally, Kara was able to dislodge Cade's arm, enjoying a deep breath from her liberated lungs. Moaning with the slight disruption of his sleep, Cade turned over on his side and removed his leg from Kara's waist. Free at last, Kara stretched out on the bed, groaning as her body revolted at the exercise.

Fuck, last night had been brutal, and that wasn't even considering the torture she endured *before* Cade had taken her to bed. Not that having her pussy licked, finger fucked, and thoroughly filled by a British lord's magnificently formed cock was anywhere near torturous. Last night just felt different—heavier, deeper, overwhelming in ways that weren't entirely physical. Cade gave her a lot last night, but he also took more than she felt comfortable relinquishing. He demanded more than just her body. He demanded her *submission*. And, for some baffling, logic-defying, earth-shattering reason, she gave it.

In her sex-addled state, she had allowed Cade to claim ownership of her body, she had begged and pleaded to come and to be fucked, and she told him that her goddamn pussy belonged to him. A tsunami of embarrassment washed over her, drowning her in her own humiliation. And honestly, she might have preferred drowning to beholding Cade's smug face when he woke up next to the woman he purportedly owned.

I'm yours.

God, hearing those words, *her* words reverberating through her memory made her want to reach over and smother Cade's delectable

Hideaway

face with a fluffy pillow and be done with it. Technically, she was still his prisoner, so she could chalk it up to self-defense, get off scot-free, and never have to face the humiliating repercussions of whatever idiocy last night had been. Truthfully, she was considering it.

With a loud sigh, Kara opted for breakfast rather than murder, sliding out of bed carefully so as not to wake sleeping beauty. At least he would wake up alone. The thought gave her a measure of satisfaction. Kara rifled through the closet until she found a silk nightgown and matching robe. She wasn't sure why Cade had even bothered to purchase nightwear since the only thing she seemed to have on her at night was him. She dressed quickly, throwing on a pair of slippers to protect her feet from the cold, and snuck out of the room.

The house was pleasantly empty as Kara made her way to the kitchen. The guys were still working on a job, the details of which she was left entirely uninformed. On that account, she supposed ignorance truly was bliss. Surprisingly, she also found the kitchen abandoned. She was happy Cade had actually given Mrs. Hughes a day off; she deserved it after having to deal with his pampered ass for so long. Kara took a moment to appreciate the peaceful tranquility of being entirely alone. For someone so accustomed to solitude, that might have been her first moment unencumbered by mandatory company or watchful eyes since Cade had taken her. *Kidnapped* her, she reminded herself. How was it that damning transgression seemed less and less atrocious the more time she spent in Cade's presence?

Must be the magical qualities of his massive cock.

Refusing to focus on the alarming emotional attachments forming between them, Kara reduced their relationship to simply a good, albeit confusing, fuck and trudged to pantry in search of the ingredients for pancakes. Because she needed the distraction of actually doing something for herself for a change—something as simple as cooking breakfast—and damnit, pancakes made everything better.

Kara was on her tiptoes, reaching for the flour at the top shelf of the pantry, when something hit her hard from behind. There was barely a moment to register the pain of the assault before the room started to shift and blackness overtook her vision.

And then…nothing.

THE unmistakable vibration and jostle of being in a moving vehicle slowly dragged Kara into unwelcome consciousness. Her head throbbed like a bitch, and a coppery tang that she recognized as blood lingered in her mouth. She felt disoriented, possibly concussed, as she tried to blink open her eyes and gauge her surroundings. It was dim, the dark tint of the windows blocking the sunlight and distorting the view of any passing cars. Even if she tried to signal for help, no one would see. Trying to sit up, Kara groaned as gravity further assaulted her already injured head. Looking around, Kara noticed that she was, thankfully, alone in the backseat of what was obviously a luxury car. There was a divider blocking her view of the front seat, so Kara couldn't see the driver. She gathered

Hideaway

enough strength to bang on the black screen, desperate to get through to whoever was on the other side.

"Hey, asshole! Let me out!" Kara shouted angrily. There was only silence, much as she expected. She tried the doors, but they were locked. Again, no surprise there. She doubted her kidnappers would have gone through the trouble to take her from the manor and then make escape a viable option, but she would have felt stupid not trying something. Seriously, she was a little over being taken hostage. Once was an honest mistake of fate. Twice made her feel like she'd done something to piss fate the fuck off.

Kara looked out the window for any clues of where they may be headed. The scenery still looked like Illinois, but she wasn't sure how long they'd been driving. They could be in fucking Canada for all she knew. Had Cade noticed she was missing, yet? Would he think she'd run away again? Would he hate her, thinking she'd betrayed him after the meaningful night they shared together? She was seriously deranged if she was worried about hurting her captor's feelings by inadvertently being kidnapped by *another* fucking psycho. Apparently, Cade had fucked her up exquisitely, but she'd think about the massive amounts of therapy she needed later. At that moment, she needed a plan of escape.

She was dozing when she felt the car slow and then stop in front of large, iron wrought gates. The ornate, gold inlaid flourishes of hand crafted metal and the ostentatious R initial in the middle looked eerily familiar, but Kara couldn't place where she'd seen it before, her head still cloudy from being bludgeoned. The gates opened automatically, ushering them in, and Kara felt a little more panicked as she heard them screech to a close behind her. The car traveled down a long, winding drive, surrounded by perfectly manicured trees before coming upon a large, Colonial-style mansion that definitely looked familiar. Her sense of foreboding grew as the car pulled around to the spacious, multi-car garage and parked. Adrenaline thumped in her blood as Kara waited for the only thing that could happen next: her door opening. She was prepared when she finally heard the click of the locks releasing, rearing back and kicking with all her might against the unassuming assailant opening the car door.

"Fuck! Fucking bitch!" the man gasped in surprise, recovering himself quickly and grabbing her ankle viciously before she could land another blow. He twisted her ankle brutally, flipping her onto her stomach before dragging her out of the car by her legs. Pinning her against the leather seats, the man pulled her up by her hair and forced her against his body. "Stop fucking fighting, or I'll dose you again," he ordered harshly, his spit landing on her check as he spat out the words.

Swallowing her panic and revulsion, Kara stopped struggling, the threat having its desired effect. *Dose her again*? Had she been drugged? That would explain the mental haze, although her head injury definitely contributed to that as well. Fucking hell, she was getting sick of being drugged and kidnapped.

"Get going," the stranger ordered, pushing her forward and causing her to stumble slightly before regaining her balance.

"Where are we?" Kara couldn't stop herself from asking, even though she doubted she'd receive an answer.

"No questions," the man barked out as he shoved her forward again.

Hideaway 341

Kara walked up some steps and exited through a door at the back of the garage, the unknown man close behind. He pushed her down a well-lit hall and then up toward a huge staircase that reminded her of the manor. Not that the house was anything like Cade's. Where Ashford Manor was all dramatic hues, history and art, golden fixtures, and intentionally obnoxious opulence, the mansion in which she was currently being held prisoner was stark. Everything was bright and white, so much so that it hurt Kara's eyes to take it all in. At that moment, she missed Cade's garish taste, even his fucking chandeliers. In spite of everything, the manor had started to feel like something more than a prison. And, as Kara looked around her, she had a feeling she would fare far worse in the new prison.

The gruff, un-talkative man forced her down the hall on the upper level, all the way to a room at the very end. Opening the door, the man thrust Kara inside and shut the door without another word, locking her in. Kidnapped, drugged, held hostage, and no escape in sight—it was all starting to feel very familiar.

Resolved not to make things easier for anyone by being a good little prisoner, Kara immediately scoured the room for a chance of escape. Upon closer inspection, her situation was growing more grim by the moment. The room was nearly bare. All furniture had been removed save for the large bed in the middle of the room. Heavy drapes obscured windows that were sealed shut, offering no way of escape. The adjoining bathroom housed the bare necessities: a toilet, a large bathtub, and a sink with empty cupboards underneath. There was nothing that could be fashioned into a weapon. Nothing that could serve as any sort of protection or defense. Nothing that could help her evade her entrapment. Kara could do nothing more than sit in silence and wait for whatever dreadful fate loomed in the distance.

She wasn't kept waiting long. A demanding knock sounded from the door, disrupting Kara's fixation on the textured patterns in the ceiling while she sprawled out on the bed. Clearly, the knock was more a warning than a courtesy as the door swung open with no admittance from her. Cautiously, Kara rose from the bed to look at her kidnapper. Her brows rose in surprise at the man haughtily filling the space of the doorway.

Avery Reed.

Of course, that's why the sprawling mansion felt familiar. She'd attended an academic fundraising event held by Mr. Reed and his wife at their home. Though she hadn't been occupying an isolated bedroom clearly fitted for suspicious purposes the last time she was there, Kara remembered seeing the lower levels at the charity function. But why had he personally overseen her abduction and captivity? He certainly didn't seem like the type to soil his own hands with such matters; that's why he had hordes of money to buy off criminals to do the dirty work for him. Criminals like Cade. The thought gave her a chill.

Kara tried to summon what she had gleaned of the man's character from social events at the university. Avery Reed was intelligent—or at least well-educated, as the two traits didn't always go hand in hand—charismatic, and a pleasant conversationalist. He was quite indulgent with his wife, a bit overzealous with his alcohol, and incredibly wealthy. Though Kara didn't have an encyclopedia on the man, perhaps she had intuited enough information to negotiate with him rationally. Hoping to appeal to the congeniality she had experienced with him many times before, Kara decided on an approach that was friendly and conversational, playing into the farce that this was all just an unfortunate misunderstanding.

"Mr. Reed, this is a surprise," Kara greeted with an ease she didn't feel.

"Call me Avery, please," he answered, all charm and good manners. "I believe we have been acquainted quite long enough for the familiarity of first names. I'll extend you the same courtesy, Kara. I am slightly disappointed that you didn't recognize my estate when you arrived."

"Oh, I definitely recognized your estate when we reached the gilded gates *emblazoned* with your initials," Kara retorted, voice dripping with sarcasm. "I was merely surprised that a man of such prominence would involve himself in criminal activities and kidnapping."

"Desperate times call for desperate measures, I'm afraid," Avery responded without remorse. "It is not yet common knowledge, but my wife of twelve years is endeavoring to divorce me."

"My condolences to Mrs. Reed on having been married to you for so long. I expect a rectification of that unhappy union was long overdue," Kara responded in contempt.

"Yes, well, it's Mrs. Hall-Reed, actually. And I wouldn't cast your pity too quickly if I were you. As it happens, the Halls are endowed with more money than God or even I."

"I am pleasantly surprised you're still able to make the distinction between yourself and divinity. I've found that unbecoming amounts of wealth and over-inflated egos addle the mind in that regard."

Exhibit A: Caden fucking Ashford.

Avery fixed her with an unattractive glare before continuing his self-indulgent tirade. "All that Hall money will certainly be put to good use ensuring their prenup is upheld and the divorce lawyer is able to rob me of everything I have. Thanks to the meticulous prying of my soon-to-be ex-wife's private investigator, the accusations of my alleged infidelity got a whole lot more provable. Video footage of prostitute solicitation is not a great look for me, as I'm sure the judge will agree."

"I bet that's not the sex-tape release you'd envisioned for yourself," Kara responded with a laugh. "Also, in addition to being distinctly compromising, isn't soliciting sex also illegal?"

"So my wife tells me. Whores really should come with a disclaimer, 'abandon hope all ye who enter here,'" he proclaimed theatrically.

"That is a tragic misuse of Dante," Kara retorted disparagingly.

"Oh yes, I forgot I was keeping company with Dr. Caine, the great defender of academia," Avery said with an air of mockery.

"Trust me, you wouldn't be the first to forget," Kara responded, fond remembrance stirring at the thought of another man who seemed all too keen to dismiss her earned title because he knew it pissed her off.

Cade.

Kara hoped against hope that he had discovered her missing and would somehow happen upon the correct source of her disappearance. Had Avery's men been sloppy and left some trace of her being taken? If not, would Cade think she'd run away from him again? She had already broken his trust once, so he wouldn't be

Hideaway

unjustified if he suspected her treachery. The thought of experiencing Cade's wrath was almost as terrifying as whatever plans Avery had in store for her. Avery may intend to kill her, but if Cade thought she had betrayed him, he would destroy her in more ways than one.

"Well, Dr. Caine, perhaps you can enlighten me as to the location of my esteemed collection of *The Canterbury Tales*?"

"I believe you mean the university's esteemed collection of *The Canterbury Tales*, as you were so generous as to donate it to our library, in your wife's name I might add. Adds a certain touch of irony to the whole situation, don't you think?"

"I could do with a little less irony in this situation, as it were," Avery bit back spitefully.

"Why do you even need them? You obviously have more than enough money."

"I don't believe you comprehend the direness of my predicament. Everything you see around you isn't solely mine; it is equity shared with my bitch of a wife who is determined to take everything in a messy, public divorce just because I screwed a few whores." Avery began to pace the room, his frustration starting to put cracks in his composed facade.

"Oh yes, poor little rich boy who can't keep his cock in his pants," Kara taunted, earning her a hateful glare as Avery's frantic movements stilled.

"I've been donating numerous historical items—across a vast range of regions and institutions, of course—with the distinct intention of having them all back in my possession in due time. My wife thinks I'm engaging in a futile attempt to win her back—as you realized with the university's collection, all donations are made in her name—but really I'm establishing a portable fortune that my wife will have no claim to once the divorce is finalized. The pieces will discretely disappear over time, the talents of men such as Caden Ashford allowing them to make their way into the hands of collectors more than willing to pay a generous sum, and I will have some capital to rebuild my life amid the ruins. The plan is infallible."

"Apparently not," Kara responded scathingly, finding the grand reveal of his master plan a little underwhelming. All that scheming so that a privileged man wouldn't have to endure the full consequences of his sins. Maybe the cheating bastard shouldn't have been as quick to violate his vows as he was to sign a prenup.

"Yes," Avery said with a pause to consider the full extent of his failure. "I must admit, I hadn't expected a librarian to impede a simple operation that had already proven to be successful. The Chaucer text was not the first to be extracted; others have already been re-acquired. I must say, your institution's system is flawed if you are the only individual capable of summoning a rare text. Whatever would happen if, heaven forbid, you were to disappear indefinitely? All would be lost."

"Of course we have taken the necessary precautions to maintain the safety of the texts, but I don't see the necessity of discussing backup procedure with you."

"Not to sound desperate, but I really must attain that book. A buyer has already been selected, and I fear they grow restless with the delay. Perhaps I would make more headway with your replacement on the occasion that the department of rare books had a sudden vacancy," Avery commented darkly, watching as Kara carefully considered her response to the inferred threat.

"I'm afraid you'll find most individuals of my profession possess a certain inherent protectiveness regarding historically rare texts. And you needn't bother kidnapping yet another librarian as your donated edition of *The Canterbury Tales* is no longer housed on university grounds."

"What? Where is it?" Avery asked impatiently, panic flickering across his face at the new information.

"I haven't the faintest idea," Kara answered flippantly, inspecting her nails as though she wasn't bothered by his threats in the least.

"Perhaps your memory needs rousing," he said dangerously as he stalked toward where she sat primly on the bed.

"You may try, of course, though I doubt you'll have any more progress on that account than your predecessor. And he possesses more impressive methods of persuasion than you could ever dream of having," Kara taunted suggestively with a pointed look at the space between Avery's thighs. She knew it was dangerous to toy with an already desperate man, but Kara couldn't help herself. It was one of the great flaws of her nature to lash out when she was cornered and helpless.

"I tried to handle this situation civilly, Dr. Caine," Avery addressed formally, his eyes turning hard and cold. "But you refuse to act reasonably. Whatever happens next is on your conscience, not mine." With those ominous last words, Avery walked out of the room and locked the door behind him.

Once again, Kara found herself enveloped in the silence of solitude.

Hours passed. Truthfully, whatever her captor had planned for her would be far less agonizing than slowly waiting for it to happen. The delay was likely just another layer of torture. And she thought Cade was the only man in her life obsessed with punishment. Clearly, Avery was just as sadistic as he was. "Get the fuck on with it!" Kara shouted into the emptiness of the room, prepared for whatever Avery might throw at her if only it would end the mind-numbing purgatory of waiting.

Pointlessly, she threw her fists into the door, relishing the way the loud *bang* ungraciously disrupted the silence and the sharpness that flooded her nerves when her flesh met with the wood. Kara continued her assault on the unrelenting door, throwing her whole body into the barrier to her freedom. She slammed herself into the door until her shoulder burned, protesting the useless violence. Stepping back, Kara heard the unmistakable sound of footsteps descending toward her room. Finally, Avery would put her out of her misery. Kara stood dispassionate and resolved as she eyed the door expectantly, a key rattling as someone unlocked the door. There was no knock this time, signaling the time for pleasantries at an end. Swiftly, the door swung open, announcing Kara's doom.

CHAPTER SIXTEEN

AT the sight of the dark figure looming in the doorway, Kara had to resist the urge to lean over and spill the sparse contents of her stomach onto the floor. She'd spent the better part of the day in hell, but now she beheld the devil himself.

Jace.

The room echoed with a dark laugh as Jace devoured the horror in her eyes. "Not who you were expecting, sweetheart? Pleasant surprise, I hope," he taunted cruelly.

"What the fuck are you doing here?" Kara asked angrily once her initial surprise waned and she regained her ability to speak.

"Come now Kara, I thought you were supposed to be intelligent. What do you think I'm doing here?"

"It was you," Kara gasped as realization dawned.

The sickeningly familiar scent of cologne that she couldn't quite place—it had been him. Jace was the one who had knocked her out and taken her from the manor. And it made sense, really. How else would an intruder have made it past Cade's heavy security without any warning? Because the intruder wasn't an intruder; he was a resident. But Jace was Cade's closest companion and business partner. What reason would he have to cross Cade? "Why? Why betray Cade to align yourself with an incompetent bastard like Avery? What's in it for you?"

"Quite simply—you. You, Kara, are the answer to all of your questions."

Kara stared at him quizzically, the sense of his riddling answer eluding her.

"Again, your powers of deduction disappoint, Dr. Caine. Must I spell it out for you?"

"Please," Kara requested through gritted teeth, irritated to be so invested in his explanation.

"Oh, I do like it when you beg," Jace acquiesced, a cruel smile spreading across his face as he inched closer to her. "*You* are the reason I left Cade. I could no longer stomach his weakness concerning you. He was willing to jeopardize our business, our clients, our livelihood just so he could fuck around with a high-strung bitch with more morality than common sense." Jace stalked toward her slowly, a barely concealed threat of danger hidden within the predatory movement.

Warily, Kara retreated until she felt the bed brush against the back of her legs.

Shit.

Hideaway

Left with little alternative in the enclosed room, Kara jolted away from the bed as Jace's approach pressed her toward the corner of the room. A soft thud emanated as her back collided with the far wall, announcing that she had run out of room to hide. Jace drew nearer, closing the space between them until he hovered above her, the searing warmth of his body assaulting hers. His light blue eyes smoldered with passion, though whether it was based in violence or lust or greed she couldn't ascertain. Kara stood frozen, unnaturally deprived of the ability to fight or flee, as Jace's hand shot out, his fingers entangling themselves in her hair. He tugged sharply, forcing her head up to look at him. Unable to disobey the unspoken command, Kara met his gaze with all of the hatred and loathing and revulsion that had begun to boil within her. Jace merely laughed at her disdain, amused that someone so weak and inconsequential could even presume to feel powerful in their emotions.

Very soon, he would instruct her on just how powerless she was, and he would immensely enjoy putting the bitch in her place. "As for your last question," Jace continued, bending low till his lips brushed against her ear. "You are what's in it for me. *You* are my reward for helping Avery." Jace waited for his words to sink in, enjoying the delicious scent of fear seeping from her pores as she began to realize how he would be claiming his reward. "I am going to fuck you until everyone in this fucking house can hear you scream, and no one will do a damn thing to stop me. This time, Ashford won't be here to interrupt. This time, you're mine," Jace threatened in a tone of violence that masqueraded as seduction, his teeth grazing her earlobe.

In equal parts rage and terror, Kara slapped Jace as hard as she could and attempted to make a run for the door. She only made it a few feet before Jace jerked her back toward him, his face the very picture of rage, as he viciously pulled on her hair as though it were a leash tethering her to him. His fingers twisted brutally at her scalp, punishing her for the red imprint of her hand that marred his bristled cheek.

"You'll regret that, bitch," Jace hissed.

"Whatever regrets I may have in my life, I can safely say, hitting a bastard like you will never be one of them."

Cruel fingers wrapped around Kara's throat, pressing dangerously tight as she felt herself being forced backward. She staggered back awkwardly, Jace's unforgiving hold on her neck the only thing that kept her upright. When the backs of her knees hit the bed, Jace lowered his hands to her hips, his thumbs digging into her tender skin bruisingly. In one swift move, Jace lifted Kara and threw her unceremoniously onto the plush, white bed.

Kara gasped in panic, trying to drag herself away, desperate to escape Jace and whatever hateful fate awaited her amid the stark white sheets of a stranger's bed. Jace grabbed her ankle and flipped her onto her stomach. There was a muffled screech of terror as Jace rolled on top of her, crushing her beneath his full weight and effectively smothering her within the stifling fullness of the duvet. Kara kicked uselessly beneath him, unable to throw him from his position on top of her. Her lungs begged for air.

"If you stop struggling, I'll allow you to breathe," Jace negotiated calmly as though he were the level headed one between the two of them.

Fucking bastard. Heavy as fuck, fucking bastard.

Try as she might, Kara couldn't seem to override her body's instinctual need to resist suffocation. Her body warred against her mind for survival. She knew giving in would save her, she screamed at her limbs to stop fighting, but they couldn't welcome Jace's assault peacefully. Gradually, numbness spread, a blanketing darkness that felt different from the blackness evoked by having her eyes covered. Then, there was nothing.

Kara awoke to a sharp stinginess in her cheek, her lungs hungrily devouring the precious oxygen they had been denied. Jace hovered above her, his knees tightly encasing her hips, his hand raised should she require another slap to rouse her. She bucked beneath him, trying to dismount him from her body, but he held firm, knees digging into the nearly naked flesh of her hips painfully.

"Get the fuck off of me!" Kara screamed in frustration.

"Come now, Kara. Didn't you learn your lesson earlier? Do not fight me," Jace scolded.

Kara screamed. Not for help. Not for mercy. Not out of fear. But out of a completely overwhelming, mind shattering, soul fracturing sense of futility.

"Save your breath, sweetheart. I haven't given you a reason to scream. Yet," Jace cautioned darkly.

Slowly, the will to fight for her freedom faded, replaced by the bleak acceptance that she was at the mercy of whatever destruction Jace intended. Kara stopped fighting, relaxing into the softness of the bed as it welcomed her surrender with open arms. A noxious glint of satisfaction filled Jace's eyes as he felt Kara submit beneath him.

Warm hands seared her skin as they traveled down the length of her body, assessing every curve with lascivious scrutiny. Jace relished the foreplay of heightening fear before an act of violence. With Kara in particular, he was more than happy to savor the buildup. He had waited weeks for that moment, and he had every intention of enjoying himself to the fullest extent.

"We enjoyed a night like this once before, didn't we Kara?" Jace reminisced fondly, the venomous words as sweet as honey on his lips. "Ashford had no right to stop me from claiming what was rightfully mine," Jace continued, traces of unresolved anger in his voice.

His hands moved to the top of her nightgown, tracing his finger along the low cut neckline but not dipping below. Kara held her breath, bracing herself for violence, but it didn't come. Jace ran his knuckles down her neck, across her collar bones, and over the exposure of her chest, as light as any caress Cade had offered. The gentleness surprised Kara, leaving her more uneasy than any of Jace's characteristic roughness might have.

"I saw you first, you know, so small and helpless as you carried a stack of books almost the size of yourself. I told Ashford, when the time came, you wouldn't give us any trouble. You took me by surprise, Kara. Such determination. No fear," he said, sounding almost reverent, as he slipped his hand slightly beneath the top of her nightgown.

Kara shivered in dread.

"Then the boss in all his gallantry stormed in before I had a chance to crack the dauntless exterior and compel your surrender.

Hideaway

But I bided my time, waited for you to come to me willingly, and you did."

Kara shut her eyes tighter against the haunting memory of her naivety as she felt Jace's hand slide further down her nightgown.

"And there Ashford was again, stealing you from beneath me where you belong. That night, he took you for himself didn't he?"

Kara made no move to answer or look at Jace, but he could read the truth on her face. Though they had not been intimate that first night, she had shared Cade's bed. It had been the contrast of Cade's protection and empathy to Jace's violence that had opened Kara to the prospect of falling for him. Whether or not Kara had been aware of it before the moment of Jace's question, she knew that the night Cade had saved her was the night that he had taken her heart as well.

"He must not have been man enough to keep you because you ran not long after. And who came after you and escorted your return to the manor? Him? No, he had more important things to do. I knew you well enough to guess where you'd gone, and I was the one who brought you back. He didn't take your escape very well did he?"

Kara blushed at the memory. Though she cared for Cade deeply, he had his own collection of flaws. His affinity for corporal punishment made the top of the list, right beneath criminal entrepreneurship and kidnapping. She had to admit, it was a rather daunting combination of vices.

"You see, Ashford likes his companions kept in line. Docile creatures ready to do his bidding. Unlike him, I prefer my women with a little more fight," Jace said as he cupped her breast beneath the thin silk of her dress.

Tightly shut lids startled open as the indecent caress awoke the fighter slumbering beneath the surface of Kara's detached existence. She pulled away sharply from Jace's touch, no longer resigned to stoically suffer his advances. Kara was offered a gratified smile in return as Jace grabbed her and continued groping beneath her clothes.

"There's my girl," he commended proudly, his voice husky with arousal as she fought against him. "I was afraid Ashford had extinguished that fight I was so drawn to from the moment we met. Glad to see the fire can still be roused."

Struggling against him as fiercely as she could, Kara got in a few good blows that were more nail than strength before Jace climbed on top of her and straddled her hips, the weight of his body rendering her immobile. She struggled to keep tears of frustration at bay as Jace took hold of both her wrists, holding her down as he bent low to take his fill of her mouth. Unable to pull away or resist, her protests were smothered beneath the vile kiss that nauseated her every sense.

"That's it baby, make me work for it," he said when he finally freed her lips, feeling the rush of adrenaline as her struggling made the conquest all the sweeter.

Kara aimed for his face as she spat the taste of him from her mouth in disgust. Jace seemed to relish her hatred as he calmly wiped her saliva from his face before administering a punishing backhanded blow to her right cheek. Kara gasped in pain and shock, turning her reddened cheek into the pillow and willing herself not to give Jace the satisfaction of seeing her cry. Jace grasped her jaw in one hand and turned her to face him.

"Do you like it rough, Kara? Is that why you like to provoke people who hold all the power over you? Because you enjoy feeling the brunt of their anger?"

With a glare of animosity, Kara kept silent, though she knew there was some truth to his words. That was not the first time that she had found a sense of power in acting out when she felt powerless, regardless of the consequences, and she prayed it would not be the last. Kara searched the depths of her being to find some minuscule semblance of submission that might save her from inciting Jace's anger to the point of destruction. But as she met the arrogance of his challenging gaze, she felt any pretense of subservience vanish as a wave of resolute defiance took its place.

"I will take that as a yes. Now, would you care to see if your initial assessment of my kinks was correct? See, I am able to fuck just fine without tying up girls and beating them, but it makes it a hell of a lot more fun when I do," Jace stated threateningly as he momentarily released Kara's arms and grasped the top of her nightgown.

In one swift move, he ripped the dress all the way down the middle, fully exposing the nakedness of Kara's body beneath. As she struggled to conceal her most intimate areas, Jace ripped a strip from the nightdress, caught one of Kara's arms, tied the cloth tightly around her wrist, and knotted the ends around one of the bedposts. Quickly, Jace ripped another piece from her dress and subjected her other wrist to the same treatment. Kara found herself naked, restrained, and stretched to the point of discomfort beneath Jace, completely at the mercy of the man's twisted desires. She had never in her life felt quite so powerless, and the vulnerability she felt in that moment was like a crushing weight.

With his task half complete, Jace removed himself momentarily to admire the full view of his work. He wasn't sure if he had seen anything quite so enticing as Kara—naked, tied, teary-eyed, mere moments from breaking beneath his will. Yes, she was a gorgeous sight to behold. And at that moment, she was all his. "Just like when we first met," Jace said in a tone that bore a resemblance to nostalgia, stroking the makeshift bonds holding her wrists high above her head. How many times had he imagined ripping off her dress and tying her up like he had when he interrogated her in that basement before Caden fucking Ashford saved the day? He'd never kept count, but it could safely be considered a fair amount. Lost to his own fantasies, Jace trailed eager fingers along Kara's thigh, inching his way higher.

Pleased that her legs had full functionality even if her hands did not, Kara waited for the opportune moment to make use of the last weapon at her disposal. As Jace's invasive exploration met with the apex of Kara's thighs, her foot made forceful contact with the delicate, organ-housing region of his abdomen.

"Fucking bitch!" Jace swore in surprise as he clutched his aching stomach.

Taking advantage of his distraction, Kara attempted to land a second kick. Prepared for her offensive strike, he caught her foot in the air before it reached her intended target. In retribution, Jace held her with a punishing grip that felt as though it crushed bone, lowered his mouth to Kara's ankle, and bit deeply. Her resistance temporarily subdued, Kara cried out at the shock of pain radiating from the tender curve of her ankle. Jace grabbed what was left of Kara's gown and tore two more strips of silk as she struggled beneath him. Grasping her ankle tightly, he pulled her leg toward the edge of the bed and latched her to the bottom post.

Taking his time as he walked around to the other side of the bed, Jace appreciated her helplessness with cruel satisfaction. She panicked when he mounted the bed and reached for her other ankle, fighting against him like a trapped animal. In spite of her final attempt to delay the inevitable, Jace captured her foot easily, digging his fingers into her heel as he spread her open as wide as possible before tying her to the bedpost. Crawling toward her, Jace knelt between Kara's thighs, reached for her panties, and impatiently ripped off the last, thin piece of protection that kept her from full exposure under his salacious gaze.

Kara felt the hot tears of fury, frustration, and futility roll down her cheeks as she stared at the despicable man forcefully situated between her legs with a loathing that was immeasurable. Even if she spent every breath of the rest of her life cursing him, she knew the expression of her hatred would never be satisfied.

Evaluating her restraints, nakedness, and tears, Jace determined that he was sufficiently satisfied to proceed to the main event. Kara grunted beneath the crushing weight of him as he mounted her, jean sheathed legs straddling her bare hips. He rather enjoyed the view of Kara trembling beneath him like a timid virgin; he would take it slow with her and savor the experience. She flinched from his touch as he stroked his finger along her jaw, instinctively keeping her eyes downcast as though she could ignore his advances if she didn't see them. A stinging slap to her left cheek drew her shocked attention once again.

"Look at me," Jace commanded. "I want you to be fully aware of *who* is fucking you."

Kara met Jace's gaze with a look of determined opposition and watched as he resolved to deprive her of her last remnants of stubborn pride. Strong, bruising hands moved to Kara's upper arms, still suspended from each bedpost, and found the most tender point of exposed flesh. Jace's grip tightened cruelly. Kara let out a whimper of pained protest, but did not avert her gaze.

"I am going to mark you, Kara." Jace moved his mouth to her shoulder and bit down, hard. "I want you to see my handiwork on your body when you look in the mirror." He marked her other shoulder with the deep imprint of his teeth. Kara bucked beneath him, longing to escape the torture. "I will brand you—body, mind, and soul."

Jace took to her bare breasts and dealt each a punishing blow. Kara let out a sharp gasp. Jace moved his hands lower to Kara's hips and dug his fingers into the hallows. Kara looked upward to avoid spilling the traitorous tears that had begun to pool. The break of eye contact drew another reprimanding blow to her already stinging cheek. Jace grabbed her jaw violently and captured Kara's gaze once again. "When I finally deliver you to Cade, I want him to know every place I touched you." Jace clawed his way down her inner thigh. "Used you." He marred the other thigh with the mark of his teeth. "Fucked you." And, as if to emphasize his meaning, Jace lowered his jeans and boxers and entered her suddenly with all the force of his body.

Hideaway

Kara cried out in protest, but could do nothing more than lie prostrate beneath his weight. She looked at Jace through shimmering eyes of unadulterated hate as he maintained a steady onslaught of thrusts. Jace lowered his lips to hers and delivered what resembled more of a punishing assault than a kiss. Vengeful lips crushed her own, his tongue claimed her mouth as unwilling territory, and his teeth drew blood from her bottom lip. Kara's teeth found their own easy target and bit down on his unwelcome tongue as hard as she could.

Jace gasped in shock and rage as he wiped the stain of red from his lips and wrapped a firm hand around Kara's neck in retaliation. His thumb pressured her windpipe until she was at the brink of passing out. Kara looked into Jace's eyes and dared him to press harder. She'd rather he amused himself with her unconscious body than be aware and awake for the festivities. Jace understood her longing for oblivion and cruelly kept her just at the edge of pain without tipping over into unconsciousness. His pace quickened as he continued his assault, pounding into her weakened body eagerly. Finally his release neared, and he lowered his mouth to her breast, biting with a violent force equal to his punishing thrusts as he finished inside her. Kara cringed inwardly as she felt his essence fill and merge with her body. She didn't know if she would ever be free of his scent on her body. Even if she peeled flesh from bone, Kara felt her spirit would always bear the dark mark of Jace, like he possessed a piece of her soul.

Finally finished with his task, Jace removed his body from hers, cleaned himself on the sheets of the bed, and walked out of the room without another word, shutting the door behind him. Kara tugged hopelessly on the restraints Jace hadn't bothered to remove, finally giving in to exhaustion after a few minutes of struggling. She liberated the desolation that had taken root in her core and allowed it to consume her. Kara wept away her endless grief until her body had no more tears to give and then slipped into the welcoming oblivion of sleep.

Kara startled into consciousness with the sound of fabric tearing and the sickening scent of cologne. Jace hovered above her, his hands on her wrists as he freed them from his makeshift restraints. Wishing she had the strength to pull away from Jace's touch, Kara trembled beneath him, fearful that he was merely giving her the false hope of freedom before continuing his assault. Without a word, Jace dropped her abused wrists on the bed, removed himself from his position on top of her, and moved to her ankles. Free at last, Kara attempted to rub the life back into her deathly cold hands, watching disinterestedly as crimson rings blossomed on her wrists in the wake of the tight ties. The marks were merely another memento of her night spent in hell.

As soon as her ankles were unfastened, Kara closed her legs and drew them up toward her chest, her aching muscles protesting the swift change of position. Kara's eyes filled with tears of relief as she relished the first chance she'd had at comfort or privacy in countless hours. Jace watched her stoically, making no move to touch her or talk to her. Slowly, Jace's hands drifted to the front of his shirt, unfastening the buttons one at a time as he kept his eyes locked on her. Cowering with dread, Kara wrapped her arms tighter around her knees, rocking slightly back and forth in an attempt to calm her nerves as she watched Jace undress. She flinched as Jace walked toward her, his chest and abdomen bare and the top of his boxers visible from the low rise of his jeans. Keeping a slight distance, Jace stopped in front of her and offered his shirt with an outstretched hand.

"Here," he said coldly, the harshness of his tone eliminating any gallantry that his actions might have portrayed.

Kara looked at the proffered article of clothing and shook her head, not trusting herself to say anything to Jace without sobbing after what he'd done to her. No matter how cold she was, there was no fucking way she was wearing his shirt.

"I suggest you swallow your pride and take it, sweetheart," Jace retorted cruelly. "Unless you want to walk out of here completely naked. Trust me, you'll get no complaints from me. And I'm sure Avery's men wouldn't mind a nice show either. The choice is entirely yours."

Jolting with equal parts horror and hope at the announcement that she was being released from the room, Kara summoned her strength, sat up, and reached for Jace's shirt, being very careful not to touch him in the process. She cringed as the material made contact with her skin, still warm from Jace's body. The lingering smell of his essence and cologne on the pale blue fabric made her want to wretch as she held the shirt in front of her to shield her body from Jace's gaze.

"We're leaving. You have five minutes to be ready," Jace ordered before walking out of the room and locking the door behind him.

Jace's shirt still clutched tightly to her chest, Kara exhaled shakily. They were leaving. Perhaps, she still had a chance at freedom. The hopeful thought granted her enough motivation to pull herself from the bed and head for the adjoining bathroom she hadn't had the privilege of using in god knows how many hours.

Five minutes.

She used her few minutes of freedom to attempt to gather the shattered pieces of her soul and rearrange them in such a way that she would be able to survive whatever trials came next. Swallowing her revulsion, Kara slipped into Jace's shirt, thankful to at least have some form of covering. She had no undergarments, but the shirt was long enough to cover her mid thighs and provide some level of modesty. The sleeves were far too large, so Kara rolled them until they hung at her wrists. Though she had no underwear or shoes and was dressed in merely a shirt, Kara exited the bathroom feeling a little more human. She'd avoided the mirror entirely; she had no desire to see Jace's handiwork reflected back at her. In fact, she wasn't sure if she would ever be able to stomach looking at herself again. Far too quickly, the door opened again revealing Jace dressed in a new shirt, jacket, overcoat, scarf, and boots. If Kara wasn't already feeling underdressed to be venturing out into the winter weather, she definitely was at that moment.

Jace eyed Kara appraisingly, taking a keen satisfaction in seeing her dressed only in his shirt, knowing Cade would be forced to smell himself on her. His marks were all over her body, his shirt doing very little to cover the bruises and bite marks. Jace's cock hardened at thought of the agony Cade would feel in discovering each and every one. The bastard would be able to see every place he touched his little whore. Every spot he used her and hurt her. Jace only wished he could keep her longer and fuck her more before disposing of her, but he had to stick to the plan.

There was no way Cade would risk Kara's safety again. He would know Kara would never be free from danger unless the book was in Avery's possession. Kara was more than willing to sacrifice herself for the stupid fucking book, but Cade absolutely would not allow that to happen, not with how far gone he was for the bitch. So they'd borrowed Kara, *briefly*, to give Cade a little taste of what would happen if he didn't cooperate and get the librarian to hand over Avery's book. After delivering his girlfriend in her current state, Jace had little doubt of Cade's assistance in acquiring the text. Avery would get the book. Jace would get the commission. And Cade would get to keep his slut in one piece. Win-win for everyone without a bit of bloodshed. Of course, the violence was the fun part, but their plan was one of convenience not amusement. As long as he got the money, Jace was happy.

"We are going on a little trip, sweetheart. Time to pay the boss a visit," he announced darkly.

Kara blanched. Though Cade was the one person in the world she longed to see, the thought of him seeing her in that state had the chilling effect of ice in her veins. Jace looked at her with sadistic glee, and Kara remembered that Cade was the exact audience for which her body had been destroyed. Jace may have used her for his pleasure, but the marks he had ensured would remain afterward like a receipt for services rendered were specifically for Cade's perusal.

"The car is waiting outside." He took a moment to admire the view, and Kara wrapped the shirt around her body even tighter, hoping to conceal as much as possible. Jace noticed her tension and endeavored to increase it, wrapping his arm around her shoulders, pressing his body against hers, and very physically escorting her from the room down to where the garage was housed.

"Is the manhandling really necessary? I am perfectly capable of walking to the car without your assistance," Kara complained, trying to escape Jace's hold.

His forceful embrace tightened as he lowered his head to hers, his breath chilling her heart as it warmed her skin. "Where is the fun in that, sweetheart? And we need to be keeping up appearances. Can't have the hostage escorting herself to the getaway car, now can we?"

Kara scowled but said nothing as Jace continued to physically push her toward their destination. Avery Reed's estate was nearly as grand as Cade's, and they walked for some time. Finally, Jace stopped in front of a door in the middle of the hall and a large garage full of black vehicles of various sizes awaited on the other side. Leading her down the stairs, Jace pulled Kara to an SUV with the headlights already on and ready to go. As a driver was being utilized, Kara assumed Jace would be keeping her company in the back.

Lovely.

"Ladies first," he said as he opened the side door and ushered her in.

Kara took a steadying breath and stepped up into the car, sliding as far to the other side as she could. After signaling the driver on, Jace entered behind her and shut the door. Kara looked around the car and was both revolted and relieved to find herself alone with Jace. "Was Mr. Reed not interested in seeing his endeavor come to fruition?" she asked warily, cautious of Avery's absence.

"Were you disappointed not to have received a farewell from my client? I believe he thought it best not to implicate himself further in the situation."

"He didn't seem to have any trouble implicating himself last night," Kara couldn't resist retorting with tart sarcasm.

Jace laughed with tainted amusement as he stroked the bruises on her neck, then his fingers trailed suggestively lower to the button of the shirt over her chest. "Care for round two?" he asked as a single finger slipped beneath the thin material and found the mark he left on her upper breast. Kara shivered, her fear palpable. Jace relished her terror; he inhaled the scent of it hungrily as if he could feed on it. To savor that feeling, he claimed her mouth in a kiss that was neither passion nor violence, just a final expression of power and control. Kara sat frozen to the point of empty surrender until at last Jace withdrew his lips.

"Lucky for you, I don't enjoy having an audience," he said, gesturing to the driver ahead. "I'll have to save it for next time." Her safety momentarily assured, Kara relaxed slightly in her seat and observed from the window as the barren trees of winter passed in a blur.

Kara had no account of the time elapsed, but she eventually found herself in familiar territory. They would be nearing Ashford Manor soon. The cold silence of the car was filled with the incessant patter of water droplets upon the roof and windows as a sudden rain covered the outside world in a blanket of bleakness. Kara wrapped the thin material of Jace's shirt tighter around her chest, but it aided little against the internal chill that threatened to consume her. Finally,

Kara saw the welcome gates of Cade's estate come into view, and a thankful sigh escaped her lips. She was home.

The driver pulled up to the speaker at the gates, and Jace lowered the window to announce their arrival. "Special delivery for Caden Ashford."

Kara didn't hear the response coming from the intercom, but the gates began to open.

Jace leaned over Kara, too close for comfort, and opened her door. "Out you go, sweetheart," he said nastily, beckoning her into the mist of rain that waited outside the car.

Kara looked at him incredulously. The distance from the gates to the actual house was quite vast, and she was keenly aware of having no proper clothes or shoes. "Forcing me to risk pneumonia on top of your other offenses is a little passive aggressive, don't you think?"

"I think you'll survive. And I have no intention of being within shooting distance when Ashford discovers how you were entertained in his absence."

Kara shot him a dark look in response to his cavalier attitude regarding the atrocities she'd endured at his hands. "Fine," she said sullenly as she headed for the exit and braced herself for the chilly downpour.

"Until next time, Kara," he said threateningly, shutting the door behind her. Kara watched as the car drove off, afraid to turn away until it was finally out of sight, and then proceeded down the muddy trail toward sanctuary. Finally alone with her thoughts, Kara surrendered to self pity and felt warm tears mingle with the rain.

CHAPTER SEVENTEEN

AT last, the beacons of Ashford Manor illuminated through the misty haze, a specter of a man adorning the entry steps. *Cade.* The darkened figure, having caught sight of Kara on the road, hastened down the steps and ran the remaining distance to her side without a care for the mud or rain. Kara found herself engulfed in a strong embrace, the warmth and security of which had never been equaled until that moment. Kara inhaled the crisp and refreshing scent of the man whom, twenty-four hours earlier, she had feared she may never see again. Cade's embrace was pure bliss, until Kara's nerve endings at last awoke and screamed for a reprieve from the crushing grasp. Unwillingly, she groaned in discomfort. The sound broke the spell of happiness that had been prematurely cast. Cade stiffened, pushing Kara away from the warmth of his body as his countenance morphed from relief into something that very much resembled fury. But why on earth would he be angry at her?

"Where in the *fucking hell* have you been?" Cade thundered at her furiously, his gladness at her return overwhelmed by the reminder that she had left without a single goddamn word.

Kara looked at Cade in astonishment, the vitriol in his words crushing the sense of joy and safety she'd felt at seeing him come running down the drive like a beacon of salvation. Her eyes brimmed with the unwelcome sting of tears at the accusation in his words and the furious glimmer in his eyes, but she took a shuddering breath and stood tall beneath the hurtful iciness of his glare. "I-I can explain," Kara answered shakily, longing for Cade to know the true reason for her disappearance, but also dreading the thought of having to speak her torture with Jace into being. To reopen the scars now painfully etched into her mind and body.

"Oh really?" Cade scoffed, a sharp bitterness in his tone. "You can *explain* why I woke up yesterday morning to find my bed empty and you gone without a trace? Were you plotting your escape the entire time we were fucking the night before, or did you do me the courtesy of making a decision rashly when you found me with my guard down—unconscious and naked in bed beside you? You bolted the moment an opportunity presented itself, for the *second* time I might add."

"It's not what it looks like," Kara defended, insulted that Cade didn't think any better of her.

She had thought the night they shared together before Jace took her had meant something more than just a convenient fuck. Their connection had felt stronger, deeper, bordering on something she didn't dare consider at the moment. Cade thought she had used sex to manipulate him as a means of escape? If she had a single speck of intelligence or self-preservation or rationality, that was *exactly* what she should have done. But no, where he was concerned, she was completely and utterly fucked.

"Is that so? Because it looks like you betrayed me, *again*," Cade seethed, barely resisting the urge to start shouting as he grabbed her arms and pulled her toward him. Though his grip was firm rather than harsh, Kara whimpered beneath his touch. Startled, Cade released her, his brows furrowed in sudden concern. That was the second time a pained sound had escaped her lips since he'd discovered her walking down the drive. Momentarily sheathing his anger, Cade took a moment to assess the state in which Kara had returned to him. It took a mere moment for Cade's initial fury to morph into horror. Kara was barely clothed, enduring the cold, winter rain in only a shirt, a *man's* shirt, that had turned transparent with wetness and revealed disturbing dark blotches on the pale skin beneath. She wore no shoes, her feet filthy and bare. Cade growled in rage as he looked at her face and discovered a large bruise prominently displayed on her left cheek.

Whether Kara had left of her own free will or not, she had clearly been through the worst sort of hell, and the thought of Kara in pain shook him to his stone cold core. "What the fuck happened?" Cade asked, his voice low and rough as he allowed the anxiety of the past twenty four hours to seep into his words.

"J-Jace," Kara answered, her voice trembling from the cold and from having to speak the detestable monster's name into existence.

Cade's face contorted with confusion. "What does Jace have to do with this? He's meant to be in Prague working on an acquisition." Cade's expression darkened with rage as he realized exactly what she was insinuating, anger setting the blood in his veins ablaze. "Did *Jace* do this to you?"

Kara nodded miserably, her teeth beginning to clatter together so painfully that she couldn't form a response as the freezing rain wracked her body with shivers.

Overwhelmed by the pure, unadulterated hatred coursing through his bloodstream like venom aimed straight for his heart, Cade's eyes fluttered shut for the briefest of moments. When they opened, the green and gold orbs blazed with intensity, glittering with a fiery need to raze the whole goddamn earth. "I swear on everything that is holy and unholy, that motherfucker will regret the day that his bitch of a mother brought him into existence."

Kara shuddered from the sheer animosity of his words. She knew, without a single doubt, that Cade would make good on his threat, and that level of violence and passion on her behalf thrilled her as much as it frightened her.

Her shivering startled Cade from his darker thoughts as a wave of guilt washed over him; he'd negligently kept her out in the rain for far too long. "Come here, you must be freezing." He reached for her, longing to warm her against his body and chase away all the pain she'd endured. Pain that was his fucking fault.

"I can manage," Kara declined stubbornly as she pushed away from Cade's attempt to lift her into his arms. "I don't need to be coddled." She already felt weak and broken; allowing him to carry her down the drive like a child would merely affirm her helplessness. As usual, she preferred her pride over her comfort.

"I don't recall asking for your opinion on the matter. You've just been through hell and are hardly a reliable authority on your coping capacity right now," Cade scolded as he bent to take her frail, shivering frame into his arms.

"Cade, please," Kara pleaded as she pushed him away again, realizing that she was probably fighting a losing battle at that moment. "I'll get you all wet."

"It's raining, love. I'm already soaked." And with that, Cade swept her off her feet and into his arms, cradling her to his chest like she was the most precious thing in the world as he carried her toward the house.

The moment Cade carried her over the threshold, they were bombarded by Ortega, Brax, and Mrs. Hughes all wearing various expressions of concern. Cade barely even noticed the swarm of people, his gaze fixed solely on Kara as he set her down gently on a plush, green settee in the foyer.

"Ortega, track that fucking car. Braxton, get ahold of Declan and Randall. Mrs. Hughes, tea. Now." Cade never took his eyes from Kara as he shouted his orders like a man on the brink of detonation. The others raced out of the room to meet his decrees, leaving the two of them in heavy, somber silence. "Now," Cade said, his voice rough as he got down on one knee before her and placed a tender hand on her cheek. Closing her eyes, Kara instinctively leaned into his touch, and he stroked the backs of his knuckles along her jaw before cupping her face with both hands and gently coaxing her eyes to meet his. "Tell me *exactly* what happened."

Kara took a deep breath, searching for a way to unravel the events of the past day and a half. "I woke up before you yesterday morning—an unusual occurrence, I know—and snuck downstairs to make you a stupid surprise breakfast in bed. I couldn't find everything I needed in the kitchen, so I went to look in the pantry. Someone came up behind me. I thought it was *you* being a prick like usual, but…" She trailed off, remembering the shock of the experience. "It was Jace," she finished after a moment of hesitation.

Cade's expression darkened beyond recognition, and Kara hastened to continue her story before he called an intermission to go kill someone. "Anyway, Jace knocked me out with something; I'm still not sure what. When I woke up, we were in a car. They hadn't taken any precautions to blindfold me, so I started to assume the worst. I don't know how long we drove, but I eventually recognized the destination. Avery Reed had commissioned my kidnapping in the hopes of attaining the Chaucer text and as what he thought would be a personal slight to *you* for screwing him over. Jace, apparently, was all too happy to oblige him."

"So you were taken against your will and brutalized because of some personal vendetta against *me*?" Cade asked in utter shock, viciously raking his fingers through his dark hair as he began to feel his control slipping away. "*Fuck*, I should have made sure Reed was handled. I knew he was pissed about how everything played out. But I let myself get distracted. My guard was down, betrayal found its way into my own home, and I nearly lost something that I value most highly." A glimmer of sorrow mingled with the fury in his green-gold eyes as Cade gazed into Kara's tear filled eyes and implored her to read the utter remorse in his own.

"It's not your fault, Cade," she said in earnest, desperate to erase the self-loathing marring his features.

"Like fuck it isn't," Cade retorted angrily, disgusted with himself and his inability to keep her safe. Hell, he'd practically thrown her into a cage full of wolves and allowed them to do their fucking worst. Suddenly, he realized that Kara had completely glossed over the details of Jace's involvement, never explaining just how far the bastard's assault had gone. A sickening sense of dread leadened his stomach as he considered a horrifying possibility. "Did he—" Cade paused, searching for the words to a question he never, *ever* wanted to ask. But he had to know. "Did Jace rape you?"

Kara looked away, unable to bear the painful mixture of fear and despair in his eyes. She wanted to lie. She wished with every atom in her body that she *could* lie. But Cade would know; he could probably already read the dark truth in her eyes. She already felt crushed beneath the suffocating weight of knowing exactly what Jace did to her. What he *took* from her. And sharing that knowledge with Cade wouldn't lighten the load, it would double it. But he deserved to know, and she deserved to not feel ashamed of voicing something that had been done without her consent. Slowly, Kara raised her head, peeking up at Cade from a veil of long, dark lashes. "Yes," she answered finally, managing to mostly keep the tremble from her voice.

Cade's composure shattered, his face contorting into an expression so dark it made devastation appear ecstatic by comparison. "Kara," Cade uttered bleakly, putting all the anguish and guilt that the human voice was capable of conveying into a single word. Aching to touch her, to soothe away every detestable detail of the past day, Cade pulled her from the settee and into his arms. They sat in a wet puddle of limbs and despair as Kara allowed herself to fall apart and give in to the tears that had been building since Jace had walked into that goddamn room and left with a shard of her soul. Cade stroked her damp hair softly, quietly whispering apologies like chanted prayers for repentance.

"What if he broke me?" Kara asked softly as she burrowed into the warmth of his chest, soothed by the comforting melody of his heartbeat.

"He didn't," Cade answered with certainty, knowing the truth of his words in the very depths of his being. "Even Jace cannot accomplish the impossible."

"How can you be so sure?" Kara questioned timidly as she looked up at Cade's face.

"Because you're the strongest person I know," Cade assured her as he moved his hand from her hair and brushed his fingers over the bruises on her face. "Because even when I tried my hardest to break you, you ended up breaking me instead."

"I didn't break you," Kara replied, her brows twisted in confusion at his words.

"Oh, you most certainly did," Cade answered with an indescribable sadness in his tone.

For what might have been seconds or minutes or hours, they huddled in silence, wrapped in an embrace of sadness and surrender. "Would you like to go upstairs?" Cade asked softly, his words reverberating through the emptiness of the room.

Kara couldn't respond. She lacked the energy, the strength, the fucking will to make her lips move and her vocal chords distribute sound. She merely nodded, the small action sorrowful and broken in itself.

Without waiting for her objections, Cade lifted her into his arms once more and headed for the stairs. "I'm sorry," he breathed with his lips against her wet hair, kissing her head tenderly as he held her tightly against his chest. "I'm sorry. *I'm so fucking sorry.*" Cade continued to whisper apologies as he carried Kara to his room. By that point, his words were less meant for her and more an unconscious attempt to quell the nauseating barrage of guilt overwhelming his senses. It was *his* fault. Everything that fucking happened to her was *his* fault. And he needed some way to assuage the guilt before it poisoned him from the inside out.

When he reached his bathroom, Cade set Kara down gingerly on the edge of the tub before moving to draw a bath. Kara shivered with the contrast of heat against her frozen skin as the room started to fill with a warm haze of steam. Slowly, Cade turned toward her, his eyes clouded with a darkness that begged to be unleashed. With sheer force, he kept the darkness contained, but barely.

"Take off that damn shirt," Cade ordered, his voice more harsh than he intended as he stared at the dreadful reminder of Jace clinging to her wet body. He hated her subtle flinch at the sharpness of his tone. He hated to hurt her even more than she already had been, but there was a fury coursing through his veins, begging to seep from his body and attach itself to the first available victim. He wouldn't allow that victim to be her. Briefly, Cade closed his eyes, caging in the anger, subduing it like every other thing that threatened his control. When he opened his eyes, they were lighter, the storminess subsiding slightly. "Please," he amended, brushing her damp hair from her cheek.

"Can you do it?" Kara asked softly, her eyes pleading. Her whole body felt numb; she wasn't sure she could lift her hands to remove Jace's shirt if she tried.

Wordlessly answering her plea, Cade's fingers found the buttons on the shirt, carefully undoing them one by one. An unearthly growl escaped his throat when the shirt opened enough to reveal the bruises on Kara's neck and chest. She hadn't seen them, but she knew they were there. She could feel the soreness of them with every breath of her body.

"*What the fuck* did he do to you?" Cade asked in horror, his voice so black and abysmal Kara wasn't sure if she'd ever hear light in his words again.

"I'm sure it looks worse than it is," Kara brushed off, uncomfortable with the all-consuming violence of his gaze.

"I'm sure it *looks* as bad as it *feels*," Cade retorted angrily as he undid the rest of the buttons hastily and threw the abhorrent piece of clothing on the floor. If possible, Cade's expression darkened even further as he scrutinized her bare skin.

Slowly circling her, Cade took inventory of her injuries, painstakingly categorizing the bruises and bites and scratches etched into her skin—a map of Jace's violence on her body. Cade brushed aside her hair and found the handprint left against her throat. He moved lower and touched the matching set of bite marks on each

Hideaway

shoulder. His fingers grazed her bruised breasts, found the tender spots along her hips, stroked the markings on her inner thighs. Finally, his hand settled on the mark above her heart, covering the abomination of deep, bloodied crescents left unmistakably by a bite of brute force. Something about *that* hateful mark felt even more personal than the rest.

"Step in," Cade ordered gently, taking her hand and carefully helping her into the bathtub.

Kara flinched as the hot water burned her chilled skin, but she delighted in the painful warmth as it spread throughout her body and thawed the iciness of her limbs. Still holding onto Cade's hand, Kara pulled him toward her, begging him to join her. Needing to feel the hardened strength of his body against hers. Needing to re-memorize his delicious scent so she could banish the stench of Jace's musk from the furthest recesses of her mind. Needing the reaffirmation of his feelings for her after everything that happened. Needing something that was real and true and good and *him*. She needed *him*. That was the first time she had allowed herself to admit how much Cade had imprinted himself upon her soul. She cared about Cade with an ardor that had seeped into the blood in her veins, melded with the very marrow of her bones, wrapped itself violently around her heart and squeezed until the rhythm of its beats were in tune with his own.

Unexpectedly, Cade pulled away, disrupting Kara's sudden, awful realization that she might actually love the bastard. *Fuck*, she was almost certain she loved him. The idea was terrifying and exhilarating and everything in between.

"Please get in," Kara pleaded, her voice unfamiliar with sheer desperation. "I need to feel you."

Cade studied her for a moment, his expression conflicted, before shaking his head. "Not this time, love," he answered sadly, his eyes guarded. He turned off the water before bringing over a washcloth and bottles of body wash, shampoo, and conditioner. Silently, Cade knelt in front of the tub, poured some soap smelling of citrus and clove on the cloth, and began to bathe her. His strokes were gentle as he brushed the cloth over bruises and tender skin with the utmost care. Kara squirmed uncomfortably as he lifted her arms to clean underneath them. He washed her breasts, but, unlike usual, his touch didn't linger. In fact, he didn't touch her at all, being very careful to use the cloth as a barrier between his hands and her bare skin. Kara longed to feel his touch so much that it physically ached.

"You know, you could do that easier if you were in the bath with me," she suggested softly, the breathy hoarseness of her voice coming across seductively.

"I'm not getting in there, Kara," Cade answered tensely, his voice rough. The sadness in her eyes was whittling away at his hardened resolve, but he steeled himself and his heart. If he got in that bath, if he *touched* her, he wouldn't have the strength to do what he needed to do. He would hold onto her and never let her go.

"But, why?" Kara asked, trying not to sound as though her heart were shattering into pieces. She was fairly sure it *was*.

"Because I can't *touch you*." As much as he desperately wanted to hold her and kiss her and wipe away every disgusting, vile thing Jace had done to her body, he didn't deserve that privilege. She deserved freedom from him. And he deserved a life of purgatory without her.

Kara gasped, unable to silently contain the pain of his words directed at her like tiny blades aimed to draw blood. "Is it…because of what happened with Jace?" she asked hesitantly, agonizing with every word.

"In part," Cade responded vaguely.

"I thought that wouldn't matter to you," Kara answered softly as she avoided his gaze.

"Of course, it fucking matters!" Cade shouted, his anger cracking through the control he tried so desperately to erect. If he had to keep talking about what Jace had done, he was going to obliterate something—anything.

"I'm sorry," she whispered, her voice choked with pain as she felt tears of helplessness and anguish flood her eyes.

Cade remained silent as he continued to wash Kara's body. If he allowed himself anywhere near *that*, he'd strangle the fucking apology from her fucking throat. She had always been too quick to blame herself. The fact that she felt guilty for the abhorrent situation *he'd* practically thrust her into left him feeling emotionally disemboweled. "Lay your head back," Cade commanded softly as he poured shampoo into his hands and began to work it into her silky blonde strands.

Kara's eyes fluttered shut as she allowed herself to be enveloped by the intoxicating scent of mint and cedar as he rubbed his shampoo into her hair. His fingers massaged her scalp, pulling moans from her lips at the blissful strength of his hands. For a moment, she allowed herself to forget Jace's violence and simply enjoy the feel of Cade's rough hands in her hair. The moment was far too fleeting.

"I'll handle Reed," Cade explained as he rinsed the soap from Kara's hair. "A man like that is simple and easily bought. I should have taken care of him earlier when things became…complicated." He wrang the water from Kara's hair before applying conditioner. "Jace will be more difficult, but I'm certain I can appeal to his mercenary side."

Cade rinsed the conditioner from Kara's hair and then motioned for her to sit up in the tub. With painstaking tenderness, he towel dried her hair before combing through the strands to remove the tangles. When he'd deemed his task of tending to her finished, Cade rose to his feet and turned toward the door, clutching the handle so hard his knuckles whitened beneath the force. When he finally looked at Kara, he wore a mask of resolve, though slivers of anguish still cracked through. "When both men have been taken care of and your safety is secured, you are free to go," Cade announced as dispassionately as he could—as though the words didn't obliterate every small fraction of hope and happiness he possessed.

As though those weren't the very words Kara had been begging to hear since he'd taken her to Ashford Manor.

As though those words didn't rip out her heart and tear it into bloody, mangled shreds of flesh and gore.

"Why are you doing this?" Kara choked out when she'd finally gathered the composure to speak.

"What do you mean *why*? Do you not want your freedom?" Cade answered, a note of frustration seeping into his voice.

"Of course I do," Kara responded, somehow sounding defensive and desolate at the same time. "But why *now*?"

"I think I've kept you long enough, Miss Caine. Don't you?" Cade said bleakly, the words intertwined with utter desolation. Before he could allow himself to beg her to stay, Cade walked out of the room, shutting the door behind him.

Alone, Kara tried to breath through the panic and despair, but her lungs seemed to have abandoned their sacred duty the moment Cade walked out on her. Deciding to say *fuck you* to the unruly organs, she held onto a shallow breath and disappeared beneath the surface, allowing the warm, inviting water to swallow her whole.

One, two, three, four, five, six, seven, eight, nine, ten.

Slowly, Kara counted as she willed calmness into her body.

Thirty-one, thirty-two, thirty-three, thirty-four, thirty-five.

Slowly, calmness came, though it was an uneasy sort of peace in which total decimation resided on the boundary's edge. If there was one thing of which Kara was absolutely certain, she was completely and unequivocally *fucked*. Cade had fatally embedded himself in her heart like an arrow to the chest, and she feared there would be no removing him without bleeding to death in the process.

CHAPTER EIGHTEEN

IT had been days since her return to the manor. Days since Jace had kidnapped and destroyed her. Days since Cade had touched her or looked her in the eye or given her more than a passing greeting. Everyone else in the house couldn't seem to leave her alone. Mrs. Hughes pestered her with tea and biscuits literally every waking moment; apparently, that was the British way of combating irreparable physical and emotional trauma. The morning after her return, a *get well soon* card was slid under her bedroom door, where she'd woken up alone. The card was signed by Declan, Brax, and Ortega; she wasn't exactly sure that the card was the most socially appropriate gesture for a sexual assault victim, but she was touched by the thoughtful sentiment. The men of the house may not be well-versed in the emotional side of things, but they were trying their best.

Hideaway 385

Later that day, Brax had come to her room to deliver the phone she hadn't seen since Jace confiscated it at the library. After checking it for any bugs Jace might have planted and giving the device the all clear, Brax installed tracking apps of his own. For the sake of her privacy, Kara had strongly refuted any need to have her whereabouts monitored, but he brushed aside her objections with a firm "Ashford's orders." Cade couldn't fucking talk to her, but he'd send his minions to install spyware on her private property.

Fucking typical, control freak.

Though she was happy to have the privilege of a phone for the first time in weeks, Kara couldn't be sure if the offer of more freedom from Cade was actually a good sign.

The next afternoon, Kara had received an unexpected visit from Ortega. He'd come with a dainty black box tied with a pretty silver ribbon. To her surprise, it looked suspiciously like a jewelry box. And it had been—a delicate gold bracelet with a lovely little gold heart charm, so pretty and entirely her taste that she happily put it on immediately. But, because no one in the house was *fucking normal*, Ortega explained that the lovely little heart inconspicuously housed a goddamn tracking device. Very seriously, Ortega asked her never to take it off, and she had been surprised by the tender concern in his eyes. Then, he threw her for a loop by saying that the bracelet had been a compromise because "Ashford suggested we give you a tracking implant while you slept."

What in the ever loving fuck, Cade?

Kara rubbed at her wrist, the small bracelet somehow uncomfortably heavy now that she knew it was merely a fashionable ball and chain. What the hell was going on in Cade's fucked up head? He went through all the motions of safeguarding her safety, of keeping her monitored and within his vicinity, but he hadn't actually engaged with her in any meaningful way since Jace had kidnapped her. In fact, he avoided her like the goddamn bubonic plague. And Kara was fucking sick of it. She was over Cade acting as though she didn't exist.

So why didn't he just end it? Why keep her suspended in perpetual purgatory? Sleeping alone in rooms down the hall from one another. Sharing meals in quiet silence, though Kara rarely had enough of an appetite to venture into the dinning hall. Cade busied himself with work. He allowed her the undisturbed sanctuary of the library. Life seemed to stagnate—never changing, never progressing. An un-altering, meaningless existence.

Fuck it.

Kara preferred to burn in the fiery flames of the demise of her relationship than be smothered by the smoke of lingering embers that slowly extinguished into nothingness. She would confront Cade, if only for a moment, and force him to admit the truth of his feelings. If he was through with her, she would end things. Right that fucking minute. Even if it hurt. Fuck, she *knew* it would hurt. But she had enough self-respect not to linger for scraps of affection from a man who lacked the capacity to offer her anything more. She just hoped, when the time came, she had the strength to walk out the door and not look back.

Kara walked toward his office slowly, her steps weighed down by dread and uncertainty. Cade had been barricaded in his office all day, even neglecting his usual, distant appearance at breakfast. As much as she hated to intrude upon his inner sanctum, Kara was done waiting for the bastard to give her the time of day. She knocked on the office door twice, the sound of her knuckles against the hardwood making a far more assertive impression than she personally felt.

"Come in," Cade answered, his voice curt and his words short. He was stressed and not in the mood for interruptions.

Trembling ever so slightly, Kara opened the doors, appreciating the scent of leather and parchment mingled with the hints of wood and mint that assaulted her senses. It smelled like Cade. God, she'd missed him. The warmth of his hands on her body, his lips on her skin. The richness of his laugh when she said something moderately clever. The fiery wit of his retorts. His stupidly perpetual insistence on calling her *Miss Caine* because he knew it drove her to insanity. The way his eyes darkened with need when she fought him. The way they melted into warm pools of desire when she didn't. She was ardently, irrevocably intoxicated by every facet of Cade's composition. Unbidden, her heart had dared to falter for the bastard.

And he was going to fucking break it.

"Kara," Cade said with a startle when he finally glanced up from the reports consuming his attention. There was a note of irritation in the way he said her name that had Kara's face falling in disappointment.

"I'm sorry to disturb you," Kara apologized hesitantly, the emotional part of her consciousness begging her to run before her feelings endured irreparable damage. "Can we talk?"

Cade's expression twisted with unease as he heard those three little words no one ever wanted to hear. "I'm very busy at the moment, Kara," Cade answered dismissively, though not unkindly. "Perhaps another time?"

"Another time? And when exactly would that be?" Kara asked, her voice heating with an anger that had remained buried under hurt feelings and insecurities. "You are never around! We never talk. You haven't touched me since…before. Fuck, you barely even look at me. It's like I don't even exist."

"What the hell are you talking about?" Cade questioned in frustration, feeling very underprepared for the fight she had clearly walked into his office with the intention of instigating. He'd given her space for her own good. He wasn't so cruel as to continue sleeping with her when he knew he needed to let her go. His days had been spent tirelessly ensuring her future safety. He'd placated Avery Reed—at great personal cost to himself. Although, whatever the price, he would have happily paid it.

"I'm *talking* about you treating me like spoiled goods ever since Jace dropped me off at your doorstep bruised and used."

"I have done no such thing," Cade replied indignantly, habitually raising his hand to run his fingers aggressively through his hair.

"Yes, you have," Kara answered firmly, noticing as Cade shifted restlessly in his seat. "You can't even stand to be in the same room as me." Kara wrapped her arms around her chest in an effort to protect herself against the chill of his apparent distaste. Kara felt the sting of tears, but she held them back—barely. "Please, don't hate me for what happened."

That had Cade abruptly abandoning his chair as he stood and slammed his fists on the desk, his features contorted with fury. "You think I *hate* you?" he asked in sheer disbelief, his voice rising in anger.

"I know you do," Kara answered with a shrug of her shoulders as though her observation was entirely obvious.

"Your absurdity never ceases to astonish me. I do not *fucking hate you*," Cade spat back, his eyes narrowed as though he could glare Kara into seeing reason. He took a deep breath as he wrestled with how much of his inner turmoil he should share with her. "I hate myself."

Kara's brow furrowed in confusion. "What do you mean?" she asked, truly baffled as she tried to understand his confession and how it related to his recent treatment of her. But it simply didn't make sense. "Why?" Kara questioned finally. "It wasn't *your* fault."

"Yes, it *goddamn* was my fault," Cade thundered back, his voice a mixture of anger and self-loathing. "I took you from your life. I kept you here. I promised you protection while housing you with a man I *knew* was a murderer and attempted rapist. He attacked you in the library, and I made excuses for his behavior. I allowed him to stay. I fucking sent *him* out to drag you back when you'd successfully escaped me instead of letting you go."

Cade scrubbed a hand over his face, wearing the expression of a man unaccustomed to regret. "I should have fucking let you go, and none of this would have happened. But I was a selfish, arrogant bastard, and—in trying to keep you—I damned you to *this*." Cade glanced at her briefly before looking away, his hands flexing at his sides as though maybe he wanted to reach for her. But he didn't. He just stood there, his face composed of anguish as an unconquerable sea of distance lay between them. "Fuck, Kara, I would carve my own heart out of my chest and lay the bloody, beating thing at your feet if it would offer even the slightest atonement for what you have endured because of me."

Kara stood in stunned silence, not quite sure how to respond to *that* declaration, though she could appreciate the romantically morbid imagery. "So…you don't hate me?"

Cade exhaled a huff of vexation as he mindlessly rustled the papers on his desk. "No, love, I don't hate you."

"Then look at me, Cade, for fuck's sake," Kara demanded, equally exasperated.

"I can't!" Cade shouted, violently swiping all the papers on his desk to the floor. "I can't stomach the fucking sight of his marks on you! The nauseating reminder of what he did to you. The damning proof that I *failed to protect you*."

"Then wipe them away," Kara suggested, Cade's confession sparking an idea—an absolutely deranged idea.

"What the fuck do you mean?" Cade asked in irritation, hardly in the mood for riddles, as he stared at the mess of papers on the floor.

"Rewrite the pain that he carved into my body. Make it your own," Kara continued, her voice taking on a darkly seductive quality she hadn't intended.

Cade looked at her then, for the first time since what happened with Jace, he truly *looked* at her. And his eyes held something indescribable and hungry and terrifying. He stalked toward her, closing that gaping sea of distance in what seemed to be a few strides. He stopped in front of Kara, his chest nearly brushing her forehead if not for the few inches of space between them. He was so close Kara could feel the warmth of his body radiating against her.

Hideaway

She ached to touch him, to close the space between them and wrap her arms around the familiar breadth of his chest. But she couldn't, not until they had resolved the issue at hand. And she had an inkling that resolution would come at a cost.

"And how am I supposed to do that?" Cade asked, his deep voice intense as he tilted her chin up to meet his gaze.

"Hurt me. Like he did," Kara said softly, averting her gaze as she felt an irrational wave of mortification at the suggestion. Her heart fluttered anxiously, her skin flushed with the heat of embarrassment as she awaited his answer, the room filling with a tense silence.

"You want me to hurt you?" Cade asked dangerously slowly, enunciating each word carefully as though talking to a delusional child.

"Yes," Kara answered calmly, her voice quiet but assured.

"You're fucking insane. I'm not going to *hurt* you, especially not in your goddamn condition. You don't know what you're asking."

"Do not presume to tell me what I know, Caden Ashford. I know what I want. What I need. What we *both* might need if you actually took a moment to consider it instead of immediately stooping to insults and belittling." Kara was getting angry. He had the audacity to throw her vulnerability in her face and declare it ignorance.

"Alright, let me *consider* the asininity you're suggesting. You want me to *what*? Hit you? Violate you? Paint your body in bruises and violence? Why? Why *the fuck* would you want that?"

"Because it would be *my* choice, Cade. You think the worst thing Jace did was violate my body? No. He stole my freedom. He took away my ability to choose what happened to me. I want that power back. I want you to help me find it again."

Cade's body vibrated with fury at her suggestion, but the blood in his veins also sung with the need to fulfill her violent desires. His face was a collage of conflict between the two as he stared at Kara in wordless indecision. Could he do it; could he hurt her? Would he be able to live with himself after? Would she?

"What's wrong, Ashford? Scared to hit a girl? Lost the taste for it since the last time you hit me with your belt?" Kara goaded, resorting to desperate measures if it would get her the reaction that she wanted. And she wanted him angry. Angry enough to fight back. Angry enough to prove that he wanted it just as much as she did.

"Careful, love," Cade growled, seething with anger at her dangerous attempts to rile his darkness. "You're taunting a monster, and I don't think you'll like it when he unsheathes his claws and comes out to play."

"Fucking *try me*."

An eerie stillness pervaded the room, like standing in the tranquil eye of a hurricane before total chaos and destruction came to obliterate everything in its path.

"As you wish," Cade said ominously. Without another word of explanation, he grabbed her wrist and dragged her out of the room.

Kara tripped over her own feet as she tried to keep up with Cade's furious strides, his crushing hold on her wrist the only thing keeping her upright as they stormed down the hall. Prickles of fear danced along her spine as she realized she'd provoked a menacing man who's limitations she didn't really know. Was he capable of actually harming her? Had she just made the stupidest mistake of her life? Her head screamed at her to escape while she still could, while her heart knew that she could trust him, even as he hauled her through the manor with a fiery glint in his eye.

Kara was puzzled when Cade came to a sudden halt in front of the library doors, swiftly dug out his keys from his coat pocket, and unlocked the door. He forcefully pulled her inside the room and left her standing alone and confused as he turned toward the doors and locked them, the scrape of the key sounding sinister and foreboding. Returning to her side, Cade reclaimed her wrist and pulled her toward the bookshelves at the far end of the library. He stopped in front of a particular shelf that housed navy rows of identically bound, numerically organized texts on nautical law; it was one of the few areas in the library that Kara had never taken any interest in.

"Are you sure you want this, Kara?" Cade asked seriously, his back pressed against the shelf as he loomed over her, studying her with the intensity of a predator about to go in for the kill.

Trembling from head to toe as fear and anticipation wracked her body, Kara could only summon the strength to nod.

"I am going to need verbal consent," he demanded sternly.

"Yes, I want this," Kara answered, surprised by the strength and determination in her voice.

His eyes alight with excitement mingled with resignation, Cade turned toward the bookshelf and tinkered with something on one of the higher levels. Instantly, the wall gave way to reveal a hidden passage with a staircase leading down into dark, unknown depths.

What. The. Fuck.

Instinctively, Kara took a step back, that alarmed voice of reason in her head screaming at the top of its lungs for her to get the fuck out while she still could because nothing about that dark, secret passage looked *safe*. Cade noticed her hesitation and allowed her a moment to adjust to the situation, his hands kept non-threateningly at his sides.

What the hell was she doing? She knew Cade was dangerous; she knew he was a criminal. Technically she still was his fucking prisoner. Maybe she wasn't the first. Maybe there had been others. Maybe he had a bluebeard complex, and this was where he lured his victims and stored the fucking bodies. Had she really succumbed to Stockholm Syndrome so completely that she was willing to follow a man she truly knew very little about into a hidden chasm, tucked away from the rest of the world with no visible escape? Absolutely everything about the situation said *run*, and yet, there she stood, contemplating if her curiosity outweighed her fear.

Cade watched as Kara's internal conflict played itself out before offering his own encouragement. "Do you trust me, Kara?" he asked in earnest, extending his hand as he walked through the opening in the wall and settled on the first step of the darkened staircase.

Kara's brow furrowed as she considered his question, her teeth tugging on her bottom lip anxiously as she pondered her answer as though it encapsulated her very fate. And perhaps it did. "Yes," she answered finally. And whether or not it was folly, she meant it. With a sigh of finality, Kara took Cade's hand and began her descent.

With the library door closed behind them, the way down on black steps was dimly illuminated by small, antique sconces along the wall. The aesthetic was very dungeon-esque, and Kara had to suppress a shiver as she slowly walked further down. She relied on Cade's guidance, holding his hand close to her chest as they navigated the enclosed tunnel of steps until they finally reached level ground. Through a shroud of shadows, Kara attempted to discern the purpose of the secret room as Cade left her side, presumably to locate a light source. With a *click*, the space ignited beneath the radiant gleam of an exquisite black chandelier adorning the center of the room. And the huge chandelier was not the most conspicuous item in the room, which was saying a lot.

Black wallpaper with elegant silver patterns decorated walls lined with racks upon racks of torture implements. These weren't the toys of someone who dabbled in deviance. These were the tools of a professional. Terrifying whips, canes, paddles, and other sinister weapons she couldn't even begin to describe draped down in organized rows. Other racks held ropes and cuffs and chains. There was a black leather bed with dark sheets and no pillows, a matching leather couch, a black bench that seemed designed for something other than sitting, an imposing desk in one corner that seemed to be a replica of the one in Cade's office, and a monstrous wooden X looming in the other corner.

What the fuck had she gotten herself into?

"So...you *do* have a sex dungeon," Kara commented blandly after the shock of the room had finally dissipated enough to allow her the ability to speak. She supposed his remark the first time she was in his room hadn't been a joke after all.

Fucking fantastic.

"I do have a sex dungeon," Cade answered, his expression amused. He'd expected some sort of panic or outburst when she saw the dirty secret that had been hiding beneath her precious library all along. What he hadn't expected was stoicism. She did have quite the knack for surprising him. "Although, I prefer to call it the Hideaway."

"Well, it's better than the alternative I'd imagined."

"And what exactly were you imagining?" he asked, thoroughly intrigued.

"A kidnapping criminal with a hidden door leading down to a mysterious room? I was starting to assume your hobbies were of the murderous variety," Kara answered with an expression that was deadly serious.

Cade laughed as he realized that Kara was taking the sex room so well because she had been entertaining far worse alternatives. A little hardcore sex looked harmless when compared to fucking *murder*. "Well, if that's what you thought of me, I'm surprised you followed me down into my den of horrors. It really exhibits a terrible lack of judgement on your part," he scolded as he moved to caress the back of her neck. "I would expect a woman of your education to be more prudent, Dr. Caine."

Kara gasped at the use of her proper title. It was perhaps the first time he had *ever* called her Dr. Caine, and he was doing so merely to call into question her intelligence.

Fucking. Bastard.

"Besides, we've yet to rule out the murder bit. Perhaps I merely like to play with my victims first," Cade whispered ominously in her ear. His mockery was met with a hard jab in the ribs as Kara punched him with all her might. "Ow!" he exclaimed in surprise, rubbing at the tender spot where her fist made contact. It was probably the first time he had received a bruise in the Hideaway rather than delivered it. The thought amused him; she clearly had no

Hideaway

idea who she was playing with. That sort of behavior from any of the women in his previous relationships would never have been tolerated. Clearly, the situation with Kara was singular in that she wasn't aware of the conditions that preceded involvement with him. It was a lapse that Cade planned to rectify immediately. "Careful, love. You don't want to provoke me in this room. In here, I have all the power."

Kara shrank back slightly at the warning. "Sorry," she apologized quickly as she looked about the room and considered all the ways Cade could retaliate. Pulling her eyes away from the intensity of his stare, Kara studied the imposing room before her, overcome with a sense of fear mingled with something she couldn't quite place. Curiosity? Excitement? The fear seemed appropriate, but she was unsettled by the thought of other feelings inspiring the adrenaline rushing through her veins.

Hoping to find something amid the madness to placate her need for rationality, Kara examined the walls and racks lined with implements and toys, some familiar and others a complete mystery as to name and function. There was something about the overall organization of the room that slightly quelled her uneasiness. It was precise, everything in its place according to a specific code, much like the texts on her archival shelves. She could appreciate that. Kara walked toward the far side of the room, drawn to where a row of canes lined the wall in succession from largest to smallest. She glanced at Cade as if to ask his permission before touching his implements of pain. He nodded in consent, seeming pleased that she recognized his authority. Kara lifted one of the thinner canes from its place on the wall, stroking the smooth edge with a single, curious finger.

"It's so light," she said in surprise as she turned the cane in her hand.

"It is. But don't let that fool you; it's got a wicked bite," he said with a soft laugh. He was surprised that Kara had gravitated toward that particular area of the room. Perhaps she was naive enough to assume, incorrectly, that the simple rod was one of the tamer objects housed in the Hideaway. Kara seemed inadvertently drawn to danger, himself included. He could only hope that her infatuation with danger survived the night.

Cade reached a hand to cover one of Kara's own, a tender embrace that encircled one of the cruelest of implements. "Canes leave the loveliest lines on the skin," he said in a silky, seductive tone, tracing a pattern along her inner arm with the tip of his finger. "It's the kinky embodiment of art; someone with a skilled hand can paint perfectly symmetrical marks that are an exact imprint of each blow that falls. Canes happen to be one of my favorite implements to play with," he said, reaching for a thicker cane two down from the top. "Try this," he said, handing her a cane that looked formidable enough to make her stir anxiously at the thought of it touching her skin. She returned the thin cane to the wall and took the other from Cade's hand. The dark, flexible rod felt as vicious as it looked.

"I can't imagine using something like this to play with. Wouldn't it cause a lot of damage?" she asked with a furrowed brow, questioning whether she would be able to endure the pain that she had practically begged Cade to administer. If she'd had any idea that she was fucking some kind of sadist, she wouldn't have made the request so lightly. Her breath quickened in panic as she held the cane, imagining Cade's use of it on her. Her eyes darted to Cade and found his face full of calm reassurance. His certainty was like a balm to her fears, and she felt a portion of her panic fade away.

"I am not going to harm you, Kara. And I am not going to hurt you any more than you want me to. In all honesty, this cane, along with many of the tools in this room, can cause irreparable damage if not handled properly. I am highly skilled at delivering pain, and it is not an act that I take lightly. It takes some practice to be able to withstand the strokes of a cane without anguish," he commented with professional certainty, taking the implement from Kara's willingly relinquishing hands.

Having secured her trust, at least for the moment, Cade paused to assess how to best proceed with Kara. She appreciated facts; she liked to be made aware of all aspects of a subject so that she was able to make an informed decision or opinion. He could imagine it was difficult for a woman used to being one of the smartest in the room to be placed in an unfamiliar situation where she had almost no knowledge or experience. Provided she was willing, Cade could offer both. "With a light hand, this cane delivers a sharp sting and leaves red welts that turn to bruises. With a firm hand, it will break the skin easily. It is one of the harshest tools that I am willing to play with. Some opt for much harder impact play, others aren't comfortable using anything harder than a crop. It is all a matter of preference between partners," he elaborated as he moved to reunite the cane with the others on the wall.

Kara remained silent, her expression dark and troubled as she absorbed the information. Cade waited patiently in accompanying silence as Kara gathered enough bravery to formulate a question. "So, do all of your relationships involve BDSM?" she asked as evenly as possible.

Cade arched his brow in surprise at her use of the specific terminology for his kinks. Maybe she wasn't quite as naive as he thought. "Personally, I find that bondage always enhances the sexual experience, but it's not a requirement. We've fucked countless times, and I haven't tied you down, have I?"

"No," Kara replied cautiously.

Not yet.

"On the other hand, discipline, along with dominance, serves a vital role in maintaining the control I strive for in every relationship, sexual and otherwise. I expect to have my orders obeyed by every person under my command, whether it is you or someone in my employ. Disobedience incurs disagreeable consequences, as you well know. Because we share an intimate relationship, your consequences are far more physical and subject to my creativity." Cade's face filled with malicious glee at the thought.

The thought of being punished by Cade with any of the menacing objects in that room filled Kara with dread. The thought of him enjoying it was even more troublesome. Cade sensed her fears and moved to ease the furrowing of her brow with the gentlest caress. As the tension in her face softened, Cade grasped her chin firmly and raised her eyes to his. He met her gaze with an earnest sincerity, longing for her trust.

"My relationships don't require an SM aspect. I am not a sadist, and I don't need to hurt someone in order to achieve sexual gratification. That being said, I do seek out relationships defined by

Hideaway

an unequal balance of power. I am undeniably dominant in all aspects of my life, and I crave submission, most of all in the bedroom. I have found that, for women who enjoy relinquishing power in a relationship, the experience is enhanced with the inclusion of sadomasochism. Being driven to release through the application of pain is an intimate and intense encounter for both participants."

A tumult of thoughts churned in Kara's head. Cade's words were comforting and reasonable, and had she heard them with closed eyes, her fears and insecurities would likely have evaporated. But hearing Cade proclaim that he didn't need to exact pain while standing in a *literal* sex dungeon full of whips and canes was a bit like hearing an addict profess that they didn't need the drugs while standing in a crackhouse. Kara kept her gaze focused on the damning proof, rather than the man with silken words and smoldering eyes that could banish her reason to the farthest reaches of her mind.

Cade addressed her unspoken accusations through gritted teeth. "Listen, I am not some sort of predator who delights in beating women. A man like *that* left those fucking marks on your body, so if that is what you think, we are turning around and walking up those stairs right now." Cade's face was full of seething anger at the unjust comparison. "It is a discredit to me and a discredit to your sensibility for staying with me if you think I am anything like that bastard."

"You aren't like him," she admitted softly, sounding sincere, but her lowered eyes still held hesitation.

Patience nearly spent, Cade raked his fingers through his hair roughly. There was nothing quite so taxing as attempting to make an *educated* woman understand facts that go against their own sensibilities. In fact, the success of such an endeavor was damned near impossible. "Close your eyes, Kara," he said firmly. She looked at him questioningly, but made no move to comply. Cade was hardly surprised; it was a difficult task to disadvantage yourself willingly, especially in a situation of tension. It was much like asking a sub to hold still without the use of restraints. The body's natural response was to maintain control; sometimes compliance required assistance. Cade walked away from Kara toward the desk at her back and rifled through the top drawer.

"Cade," she implored in a voice shaky with trepidation. She eyed the point of escape, wary of his intentions, mind racing with images of what horrifying objects could lurk within the confines of that drawer. Cade walked back toward her carrying an unassuming piece of black cloth.

"May I?" he asked in polite request, holding up a silk blindfold. She was so relieved that he hadn't come bearing some instrument of torture that she nodded her head in acquiescence. A blindfold was familiar, and she felt just a little more at ease as he slipped it gently over her head and the view of that terrifying room disappeared.

The darkness was comforting.

Cade moved to stand behind her. She inhaled the cool, familiar scent of his cologne as intoxicating as the first time she'd breathed him in. She felt the warmth of his body pressed against her back, the tingle of his touch as his hands traced unfamiliar patterns along her bare arms, the pleasant burn of his stubbled jaw grazing her neck as he leaned in to kiss her throat. He rested his cheek on her shoulder, his lips by her ear.

"I believe the sight of this room and all its unknowns has robbed you of your ability to assess the situation with a level head," he whispered in a low, husky voice. "Perhaps if I take away one of your senses, your sense of reason will heighten."

Kara felt herself being gently pulled across the room. Cade placed a hand on top of hers and moved her fingertips to explore a diverse row of implements hanging along the wall. The smoothness of the soft leather strands caressed their joined hands with a feather light touch. Kara could imagine the multiple strands being used on her body like silk against her skin.

"I enjoy the extraction of pain to the extent that you enjoy it," Cade whispered against her ear.

He trailed her hands over firmer objects that were smooth and braided. Perhaps they were whips? They felt so much less threatening when she didn't have sight to inspire fear.

"In the case of punishment, I enjoy the pain to the extent that you require it. The pain is an extension of control. It is the act of taking possession of your body and making you feel what I want you to feel. It is a similar type of physical dominance as sex, just with a different sensation."

Cade moved her fingertips along a row of ropes, some thick and coarse, others thin and satiny. He brought her back to the collections of canes, and they felt more like smooth twigs than instruments of destruction. He moved her around the room and brushed her hands over the leather couch and silk sheets and the cool, wooden surface of the desk.

"I reach the same high fucking you, demanding pleasure from your body, as I would flogging you to demand your surrender to the pain. In both situations, it is the power of control that fulfills me."

He spread her arms above her head, pressing her against what felt like the wooden cross as he stroked his hands down her body from wrist to ankle. She gasped as he placed a lingering kiss on the top of her foot, trembling as her body begged for more of his touch.

"From personal experience, the most intimate, tender sex can follow the most excruciating SM session." Cade breathed against her skin as he continued to brush his lips over her body, kissing his way up until he reached the sensitive curve of her neck. Placing one hand possessively across her throat, Cade moved to untie the blindfold nestled in her hair, letting the black cloth fall to the floor.

Kara blinked in the newness of light, readjusting herself once again to her surroundings with full senses. The room hadn't changed form, but its contents no longer inspired fear, the strangeness banished thanks to Cade's unorthodox introductions. More than that, Kara found herself intrigued by the thought of submitting to Cade and the contents of his secret hideaway. The overwhelming need she felt in that moment was startling. All the rationality of her mind was fighting a losing war with the erogenous areas of her body. She knew a single look from Cade would send her hurling over the brink of surrender.

"If you don't want this, we will leave the Hideaway and pretend that I never showed you what lies below. If you do want this, own up to it. You aren't less of an independent woman or less of an academic or less of a rational human being for consensually claiming what your body desires, no matter how unconventional that desire may seem. The choice is yours alone."

Kara drew a deep, shaky breath, her eyes fixated on the exit. Escape was hers if she truly wanted it. But the starling, nerve shattering truth was—she wanted complete surrender with Cade more. "I want this. Please."

"Brave girl," Cade responded in a voice husky with emotion as he breathed a deep sigh of relief. His eyes shone with the light of admiration that she was willing to wade into the unknown, trusting that he would be there to hold her and guide her. And he would be. Every step of the way.

CHAPTER NINETEEN

CADE looked at Kara with a mixture of admiration and hesitation. She was offering herself to him so trustingly, and, as hard as it would be to restrain his darker nature, he would need to keep himself in check. "You need a safe-word. Something to use as a signal if you think I've given all you can handle. It doesn't need to be anything specific or significant, but it should be memorable enough that it is easily recollected if you are at your limit. As this is your first time, I intend on being cautiously receptive of your tolerance and needs. You should have no need of a safe-word tonight, but under normal circumstances, the safe-word serves as a precaution in situations where *stop* is more of an encouragement than a deterrent."

"O-okay," Kara responded nervously. She felt a general sense of unease at the thought of allowing a man who seemed to have an entirely different definition of the word *stop* to have full control over her body, but the indescribable need she felt outweighed her misgivings. The idea of two consenting adults needing a code word to play safely seemed rather juvenile, but Kara was willing to meet his conditions, whatever they may be. "Thornfield," she decided finally, paying homage to her favorite piece of literature.

"I believe that is rather suiting," Cade replied with a smile. "The Brontës definitely had a robust understanding of the darker side of human nature, and I am sure Mr. Rochester would find himself rather comfortable in a BDSM setting," he added with a wink.

A kinky Mr. Rochester?

In all her many readings of the text, Kara had never once considered *that* possibility, but she supposed it wasn't hard to imagine that the man who kept his wife locked in an attic and emotionally tortured and manipulated the woman he loved might have done so out of sadistic pleasure.

"Now, for my second condition," Cade continued, reclaiming her attention. "I would like you to address me as *sir* from this moment forward."

Kara giggled at the ridiculous suggestion, earning her a withering glare from the imperious man before her. "You can't be serious," Kara demanded, her expression horrified.

"I bloody well am serious," Cade responded darkly, his eyes glittering with a need to punish.

"That's absurd! I'm not going to call you *sir*," Kara argued, crossing her arms angrily over her chest and very narrowly resisting the urge to stomp her feet in protest.

"Then leave," Cade answered, his voice deadly calm as he nodded toward the stairs. He knew that she needed his dominance more than she needed her pride at that moment, and he was calling her bluff.

"Fine!" Kara shouted in exasperation, throwing her arms into the air in surrender.

"Fine, *what*?" Cade questioned with a raised brow.

"I would like to stay," Kara responded sullenly.

"Are you sure you can handle it, love?" Cade asked with false concern as a taunting smile spread across his lips.

"Yes," Kara replied curtly. With a chastising glance from Cade, she added, "*sir*."

"Good girl," he praised tenderly. "Remove your clothes," he ordered, a subtle change to the tone of his voice evoking pure dominance.

After a single moment of hesitance, Kara obeyed, trembling fingers moving to undo the buttons of her dress before allowing it to slip off her shoulders and fall to the floor. She stood before him in only her bra and underwear and waited.

"Everything," he corrected impatiently as though it had been inherently implied in his first command.

Feeling suddenly modest in front of the man who had already seen her naked on numerous occasions, Kara reluctantly reached behind her back to unclasp her bra and let it fall to her feet. Her heart pounding with anticipation, she brushed the lace of her panties and slowly slid them down her legs, stepping out of them a foot at a time. Impulsively, Kara balled up the panties and tossed them in Cade's unsuspecting face. They landed at his feet in a puddle of pink lace.

Hideaway

"My, aren't we cheeky today?" he chided, his face a picture of amused shock. "For that, I think I'll keep these," he decided, stooping to pick up the knickers and place them in his back pocket.

Pleased with her submissive nakedness, Cade walked toward her purposefully, drew her mouth to his, and tasted her lips softly. Kara accepted the gentle kiss eagerly, absorbing the warmth of his mouth as though it could banish every chill that wracked her naked body. Cade wrapped both of his hands in her hair and pulled her away so he could read her expression with his next question. "I am going to cuff you. Are you comfortable with that?" he asked, aware that such an activity might invoke trauma of the past. Since the ultimate goal of their exercise was to allow Kara to overcome the dreadful assault and gain some sort of normalcy again, Cade was willing to take her as far as she was able to go.

"Yes, sir," Kara answered shakily.

"Very good," he said proudly, bending low to bestow a soft kiss to her temple. "Come with me," he ordered gently, offering his hand. Kara took it and followed his lead across the room to where an assortment of cuffs hung in a line against the wall. He pulled up a pair of black leather cuffs, each adorned with a single loop of silver. "Wrists," he ordered as he turned to face Kara.

She complied quickly, presenting both wrists face up before him. The posture felt a bit as though she were offering herself to be sacrificed, but the inherent submission of the gesture left her feeling pleasantly tingly in all the right places. With a steady concentration, Cade took her wrists one at a time and set about fastening the cuffs, ensuring with professional caution that they were tight enough to keep her safely in place, but not too tight to cause harm. Satisfied with his work, Cade released her wrists and allowed her to adjust to the new accessories. Kara eyed the cuffs curiously, feeling the unfamiliar weight of them as she moved her arms. The smooth black leather and silver details definitely had more class than Jace's choice of restraint.

"Feel good?" Cade asked, watching in amusement as Kara adapted to wearing real kink accessories for the first time. They looked damned good on her.

"In a strange way, I believe they do, sir."

"I am pleased to hear it. I could certainly get used to the sight of you in cuffs," he said, his voice husky.

"Is that so?" she inquired temptingly. She closed the small distance between, placed one hand on his jaw and the other behind his head, and pulled him down to her lips. The taste of his mouth was so intoxicating that Kara was nearly ready to forego their whole endeavor, take him upstairs, and enjoy a rather hard fucking. Cade broke off the kiss before she could reach complete abandonment and set her a few spaces away from him.

"I don't believe I gave you permission to kiss me, Kara," he said with a stern displeasure that she couldn't classify as jest with any certainty.

"Do I need permission, sir?" she challenged.

"Tonight I will allow it, but don't expect me to extend mercy the next time you take liberties," he replied darkly, but his eyes held the glint of a smile.

Arrogant bastard.

"Don't be expecting a next time," she answered scathingly.

"I should hope you find yourself in a better state of humility by the end of the night. I have a low tolerance for bratty behavior."

Hooking a finger in the silver loop of one of the cuffs, Cade dragged Kara to the center of the room. With her wrist still in his possession, he lifted her right arm above her head and attached the cuff to a grate in the ceiling that she hadn't noticed until that exact moment. With the shocking display she was presented with upon entering the room, Kara had never thought to look up. Her wrist firmly locked in place, Cade moved to fasten the left cuff in a similar manner. After both arms were restrained and suspended above her head, Cade took a step back to appreciate the satisfying sight of submission at its finest.

"You look lovely," he praised, fairly certain he'd never seen a more stunning view in his entire life. Cade had never considered approaching Kara to participate in his lifestyle; he had thought her too uncomfortable with exhibiting weakness, too stubborn to follow his lead, and yet, she was in the Hideaway of her own accord. Even if one night of catharsis was all Kara ever needed or wanted, Cade would cherish Kara's submission as the precious gift it was. "How are you feeling?"

"I'm a little anxious," she answered, glancing up at her restraints hesitantly. "Jace tied me up before—" She shut her eyes as though it could shut out the memory of his hands on her. "Before it happened."

"I know; I saw the marks," Cade said softly, recalling the familiar reddened burns on her skin. He often made those very marks on his own willing participants. Cade reached to grasp Kara's wrist as he bent to kiss her neck. "Now it will be my marks left on your skin," he whispered against her ear. "Are you okay with that?"

"Yes, sir," she responded breathily.

"Good. Are you ready to begin?"

"Yes, sir."

Cade attempted to quell the excitement that began to build at her words. Though he had continued to engage in sessions at his private club, Cade had not used the Hideaway and his personal collection of toys and implements in quite some time. Enticing options coursed through his head as he contemplated which implement would be best used on his girl. Unaccustomed to playing with someone so inexperienced, Cade decided it would be sensible to establish some foundation as to Kara's expectations and tolerance.

"Have you ever engaged in pain play, Kara?"

"Not really, sir."

"I am afraid I'll need a more concise answer than *not really*."

Kara blushed as she pushed through the embarrassment to be more descriptive. "You know, standard sex stuff—light spanking, playful biting, hair pulling. Nothing quite so professional as this."

"I see," Cade said with a smile. His sweet, vanilla girl was about to get an education. "How would you rate your pain tolerance?"

Kara thought back to that night with Jace. Even with everything he put her through, it was almost as though she had disappeared from her body. She could hardly feel a thing until after he had left the room. That was when she allowed herself to acknowledge the pain, when her tears would belong to no one but her. The only other time she had experienced pain like that was after the car accident. Kara had used the pain from her injuries to keep herself from going numb after the loss of her parents. The doctors had been baffled by her ability to persevere and recover without the use of pain medication. Kara supposed she had always treated pain as a mental obstacle; she could revel in it when she wanted to feel its power or she could overcome it to keep from breaking.

"High," she answered after a moment of self-reflection.

Cade's brows lifted in surprise. "High? Are you certain?"

"I'm sure, sir."

"Well, you are full of surprises this evening. How far do you want me to take you?"

Kara bit her lip as she contemplated his words. How far did she want to go? "To the point where all I feel is you on my body. Erase the memory of him on my skin. Write over the pain he left, the marks he made. Make them yours. Make me yours. Please," she begged almost desperately.

Cade had to wonder if she knew what she was asking for with such determination, such trust. He moved his hand to tenderly caress the smoothness of Kara's bruised cheek. "Are you completely certain that you want your entire body—every mark—to belong to me?"

"Yes, sir," Kara answered with finality.

Before she had a moment to reconsider her decision, Cade drew back his hand and slapped her across the face. Hard. Hard enough to bruise. Kara's wide eyes filled with tears of shock and pain at the brutality of the act as she pressed her burning cheek into the cool skin of her shoulder. She couldn't believe that he had *hit* her. Kara understood the irony of her infuriation, considering Cade had merely met her demands, but there was something inherently degrading, something intrinsically barbaric about hitting a woman in the face.

Embarrassed and confused, Kara kept her eyes lowered as she reconsidered what the hell she was doing.

Cade read the tension in Kara's body as he held himself at a distance, allowing her to process exactly what the session with him would entail. He hadn't wanted to hurt her, especially in a way so lacking in pleasure, but it was what she needed. She deserved to own her body once again, and he intended to give it back into her possession one piece at a time. Tentatively grasping her chin and raising her head up to face him, Cade searched her eyes as fresh tears pooled and spilled down her flushed cheeks. She was breathtaking, perhaps more so than ever before, as she slowly shattered into lovely, fractured pieces in front of him. Cade lowered his mouth to her bright red cheek and softly brushed his lips over the dark mark of his hand marring her pale skin. His tongue found a trail of her tears and licked her from chin to cheek bone, savoring the saltiness mingled with the sweet taste of her.

"Mine," Cade declared roughly, looking deeply into her eyes and willing the truth of his statement to penetrate the farthest recesses of her mind. She had asked him to erase the memory of Jace from her mind and body. Cade planned to be meticulously accommodating.

Kara looked at him incredulously as her conflicting emotions incited inner turmoil. The burn of his blow mingled with the warmth of his kiss, barbarism tempered with tenderness. The contrasting combination of the two sent the blood in her veins singing with the sweetest sensation that could only be likened to euphoria. Cade read the realization in her face and couldn't help but smile.

"Would you like more?" he asked knowingly.

"Yes, please, sir," Kara answered, startled by how much she did.

Cade circled her, appraising the extent of the damage left behind by Jace. The bastard had marked her thoroughly. Kara would have to withstand a considerable amount of blows if Cade was to reclaim her body completely. He contemplated the best choice of implement with a professional prudence. "I think we can find something with a little more finesse than my belt," Cade remarked playfully as he walked around the room to survey his vast collection.

Kara followed his movements in suspense, growing a little anxious as he disappeared beyond her sight. Considering it was Kara's first time and the application would cover much of her body, Cade needed something light. Though he rarely used such a low impact tool in a typical scene, Cade decided a flogger would best suit Kara's needs in their particular situation. Lifting the unthreatening instrument from where it hung on the wall, Cade presented the item almost ceremoniously before Kara.

"A flogger," he announced by definition, correctly assuming that Kara would be unacquainted with its name.

As she eyed the mild looking tool in Cade's hands, her face distorted into an expression reminiscent of disappointment. From her unconventional tour of Cade's room, Kara remembered the feel of the flogger, soft strands that emulated caresses. But a caress was not the sensation Kara ached for; she needed more and was slightly hurt that Cade had determined she only had the strength to endure softness.

"Is something wrong?" Cade asked in confusion, noticing the furrow of her brow as she looked at the flogger in distaste.

"It's just…well…I suppose I had been expecting something a little more menacing than *that*," Kara answered, gesturing with her head to the flogger in his hands.

"I see," Cade remarked dangerously. "So you take issue with my choice of implement? Or perhaps with my ability to wield it?"

Shit.

As she heard the darkening of his tone, Kara felt the chill of panic wash over her. "I am sure you are more than capable, sir," Kara placated hastily. "I just think I can handle something that hurts more than a flogger."

"Kara, I am skilled enough to inflict pain with even the most mundane of objects. With an instrument that is specifically designed for both pleasure and pain, I assure you, I can *make* it hurt."

She believed him wholeheartedly, but she was willing to further risk his displeasure with one more question. There was a single thing she hoped most to gain from their endeavor, and she seriously doubted the flogger had the potential to satisfy her desires. "Will it leave a lasting mark, sir?"

The question caught Cade off guard. He hadn't chosen the flogger with the intention of leaving a lasting imprint on her skin, and he hadn't considered that she would care. In his world, it was typically masochists who relished the marks left by their Dominants, a way to savor and remember the pain they'd received after a scene was finished. From their previous encounters, Cade could safely assume that Kara was not a masochist—at least not entirely—but he had failed to remember that she had been intimately acquainted with a sadist in the worst possible way. With slow, dawning awareness, Cade realized that Kara had been literal in her request that he write

Hideaway

over the pain Jace had left, and, in some singular way, her need for physical proof that Jace was not the last person to touch her made sense.

"You want me to mark you, Kara? Like he did?"

"Yes, sir," she answered, aware that she sounded marginally insane.

"It will hurt," he explained unnecessarily, wholly certain of what her response would be.

"I know, sir."

"As you wish, though I dare say you've quite removed any element of dominance from this session," Cade conceded moodily as he walked to return the flogger to its appropriate place. "You merely have me playing the sadist for your own personal needs. Truthfully, I feel quite used," he lamented with a tone of playfulness.

"Caden Ashford, exploited at the hands of a woman? My, what a novel experience that must be for a man who gets off on dominating the weaker sex."

"Watch your tone, love. I have yet to determine my choice of weapon, and your continued provocation ensures that you will not appreciate my decision," Cade threatened darkly as he continued to test and consider multiple implements around the room.

"My apologies, consider me fully submissive and at your disposal, sir. Happy?"

"As a matter of fact, I am, though you likely won't be in such a cheeky mood much longer," Cade remarked as he came into view holding the first item Kara touched upon entering the Hideaway—a thin, flexible cane.

Fucking. Shit.

"Satisfied, love?" he asked pointedly as he turned the cane in his hands, gratified to see a glimmer of apprehension appear in her eyes.

"Terrified," she answered truthfully. Kara knew that she'd asked for pain, she'd asked for marks, but she had never asked for *that*.

"Finally, she shows some capacity for self-preservation," Cade commented with a sardonic roll of his eyes. Kara merely glared in response. "Has your resolve faltered, or are you still intent on continuing?" he asked, striking the cane against his thigh loudly for emphasis.

Kara flinched, both at the movement and at the thought of the cane on bare skin. "Yes," she answered softly after the smallest hesitation, her eyes locked on his.

"To which question?"

"Both? Yes, my resolve is slightly shaken as you brandish that weapon so menacingly, but yes, I want to continue."

"Do you remember your safe-word?"

"Thornfield," she confirmed after a shaky breath, aware that she was now past the point of no return.

"Good. I'll remind you a final time that I am to be addressed as 'sir.' The next time you experience a lapse in the appropriate respect you won't enjoy the outcome," he responded firmly.

"Yes, sir," Kara agreed hastily.

Cade traced the tip of the cane along her skin, sliding it down her neck, circling her breasts, trailing across her abdomen, grazing the softness at the junction of her thighs before continuing lower down her legs—adjusting her senses to the feel of the rod. He hoped an introduction of intimacy before pain would help to lessen her apprehension.

Slowly, Kara warmed to the sensation of the cane gliding across her skin, welcoming it as an extension of Cade, caressing her body as he would with his hands, and she opened herself to his exploration. Having thoroughly christened the front of her body, Cade moved behind her to continue his attentions. Kara felt the tip of the cane travel down her spine and shivered as it skimmed the delicate nerves along the center of her naked back. Cade paused when he reached the curve of her bottom, dragging the cane across the fullest swell of her backside back and forth as though he held a bow and her body was an instrument to be played.

"I am going to hit you here, Kara," he warned, his voice rough and full of emotion. "Take a deep breath, love."

Racked with anticipation and dread, Kara inhaled shakily. As she exhaled, the first searing strike of the cane sliced across the tender skin of her backside, leaving a cruel, red stripe in its wake. Kara cried out. She hadn't meant to, possessing every intention of enduring the pain in silence, but she could not contain her body's instinctual reaction, her courage surmounted by the overwhelming agony so new and unfamiliar. Kara had known pain in her life, but somehow Cade's version felt like an entirely new variety of sensation.

"Are you okay?" he asked, a hint of concern in his tone.

Kara nodded, unsure if she could trust the strength of her voice to speak.

"Answer me," he commanded, unsatisfied with the slight nod as proof of her well being.

"I'm okay, sir," she answered weakly.

Satisfied, Cade stroked her gently with the cane, perhaps an inch below the first blow, as he prepared her skin for the next strike. When he hit her the second time, Kara gasped sharply, clenching her teeth to keep any louder reactions at bay. She felt more prepared when Cade aligned the cane with her skin the third time. Biting her lip as the blow fell, she was able to remain silent, much to her satisfaction. She whimpered softly as the fourth strike took her by surprise. After Cade delivered the fifth cut of the cane to the lowest spot on her backside, Kara felt tears on her cheeks. Every nerve in her body cried out against the injustice of Cade's assault, but her resolve held firm. Tensing for the next blow, Kara was startled when she felt the cool touch of Cade's lips, rather than the cane, on her burning skin.

There were five lovely marks, perfectly spaced red lines against pale skin, and Cade delivered a soft kiss to each. They belonged to him. With every strike, every kiss, Cade felt as though he took complete possession of Kara as well.

After the brief reprieve, Kara once again felt the touch of the cane on her skin, this time aligned with her upper thighs. Considering the introductory period concluded, Cade made no attempt to ease the blows on her thighs, bringing the cane down harshly and swiftly as he marked her with consecutive stripes. Kara counted the blows silently, envisioning where the next would fall. She preferred the rapid succession of strikes; it allowed her to focus less on the point of pain and more on the culmination of stinginess that spread through her legs. Transcending the previous agony, Kara endured five cuts of the cane to the backs of her thighs with little more than a whimper. She allowed herself to relax slightly as the strikes of the cane subsided, assuming Cade had met his quota with a total of ten blows. The sound of the cruel implement slicing through the air once more caught her off guard, a belated warning of anguish to come. An unfamiliar shriek escaped her lips as the cane landed diagonally across all five of the stripes etched into the back of her thighs.

Fucking. Sadist.

Kara wrestled with feelings of hatred as Cade knelt behind her and continued his ritual of kissing her new marks. He had hit her harder the second round, and the feel of his lips burned as though he chafed an open wound. If one thing was certain, Kara would no longer remember Jace when she succumbed to agony with the smallest movement thanks to Cade's more than diligent torture. She supposed the vicious efficiency was to be expected when you employed a professional.

Having atoned for his deeds with six kisses, Cade walked around to face Kara, anxious to gauge her physical and emotional state. She had taken a considerable amount of pain in near silence, a feat that was difficult to accomplish when a cane was involved, even with experience and training. Astonishingly, her assessment of her pain tolerance appeared to be accurate. When he stood before her, Kara raised her eyes boldly to meet his gaze. Accustomed to a version of Kara that was always perfectly composed, Cade appreciated how vulnerable she looked in that moment with tear-dampened cheeks, mascara smudged beneath her eyes, and her bottom lip unnaturally red as though she'd bitten through the skin to keep silent. He doubted if anyone had ever looked lovelier.

Cade searched her expression for any sign of devastation or surrender, but he found only determination. There was a burgeoning sense of pride blooming within his chest as he considered how the girl who appeared so delicate could be so unbelievably strong. Kara had proved that tenacity over and over from the moment they met. Cade lifted his thumb to her mouth and lightly stroked her full bottom lip, denying every instinct that told him to conquer that mouth and make it his that very instant. He read the language of her body as she leaned into him, pleading for the embrace he withheld, but satisfaction for the both of them would have to wait.

"I'll continue here," Cade informed brusquely as he pulled away from her, using the cane to stroke up and down the fronts of her thighs marred by the imprint of Jace's hands. Kara swallowed anxiously. Her bruised thighs already felt sensitive to the soft touch of the cane; she couldn't imagine how excruciating it would be to have the full force of Cade's blows cutting into the tender skin. Even worse, she would be able to anticipate the moment of every strike and see the damage that was done.

"May I close my eyes, sir?" she asked timidly.

"You may," Cade allowed, surprised that she was getting suddenly squeamish after she'd already been hit quite a few times. He made a mental note to implement a blindfold the next time they engaged in impact play. If there was a next time.

Shutting her eyes tightly, Kara took a deep breath as she prepared for the next onslaught. The first blow fell unexpectedly high, grazing her most sensitive region, as she exhaled sharply. She hoped against reason she would never feel the sting of the cane a couple inches higher. The next two came quickly as Cade made his way down her legs. She groaned through gritted teeth as the fourth landed on a particularly tender spot where Jace had grabbed her, washing away the past violence with Cade's variety of brutality. Kara prepared for the worst after the fifth strike came. Never failing to disappoint, Cade brought the cane down hard on top of the preceding red welts. Kara sobbed softly in relief as the sixth brought with it a brief intermission from the pain.

As Cade sank to his knees to administer his six caresses, Kara focused on steadying her breathing and absorbing the sensations reverberating through her body. More curious than courageous, Kara tentatively opened her eyes to view the damage Cade had dealt. The sight of Cade knelt between her legs with his mouth on her skin sent a thrill through her body that momentarily wiped every other thought from her mind. She spread her legs slightly wider, willing his lips to travel upward to where her most sensitive region waited impatiently. If Cade had any inkling of Kara's more than obvious hint, he certainly didn't show it, keeping his attention infuriatingly focused on her thighs only. Resigned to remaining unsatisfied, Kara sought out her initial point of focus.

Shockingly, the marks of the cane appeared to look even worse than they sounded and felt. Angry red welts streaked symmetrically across her thighs, the skin broken slightly at every point where the final blow had met with the other five. She hadn't expected Cade to draw blood; the sight of her abused skin incited emotions she couldn't quite describe. If she were honest, she might admit that the marks of ownership inspired arousal, and she could not tear her eyes away from the sight of those red lines.

"Are you ready?" he asked, startling her from a fascination with the new adornment of her thighs.

"Yes, sir," Kara answered almost eagerly, curious to see where he would aim his attentions next. She blanched as he laid the cane across the tops of her breasts in response to her silent inquiry.

Certainly he wouldn't?

Kara had serious doubts about that particular part of the body being an appropriate point of application for a cane, or any instrument really. After a moment of stroking the cane against the skin of her breasts, he drew back to deliver the first blow.

"Cade!" Kara shouted in horror, breaking her pretense of submission.

Cade stayed his hand as an expression of concern washed over his features. "Are you okay?" he asked worriedly, gauging her breathing and heart rate for signs of distress. Had he gone too far? "If you would like to utilize your safe-word, do so now," he instructed gently. He didn't want to push her past her breaking point, but he also was hesitant to stop until her needs had been fully satiated. The choice was entirely up to her.

Kara remained silent, shamefully aware that she had attempted to stop Cade without having reached a point where she was prepared to use a safe-word.

"I see," Cade commented with a hint of chastisement, his brows furrowed in displeasure. "As you still consent to submit to my authority, that little outburst has incurred an additional strike as punishment," he said right before bringing the cane down hard across the center of her ass and pulling a whimper of pain from her lips. "Now, do you have any complaints of which I need to be apprised?"

"No, sir," she answered with heaving breaths, still reeling from the discomfort of having her ass further assaulted.

"Good." Without another word, Cade continued with his work at the top of her breasts, delivering slightly lighter strikes to the delicate area. Though the cane hit a new spot every time, Kara felt as though she was becoming desensitized to the pain of it, the sensation morphing into something entirely unfamiliar, almost akin to elation. Kara was aware of the pain, but she found herself being pulled toward it, craving the next strike rather than shrinking from it. Slowly, the pain that had threatened to overwhelm her senses seemed to be driving her toward release. She lost count as the blows fell in a haze, slicing across her skin with the sweetest sting. Cade layered a final, brutal strike upon the imprint of Jace's teeth on her breast before concluding the caning.

When the pain ceased, Kara's body ached in its absence, like cold-numbed nerves upon their first, jarring introduction to warmth. As the dull desensitization slowly faded, her skin burned like fire, but the heat felt invigorating after so many days spent in numb desolation. Cade had shocked her senses from the slumber of surrender, and they screamed in agony and bliss.

Cade reverently bent his head to bestow kisses more tenderly than ever upon the raw skin of her breasts. He began with the lowest stripes, kissing and running his tongue along the entirety of the red lines. When he reached the center of her breast, he took each nipple into his mouth and sucked deeply. Kara moaned as the arousal traveled straight to the soaked slit between her legs. Far too quickly, Cade moved his lips from her nipples to the higher marks streaked across her chest. When his mouth found the twin crescents left by

Jace upon her upper breast, Cade bared his teeth and bit down hard, hard enough to draw blood as Kara whimpered in both agony and ecstasy. Having finished anointing her marks with his mouth, Cade raised dark, smoldering eyes in search of hers, his body tense with passion that seemed just barely enslaved by the bounds of self-control. Were she not restrained herself, Kara would have extended every effort to set his passions free, gladly reaping the consequences of both his ardor and his violence unconstrained.

"One more to go," Cade announced gruffly, forcing himself to draw back when all he wanted to do was be inside her that very moment. With one more spot to claim, she would be his in every sense of the word. "Spread your legs, Kara."

She hesitated merely a moment before opening herself for whatever purpose Cade deigned, uncharacteristically willing to obey his command without question. Perhaps she had been lulled into submission due to the onset of pain induced delirium. The notion seemed plausible, but what didn't satisfy logic was the fact that she was covered in welts and bruises and somehow felt nothing that remotely resembled pain. Somehow, Cade had mended her spirit even as he destroyed her body. Perhaps there was something to be said for the lifestyle of dominance that Cade was drawn to.

"Wider, love. I have a very specific target in mind."

Kara complied instantly, spreading her legs as far apart as comfortably possible, his words warming her insides in anticipation. Satisfied with her stance, Cade touched the cane to the spot between her legs, gently sliding the wooden rod along the folds of her pussy, stroking her from clit to slit. Finally receiving the attention she'd been craving all night, Kara moaned as the cane slipped easily back

Hideaway

and forth, aided by her own, dripping wetness. Cade allowed her to enjoy a moment of pleasure, appreciating the sounds that escaped her lips every time the cane made contact with her clit, imagining how she would sound when he replaced the cane with his cock.

As Kara neared release, Cade drew back the cane and delivered a final, piercing blow to the most intimate part of her body. An unearthly scream that encompassed all that was torment and euphoria and everything in between rose from the depths of Kara's being. Cade heard it like the call of a siren, threw the cane to the floor, and made all haste to claim the reward he had endeavored all night to earn. Without the patience to remove her restraints or move her to a more comfortable position, he violently threw himself against Kara. Fervent hands tangled in her hair; he pulled sharply, forcing her mouth to his, devouring the taste of her as though he was at the brink of starvation and Kara was all that could sustain him. Keeping a firm grasp on her hair, Cade slipped one hand down Kara's neck and wrapped his fingers tightly around her throat, pressing hard where Jace had left his fingerprints in bruises.

"You are mine," Cade whispered harshly in her ear, appreciating the surge of dominance he felt as he held her very consciousness in his possession.

As Kara felt her vision slowly start to darken, Cade loosened his grip on her throat and moved his hands over her body greedily, tracing every inch of her skin as though it was the first time he had ever touched her, the first time she was truly his. And for the first time, Cade held nothing back. Kara gasped as rough hands brushed against fresh bruises and welts, desperate fingers clawed at raw skin, every sensation igniting the need for more. She ached to touch Cade, pulling against the restraints that rendered her powerless to unleash the raw passion that had been building inside her, like a balloon about to burst. The feeling of being cuffed in place was infuriating, and yet, she knew this was how Cade liked her—helpless, exposed, entirely pliant to his demands.

Strong fingers dug painfully into her thighs as Kara felt herself being hoisted high enough to meet Cade at eye level. Instinctively, she wrapped her legs around his hips and tightened to draw him closer to her body. Though she didn't have the use of her hands, Kara could certainly make due with the lower half of her body. Cade growled appreciatively at Kara's eagerness, pleasantly surprised that the rather extensive caning had done little to quell her carnal appetites.

"Fuck me, please, sir," Kara pleaded between breathless kisses—desperate, aching, and near death with a sheer, indescribable need to be *filled*.

Cade groaned into her mouth, her begging and her submission sending an electrifying shock of arousal straight to his cock. "Hold on tight, love," Cade instructed, releasing his hold on Kara as he frantically worked to undo his belt and lower his pants beneath the grip of her legs around his waist.

Finally, his cock sprang free, the steel-like hardness jutting into the painful lashes on the backs of Kara's thighs. She whimpered at the feel of him against her tender skin, both in pain and in the need for more. Cade's fingers savagely gripped the raw skin of her ass as he spread her open and lined up his cock at her drenched pussy. In one brutal thrust, Cade impaled her completely, drawing a scream from her open mouth as his cock stuffed her full, almost too full as she struggled to accept his overwhelming size without agony. It was impossible; sex with Cade would always mean a mingling of pain and pleasure even if the only weapon he wielded was his cock.

The room echoed with the sound of flesh violently meeting flesh as Cade fucked her ruthlessly. With her arms restrained, Kara could do little more than latch on with her legs as best as she could while her body was wrecked and ravaged. Cade fucked her as though it was the last thing he would ever do; Kara reveled in his punishing thrusts as though it was the first time she had ever been fucked, truly and completely. She had never felt so dominated, free, pleasured, and split entirely fucking open.

"You are mine. Do you fucking hear me? Every scream, every tear, every breath," Cade squeezed his fingers around Kara's throat until he stifled the very air in her lungs, "every *fucking heartbeat* is mine. Do you understand?" His voice sounded violent and manic and unfamiliar to his own ears. Kara had unleashed the ferocious beast that lurked beneath his calm, calculated composure. The possessive demon whose thirst for dominance and blood he had taken great pains to keep carefully satiated instead of allowing the monster to devour at its pleasure. Now that the beast had fed, had tasted the sweetness of Kara's tears and pain and *submission*, there would be no stopping it. Kara no longer had any hope of escape. "Answer me," Cade commanded harshly as his fingers pressed deeply into her throat with bruising strength.

Kara nodded frantically, her ability to speak stolen by the delicious agony of his hand constricted around her vocal cords.

"Say the fucking words, Kara," Cade growled with his mouth against hers, their lips nearly touching as though he meant to kiss her. Or bite her. He loosened his hold enough for Kara to draw small gasps of breath. The demon inside needed to hear her *say* she belonged to him.

"I'm yours, Cade. I'm all yours. Take everything. Everything that I am belongs to you," Kara answered in heavy breaths, her pupils blown and her lips quivering with the need to feel the warmth of his mouth on her.

"Fuck, baby," Cade groaned in ecstasy at her surrender. His hand moved to her hair and gripped painfully, dragging her lips to his as he devoured and ravaged, his teeth drawing blood and his tongue lapping it away as though it were the most intoxicating thing he had ever tasted. Because it fucking was. His other hand dug into the welts on her backside, slamming her onto his cock while she struggled to keep her legs wrapped around his waist as he fucked her mercilessly, his rhythm vicious and unmatchable.

Kara felt the pleasure building deep in her core as Cade's cock and hands and lips tore unearthly moans from her body. The fire pulsing through her veins was unlike anything she'd ever felt before. He was incinerating her and creating her anew with every thrust of his body.

"Come for me, Kara. Fucking scream my name while you shatter on my cock and soak me with your cum." Cade slapped the angry red welts on her arse so hard that she cried out in intertwined agony and bliss. "Show me who fucking owns you." Cade gripped her ass with both hands, possessively digging his nails into the broken skin as he fucked her harder than he had ever fucked in his life, as though he were trying to fuck her very soul from her body.

"Cade!" Kara detonated, fracturing into a million shards of pleasure and pain and every emotion in between. "Cade, Cade, Cade," she breathed his name over and over, like a prayer on her swollen, aching lips. Her arousal flooded out of her, drenching his cock and thighs and the marble floor below as he continued to savagely fuck her. The wet sound of their flesh fervidly colliding was the most lasciviously entrancing symphony she'd ever heard. She couldn't help but stare at the beautifully obscene sight of his hard cock entering her dripping pussy like it belonged there.

"Kiss me, Cade," she pleaded, her voice half-dazed. "Please." She desperately needed to touch him, to show him just how much she possessed him too. With his hands still on her ass, Cade crashed his lips into her. There was nothing gentle about their kiss; it was a battle—a brutal, vicious collision of lips and teeth and tongue. This time, rather than letting Cade consume her, Kara matched his violence with her own. If he was out for blood, if he was out to devour and conquer, then so was she. "You're mine, Caden Ashford," Kara declared forcefully, her voice full of a power and dominance she had never known existed before Cade. Her teeth tore into his bottom lip and pulled as hard as she could, her tongue tasting copper as his skin broke beneath the force. Cade groaned into her mouth, the sound guttural and primal.

"*Fuck me*," Cade growled as he came undone, his cock swelling as he filled her with his cum. He felt Kara's cunt convulse around him, strangling his cock with spasm after spasm of pleasure as she came again, this time wordlessly, breathlessly, her energy absolutely spent. Cade stayed inside of her, not wanting a single drop of his cum to escape her still throbbing pussy. When Kara seemed to be on the verge of passing out from exhaustion, Cade finally withdrew his cock, using his fingers to capture the cum that dripped down her thighs and fucked it back into her with his fingers.

Fucking. Mine.

Cade released Kara from the restraints, carrying her over to the bed and laying her gently on the sheets. Her eyes fluttered as she tried to hold onto consciousness, the lull of sleep begging to overtake her. Cade stroked her cheek, sweeping aside her sweaty hair and brushing away tears she'd cried in ecstasy. She looked absolutely wrecked and absolutely breathtaking. "You have exceeded my every expectation, love," Cade said in awe as he trailed his fingers down the side of her neck, noting the bruises left by his hands. "You are so much more than the meek little librarian I watched from the windows at the university."

Kara peeked open heavy eyes to glare at him. "The fact that you think that's a normal statement proves I've fallen for an absolute lunatic. I'll add stalking to your lengthy list of offenses."

"You've *fallen* for me, have you?" Cade asked, a mischievous glint in his eyes as he glossed over the rest of her insults and focused on that one, weighty word.

Kara flinched when she realized he'd caught the slip of her tongue. Whatever she felt for Cade, she wasn't in an appropriate state of mind to make that sort of declaration, not with his cum dripping down her thighs and his bruises decorating her skin. Kara cleared her throat nervously. "Yes, fallen, as in I've leapt from the edge of reason and plummeted into the chasm of whatever blissful insanity this is."

"What lovely evasion, my dear," Cade teased playfully as he bent to steal another kiss from her lips. "To think, all of this happened because you wouldn't hand over a fucking book. As much as it generally vexes me, perhaps I should be thanking you for your stubbornness. I couldn't bend you to my will if I tried. And, as we both are intimately aware, I have tried. *Endlessly*."

"I wouldn't be so sure of that," Kara taunted with a mischievous smirk.

"Is that so? Meaning what, exactly?" Cade asked in confusion.

"*Meaning*, I wouldn't be so sure of your failure to attain the Chaucer text. And, if you were to currently peruse your library, you might find yourself in possession of an extra first edition," Kara elaborated smugly.

"You've hidden *stolen* contraband in *my* library?" Cade asked with feigned outrage.

"Well, I'm sure it wouldn't be the first time," Kara replied with an eye roll as she tried to swat at him before he darted out of reach.

"Really, though, however did you manage that?" Cade inquired in astonishment.

"Remember that time I ran away from you?"

"How could I forget?" Cade answered fondly, the sadistic gleam in his eyes hinting that the experience was memorable for entirely different reasons than her own.

"Well, I had more than one reason for making a *temporary* trip to the university. I wanted to make sure that *The Canterbury Tales* was secure, and what better place to conceal it than the house of the man commissioned to steal it? Even if Avery had managed to gain access to the archives, he wouldn't have found his generous donation among the texts."

"That was surprisingly devious of you, love. I'm thoroughly impressed."

"Now do you feel bad for beating me with a belt?"

"Not in the least," Cade replied without a touch of remorse.

"Fucking sadist," Kara huffed before closing her eyes and curling into the warm safety of Cade's embrace.

Cade wrapped his arms around her, pulling her into his body as tightly as he could without suffocating her. Barely. She fit against him perfectly, filling all the empty spaces as though they were two jagged halves of the same whole finally pieced together. One thing was certain, he'd never allow her to fucking escape him again.

CHAPTER TWENTY

JACE had vanished like a cockroach in the dark. As hard as Cade, Braxton, and Ortega had tried to find the son of a bitch, he was gone without a fucking trace. That was, until the prick found the opportune moment to come crawling back. Cade stared grimly at the ominous text he'd received the night before.

bring me the book...or the next time i take kara i'll cut her up piece by piece and leave her remains scattered for you like a goddamn scavenger hunt. you like games don't you ashford? give me what i want or we'll see how dangerous you like to play.

Cade would have offered the cunt any sum of money to keep him the fuck away from Kara, but—as was goddamn typical—Jace was asking for something far more costly than money. Cade had made the mistake of allowing Kara to become his one weakness, and the fucking bastard was more than willing to exploit it to his advantage. As much as Cade wanted to tell Jace to go fuck himself, he knew he couldn't risk Kara's safety. Much like himself, Jace wasn't one to make idle threats.

meet me by the den of iniquity at 10pm tonight…come alone.

A second text had come in early that morning. The sound had startled both of them awake, and Cade had turned over to shield his phone from the sleepy, prying eyes of the beautiful woman lying naked beside him. The fact that Jace's threats had put a damper on his intent to have a lazy morning fuck with Kara already had him storming around the house in a fury. If Kara could tell he was being secretive, she didn't let on. He'd deleted the messages just to be safe, but he would only be half surprised if Kara somehow manage to tail him and show up at the rendezvous that night. As a precaution, Cade had arranged a distraction for her—courtesy of Declan and Mrs. Hughes.

The guilt of having to betray Kara's trust to protect her safety twisted in his gut like a knife. She was wiling to give her life to protect that damn book, but Cade no intention of allowing that to happen. He would do everything in his power to keep her from harm, even if there would be hell to pay later on. But he wouldn't be the only one paying. It might not be that day or that week or that year, but someday soon that traitorous piece of shit was going to pay with his life. And Cade would be there to delight in every scream, every beg for mercy, every drop of blood wrung painfully from his miserable carcass. And the thought of torturing Jace into his reservation in hell was the first thing to put a genuine smile on Cade's face that day.

THE seedy streets of Chicago's underbelly were sweaty and crowded. Whores beckoned seductively with spread legs and red-painted lips. Junkies chased their highs in a variety of ways. Everyone who came to that part of town was seeking either release or profit. Or perhaps a bit of both.

It was a licentious playground where one's wildest fantasies could be granted, one's darkest desires explored without prejudice. There was once a time when Cade had been lured to those very streets, enticed by the promise of freedom in all respects. He had since found more established venues for his particular appetites, but the wanton abandon being experienced all around still called to him like a soft, familiar hum. Cade ignored it and continued toward Jace's chosen meeting place.

Jace had picked the perfect location for their exchange. There were hundreds of witnesses, all with eyes blind to the illicit, though some may take offense if Cade decided to take Jace's life rather than accepting his cowardly extortion. Regardless of the consequences, Cade knew he would be tempted to try as soon as he saw the traitorous cunt.

The cathedral stood out pristinely amongst the other decrepit buildings in a state of disrepair due to overuse and neglect. It was a beacon to all sinners, though with an entirely different message than eternal salvation. More like delight in damnation. And hundreds flocked to the revamped kink club to do just that.

Its facade was uncharacteristically gothic for a chapel built in a country of such young architecture, reminiscent of thirteenth century cathedrals that embellished the timeworn cities and countrysides of France and Germany. The stained glass windows depicting biblical narratives were blacked out, shrouding its internal activities in mystery. Crimson tinted spotlights illuminated the stone spires, transforming the sanctuary into a hellish palace. Music thumped entrancingly, like the call of a siren, from the open doors. After his business was concluded, Cade had half a mind to return with Kara and introduce her to Chicago's sexual underworld. He had given her a taste of depravity, and she hadn't shied away. Perhaps, she was ready for more.

Cade's musings were disrupted when he spotted a familiar figure amongst the throng. *Jace.* Cade felt like a daft twat for keeping such a deplorable specimen in his confidence and on his payroll for years. Kara had revealed Jace for who he truly was, and Cade would never recover from the overwhelming guilt at what she had suffered at his hands. Jace would receive his recompense for harming Kara. One day, when Jace was happy and free and enjoying life, Cade would come to rip away everything Jace held dear. And then he would take his miserable fucking life. And his death would be as excruciatingly torturous as humanly possible, for pain was a tool Cade wielded all too easily.

Hideaway

Jace signaled to Cade from among the crowd, unperturbed by the threats of death and destruction written upon his face. He had chosen their location for a strategic reason, knowing his safety was guaranteed among the mass of witnesses, knowing Cade wouldn't risk being caught regardless of whatever indecencies Jace had committed against his precious little pet.

"Ashford," Jace greeted causally as he had done nearly every day for years, as though nothing had changed between them.

"Jace," Cade answered cautiously, as though meeting a stranger wearing a mask of the man with whom he had been so well acquainted. Cade toyed with the idea of peeling flesh from bone to discover what truly lay beneath—monster or man.

"How is dear Kara?" Jace asked, sounding deceptively conversational as though commenting on the weather.

Cade knew the comment for what it really was—the stab of a knife aimed straight at his heart. "Keep her name out of your vile, fucking mouth," Cade answered through gritted teeth, his eyes glittering with the dark fury of death.

"Oh, I've had more than just her name in my mouth. I've tasted all of her. *Thoroughly*," Jace responded, running his tongue along his top lip at the delicious memory.

Cade clenched his fists at his side, using all of his self-control to remain stonily silent in spite of Jace's taunts.

Jace took Cade's silence as permission to continue his brutal assault. "Did she tell you how she screamed when I thrust my cock inside her? How she begged and cried for mercy as I fucked her within an inch of her sanity? How sweet she tasted as I devoured her mouth and her breasts and licked the saltiness of tears from her skin? How hot and tight her cunt was as I poured my cum inside her?"

"You motherfucking piece of shit!" Cade shouted as he strode toward Jace and punched him squarely in the jaw, his self-control losing a battle with his body's primal demand for vengeance and violence and blood.

"Damnit, Ashford," Jace gasped in surprise as he clutched his smarting face, spitting out the acrid taste of blood that filled his mouth. "Why so fucking angry? Is some bitch really worth all this animosity between us? You and I have been partners for five years. You've known this girl for all of two months. Don't get me wrong, she's a great fuck, but she's nothing special." Jace wiped a trickle of blood from the corner of his mouth, glancing at the red stain on the back of his knuckles thoughtfully. "Tell me, do you think of me when you fuck her?"

"Neither of us have given you a moment's thought since you left," Cade bluffed, his hand twitching to deliver another blow.

"Oh, I highly doubt that. I marked her just for you. A memento to remember me by. I bet some still linger on her skin even now," Jace tormented.

Cade flexed his jaw tightly at the reminder. Jace's horrific marks on Kara's body had been dealt with rather drastically, effaced by his own form of violence as Kara had requested. Cade's bruises mingled with Jace's, the owner of each indecipherable. It was the only way he had been able to sleep with Kara with a measure of his sanity still intact.

"This immature taunting is befitting a child, Jace. Not a grown man supposedly in possession of both his balls. I believe an exchange is in order? Stop stalling and get to it," Cade demanded gruffly.

"So eager to barter away the sacred item your precious fucktoy was willing to give her life to protect? Is she aware of our little deal, or are you already keeping secrets from her?"

Cade glared at Jace; the evil bastard was fully aware of the shitty situation he'd forced him into. Doubtless, it was why Jace had asked for the text rather than extorting him for money. He knew that Cade's betrayal would devastate Kara and put their already shaky relationship at risk. Which was why Cade had every intention of making sure she never found out. He already had Braxton tracing any mention of a first edition Chaucer being bought or sold in the hopes that Jace had already secured a buyer for the text. He'd also put the word out with his international network of contacts, asking for any information on *The Canterbury Tales* first edition. Cade was a thief, for fuck's sake; did Jace really think the book would be secure once he had it in hand? Cade had every intention of restoring the priceless text to his stubborn librarian, even if it meant relinquishing a large portion of his time and wealth to do so. For the sake of his very selfish cock, Cade hoped it was *before* Kara discovered the book missing from his library and expressed her fury by revoking sex privileges. Repressing a cringe at *that* unthinkable outcome, Cade made a mental note to commission a counterfeit Chaucer as soon as possible just to be safe.

Jace took Cade's silence as affirmation that his scheme had been executed perfectly. "Well I do hope this little deception doesn't get you into too much trouble when she finds out. Because they always do."

"Let me worry about Kara. You worry about keeping your end of the bargain."

"Of course. The book, if you please," Jace requested amiably, outstretching his hand.

Cade reached into his bag to pull out the heavy, parchment wrapped book that had been the cause of so much trouble. And so much unexpected joy in the form of the delectable, fearsome woman waiting for him at home. Not one to simply take a man at his word, Jace tore open the brown paper and inspected the book critically. Satisfied that it was indeed the original text, Jace gave a nod of approval and thrust the book into his black bag without a modicum of caution or gentleness. Cade involuntarily cringed at the thought of how a certain librarian would react to seeing the fragile text treated so indelicately.

"Are you satisfied?" Cade asked impatiently, his tolerance for being within strangling distance of Kara's rapist growing thinner by the minute, his hands itching to steal Jace's last breaths. He couldn't squelch the impulse to murder much longer, and it would be a great inconvenience for him to take Jace's wretched life amongst hundreds of witnesses. But another couple minutes in Jace's presence, and he would welcome the inconvenience with open arms.

"Very satisfied," Jace answered with a smug smile.

"And your end of the deal?"

"You have my word that you'll both be left in peace," Jace answered as though he were the pinnacle of magnanimity.

Cade scoffed. "And what exactly is the word of a traitor worth?"

"I do admit, I'm getting the better end of the deal," Jace said with a humorless laugh. "You'll just have to trust me."

"And Kara? You have your bloody book, so you'll have no need to be in her vicinity ever again. Agreed?" Cade asked, his voice black and lethal.

"I give you my word as a gentleman, I will never again lay eyes upon Kara Caine," Jace promised, holding up his right hand as though making a solemn oath.

"A gentleman?" Cade questioned incredulously. "Now *that* I trust even less. Consider yourself forewarned, if you break your word, your eyes will be forfeit, along with the rest of you."

"I would expect nothing less from a savage bastard such as yourself," Jace quipped breezily.

"Then we're done here. I never want to see your goddamn face again."

"Likewise," Jace answered in parting, issuing a small nod of goodbye.

Both men turned and walked away in separate directions. Both men had lied. Cade and Jace knew that unfinished business would draw them together once again. They knew that, eventually, only one of them would walk away. But both were resigned to bide their time until the opportune moment for vengeance and destruction presented itself.

CHAPTER TWENTY ONE

AFTER their time in the Hideaway, life had somehow acquired a semblance of normalcy. Or rather, as normal as it could be under the circumstances. Technically, Kara was no longer a prisoner, but she continued to reside at Ashford Manor and spent her nights in Cade's bed. She had tried to explain that the most logical decision would be for her to return to her Chicago residence, but she'd lost that argument in favor of her *safety*. Sometimes she got a little sick of being protected. She'd finally returned to work at the university library, an argument she *had* actually won, provided she allowed Declan to drive her to and from work. The kid stayed on campus the entire time, not necessarily spying on her, but not letting her out of his sight either. Cade's control issues were something she hoped would soften in time.

Hideaway

Then again, he hadn't exactly been anything *other* than controlling in any aspect of their relationship the entire time she'd know him. It was as if his need to dominate was an inherent aspect of his very nature. And hell, maybe it was. She didn't mind when it came to sex. Who was she kidding, she fucking loved his dominance in the bedroom, but she found it harder to sacrifice her independence when it didn't come with an orgasm. And Cade wanted her submission every hour of the day.

In addition to agreeing to stay and explore whatever the fuck their twisted relationship was, Kara had suggested that they try things Cade's way—which included making the Hideaway a regular part of their routine. She still couldn't believe she had spent so much time innocently lounging in the library with a complete sex dungeon a few feet below. Cade had fought her on the idea, suggesting that she perhaps wasn't ready for the extremity of his darker desires, but she told him to fuck off. If he could handle it, she could fucking handle it too. He finally acquiesced with a mischievous smile that suggested he would greatly enjoy proving her wrong.

And it was that salacious smile that haunted her when she entered the library and found a suspicious, bow adorned box resting in her favorite reading chair. She approached the package hesitantly, remembering the last time she'd been ambushed by one of Cade's revenges wrapped in ribbons. She read the inscription on the little black card.

Put this on and meet me in the Hideaway precisely at six o'clock.
Do not be late.
-C

Cautiously, Kara undid the bow and lifted the top of the box with a cringe of apprehension. A gasp of mortification escaped her lips when she found a fucking *sexy schoolgirl* outfit elegantly tucked between crisp layers of tissue paper as though it was a luxurious present, *not* goddamn kink clothes. Blushing with embarrassment, she removed the items from the box and held them up for inspection. There was a very fucking short pleated red mini skirt, a matching tie, a cropped white shirt that boasted an astonishing *two* buttons to keep her tits barely covered, and plain white thigh-high stockings.

The ensemble was a goddamn monstrosity, and that wasn't even considering what it would look like *on* her. She understood the irony—really, she did. She worked in academics, she was an avid learner, and she considered herself a perpetual student in all things. However, the schoolgirl outfit was taking it *way* too fucking far. She had PhD's for fucks sake—plural—and hated the idea of being boxed into an insulting, juvenile, academic stereotype for the sake of Cade's twisted sex games.

Professional and feminist outrage aside, Kara could not deny the aroused quickening of her pulse and the damning wetness gathering between her thighs. Dignity be damned, she was going to wear the damn sex outfit. She had asked for Cade's dominance, and, in return, she had promised to offer as much an effort at submission as she could. Having spent her entire life prioritizing independence, submission was not something that came naturally to her by any means.

Frantically, Kara glanced at the clock, remembering that her *sir* had demanded that she not be late.

Shit.

It was five minutes until six o'clock. Five minutes until she earned herself some sort of excessive punishment in Cade's Hideaway of horrors. The thought frightened her as much as it soaked her panties, so much so that her thighs slid together slickly with the overflowing dampness of her arousal. For her own sake, she endeavored to obey Cade's command, but opted to be a few minutes late. Just to make things interesting.

Kara knew she would never be able to make it up to her room to change without evoking severe consequences for disobedience. A few minutes tardy might be fine, but the fifteen it would take her to travel up to her room, switch her clothes, and then make it into the Hideaway and in the appropriate position might be pushing it. Glancing about the library anxiously and listening for anyone coming, Kara decided *fuck it* and started to strip out of her clothes.

The pleated skirt fit her hips perfectly, accentuating her slim waist and making her feel a bit like the cheerleader she never would have sacrificed her self-respect to be in high school. The hem of the red plaid material covered—literally—two thirds of her ass, leaving the bottom third of her buttocks hanging out in the open. With her panties already unbearably drenched, Kara decided to go without, slipping them down her legs quickly and tossing them on the leather couch. Kara stared at the cropped shirt indecisively, not sure whether it would look more slutty to have half of her red bra hanging out of the see-through top, or to go without the bra entirely. Since she was already sans panties, she went all the way and took off her bra too. She was sure the bastard would be more than thrilled to find her so underdressed for the occasion. Kara slipped on the tight shirt, groaning in annoyance at the sight of her hardened nipples poking noticeably through the white material. Taking off her black heels, Kara sat on the sofa and pulled the stockings up over her thighs. They were by far the most innocent part of the outfit, and she actually quite liked them. Rolling her eyes at the ridiculousness, Kara lastly slipped the tie over her neck.

Nope. Too fucking stupid.

Deciding that the school uniform tie was too over the top, she ripped it off and tossed it on the couch with her discarded undergarments. Unfortunately left with no other option than going barefoot, Kara slipped her black heels back on, hating how much more exposed they made her feel, as though her bare pussy and ass were literally on display. As a finishing touch, Kara slipped the red ribbon from her messy braid and gathered her hair into a high ponytail, tying the ribbon into a bow at the top of her head. A mere three minutes late, Kara headed for the secret entrance to the Hideaway feeling nervous, excited, sexy, and horny as fuck.

The lights were already on, guiding her way down. Kara stopped on the last step when she realized she wasn't alone. Cade sat at the desk in the far corner, dressed in his usual three piece suit and tie, his expression strict and chastising as he glared at her with eyes darkened with disapproval mingled with insatiable lust. In his hands, Cade twirled a twelve inch gold ruler.

Hideaway 449

"Miss Caine," Cade greeted sharply, loving her small jolt of fear at the sternness in his tone. "You're late."

"Only by three minutes, sir," Kara argued in her own defense, her voice sounding stronger than she felt.

"Excuses already, Miss Caine?" Cade asked with a condemning scowl. "Come here and stand in front of my desk."

Dragging her feet each step of the way, Kara sullenly walked the short distance to the desk and obediently stood before him. She tried not to wither beneath his reproachful eyes, but it was an impossible task. As an act of self-preservation, she lowered her eyes to the floor and awaited Cade's judgment.

"Now, what time were you told to be ready and waiting in the Hideaway?"

"Six, sir," Kara answered petulantly, her eyes still downcast. It wasn't exactly her fault that she was given so little time to follow his orders.

"And what time did you make your way down those steps?"

"Three minutes after six, sir."

"Look at me," Cade ordered. She listened hesitantly, meeting his eyes with an expression that could only be defined as defiance. Cheeky brat. "Did you obey my instructions like a good girl?"

Kara smirked slightly before quickly covering it with a pliant expression. "No, sir."

"Indeed, you did not," Cade agreed, momentarily pausing to rake his eyes over Kara's entire, incredibly exposed body. The delectably filthy sight of her in the revealing school uniform—her tits nearly spilling out of the top, her nipples so stiff they could practically cut through the thin material, her exposed abdomen and hips that begged to be licked, and her just barely covered pussy—sent all of the blood in his body straight to his throbbing cock. It would take all of his self-restraint not to bend her over the desk, flip up that fucking short skirt, and fuck her that very second. But he wanted to play with her before he tore into her cunt and claimed her screams of pleasure as she clamped down on his cock in ecstasy. Fucking could wait; first, he wanted to make her writhe and beg.

"Do I need to teach you how to be a good girl?" Cade asked after he finally finished eye-fucking her, his words weighted with the possibility for punishment and pleasure.

"Yes, sir," Kara answered softly, biting her bottom lip to keep it from trembling with anticipation and arousal.

Those two, sweet words had never come from a more delectable mouth. A mouth that he had every intention of using very soon. Accepting her surrender, a sinister grin spread across Cade's lips before his expression morphed into one of chastising displeasure. "Tell me, Miss Caine, do good girls go to class without knickers?" Cade inquired sternly, judging her reaction intently as he purposefully fidgeted with the metal ruler on the desk.

Kara squeaked slightly in surprise, not sure how he could have known *that* without so much as an inspection beneath her skirt. "No, sir," Kara answered dutifully, seriously second guessing her decision to taunt Cade with a bare pussy.

"I see," Cade responded, nodding his head in agreement as he continued to play with the ruler, sliding it smoothly from one hand to another.

Kara had to smother a giggle as she shifted awkwardly beneath his stern gaze. Cade had explained the concept of a scene to her—the

Hideaway

idea that sexual encounters would be staged to enhance the experience—but the play acting and her ridiculous costume seemed like a bit much to suffer with a straight face.

"Is something amusing, Miss Caine?" Cade asked deprecatingly, startling Kara from her inner thoughts.

"No, sir," Kara responded hastily, wiping the subtle grin from her face. Perhaps she lacked the seriousness to participate in his games. The last time they had used the Hideaway, everything had been so real. The emotions. The pain. The *need*. This time, under contrived circumstances, there was a hurdle of awkwardness that Kara was struggling to overcome. The need was there—the raging appetite to feel and fuck and hurt and surrender—buried beneath inhibitions she couldn't quite shake.

Cade watched Kara closely, recognizing the inner turmoil. It wasn't an easy thing to surrender your basest desires into the hands of another, and it wasn't meant to be. Complete mutual trust was one of the elements that made a Dominant/submissive relationship so intoxicating, and it was something on which Kara needed to be educated. Cade could read the hesitation in her body; he could sense her fear. She didn't fear him or the many torturous things he could do to her in his well-stocked dungeon. No, she feared that voice in her head that told her what she craved, what she needed to sustain her body as much as her lungs needed oxygen, was wrong. Unnatural. The subconscious echoes of a repressed society that deemed an appetite for pain as deviant and depraved, a longing for submission as anti-feminist and degrading.

Cade burned with the overwhelming need to thrust Kara from the limitations of what upstanding society deemed as normal desires. To shake her from her own inhibitions. To give her something tangible and real of which to be truly scared. Cade was an unequivocally possessive man, and the fact that any of her fears didn't belong to him was goddamn unacceptable.

A loud *smack* pervaded the room, disrupting the tense silence as Cade slapped the ruler hard against his open palm. Kara jolted in surprise, eying the instrument in Cade's hands with a newfound sense of mistrust and dread. Cade appreciated the sudden heaving of Kara's chest as she shifted anxiously before him, fearful of his intentions. Good. He was finally getting somewhere, her fear turning to him where it belonged. Where it would always belong.

Cade stood from behind the desk, his form appearing somehow larger, more menacing than usual, as he stalked toward Kara. He clenched his right hand, reveling in the burn that reverberated through his palm courtesy of the ruler he still held. He imagined how Kara's skin would heat beneath the blows, how the metal would sound clashing against her skin. His erection grew painfully hard within the confines of his trousers at the thought of her ensuing cries for mercy—and more.

Kara flinched as she felt Cade's firm body pressed against her, forcing her into the hard edge of the desk, his hardness thrust against her backside. All it would take was one push, and she would be sprawled out across the desk. His for the taking. He knew the damn girl had no knickers underneath that short, little skirt. One lift of his finger, and she would be bare beneath him. His cock ached to be deep inside her sweet cunt, riding her until she screamed his name in surrender. But he wanted to claim more than just her body. He wanted her mind as well.

Slowly, Cade dragged the sharp corner of the ruler down Kara's neck, over the curve of her shoulder, and down the side of her arm, resting at her wrist. Kara's whole body shivered at the sensation, her skin prickling in its path. Ever so softly, Cade drew the ruler back up her arm and then slid the edge down her back, following the ridge of her spine. This time, Kara moaned quietly beneath his touch. Stroking the tip of the ruler along the curve of her hip and then down the front of her thigh, Cade leaned in close until his lips rested against her ear.

"Tell me, Miss Caine, do good girls take off their clothes in the middle of the library when anyone could walk in and see them indecently exposed?" he whispered, the quietness of his tone ill at ease with the dark threat that laced his words like poison.

"Hmm?" Kara mumbled incoherently, confused by the question and distracted by the cool metal sensually caressing her skin.

In reprimand, Cade used the ruler to administer a harsh slap to Kara's thigh.

"Ow!" Kara screeched, rubbing her hand against the sting as she attempted to pull away from Cade's hold.

Cade wrapped his hand firmly around the back of Kara's neck and jerked her tightly against him. "Remove your hand from your thigh, or I will smack it as well," Cade commanded sternly, rapping her lightly against the knuckles for emphasis.

Trembling, Kara let her hands fall to her sides, trying to relax as much as she could in the hold of a threatening man wielding an unexpectedly harsh weapon against her bare skin.

"Good girl," Cade praised as he felt her softening against him. "Now, answer me."

"I'm sorry, sir, can you repeat the question?" Kara pleaded, the heightened sensations of her body hopelessly overwhelming her thought processes.

Cade's hand slid from her neck to grip her jaw, forcing her head to the side to look at him, the seriousness of his gaze boring into her and demanding her absolute attention. "Do good girls get naked in libraries and leave their arse, tits, and cunt on display for everyone to see?" Cade asked very slowly, allowing her to absorb the full insinuation of his words as he continued to stroke the ruler threateningly against her thigh.

Yet again, Kara gasped in surprise. First, because he knew exactly what she had done when she discovered his *gift*. Second, because there was absolutely no way he could have known she undressed in the library. There was no one near that area of the house. She'd checked, obviously. She might be exploring her kinks, but she was nowhere near a full-blow exhibitionist.

"Cameras, darling," Cade explained in answer to her unspoken question. "Do you really think a man of my profession wouldn't have security measures in place, particularly in an area where items of value are held?"

Blanching, Kara turned away in embarrassment. The fucking bastard should have warned her there were cameras hidden in the house. They'd had sex in the library for fuck's sake.

"If you're wondering if there's a video of me fucking you against the stacks to heaven and back, there is," Cade said with a salacious grin.

Kara tried to pull away in disgust, but he gripped her tighter, sharply smacking the ruler against her thigh in warning. "The next one will be harder if you don't answer the question," Cade threatened.

"No."

Another, harder slap landed on Kara's other thigh. She yelped in response, twisting against him.

"No, what?" Cade challenged, his ruler poised to punish again.

"No, sir, good girls don't undress in libraries," Kara answered helplessly, her thighs smarting from the blows.

"Very good. Now, one more question," Cade paused dramatically, leaning down until the slight stubble of his jaw brushed roughly against the tenderness of her neck. He placed one, soft kiss against her throat, breathing in the scent of her, feeling her pulse thunder against his lips. He tucked his thumb under her chin and gently lifted her eyes to meet his. "Have you been a naughty girl?"

Kara struggled to remain upright as all the bones in her body seemed to liquify beneath the burning fire of Cade's gaze. The desire in his eyes spoke to her body in such an effortless way that words could never communicate. She longed to obey him, please him, cry for him, scream for him. In that moment, she was his. Completely.

"Yes, sir," Kara whispered in response, her eyes unconsciously closing in anticipation of whatever delicious destruction those words would bring.

Hearing her admission, Cade smiled gleefully, bestowing another kiss behind her ear and rubbing his thumb across her bottom lip, eternally grateful for those two damning syllables that came from her sinful mouth. "Do you need to be punished, naughty girl?" Cade asked breathlessly against the skin of her neck, his control unraveling to the point that he felt the need to sink his teeth into something to keep his sanity. So he did, biting down hard on the tender curve between Kara's neck and shoulder. Cade's eyes fluttered shut at the delicious whimper pulled from Kara's lips.

"Mmmhmm," Kara moaned as she nodded her head in agreement with Cade's question, the ability for speech having completely abandoned her as her body seemed to pool all its resources to her throbbing pussy.

"Bend over the fucking desk," Cade commanded harshly, the arousal in his voice barely contained, much like his swollen, aching cock begging to be set free.

Kara bent at the waist and fell against the top of the desk, her naked thighs already marked by being pressed tightly against its edge. From her position over the desk, she knew he could already see her bare cunt peeking out from underneath the short skirt. Cade inhaled sharply at the sight of her, absolutely throbbing to be so deep inside her that she couldn't tell where her body ended and his began. She wiggled her ass slightly, taunting him with the sight of her dripping wet pussy in the hopes that she'd get his cock as punishment.

Instead, she felt the cool touch of metal sliding up her leg and flipping the edge of the pleated skirt up over her ass. The touch of the ruler disappeared briefly before landing incredibly hard against the lower curve of her ass. Kara moaned heavily in response, intense pleasure radiating throughout her entire body rather than pain. Cade slapped her again, drawing a greedy cry from her lips as she pushed her hips back against him to welcome the punishment. He hit her three times in rapid succession, each slap harder than the last. Kara cried out—the sound hungry and desperate and unfamiliar to her

Hideaway 457

own ears—wordlessly begging for release beneath the sublime fucking ecstasy of the blows.

"I think you're enjoying your punishment, naughty girl," Cade commented in amusement as he thrust the hardness of his cock against her tender spanked ass, admiring the bright, red lines the ruler made across her delicate skin.

Kara was soaked, the wetness of her arousal sliding down her thighs and dampening his pants where the rigid outline of his erection pressed tightly against her. And fuck if it didn't make him harder to see his cock christened with her cum. He fucking ached at seeing how much she wanted his twisted pleasure, how she needed it like he did.

Abruptly, Cade bent over Kara, his weight crushing her against the hard desk as every inch of her body melded into his. His hand tangled in her hair, roughly jerking her head to the side and pressing her cheek into the cool wooden surface. His mouth lowered to her neck—kissing, biting, ravaging, claiming her as his by leaving his marks on her flesh for everyone to see. Kara belonged to him, and he had no intention of ever letting her or anyone else forget it.

Continuing to use his mouth to ravage her body, Cade dragged the edge of the ruler across Kara's hip, pressing just hard enough to leave a thin pink scratch etched into her skin. He slapped the ruler lightly against her ass, taunting her with the promise of more punishment. She pressed her backside against him eagerly, begging to be used and dominated and hurt just a little bit beyond the point of pleasure.

"Do you want more, Miss Caine?" Cade asked in a husky voice that sent chills of pleasure rippling through Kara's body as he spanked her a little firmer than before, but not enough to satisfy. He wanted her to beg for the pleasure of her punishment.

Kara struggled to shake herself of the delirious haze of excitement and arousal to ponder his question. Did she want more of what Cade had to offer? More of his dominance, his need to control, his desire to retaliate in the most terrible and delicious ways when he wasn't obeyed? As much as she hated to admit it, she felt a burgeoning addiction to the darkness Cade had brought into her life. Now that she had a taste, she wasn't sure if she could ever live without it.

Cade could spank her, fuck her, destroy her—in whatever order he preferred—and she would always beg for more. Kara wanted more than more. She wanted everything.

"Always, sir."

ABOUT THE AUTHOR

Hideaway is the debut novel for author Willow Prescott. *Hideaway* is the first book in the *Stolen Away Series*. This is only the beginning of Kara and Cade's story, and there is plenty more to come. If you are hungry for more spicy romance and kinkery, please stay tuned for updates on the next installment of the series and other book releases.

Willow Prescott lives in Amsterdam with her husband and small coven of mini monsters. She spends her nights in a caffeine haze dreaming up twisted sexcapades and deliciously dark villains who make you get on your knees and beg for more.

Keep up with Willow:

willowprescott.com

willowprescottbooks@gmail.com

TikTok: @willowprescottbooks

Instagram: @willowprescottbooks

Printed in Great Britain
by Amazon